FOOTSTEPS

ON A

DRUM

Robert Mendelsohn's novels are set in the background of his own colourful and adventurous life. He is no stranger to danger in exotic places, having led the life of a roving wheeler dealer, with extensive knowledge in particular of the Caribbean and the Far East. He is now an international wine merchant, a keen yachtsman and art collector, based in London.

His novels have been translated into Spanish, Italian, German, Polish, Dutch, Russian and Hungarian and every year brings him many new readers all over the world.

Of *Footsteps on a Drum*, William Stevenson author of *A Man Called Intrepid* wrote: "An enormously romantic tale. He could be tomorrow's Graham Greene."

Other books by Robert Mendelsohn
published by Prion

Clash of Honour
The Red Pagoda
The Hibiscus Trail

FOOTSTEPS ON A DRUM

Robert Mendelsohn

PRION

Published in paperback in 1995 by PRION,
an imprint of Multimedia Books Limited,
32–34 Gordon House Road, London NW5 1LP

ISBN 1-85375-192-8

Typeset by Books Unlimited (Nottm), Pleasley, Notts NG19 7QZ
Printed in the United Kingdom

For Dawn

Contents

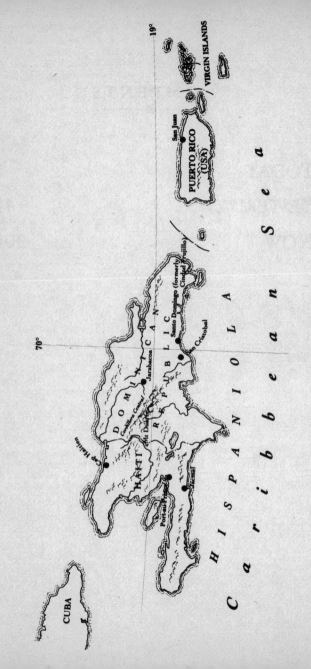

BOOK ONE
TODAY

CHAPTER ONE

◼

SUNDAY 22 JULY, 1984, 11 A.M.

Today I saw my wife's lover Cunningham walking down the street. He walked without his stick and did not limp and occasionally he stopped to look at shop windows. He played with his key-ring and smiled at passers-by and had he not been dead for seven hours at least I could have sworn it was him. He was tanned and his cruel face seemed as handsome as ever. His soft, expensive jacket clung to his trim, tall body and I felt the hand of old jealousy fan the embers of hate inside me into flame.

There was, of course, no way it could have been him. He was the last man I expected to see again in this world, yet my obsession with eliminating him willed me to think about him and smell his rare aftershave lotion and hear his cultured voice and see the blue cobalt of his eyes. Just for a moment, all at once and everywhere.

I had not always felt that way about Cunningham. He used to be someone else. Different. He was funny and considerate and charming and interesting to talk to. I did not wish him dead fifteen years ago, when we first met. He was, like so many others, having a rough time getting used to England again. He still had doubts then and his voice was gentle and on occasion one detected the look of a little boy, lost, in his eyes. I myself was only a beginner at that time, having been made assistant manager at a West End branch of the bank. The manager was on his annual holiday when Cunningham was shown into the office. I was the first to interview him, but looking back on it now I know he was there intentionally and had come to see no one else. Outwardly he did not look too different. He was always impeccably dressed and his speaking voice put one immediately at ease, as did his manner. There was something about Cunningham which made him unforgettable. People were instantly drawn to him. Wanted to be with him. Do things for him. I don't know what it was. Could have been that light in his eyes or his slight limp or that incredible smile which reached out to make you feel clever and important and the sole inhabitant of this planet as far as he was concerned. Yes, perhaps it was his smile. It was an attractive smile. It was strong and yet it had an appealing quality which made him look helpless and hexed you into thinking you were the only person in the world he could depend on.

'I wonder whether you might be able to help me.'

These were his first words to me. His eyes looked straight into mine and there was humility in them, as if he were waiting for words of infinite wisdom from me. He did not look like someone come to negotiate a loan. No. He was the type of customer we all wanted. Youthful-looking, obviously successful, full of plans and ideas and contacts all over Central and South America.

He was coming back to live in England and was looking for local financial connections. He had, he said, made his money in trade. I suspected it was not the sort of retail stuff the branch was used to, but he did not specify. He had taken rooms in the Albany around the corner and said he was going to look for a place in the country should he decide to make England his home.

'The main thing is to find something to do and someone to do it with,' he said.

He had not made up his mind what it was going to be. Money was not the object, he stressed. His own cash was mostly out of the country, but there was some his father had left him which needed attention. That investment was handled by our bank too. At a City branch near where his father had practised law. Cunningham was not happy with the way they handled the account and he planned to move it to our office if we saw eye to eye.

It was when he mentioned the Dominican Republic that he touched a personal chord. My wife's younger brother, Gerald

4

Buckmaster, had lived in the Dominican Republic for some years. His wife Marina was an American girl and Gerald worked for her father's company. I longed to ask him if he knew them, but did not. It was clearly, I thought, the wrong time to introduce a familiar note into the discussion. I did not even mention it then. Of course, I should have done. It would have saved many people much pain, myself more than most, but one learns to be less inhibited with age.

'What sort of trade did you engage in?' I ventured.

'Oh, this and that,' he said sheepishly. 'I dealt in all sorts of things. People, mainly.'

How could I have guessed he had meant just that? I did not know that the slave trade was alive and well and thriving, even then. I have only myself to blame for not realizing what he was talking about. He, I must admit, had been quite candid. He said he had recently been supplying the military regimes in Central America and the Caribbean. They were now mostly buying from the United States and he was being squeezed out. In any case, he was looking for a quieter life.

There again, I misunderstood. I did not take this to mean that Cunningham had been an arms dealer. Gun-running had bad connotations and was a world away from the retail trade in Regent Street. Perhaps I was too keen on attracting new business of my own.

I was free for lunch, but when he asked me I thought it would be best to decline.

'You may just be right for me,' he said. 'I need to learn how things are done here in England these days.'

He looked and sounded so English. One would never have guessed that he had spent more of his life out of the country than in it. He must have known more about me than he let on, but I was flattered that he had chosen me and spotted none of this. Lack of experience on my part, I suppose.

He refused a cigarette and proceeded to ask intelligent questions about the way in which his account would be administered. He seemed to like the answers, for right then he produced a draft in the amount of ten thousand pounds. He held it up for a second and then he passed it to me, looking directly into my eyes.

'I would like you to look after my affairs yourself. Could you do that for me, do you think?'

I could not help basking in the kind of comfort one enjoys when pleasing a celebrity.

He must have been in his late forties then, although he had the sort of boyish looks and optimistic energy that made his age difficult to gauge. As he got up to leave, I noticed for the first time that he had a walking stick. He said he was leaving for a short trip to the Continent and hoped his chequebook would be ready when he returned. He pumped my hand, tapped my shoulder, and then he left. He had a slight limp which hardly bothered the typist who looked at him with blatant admiration as he walked to the door.

On his next visit, Cunningham asked for me by name. He told me to call him Peter, but I have then and always will think of him as Cunningham. It was a strong name. Almost regal. It was elegant and dashing and suited him well.

And then came the time he took me and my wife out to dinner.

I know I must stop this maudlin nonsense. Find another train of thought. I can feel the jitters coming back and it's time for my Sunday walk to end.

But that man haunted me and I watched him. He stood there still, admiring an old oriental vase in the window of an antique shop. He looked as if he would have liked to have gone in to buy it there and then, but he changed his mind. He turned and walked down the hill and kept walking. When he reached the kerb, he stopped. He looked right and then left and crossed the road. They have this flea market off the high street on Sundays and he walked up to the first stall and then disappeared into the crowd. Whoever he was.

CHAPTER TWO

■

SATURDAY 21 JULY, 1984, MIDNIGHT

The window is wide open, but he does not notice the sound of the wind in the sycamores. He does not hear the footsteps that crush the gravel on the path nor the shuffling directly outside. He has just put the telephone down. He has just been told that she will not be coming back to him and he takes a deep, incredulous breath. Not coming back to him. Silently, in the warmth of the summer night, Cunningham's small world seems to be closing in on him. He is sinking. The wheelchair is tight up against the desk; his torso is drooping, shoulders hunched forward. From behind him, from the open window whose curtains swish and billow with the trees, the menacing nozzle points at the back of his neck. There is the sharp, alien sound of metal falling on metal. And then he hears a click.

'Shit,' a voice says in anger, and Cunningham turns around to face the frustrated expression behind the gun.

'What the hell?' he hears himself ask, but out there steel slides over steel and he knows a new cartridge is being slotted into the barrel. He knows there is no time and he drives himself back from the desk, ducking to one side, knocking the telephone down, the wheelchair suddenly a mobile prison.

The alarm should have gone off as soon as the phone touched the ground, but no bell sounds. Apart from the pool of light cast by the desk lamp, it is dark in the room and he is alone in the house. The fidgeting killer at the window must know it.

There is no one he can call. Least of all her. She who is the sole guardian of his hopes, she who will not be coming back.

She may have planned the whole thing. Impossible. Why impossible? An angry woman's mind is not predictable.

Surely not like this, in cold blood, after what they have been through. Why not?

He can almost hear the man's nerves jangle as he struggles to get the gun functioning. Any minute now. His desert training comes back into the Cotswold countryside just in time. An automatic response the roots of which are buried deep in the training for an ancient war. He presses hard on the wheels and zigzags to the corner. The gun barks. It spits erratic lead into the dark, well away from him. He cannot help smiling to himself. The paintings being shredded on the wall have all been willed to her and now she is losing them for the sake of his head.

He chuckles and the fear is gone. Tobruk? No. Mersa Matruh in 1942. That was where he had first met fear and the smell of gunpowder. He is on home ground now and the man at the window knows nothing of the big safe he can crawl into and hide in. No one does. Not even her.

The man is reloading just as Cunningham reaches the heavy metal door. He tips the wheelchair over and falls and rolls and stretches his arm. A piece of luck he had left the bloody thing open. His hand searches then closes around the old Mills which lies where he had seen it earlier. He crawls towards the window on his back as his fingers pull the pin. The Mills feels cool and reassuring. He turns sideways and he listens. A new magazine clicks in. The gun bursts into action again. The man shoots slowly, as if he has all the time in the world.

His Haitian friends would have said that the spirits were safer than a hand grenade. They would have summoned a curse from Diquini or the Black Mountain. They would have tied a dead lizard to the curtain with a freshly severed chicken head. That would surely defeat the man and his gun. Make him disappear like the sun behind dark clouds. Voodoo. Rubbish. Haiti was behind him now. Long gone.

From the selective rhythm of the fire, Cunningham knows the man has regained his nerve. He eases the pin from the grenade, lifts the handle and counts to three before lobbing it up and out of the window. It will drop into the flowerbed there. He pulls himself back to the safe. He waits.

Perhaps it was not her after all. Of course it wasn't. No – had to be. All his other enemies had either gone to fat or were dead. And then the explosion comes and the flame. He crawls forward and looks up. Nothing to be seen through the window.

No one in the village will have heard. They are far away and on their television screens it's Sergeant Bilko's hour or some such. The Haitian gardener must be asleep. Or busy making knotted jute dolls in the hut he has built for himself in the grounds. A place best avoided. Smells like hell with all the dead vermin the loony hangs everywhere to attract the spirits.

The last sounds die to nothing. It's all quiet now. His ears hurt. Why? He is being punished for something.

CHAPTER THREE

◼

Into Ti Allain's ear flew a frightening clutter of shots. It came from the big white house across the grass, where the one-footed foreigner lived. There were no other houses for many distances around, and he had heard no visitor. The firing must be coming from the foreigner's picture box which showed small, living images of people. That box frightened him yet it was irresistible. Sometimes he found the courage to creep close to it and look inside, to watch how the little people killed and kissed and fondled each other shamelessly, right there in the box for all to see. He did not do that often, and when he did, he always covered the eyes of the doll he had made in his own image, to repay the spirits.

How far he had come from his village and his grand-mother's friend Monique, the black witch who had dominated

9

his early time. In a way, his situation was her doing. She had caused his long exile so far from his village in the mountains of beautiful Haiti. His grandmother's bones lay there under the ground with the others and her spirit had not followed him to the white man's land because she could not leave Monique the black witch.

Many of the spirits had gone from his village, Ti Allain believed, and with their departure starvation had to come. New spirits can only be created by death. He should have felt bad about that, but he knew that man is not master of his own destiny. The spirits had sent him away. Perhaps they wanted the village to die.

And then again perhaps he had been replaced. Perhaps there was someone else now to look after Monique and his grandmother. Someone else to collect the healthy males and lead them out of the starving village, all the way across the border to the plentiful fields of Saint Domingue.

The firing went on, but Ti Allain continued to spread the herbs on the wooden floor of his hut. It was difficult to get them to dry in this, his master's land. There was much rain here. Enough to give life to many barren fields around his village. Perhaps enough water for the whole of Haiti. There was plenty of grass to cut and insects to collect, which he placed in many small boxes to offer the spirits or to take back to the place of his birth when the curse was lifted.

The kindly one-footed foreigner who was now his undisputed master seldom talked to him these days. But that did not matter to Ti Allain because he was the other half of him. The man Cunningham had become his other half back in Saint Domingue, and as long as that was the order of things they were both safe.

He would collect real soil and scatter it to cover the wooden floorboards. Then he would not be separated from the ground which was connected to the earth which was connected to his village. That bond would surely protect his master as long as it remained in place.

A big explosion came from the house and Ti Allain saw a flash of flame fill the sky. For an instant the grass was lit and he knew for sure this could not come from the magic picture box. He must dance. Dancing would clear his head as it always did.

He got up and his feet started a sliding step upon the boards. They were mostly soft and smooth now, save where he had left the grains to roam. His feet tapped and his hands flew up above his head. He danced and in his mind he knew that he would soon fly out of the window to where there was peace. He would not stay there for ever. Just for a little while. Long enough for his head to clear.

He would go up to the house and see. He would do that soon. As soon as he had finished his dance. Perhaps it was madness to persist now. And yet he must. He took his golden paper crown out of the box. The skin had dried on the two remaining chicken heads which hung from the brim. The one-footed foreigner always cursed him for the smell, but there was none. He had made the crown long ago. The bones glued to the paper were white and smooth and Ti Allain lifted it from the box and placed it on his head with great care.

Outside, a full moon shone as brightly as it had ever done over his own village. That was a rare sight, and since the moon lived in the sky it meant he had to dance for the spirits first, before he danced to clear his own mind. The spirits had not communicated with him for a long time now. Very long. How long he did not remember, but they were there all the same.

Dance, Ti Allain. He heard his grandmother's voice from the sky, near the moon. He had not heard her voice for long, and he knew it meant something of great importance. He forgot what.

She had gone to live with Jesu and black Mo of the Israelites years and years and years ago. Now she rested up on the big black mountain behind heaven. No one knew better than Ti Allain how hard she had worked the fields while she lived and how she deserved to rest. Remembering that always made him

11

cry, but now he could not because he had to keep his eyes dry and clear for the spirits to see into his soul.

Her voice was a sure sign that something was about to happen to him. A change. Perhaps he was going to be taken back to his village. But that could not be. Not while the one-footed foreigner, the one who lived in the house and was his mirror image, walked the earth alive.

They had been through a lot together. Ti Allain did not count the days or months or years. He could not say how long. The sun did not show itself every day in this land like it did in his Haiti. Here black nights were often followed by dark days and he could not be sure how many were real days and how many were not.

He thought of all this as he danced. He concentrated and did not need to sing because he danced to the sound of the insects and the swaying branches of the big tree above his shed. Far away a dog barked. He danced and he prayed.

Slowly, very slowly, the echoes of the explosion were dying away. He would soon finish his dance. He would draw a new circle with powdered chalk. White and red and green. Right there, on the floor. He danced and he thought of how he would draw it and what he would put inside it and how he would walk round it to the door. He would keep his crown on his head for protection.

Soon, he would go and see what had happened to the one-footed foreigner. The man had been kind to him. The man had saved his life. Even if the spirits had caused him to do this, the man had saved his life and that of many others. He would go and see what had happened. Soon.

As soon as he'd finished his dance.

CHAPTER FOUR

—■—

Cunningham lies on his back in the wreckage of his study. Through the window a cloudless, moonlit sky looks down on him. It is a peaceful sky and but for the debris around him he could have been in Egypt, back in 1942. There, out of the hospital window, he had seen that same moon when they were both younger. It is all back in his mind again, as if neither he nor the moon had ever left.

Heliopolis. That was where the hospital was. There was the smell of ether in the air. And iodine and vomit. Someone was leaning over him. He spoke with a distinct European accent.

'Don't feel too sorry for yourself, young man. You are alive. You must have been blown clear out of the hatch. Your friends, the other men in your crew, were not so lucky. They were caught inside the tank and were burned. Your name is Cunningham, yes?'

He nodded.

'You are twenty-one years old?'

He nodded again and his eyes wandered down to the space below his right knee. His foot was itching like mad. Why was this man asking him questions to which he knew the answers? He stretched his arm and felt a sharp pain in his side. His face contorted. Could he have broken a rib?

A look of concern flashed across the European's big, beefy face.

'I'm trying to scratch my foot,' said Cunningham. 'Stupid, isn't it?'

'It's quite normal. You'll feel that missing foot for a while yet. You were lucky we were able to save the knee. We'll give you another shot, yes?'

'No. It's not that bad. Thank you.'

The Medical Corps Major's hand was large and soft and surprisingly light on his forehead. His arm was pulled from beneath the covers and he felt the coldness of a swab close to his shoulder.

'No. Please don't,' he said, and shook his head as he felt the needle invade his skin.

'You needn't be a hero here, Cunningham,' the Major said. The room was going dark on him and the itch stopped.

'Call me if there's any change,' the European said.

Far off, Cunningham could hear a female voice.

'They all call for their mothers. But not this one. This one never does.'

He could smell the hospital cocktail in the air and hear all that was said around him. He felt no pain. His lips were numb.

No. He did not call for his mother. Why should he call for his mother? She was not there. She had not been there for a very long time. She had run off with another man three days before his eighth birthday and the party was cancelled. He dreaded birthday parties ever after.

He watched his father going about his business, pretending nothing had changed. He saw him being eaten by pain, his drawn face straining to smile each morning as he left the house to catch the London train. In the evenings they ate silently together facing the humiliating emptiness of his mother's chair. The man watched him bathe and told him bedside stories and always stayed with him until he fell asleep.

That year his father sold his law firm to a junior partner and moved to another village where he became a country solicitor. The house was large, the grounds extensive, and there, trying to lose himself among the trees, Cunningham once saw his father cry.

If there were any women in his father's life they were well hidden. His father was all his and the boy did well at school and read books and was happy on holidays. At Christmas, they sometimes went to Switzerland, where his father swished down the great white slopes with a youthful confidence he himself never felt. They went salmon fishing in Scotland in June and sometimes they went to France in August. The summers were everlasting then, with his father always at his side.

The elder Cunningham had planned a trip to the United States to celebrate his son's matriculation when war broke out. His childhood was suddenly over. He was commissioned into the Royal Armoured Corps from his second year at law school, and found himself en route to Alexandria and the desert.

He corresponded regularly with his father. There were letters passing back and forth between the two through the wartime postal system. Then, weeks before his tank blew up, he learned that the old man had perished in a bomb raid on London. He had been visiting his old law firm when the building collapsed. The report said death was instantaneous. The military jargon did not lend itself to more than plain facts. Where, when, and more or less how his father had met his end.

He had little time to think of it then, in the thick of tank battles that raged in the sand around him. He acquitted himself well. And then came his own mishap and the hospital.

He did not call for his long-lost mother or dead father. He wanted to sleep without ever waking so that he might forget he was going to be a cripple.

'You won't be with us much longer, Cunningham,' the Major said one night. 'You're stronger by the day and your walking is progressing nicely. All you need now is to convalesce. Someone will have to clear this beautiful desert from all that human waste. War stinks.'

'You'll be able to go back to real medicine.'

'It's a big step from tropical diseases to a butcher's shop like this. I told you, war stinks.'

'My father said the same thing. He spent a year in the Army during the Great War.'

'So did I. Just at the end. Long enough to surrender.'

'Where did you serve?'

'In France. I was in the Austro-Hungarian Army.'

'You were fighting against us?'

'Yes. Life is strange. You yourself may find you are standing against your own country one day.'

A pain in his back wakes him from his reverie. He stretches. He is still on the floor, and he looks through the large empty window above him. The moon sails past, over the treetops. He smiles. The medical major had been right. He had, over the years, found himself at odds with his own people.

Cunningham pulls himself upright and holds on to his desk. The wheelchair lies on its side like a carcass. He hops over to it, rights it, and sinks gratefully into its comfort. He'd have to go out there and see what had happened to the man with the gun. There is plenty of time. He is not expecting any visitors. He picks the phone up from the floor and puts it in its place. It rings.

He need not pick it up. Maybe he should. He might learn something about the shooting. Does he really want to know? He'll let it ring one more time.

'Hello,' he says softly. There's no one there.

'Hello,' he repeats, 'Cunningham here.' Someone clicks the phone down somewhere, leaving him with the night and a faint dialling tone. His number is not listed. Must be a mistake. Happens all the time.

He should be tired, but he is raring to go. Go where? With whom? He might have a little drink. This is a night on which to reminisce. He might learn about his future. Go over some of his mistakes. Tomorrow is another day. Tomorrow will look after itself. He'll think of something.

After all, he is alive and has become somebody. Just as the woman had said he would, years ago, on the train to Palestine.

CHAPTER FIVE

———◼———

'Aren't you a little young to be an officer?'

'Rommel didn't seem to think so.'

'He would have done if he had taken a closer look.'

'His boys got close enough.'

She was a well-dressed woman in her late twenties. She had long tanned legs and an oval, olive-skinned face. A pair of bright green eyes that sparkled through a mass of soft, unruly black hair. She started talking to him as soon as she sat down opposite him. She said she was going back to Palestine after three weeks with her sister in Alexandria. She was chattering away about anything and everything, and by the time the desert dunes started to advance on them through the dusty windows Cunningham knew most of what there was to know about her life.

Her husband was born in Palestine of Russian stock and was currently serving in the British Army fighting the Italians in North Africa. She had not seen him in months; had a letter from him only the other day. He was well but did not expect to get any leave for the time being. In the photograph she proudly showed him the man looked large and his strong-jawed, optimistic face smiled at Cunningham. He had a pair of piercing, intelligent eyes under a thick lock of black hair. His shoulders boasted the two pips of a first lieutenant.

'He is a captain now,' she said as she put the print back in her bag. 'He used to work for an oil company before the war, but now I think he'll stay in uniform.'

'The war is bound to end one day.'

'Not our war.'

'I'm afraid I don't understand.'

'One of these days you British are going to leave Palestine. We will have our own state then, and our neighbours won't just sit there and let us get on with it. There will be another war, and we will have to have an army. My husband and many others will form that army when the time comes.'

Around them stretched an eerie sea of moving sand. Valleys and hills and plains and mountains of it. Only the occasional camel and the odd bedouin tent hinted at their presence on earth. His stick was on the rack above and all the while he did not get up. He did not tell her about his foot.

'Have you been in Palestine before?'

'No.'

'Are you staying long?'

'I don't know. I can't say.'

'You'll love it. I know you will. It's so different.'

'How different?'

'Oh, it's new and it's old. It's parochial and it's cosmopolitan. It's foreign yet familiar. It's right in the Middle East, but it's European ... You'll hear every language, every accent under the sun there. The natives are loud but friendly and well read. There's a spirit of energy and hope everywhere ...'

'Your English is perfect.'

'It ought to be. I was born in South Africa. Spent two years in England.'

'Oh.' He was tired. He covered his face with his hands to hide a yawn and rubbed his eyes.

'You shouldn't do that. Do you have an itch? It happens in the desert. The eyes get dry. I can give you some drops.'

'Don't worry about it.'

She picked up a little brown suitcase from the floor and opened it. She handed him a small brown bottle.

'Take it anyway.'

Next came a small packet of waxed paper. 'Would you like a sandwich?'

He wasn't hungry, but he thought she might be offended if he refused.

'Thank you,' he said, and took one.

'My sister made them for me. Egg and onion. All chopped up. A Polish delicacy.'

'Very nice,' he said, and took a small bite.

He looked at the thick wedding ring on her finger. He ate and he wanted to sleep, but she kept talking. She had no children and was running an antique shop in Tel Aviv.

'You meet a lot of interesting people that way and time

passes. My parents wanted me to go to Johannesburg for the duration of the war but I wouldn't dream of it. Where are you going to stay in Palestine?'

'I don't really know. Some convalescent place. Near Jerusalem, I think. Have to report to the Movements Officer in Jaffa first.'

'What's wrong with you? It's not shell-shock, is it?'

The ticket collector passed by again and acknowledged them with a bored two-fingered salute. He hoped she'd change the subject.

'What happened to you?'

'I ... hurt my leg,' he said, and pointed at it.

'Oh, I am sorry ... Your knee okay?'

He nodded.

'That's good. Believe me, I would never have known. You take it all very well. Mind they don't send you back to the front with that healthy face of yours. At least ... at least the war is over for you.'

'That's what everybody keeps telling me.'

'I have two days' holiday left,' she said. Her face assumed its open expression. 'When do you have to report?'

'Tomorrow. The day after. I suppose it doesn't matter much.'

'How did you ... er ... where?'

'In a tank.'

'I could show you around the place if you like.'

'Thank you.'

'Is it a date?' He thought she looked lonely.

'I suppose it is.'

The woman went silent as she watched the desert flying past. What now? he thought. Go back to university? Never. He would make a bad lawyer. Travel, that's the thing to do. Look around the world and find a corner. Be alone? He'd been that before. The Major had told him he might feel low at times. Please talk, woman, his insides screamed. Say anything. He didn't know her name and he looked at her and smiled.

'Did anyone ever tell you the world is yours for the taking? With that disarming baby-face, your strong, sensitive eyes, your infectious smile ... You will always get what you want.'

A muscle flexed in puzzlement on his cheek.

'You don't know, do you? Women will spoil you and men will follow you. You have been born under a lucky star. When is your birthday?'

That was one question he hated, but the answer shot out of him unawares.

'Christmas Day.'

'Capricorn,' she said. 'I thought so. Oh yes, how easy it will be for you ... how hard on those who'll love you ... And there will be plenty of those, boychick. Plenty.'

She was trying to make him feel good. 'You don't really believe all that, do you?'

'Wait and see and live and then perhaps you'll remember what I said. Of course I believe in it. Look in the mirror one day and smile. From the inside. You'll see what I mean ... I wonder what time we get in? The seafront by night is a dream.'

The gentle clatter of the rails sang heavy lullabies. He fought to keep his eyes open. She looked at him and she whispered. 'Rest a bit. I'll wake you when we get there.'

Much later, in her apartment, the softness of her voice turned hard. Through the open bathroom door he felt the urgency of it.

'Come now,' she said. He did not answer.

The sight of his stump was strange and ugly and alien. He had tried to immerse himself in the water to hide it. The Major had said something about that too. 'It's your body, Cunningham. Don't ever hate your own body.' How easy it is to give advice.

He did not report to anyone upon arrival. The woman said two days was all the time in the world. He could come to her flat. She was gentle and sweet, if a little pushy, and now they were there and she was calling him. He crawled out of the water and reached for his stick. He wiped himself in short, hurried strokes and slipped his underpants on.

'I thought you'd drowned in there.'

'I'm still wet,' he said sheepishly.

'Come over here. I'll dry you.'

He hopped through the door towards her, his silhouette cutting through the light. He was short of breath. He sat down on the bed beside her. She took the sheet cover and rubbed his back. 'There,' she said, 'that's better.' Her hand cupped his shoulder and she pulled him closer. Her nightgown was soft and warm and transparent.

'It's been a long day,' he said as the feel of her body brought a flush of anxiety. Her skin was smooth and her long legs crawled towards him and around his hips and her hands were everywhere. She was kissing him hard. From the side table, flanked by a silver frame, her husband's rugged face smiled at him.

And then she touched him there. Her hand was warm, but it contracted. 'What's the matter?' she asked, and she looked and smiled and turned the light off. Her hands came back to him very gently and stroked and he felt himself harden. In the dark he saw her smile.

'Come on,' she whispered, and turned to him and guided him to her. He held his breath and moved against her in short, uncontrolled jerks. His mind attempted random thoughts a dozen times a second but his body had taken over and his excitement was soon spent. He fell down on top of her and grunted. She wriggled and bit his shoulder and shouted something.

'I'm sorry,' he said, and wished he could disappear.

'Your first time?' she asked, and he nodded. She lay back and lit a cigarette.

'How marvellous. I've never been with a male virgin before.'

He wished she could be less explicit.

'Don't look so worried,' she said, and was all smiles. She

21

joked and brought him a plate of fruit from the kitchen. She cut the fruit up for him and watched him eat.

'Thank you,' he said.

She got up and went to the bathroom. He thought he heard something break. Perhaps he had overstayed his welcome. By the time she came out of the shower, he was dressed.

'Where are you going? You'll never find a place at this time of night. You can stay in the spare room.'

'I thought you'd rather I went.'

'How little you know of women. I'll make you some hot chocolate. It'll make you sleep better.'

Later still, he heard her come in. He must have dozed off for a few hours and he rubbed his eyes when he felt her slip into the narrow bed beside him. He felt her nakedness along the whole length of his body. She was gentle with him now. She caressed his face and cheeks and hair and kissed his forehead and his eyes and his cheek and his lips. She told him he was sweet.

Her hands gripped his shoulders and he rolled over to find himself on top of her. He was not sure how he got there and suddenly he was firm and slipped into her easily. He was moving and she moaned but did not speak and he thought he must be dreaming. Soon his body was hammering against hers and she arched closer and dug her nails into him and whispered things in a language he did not understand. He touched her hair and she pulled wildly at his and all the while his body moved like the wind. The room was dark and he did not know where he was nor did he think about his leg. This had been someone else's woman yesterday, but now in his dream she was his and would remain so until he awoke and anyway it did not matter. He was moving with all the vigour of youth and her body closed in on him, moist and tight, and then she screamed and he woke up and saw her biting her lips. Her body sagged as she shuddered. Down there, gushes of pleasure surrounded him and he moved more as a prolonged explosion hit him and still he moved and she said, 'You're killing me, tiger,' and then she fell silent. He could wake up now because he felt strong and knew he had made her happy. He stretched his muscles and smiled in the dark and he felt her lips glide across his face and brush his lips and then she was gone.

CHAPTER SIX

He had made a few Aussie friends at the sanatorium, but only truly came alive on the two or three days she visited every week. She always had things to say he wanted to hear, and her fresh look and brisk manner lightened the slow, oppressive air of the place. On weekends she would take him down to Tel Aviv, to her flat, where she washed and ironed his uniform and polished his shoes and fed him and made love to him until it hurt. She bought him slacks and shirts and told him he looked like a boy in civilian clothes, and he hated it.

Now they were in her car and she was driving and was about to say something when the rear window suddenly exploded, showering fragments of glass over the back seat. And then he heard the shots. Some whined past them and some hit the side of the car. She looked at him with an expression of relief as she slammed her foot down. The car shot forward like a rocket down the narrow, winding road from Jerusalem. A fast-sinking red sun lit the pine-strewn hills.

'They got a whole family last week,' she said. 'They planted a bomb under a heap of cow shit on this road and detonated it as the car passed over. No one survived. Two small children. The father was a heart specialist. No politics, no nothing. Fuckers.'

He blushed at the sound of her language, but she was driving too fast to notice. She was good at everything, he thought. The tyres screeched as the car took the curves.

'Hold on, Cunningham. I've got to get you out of here. You come up and down on the train from now on.'

'I am a soldier, you know.'

'Yes, but this isn't your war. You're supposed to have come here to get away from danger, not to get shot at.'

'There must be something you can do.'

They had come out of the creek and were driving into open country, leaving the Judean hills behind. They approached a crossroads where there was a petrol station. She stopped, and they got out to clean up the car. Here the sun was still visible. In the shade of a carob tree sat a police jeep. She ignored it.

'Are you going to report this?'

'Don't be silly. What difference would it make? Nobody's interested. There's a big, bad war going on, you know.'

'You ought at least to have a revolver. Won't you take mine?'

'Don't be crazy. You'll get yourself into trouble.'

'I'll find a way. I can't have you driving about unarmed.'

'You are a very sweet boy, but no.'

'Why?'

'We're not supposed to carry guns. It's against the law.'

'They weren't using broomsticks back there.'

'Try and find them. How they get their guns is a mystery. The way they hide them is a greater mystery. The Palestine police search their villages, but nothing is ever found. Are you all right?'

'I love you.'

'Of course you love me, dear boy. And I love you too.'

'What about your husband?'

'I am in love with him.'

'How can you say that?'

'Different, Cunningham, different. We both love each other, my husband and I. We made no promises when he volunteered to go to war. He is my best friend. We are not going to interrogate each other when he comes back.'

He fell silent. He did not understand. He slept in the man's bed and washed in his bath and ate off his plates. And he had been making love to his wife. Just like the man who had taken his mother away.

'You will love him, too, when you meet him,' she said. He could not imagine how.

'I must do something about your safety.'

His opportunity came unexpectedly, towards the end of the following week. He had to go to the military hospital near Haifa for a check-up on the condition of his stump. He had to leave all his clothes and personal effects at the reception desk. The clerk surprised him by noting all his property on a cyclostyled form, and when he asked why, he told him that there was a lot of pilfering in the hospital.

'Commandant's ordered that we list everything, get it signed in and out. Puts us in the clear, like, if anything goes walkies ... We have every nationality under the sun in this establishment. Unless we list your property in an orderly fashion and lock it up in this steel box it may not be all here when you leave, sir ...'

The telephone on the shelf behind him rang and the clerk turned to answer it. Cunningham waited as he consulted a list posted on the wall, and then, quite calmly, he reached into the box and took out the heavy Webley revolver and hid it under his dressing gown.

He had never stolen anything in his life before and his heart pounded. Surely someone must have seen him. Any minute now someone would say something. But the clerk replaced the telephone receiver and turned back to him with a smile.

'Sorry, sir. It's the busiest time of day.'

'Don't give it a thought.' He looked up at the clock on the wall. 'I'd better cut along to my clinic, hadn't I.'

He had reached the end of the corridor when the clerk called him back. He turned slowly. Could the man have seen him after all?

'What is it?' he asked with an edge of impatience in his voice.

'Could you just sign the list, sir? Confirm you left all these items with us?'

'Certainly.'

He brought the house down when he declared the pistol missing. He demanded that the clerk produce the inventory form which showed it had been left in the hospital's care. Reports were written, typed and duly signed. No suspicion ever came his way and he left the hospital for Jerusalem with arrangements for a replacement revolver among his papers.

When next they met, walking in the garden of the sanatorium, he slipped the weapon to her, wrapped up in a copy of the *Palestine Post*. Speechless, she dropped the parcel into her bag. The cake she had brought crumbled under the weight of the gun. That day there was no search of visitors entering and leaving the convalescent home.

That was the start of a thin trickle of arms which Cunningham began to find for her friends. A few Sten guns and then a rifle and some more Sten guns and a two-inch mortar. Later there were a few shells and some ammunition. He found a willing ally in the Australian corporal who claimed he needed money to pay gambling debts. The man could procure almost anything at the drop of a hat.

It was a dangerous, riveting time. The clandestine business excited him as nothing had ever done before. He was buying and selling arms for love. He was breaking the law, yet underneath it all there was the excuse of a just cause driving him on, and he continued taking risks. The cloak-and-dagger, middle-of-the-night meetings with hooded, voiceless people on street corners and in fields and the backs of trucks worked on him like a drug. Often he would arrive, blindfolded, to where money was handed over for equipment with a handshake or a slap on the back and always a guttural whisper of thanks. Then the tortuous drive that would deliver him outside the gates of the sanatorium with one more transaction completed. The Australian corporal said he must have been raking in a fortune and laughed when Cunningham assured him he was selling the equipment on at cost.

The time for his repatriation was fast approaching. He tried to get demobbed in Palestine and find a position for himself in the local government. He had started to walk the corridors, looking for the right doors to knock on, when the Australian corporal was arrested one Sunday morning. At noon the same day, two CID men came knocking on Cunningham's door. He had spent that day on Lake Galilee with the South African woman, and by evening she had told him he could not go back to Jerusalem.

'Why not?'

'The Military Police are looking for you.'

'What are you talking about?'

'You can't go back. They have arrested your Australian friend.'

'How do you know?'

'We have our contacts.'

On the drive back to Tel Aviv, Cunningham hid behind a fake Jewish beard and a traditional black coat which she found for him in the holy city of Tiberias. They were not stopped and she kept telling him he should never wear that outfit again.

'You can stay here,' she said as soon as they got to her flat.

'For how long?'

'Until we find a way to get you out of the country. I'm afraid it may be a long time before you see England again. Perhaps you never will. God, what have I done to you?'

'You have done nothing to me. I don't want to go back to England. There's nothing left for me there.'

'You are a young boy. The bridge for home is made of stone. It never burns.'

Her husband was involved in the nucleus of a future Jewish defence force. A middle-of-the-road organization that had encouraged its members to join the British forces. Cunningham had met a few of the members, and over the next few months he was to hear three sentences repeatedly.

'We will not leave you in the lurch. We never forget our friends. We are not without resources.' They said it with great pathos. As if speaking of the basic tenets of their creed.

He was, from that time on, always in their company. They appreciated what he had done for them and never left him in the flat alone. And yet, in spite of all the voices and emotions, even when in bed close to her, Cunningham began to feel he was on his own.

'Life will never be the same again,' she said one night.

CHAPTER SEVEN

◼

SUNDAY 22 JULY, 1984, 12.30 P.M.

The smell of her roast reaches me right down by the gate as I return from my walk. We bank managers are creatures of habit. Even though I thought I saw Cunningham I got home in time. We eat at half past one, prompt, just after the news. I am never late and she makes sure we are finished within the hour. In time for the matinee. We both like to watch these black and white oldies, but they've been running short of decent films lately.

She looks through the living-room window and waves as a smile brightens her face. She has this transistor radio she listens to while she's in the kitchen. They might say something on the news; Cunningham was not exactly unknown. An hour to kill before lunch. Time enough to dead-head the roses or attack a patch of daisies or something. Sundays are so long.

He had some connections in the Middle East. Business-wise they were not much use since he knew no one from the oil-rich countries. He did know a lot of Israelis, however. Mostly from his time in Palestine, before he surfaced in the

Dominican Republic and Haiti. He even introduced some of his friends to us on occasion. They looked bulky and uncomfortable in their ill-fitting three-piece suits. Large fellows, almost menacing and always on the defensive. Humourless, hard to entertain, they were, and I could never understand what a man of his culture and charm ever saw in them.

Except for the one we met in Palma one Easter. I think it was the second time we'd been there with Cunningham. Little breaks-from-the-hassle sort of trips. I did, of course, pay our own expenses and Cunningham was only as generous as I allowed him to be. This particular chap spent a few days with us, and I think I got to know him quite well. He worshipped Cunningham, of that I am sure. I played tennis with him that morning while Cunningham and my wife took off for Valdermosa, where Chopin had lived with George Sand. Had it not been for his thick silvery hair and intelligent conversation he could have passed for someone's bodyguard.

He spoke English fluently, though with a thick accent. Reached the rank of captain in the British Army during the war. Went through the desert campaign and Italy. He said he spent many years in the Israeli Army where he made colonel. He was now in business for himself and had an aura of success about him, with a chauffeur-driven car and constantly being paged for overseas calls. His manner was easy, yet he did not seem to relax. He did not say what business he was in, and I, of course, did not ask.

We played for a couple of hours and then he took me through the narrow streets of old Palma. He gave me a condensed history of the Jews in Spain. He had no formal education beyond secondary school, but was an ardent reader. Went through two or three books a week. Most subjects. His favourite topic of conversation was Cunningham. I suppose he was obsessed with him, just as I am.

'I've known him for years,' he said as we sat down for a cool drink in the plaza. 'One of the best, I assure you.'

'How did you meet?' I asked.

'It was my wife. She met him first. You will laugh. She met him on a train from Alexandria. Long before Egypt became an enemy. He was very young then, even though to look at him you wouldn't think he'd aged at all. And yet his personality has undergone a total transformation.'

'How?'

'The young, insecure, shy English subaltern my wife met on the train to Palestine on his way from the war became a Latin. He is friendly and outgoing and fun and a hell of a flirt. Most Englishmen never change, regardless of how many years they spend in India or Africa or anywhere. I suppose Cunningham became a Latin because there were no British clubs or races or any of the trimmings you people surround yourselves with when you are away from home. There were very few English people in the Dominican Republic at the time.'

'I don't quite understand what you mean when you say he became a Latin.'

'He is sentimental. He has no strong political convictions, yet he will take sides in an argument. He'll try anything new. He is only conservative in the way he dresses. He is vain about that. He doesn't plan for his retirement or worry about life insurance. He'd spend his last penny on having fun. Fair play to Cunningham is what he feels is right on the spur of the moment, yet he strongly believes in justice. His own kind of justice, strictly based on the time and place and those who are about. He does not believe in interests or right or wrong as per John Stuart Mill or the Bible. His code of honour is built on a whim, yet he is the most loyal friend you could ever have.

'Interesting guy, Cunningham. Nothing predictable about him. He is an adventurer, you know. A modern-day pirate. Just like the English used to be before they got rich or bored or whatever.'

We walked along the bay, among the thick old palms, and we watched the yachts nodding their bows by the quay.

'I wonder what made the English change,' he said. 'They come up with the greatest inventions and then they go to sleep. You people have taught the world how to run governments, banks, industries and armies. You can make the best cars, build the greatest boats and design guns and planes and engines second to none. I cannot understand why you are in such a mess these days.'

He wasn't telling me anything new, but the way he spoke made me feel he had a secret admiration for us, and that was amusing.

'You two go back a long time,' I said.

'Yes. My wife met him in '42 or '43. I saw him first in 1950, after our war of independence. Until then he had kept in touch with my wife. She was the typical Jewish mama. You see, they met just after he'd lost his foot and was, I suppose, having problems getting used to it. He had also just lost his father. He needed someone to talk to maybe. Perhaps he saw a mother figure in her. Anyway, we three got on famously together from the start.

'Above all, he was a tower of strength to me when she died. Invited me to spend a month with him in Florida. That was where we became really close. When my world collapsed, he was there.'

His face assumed a sadness that embarrassed me. He was, in view of our short acquaintance, being a little too personal. Yet what he said only strengthened my own esteem for Cunningham. By that time he was living in England permanently and we either saw or spoke to each other at least twice a week.

He was supporting someone in the Dominican Republic. At his insistence I used to arrange for these payments myself. I do not know much about his life on the island. He talked little of his time there. All I knew was what my wife's brother Gerald Buckmaster had told me, and that wasn't much.

It was late in the afternoon when Cunningham and my wife got back to the hotel. She had had a marvellous time and looked radiant and I was pleased for her. I am not much of a tourist and being a housewife must be a bore. The Israeli colonel and I were having a drink on the verandah when they walked in. I could sense the bond of affection between them. I might have been a bit jealous. Or maybe I resented the way my wife looked. I do not remember. It's all academic now anyway.

The last time I saw the colonel was when he came to my office. Cunningham was out of the country and he was passing through. I took him for lunch and we talked. It was not long ago and I remember it well. We talked about zombies and voodoo and the world of the spirits. Not a subject I favour particularly. All I knew about Haiti was its economics. Poorest country in the Western world.

'Papa Doc,' I said, 'isn't that the Governor's name?'

'Oh, there's more to Haiti,' the colonel said. 'Much more. It's an exciting place – naive paintings, friendly natives, incredible music. Beautiful country, too. You should ask Cunningham. He knows it inside out. Black magic played a big part in his life at one time.'

He talked of Haiti, but everything centred on Cunningham. I didn't pay much attention. By then, of course, I already knew about him and my wife. My plans were shaping up.

CHAPTER EIGHT

—◼—

She has always been a quiet girl who blushes easily. I am exceedingly proud of the way she looks and the way she dresses. In all the gatherings we have had over the years, I could not help noticing how some of my colleagues looked at her. Even the younger ones. In today's world she could easily have been a model.

Maybe not. She is far too shy and reserved for that. I have rarely seen her in the nude; she would invariably wait for me under the sheets. Whenever I was in the room at bedtime she would undress in the dark.

I wonder how she was with him. Did she make him wait outside until she was in bed? Was she all the things she never wanted to be with me, with him? It's all back in my mind now. Frustrated anger mingled with helpless humiliation.

Lunch will soon be ready. She has this habit of watching me while I eat. She is an excellent cook and is eager for my reaction. I do not want her to see the pain or sense the depth of misery her affair has caused me. And still does. I do not believe in carrying my heart on my sleeve for all the world to see. That does not mean I have no feelings. I do, and they are killing me.

I could not function at the time. I only went through the motions of doing my job. Luckily I had good assistants. Heaven knows what they must have thought was wrong with me. I could not make love to her for months, and yet I wanted her more than anything in the world. I still do today, but I cannot get rid of this thing hanging over our alcove.

Ego, I tell myself. That's all it is. Ego. Balls. I was and am and always will be jealous. I sometimes wish I could tell her I know, but then I think she might still be in love with him. It is not difficult. For many years I was extremely fond of him myself.

How will she feel when she finds out? Will Cunningham become a martyr? She must suspect something is up. We used to talk about him a lot. I used to. We hardly mention him these days. I started to get urges to belittle him. Invent stories that would make him look ridiculous in her eyes. Anything. But I didn't believe them myself and certainly did not know how she would react.

Sometimes, at night, I would lie there and know she was awake. Not just awake, but wanting. Wanting him. Every bone in her body yearning with desire for him. For any man but me. I would sneak a glance in her direction and see her glorious shape and know that her skin was eager for a touch right then, right there under the sheet that separates us. I would know she was on the edge of frustration. On fire. But not for me to put out. How often did I try, in those terrible days, to stretch my arm towards her and be rewarded with a total stiffening of her body? I would listen to her breathing and sense that scent of woman in the heat that emanated from her side, while the room around me remained cold and lonely.

I feel weak. I feel crushed. The pain of castration is hammering under my skin. It's all back again. I have some time on my hands, but I cannot prune the roses or trim the lawn or do anything for long. I cannot concentrate. I pretend, sitting here reading the papers, but I cannot go through more than three lines before my mind begins to wander. Even now, in my own chair, on a day of rest, I get those thoughts about him and her.

I am being stupid. This happens to everybody. You hear about it and close friends admit it to you in weak moments. Sometimes you manage to help just by listening and you understand it all. As long as it isn't you. God, how I wish sometimes I were one of those hot-blooded Mediterraneans you read about. Get mad and have the whole thing off your chest by means of what the French call a crime of passion. No, no, no. How dare I even think of it. I am not an animal.

She is standing by the french windows. I can hear her breathe and feel her presence and any minute now she may come up and touch my shoulder as she does sometimes. She must not see my eyes. I cannot understand how she never noticed it, knowing me as she does. Must keep calm. We'll hear the news soon. Better not switch it on at all. I'd rather not be around when she finds out.

After the war, Cunningham found himself in the Dominican Republic. How he got there or why he went I do not know. He made his home on the island and lived there and in Haiti on and off until he came back to the UK. He could have been involved in all sorts of things and I would never have guessed had it not been for my wife's brother Gerald. He told me all about the slave trade. He did not know Cunningham had anything to do with it. He did not tell his sister and I certainly won't. It might make him even more of a hero in her eyes. She is an incurable romantic. She became one, the way women do sometimes, right under your nose. I did not notice. Perhaps she was that way all the while. I am going to get to know her better now that I have the time.

'Lunch is ready, dear,' she calls. I look up and she smiles. She takes my hand as she always does and leads me in. She does not notice a thing.

It is the usual silent ritual of a Sunday lunch. I sit down at my place and look the carving knife over. We do not speak until we are both sitting across from each other to start the meal.

The most important element in any marriage is friendship, and that we have certainly had. This must by why I never told her I knew about her and Cunningham. That was and should remain locked in her private domain. True friendship is measured by the amount of breathing space one partner allows the other. She has given me all the time and space I ever needed. She accepted the position of second fiddle to my work, and her understanding of my needs enabled me to attain the position I reached at the bank.

She endured many lonely years while I moved up the ladder. Both her parents were dead and Gerald, her surviving brother, had gone to work for his father-in-law in the Dominican Republic. She did have an older brother who was killed by one of the Jewish terrorist gangs in Palestine in 1946. She did not often mention him, but I knew how much his death still affected her.

Their relationship was rather more than the usual admiration of a girl for a brother who was a grown man. He seemed to have understood her better than anyone, and since their parents died when she was ten years old, he more or less brought her up and supported her on the small salary they paid in the colonial service.

That, and the fact that they used to have paying guests in their house, must have been the reason for Gerald's burning ambition to get on. He went through Oxford and into his career with a vengeance. Today he would be called a workaholic.

There is a picture of the three of them on the table in the living room. All tall and very distinguished-looking. Gerald looks like a larger version of the Prince of Wales. The one who abdicated to marry Mrs Simpson. She stands there between the two of them, already a stunningly beautiful woman. Tall, slim, if a bit hippy, with the face of a madonna. Her hair is greying now, but the high cheekbones, her alabaster skin, her haunting green eyes and sensual lips arouse a desire in me that is hard to contain. I am not surprised Cunningham fell for her.

She helps me to vegetables and then holds up the sauce boat.

'A new recipe,' she says. 'Tell me what you think. I got it from Delia Smith in yesterday's *Evening Standard*.'

No. She has not noticed a thing. But she is good at hiding her emotions. When we met the Israeli colonel in Majorca she never gave any indication of her true feelings towards Jews, especially Israelis, following the death of her beloved brother. She was quiet and remote, but invariably polite to him. I think I did notice some signs of strain, but no one else did. No one could have done.

Later, on the few occasions when he passed through London, I understood completely when she always pleaded a prior engagement. Of course, I had no notion then of the attachment she had formed for Cunningham, and that she found it painful to be in his company along with me, her husband, and an Israeli who could easily have been her brother's assassin. All that belongs to her and I must not and will not intrude. I pray to have the strength to keep it from her until the end.

It is that, and not the problems he caused the bank, which finally tipped the scales and made me see Cunningham for what he was. Forgive her? Yes. Forget? Never.

Sometimes I wish I had never found out.

CHAPTER NINE

■

SUNDAY 22 JULY, 1984, 2 A.M.

The moon floats past the window and away. He sits at his desk, conscious but barely awake. There are footsteps and small sounds in the garden outside the open window. Things are happening out there, but Cunningham's mind is hovering between sleep and awareness. Pictures of his past flash by. Some linger, others last but a second. He feels the danger in the air. Close by. Somewhere in this room. And yet he is at peace with himself and the world as if his turbulent years had never been.

Is he going to die today? He's heard it said that pictures of one's life pass before one's eyes, just before the end. He has no reason to believe it. He has been in mortal danger before, certainly. But he cannot remember running through his past like this, this animated picture album, then.

It doesn't matter much who is after him. Somewhere in the labyrinth of his past there must be someone with a long-lasting grudge. Unsettled accounts he has overlooked. Oh, sweet Jesus, how tired he is of being the eternal survivor.

But then he is comfortable and snug behind his own desk. The chair is soft and the surroundings familiar. He is in control. He can choose the pictures he wants to watch. Why, then, this sadness? Is he getting old? Yesterday is a tired friend.

He remembers going back on that same train to Alexandria. They sent the South African woman with him as far as the port, where he boarded a freighter to Cape Town. The Jews had died his hair and his beard and dressed him up again in the black, sombre clothes of the Hassidim. They had given him a letter from some famous rabbi testifying that he was deaf and dumb and pious, travelling to collect funds for the blind in the

Holy Land.

He kept very much to himself on the long voyage down the east coast of Africa. They met him in Cape Town and took him to a house where he would be safe. Maintaining his disguise, they kept him indoors. There was a ship, they told him, in three weeks, that would take him to New York, by way of Rio and Recife.

Time crawled by, but the ship finally arrived and sailed on time. He was about to settle for more waiting when, as the sight of Table Mountain crept over the horizon, two men came into his cabin. They told him he could abandon the charade and revert to his own appearance. He could cut his hair and shave his beard and talk. He was allowed his own name again and was given a new biography.

A descendant of British settlers in Central America, he became, overnight, a diplomat in the service of Nicaragua with a consular position in Miami. Once in Florida, he was given a crash course in Spanish. He took to the language well, and by the end of the war he was sent to his next posting, the commercial section of the Nicaraguan Embassy in Ciudad Trujillo, the capital of the Dominican Republic. He was given twenty thousand dollars and told that he was now on his own.

He fell into the local scene without any trouble. It was a place where no one asked any questions. He was an Englishman with a Central American diplomatic passport, and none of the locals enquired into the contrast his background presented. He began to enjoy the food and the climate and the slow flow of Caribbean life.

The arrangement, he was told, was good for five years. By that time he would have found his feet and his future and some purpose. The Jews said they would not let him starve and would help him in any venture he cared to involve himself in. They kept their side of the bargain with considerable efficiency and generosity, and Cunningham did carve a new life for himself. He did get involved. Especially when he ran into Francisco Martinez.

He sits up and he looks at the ceiling. The thought of that scoundrel makes him laugh out loud. Francisco Martinez. That *hijo de puta*.

'*Conjo,*' he says to himself. '*Dónde estás ahora*, Francisco, you son of a bitch?'

He knows full well where Francisco is. Why is he asking? Why is he thinking in Spanish all of a sudden?

The first blush of daylight is trying to creep into the sky. He must have fallen asleep again. He is no longer tired or morose and the dangers he had steeled himself to face have gone with the moon. He gets up and he stretches and he takes his stick in his hand. A hot bath. A few more hours of real sleep in his own bed. Might go into the village in the morning. Browse around the shops.

What of the body by the window? A shiver crosses his back. He is not scared. Must be the cool morning air. The walls are a holy mess. A mini-tornado has torn through the wallpaper and her paintings are sliced. The trinkets on his desk are in disarray.

'*Qué importancia?*' he says to himself. '*Mañana otro día.*' Spanish again.

He walks to the window and looks out. It is dark still and he can smell the fire that has eaten at the dry overgrown lawn. He'll give that lazy Haitian a talking-to on Monday. Never cuts the grass all the way to the wall. Too lazy to use the shears. Or does he hope to find a snake in the knee-high grass, in this neck of the woods?

He takes his torch out of the drawer and looks again. There are clear signs of charring on the lawn. There are cracks in the brickwork where shrapnel fragments have struck. There is a patch of something that might be blood. He cannot be sure.

But there is no body. There is nothing.

BOOK TWO
YESTERDAY

CHAPTER ONE

■

SANTO DOMINGO, JULY 1964

It was the end, and she knew it, but then she had always found it difficult to accept defeat. Her husband was coming back that very afternoon, and Cunningham had said he was returning to Europe and his beginnings. She wanted to believe him, but could never be sure. She knew he was in danger and on the run. There was nothing she could do for him. Worse still, he wouldn't have wanted her help. Certainly not her pity.

What a mess. To become star-struck by a man twenty years older than herself, a man with a secret past and a doubtful future. Why? What was Cunningham to her anyway? Everything, her whole being shrieked back. She wiped her eyes and gazed out at the sea, beyond the coast road they called the Malecon. The breaking waves groaned, lifted themselves high into the air, then thundered down in white explosions onto the honeycomb rocks below. It was a heavy, grey day, and the world was taking a troubled siesta. Or so it seemed to Marina as she sat in Antonio's Bar and watched but saw nothing.

She would have gone with him to Tierra del Fuego or Mandalay or the end of the world if he had asked her, but he had not. Nor would he ask her now because he was far away and out of anybody's reach. And anyway they were through.

'It should stay our secret,' Cunningham had told her. 'Don't hurt Gerald with a confession; you'll probably spend the rest of your life with him.'

The arrogant, condescending son of a bitch. And yet when she first met him he had cut a shabby, pathetic figure for whom one might have felt no more than pity. And still she wanted to talk about him and brag about it and scream. She wanted to grab the world by its insensitive lapels and tell it how Cunningham was hers once, too.

Oh, she knew the truth about him. She knew about his

lifestyle and his shady deals and had met the unsavoury characters he mixed with. Why, then, was she in so much pain? Because they all loved him. Because he was the sun and the moon and the stars. Baby-talk. Maybe it was, but then she didn't want to believe he was a bastard. Why, he couldn't even go back to his native England. Everybody knew that. Of course he was bad. Was she losing her marbles, yearning for him like this?

No way she was. She'd just lived through the most exhilarating two weeks of her life. 'Mature love,' he had called it. Said it didn't happen to many. Damn right it didn't.

She looked around her and sensed the hollow afternoon. Antonio, wiping his eternally wet bar, wore a bored expression. Did he think she was crazy, too? No. He had been Cunningham's friend for years, and he knew.

'Give me another beer,' she said. She didn't want to think any more or prod any more, and as the cool, bitter liquid filtered through her lips her mind crawled back into the distant past.

Marina Stone Buckmaster was the most unlikely woman to become involved with the likes of Cunningham. She was a Stone of Lexington, Vermont. They were gentlefolk whose ancestors had helped found the town. The male Stones had fought in all America's wars, thrived in peacetime and married their own.

Her husband, Gerald Buckmaster, was not seen as a foreigner even though he was born in England. She had met him one summer at Oxford, during a week's visit there. The family did not expect her to emerge from her first trip to Europe with a prospective husband, but as soon as they set eyes on him they knew he was one of them.

The Stones had always wanted a son, and Gerald had all the attributes they would have expected in a son of their own. He was tall and reserved, with just a trace of hesitancy in his beautifully modulated voice to indicate self-control. He had impeccable manners and had graduated from Oxford. Both his parents had died in his childhood and his only sister was respectably married to a banker.

Within weeks of his arrival, the best families were inviting him to their barbecues and their cocktails and tennis parties, making Marina the object of much benevolent, if slightly envious, chatter. He was a presentable, helpful young man who had immediately captured Marina's mother's heart. He blended in with their friends, causing no ripples in the local conservative waters.

After the wedding, Gerald joined his father-in-law's trading company, quickly gaining membership with the two really good clubs in town. He worked long and hard hours and made himself immediately popular with customers and suppliers alike. When the family decided to open an office in the Dominican Republic to serve the Caribbean, Central and South America, he accepted the job of running it as soon as it was suggested.

And Cunningham? How could you? her mother would have asked. What do you know of love? she would have answered. God, she knew he was different. He was English, too, just like Gerald, but that was where the resemblance ended. His arrival in Central America before the end of the war was a mystery. He had no steady income and his fortunes rose and fell and he used people. Used her, too. On their very first meeting he had used her.

While the Buckmasters and their two little girls were packing their bags to go to the small Republic, Cunningham was doing time in Puerto Rico, the American territory thirty-five miles to the west. He was held on suspicion of various offences, including murder and drug trafficking, but no evidence was found and his stay behind bars was short.

On the day the Buckmasters' Pan Am Clipper from Miami landed at the Aeropuerto de las Américas, Cunningham was in that very same customs hall. He was amusing the officers with tales of the gringo jail. He was just about to describe how he got out when he heard an unmistakably British voice flare into an argument by the conveyor next to his. Amidst the shouting and the commotion, the customs officer was insisting on Gerald opening his luggage.

The young man, who knew very little of the local habits, was fiercely objecting. 'I have already told you,' Gerald said in his best Oxford Spanish, 'that I have nothing to declare.'

This was too serious for the customs man, who was used to an immediate response. All he really wanted was to get a good-humoured look into what the gringos were bringing in. Something to gossip about later, that was all.

Marina was holding the baby in her arms while the little girl clung firmly to her skirts. She was hot and wished Gerald could be a little less pompous with the officer. The man was losing face and was becoming angry. 'Please open all the cases, señor, and empty your pockets. Do not speak back to me.'

Cunningham, who knew the man well enough to call him by his first name, drew him aside with a wink. He whispered something in his ear about the other Englishman being drunk out of his mind. After a few minutes of hearty laughter, the customs officer returned to face the Buckmasters with a broad smile.

'You should have told me you have lost the key, señor. Any friends of Señor Cunningham are welcome here.'

At the mention of his name, Cunningham touched his hat. Marina glanced at him, and then the baby stopped crying. The air-conditioning began to work and the officer waved them on.

Cunningham's suit looked old, but it was perfectly pressed. His face, clean-shaven and haggard, smiled at her. His well-worn shoes were polished, as was the black cane he was leaning on. The proud demeanour of his presence contrasted sharply with his tatty luggage. He smiled at her. It was a broad smile that extended all the way to his shining, cobalt-blue eyes. Gerald wanted to say something more to the officer, but Marina kicked his ankle.

'Just thank the gentleman and move, darling,' she said.

'Let's get out of here.'

They were now at the door, and Gerald did not notice the little packet someone dropped into the open shopping bag Marina was carrying. While they waited outside for their luggage to follow, Cunningham came up. As he addressed Gerald, another man fished the packet out again. The exercise was not really necessary, but his man inside the building had thought Cunningham's interference was a signal for him to use the gringo's checked luggage as a means of transport. Marina had been watching and she saw it all, but Cunningham's dilapidated attire evoked a spark of pity in her.

'You will find it difficult to get a cab here, young man,' Cunningham said. 'Do use mine. I have some unfinished business here. It's paid for.'

'I cannot accept any more help from you. You're British, aren't you?'

'I am indeed. We ought not to let the side down out here. You might do the same for me some time. There's a chronic shortage of taxis in this town.'

Gerald was about to protest. Marina looked about her. There was no other cab in sight. Perhaps the man was trying to make up for his indiscretion.

'Come on, take the cab, darling. The girls are tired.'

'We'll take it, thank you,' Gerald said.

'Where would you like to go?'

'The Hispaniola Hotel.'

'*Al Hotel Hispaniola, por favor, Rafael,*' Cunningham told the driver in a surprisingly fluent local Spanish.

And that was that. They had met. A nothing meeting. A trifling encounter that would have led nowhere. She might never have remembered his face or his voice; even that smile of his. And yet there was something strange in his eyes and the blatant way he had looked at her, unabashed, without a word.

If anything, she could have felt compassion for the way he looked, elegantly spreading his arms as he spoke to Gerald. At best he could have been an impoverished, social-climbing smuggler. Yet now, as she sat in the little open-air bar, she remembered what followed. It had only just ended, but it seemed to have happened years ago. She must have grown up in two weeks. Her eyes were moist, her spirits low, and her body ached all over.

She would have to get back to her hotel pretty soon, since Gerald's plane was due at any moment. They were supposed to move into the house they had rented. He would be surprised and angry if she were not packed and ready, and in a curious way she wished him to be. She yearned to tell him of the travels and the dangers and the thrills and the incredible time she'd had in Haiti. A lifetime on another planet. Yet all they'd had were two lousy weeks.

The wind rose, the palm trees swayed wildly, and the asphalt bubbled. Her beer was as hot as the day. She was not the pleading type and abhorred begging, but she had tried. He could, she said, go straight back to England and avoid whoever was chasing him. He could sneak back across the border into Haiti and ask the British Consulate for help.

Stupid, that. She knew he was travelling on a Nicaraguan passport and had wondered why, but he never said. All he did was refuse, claiming that it was a question of honour. He said that to walk the streets of Mayfair empty-handed was worse than death. He had, he said, often been poor and he knew.

At the time, her heart went out to him and she would have given him all she had and more. But she knew he would never accept charity from a woman. It was a woman's help which had started him off on the wrong road, he had once told her, in an unguarded moment.

She knew that women were the mainstay of his life. He had known them and had felt for them and loved them. He understood their moods and their whims and had identified with their frustration and their pain. She had heard about their suppressed desires to stand tall in this crowded male world of the Latin.

In his crooked way, Cunningham was a perfect gentleman. Francisco Martinez had told her how Cunningham took women into his confidence and worked with them as equals while remaining their defender, their mouthpiece and sometimes their lover. Francisco would not have lied about that. Cunningham's attitude to women was something he detested.

Here, in the eternal summer of the islands, both the Conquistadors and the vanquished Indians were buried. But while there were statues for the conquerors, their victims' blood was never avenged. This was the macho world where there were no libraries or women's clubs or the female vote to lean on. Not if you were poor. Here women endured a loneliness that increased in their winter years. Here a man could be, and often was, ostracized for taking a woman's side. She could talk about it and her mother's friends would start a collection, but no one would believe her.

She knew about Cunningham and women. Everybody did. Yet still he was liked and allowed to survive and sometimes, rarely, he was allowed to prosper. Men of the older generation hoped he would repent and younger ones laughed at his jokes, accepted his drinks and tried to sleep with his women, and hated him quietly when they failed. He had refused to take money from a woman and yet he was a slave trader, a hoodlum. Not her sort at all. Her mother would die.

Soon, in a few hours, the wind would drop with the sun. The evening lights would bounce off passing cars. There would be music in the air and the scent of frying food and flowers, and courting couples in the shadows. She should keep herself busy unpacking and arranging the house tonight. That way Gerald would ask no questions and she would not be tempted to tell him. He wouldn't boast about his trip and if she worked hard enough she might tire herself into sleep.

To sleep knowing she would not see Cunningham again was something she had been dreading, and tonight she would know. No regrets and no guilt. The little summer madness which had seized her had come late. Other girls had that at seventeen.

She knew Cunningham was in great danger and in the coming hours his battle would intensify. In the morning he might be dead, alone in the middle of nowhere. It would take the authorities months to find him and she might never know.

Drama, drama, drama. Childish bullshit. Never. This was real enough. There was nothing she could do for him. Not even wait. With Gerald in the house she would never be able to contact Francisco Martinez, the only man who could help. He never surfaced before evening, and she did not know where to find him this early. And right in her bag was all that money entrusted to her for Francisco. Her husband would want to know about the children, to hear about the Spanish lessons she was supposed to be taking, and he would want to take her to bed.

Marina paid for the beer. She might as well go back to the hotel and be ready to move out as soon as Gerald arrived. Cunningham would not thank her for talking to Francisco just to save his life. He did not want her to do anything. He did not want any part of her. He might just as well be struck down and die like a dog.

She would miss the bastard. She would cry for him in the day and long for his laughter in the evening and his arms at night. She was fantasizing again. Infatuation, that's all it was. No it was not. Yes it was. Had she not met Cunningham again, she would never have given him another thought. Yes, of course he had been kind to them, but where she came from people were always helpful.

CHAPTER TWO

A lush, palm-lined highway swung past their car as they sped from the airport into town. Red and mauve and yellow bougainvillea rose between the coconut stems, and beyond, hissing into the horizon, lay the foam-spotted, emerald Caribbean Sea. The driver, competing in a local version of the Indianapolis race, was for ever overtaking everything in sight. Ceaselessly blowing his horn, he did not reduce his speed. Not for carts, trucks, animals or children. Not even for the occasional policeman they saw, sitting uninterested in their parked cars by the roadside, immersed in their newspapers. As they approached the city, crossing the wide bridge over the River Ozama, traffic lights finally forced their progress to slow.

The car now moved at the pace of a snail and was besieged by swarms of young boys trying to clean their windows for a coin. The driver ranted and raved and cursed the boys off.

'There were no begging children here when Trujillo ruled this island,' he fumed. 'There was order. That is why the city was called after him, Ciudad Trujillo.'

'Come on, Gerald, tell him to stop the car. Give them something,' Marina pleaded.

'Shouldn't give them a penny,' Gerald said. 'They must not grow up thinking someone owes them a living.'

But this did not look like a lazy place. There was a constant hustle of movement around them. Hundreds of stalls and workshops where people sweated behind mounds of fruits and vegetables and cans and sewing machines. They looked cheerful and well fed, their bodies swinging to a continuous stream of exotic merengue music that blew out from all corners. Slowly they crawled on inside the air-conditioned car, and she felt for the people out there in the heat. They carried on over changing road surfaces and past old colonial buildings and trees.

Darkness fell with a rush as they passed the Presidential Palace and turned into the Malecon which stretched along the waterfront. It burst into life as people spilled out of the cinemas, coffee shops and bars. Old people and young ones, children and couples who chuckled, walking arm in arm.

Night girls, all ages and shapes, poured colour onto the sidewalk, looking for someone to pay for their drinks and their bodies. All this was far from New England, yet the effervescent, carefree air of unhurried fun struck a chord in Marina. It had been a long day, but her weariness was gone and for a moment, in her imagination, she wantonly joined that perpetual carnival outside. Then they reached the hotel and her budding flash of mischief gave way to the baby, who started crying, while her older sister asked for a hamburger and french fries. She returned to reality with a jolt.

The day she had walked down the aisle, flushed, fresh-faced and virginal, belonged to another age. Any minute now the constant demands would be back to remind her she was a wife and a mother. In spite of being her father's employee, Gerald was firmly in charge of the purse strings. He thought she had been pampered, and was trying to teach her the value of money by keeping her short. Her parents wholeheartedly sided with him. 'In time you will find out he is right,' her mother said. And she kept quiet because she did not want an argument. The whole world couldn't be wrong.

The flowers and distant bells of her all-too-short youth had returned for a second, and then Gerald said, 'We are here, dear,' and the dream was over. Where had the romance gone? What was so great about changing nappies and washing the same dishes every day? Housewife is a dirty word when no one appreciates you and your female elders expect you to endure the drudgery just because they had to do the same. In my day one wouldn't have dreamed of complaining. Yes, yes, yes. But this is my day, she would think but never say. At twenty-seven years of age, Marina Stone Buckmaster was a matron with a teenager's soul. Her years had come and gone too quickly.

Gerald had disappeared as soon as they were shown into their suite. She was left alone, and having gone through the bathing and changing and feeding she found a note from him on the dresser. Had to go and see our man, darling. Don't wait up for me. This was going to be like home. Some of what she had seen and heard and felt in the cab remained. She was too excited to get mad and too awake to go to bed.

Marina did not see much of her husband or the city during her first week there. None of the maids she had interviewed were suitable. Perhaps it was her apprehension about another woman looking after her daughters.

'You're far too fussy,' Gerald kept saying. 'You'll find someone if you give them half a chance. You always want something to complain about.'

He was putting her down. He said, 'I can't be with you all day. I came here to do a job.' Then later, 'I'm too tired to listen to you now. We'll talk in the morning.'

Perhaps he was right, but then she had hoped he would be a little more patient with her. A little more understanding. After all, he knew she'd never really been away from home except for that one time to England, when they'd met.

CHAPTER THREE

———◼———

The landowner kept haggling. He had been stringing it out all afternoon, hoping to tire Cunningham into reducing the price. He pronounced each syllable of every word, pausing maddeningly before each sentence as if the cane-cutting season was months away.

'It's two hundred pesos per head,' Cunningham said. 'Not a centavo less.'

'You're making a fortune at my expense.'

'Take it or leave it, Fernando. Someone will gladly have your share. There are plenty of people around these parts who would kiss my ass for any extra hands I can bring in.'

'Bring in? Smuggle, you mean.'

'Quite right. Of course I smuggle them in. That's why

they're expensive. To operate without the protection of the law costs money.'

'No wonder you're becoming rich. Every time I see your pretty face you charge more.'

'I have expenses, Fernando. There are bribes to pay on both sides of the border. You know how little the police earn. Not much more than these miserable people on your plantation. I have to pay my selectors in Haiti, transport expenses ...'

'What transport expenses? Everybody knows you make the poor bastards walk every foot of the way.'

'I'm getting a little bored with your shit, Fernando. Find something new to say.'

'*Por Dios, hombre*, it used to be such fun to negotiate with you. Come on, let's have a drink or something. Or a game of dominoes. We'll play for the difference.'

'I never mix work with gambling. You should be thinking of your cane, Fernando. The season is three weeks away. If we do not strike a deal now you'll have to cut the stuff yourself. Think of what that'll do to your nice soft hands.'

'You city rats think we're all layabouts up here.'

'Oh no we don't. We know about your drinking and your gambling and your screwing and your fiestas. Where did you last see a cow, Fernando? On the television? You'd never think of going out in the fields, except to take a piss.'

'That's better. Insult me all you like, as long as you bring the price down. You're asking too much.'

'Your voice, Fernando, sweet as it is, won't pay my bills. One last time, two hundred pesos for each one. Take it or I'm going.'

'Don't get so upset, Cunningham. We've got to negotiate a bit, no?'

He usually stayed longer. There was little excitement up here and Cunningham knew how much the landowner enjoyed a good haggle, but his interest was waning. The American woman from the airport was much on his mind. He had been thinking of her all week and had checked the grapevine.

He had found out who she was and what her husband was here for, and the gossip was that she was always alone. He remembered her skin and her intelligent eyes and her perfume. He remembered, too, the bewilderment that had turned into authority when her husband stepped out of line. He must find a reason to look her up soon. Very soon. Today.

He got up, slung his white jacket over his shoulder, and picked up his stick.

'Two hundred pesos, Fernando. Do we shake hands or not?'

'You are being too hard on me. It's too hot to rush. Have a drink.'

The porter at the Hispaniola had told him she always brought the children down for a swim at around four in the afternoon.

'I have things to do,' he said, and started for his car.

'Hold it,' the landowner said. Fernando needed the extra hands. They should be at work on his land in less than three weeks and yet he couldn't let the gringo get the upper hand just like that. He couldn't go elsewhere because Cunningham was a reliable supplier who delivered strong, healthy men and on time. The price, he knew, was right, and Cunningham was offering him more hands than he needed. He had to take them. He could sell them to his neighbours who would pay any price once the cutting season was upon them.

Perhaps he should invite him into the house proper, instead of sitting out here on the verandah. Something other landowners did not do often, chiefly because they did not trust him with their womenfolk but also because it was beneath their dignity to entertain a foreigner with his dubious past. The proud code of the old Spanish landed gentry still held sway up-country.

Fernando Bogard was certainly not of aristocratic origins nor Spanish. His Dutch grandfather had come to the West Indies in search of emeralds and gold. He landed in Colombia first, then Venezuela and Curaçao before fetching up on Hispaniola. He found no precious minerals, but instead unearthed a young childless widow blessed with a good-sized parcel of productive land. The first Bogard was a hard-working, frugal man, and with the crops he grew and the children his bride brought into the world the Bogard dynasty began. Now, in Fernando's generation, there was a Bogard in the army and another in the diplomatic service. With yet another in the government, regardless of which party was in power, the family was secure. There was never a problem with export licences or quotas, and their sugar and coffee and beans never failed to find markets.

The children of Dominican landowners married each other and their holdings were tightly tied together to keep strangers out. Fernando had married outside his peer group. His wife was a Canadian air hostess from Vancouver. She had brightened the old plantation house and produced a string of fair-skinned children of whom he was immensely proud. She was not greatly interested in the affairs of the country or in running the estate. She did not interfere with him as long as she could spend some of the money on monthly shopping trips to Miami or Puerto Rico.

These days there was little reason for Fernando to fear the Englishman's famous appeal to women. Señora Bogard had met Cunningham years before on one of her trips, and it was she who had told him to contact her husband in the first place. Cunningham always denied that they had a fling back then, but along the Malecon, people swore blind that Fernando's sixteen-year-old daughter was his child. Fernando used to take the Englishman to the best eating places in the capital and often paid his gambling debts when trade was slow. He deserved special terms.

'You owe me some money anyway, Cunningham. Who bailed you out in Puerto Rico last week?'

'I did it myself, Fernando. You put up the air fare, that's all. Three hundred pesos.' Cunningham threw a thick wad of red bills onto the table. 'There you are, take your money out of this and let me get out of here.'

'Where did you get all this money from?'

'At the casino last night.'

'You still play seven and fourteen?'

'Yes. And they came up last night. All night.'

'So that's why you look so happy. You used to look that happy only when you were in love.'

Cunningham counted out three hundred-peso bills and put the rest in his pocket. The pale face of the young American woman refused to leave his mind. She was not as tall or as buxom as his last sweetheart, but in her shy strength he saw a challenge. And she was married.

'I am not in love, but I may be soon. Two hundred pesos per head, or do I go see your neighbour El Gordo? He knows I'm in the area.'

'How many do you have?'

'Sixty-five this time. All young and strong. At least for the moment. With the crap food you give them here they're not going to fetch half that next season ... if they live long enough to see it.'

Fernando did not answer. For one thing it was true and for another he did not want El Gordo to have any at all. That way he could pass half the Haitians on to El Gordo himself and make a profit.

'Done,' he said, 'two hundred per head.'

'And fifty-fifty on whoever you offer to El Gordo.'

'You are an *hijo de puta*, Cunningham. You win, but next time ...'

'You owe me thirteen thousand pesos, Fernando, and the Haitians get two pesos a week and food and mattresses. Payment in cash and now.'

'Daylight robbery. Sugar prices are down.'

'That's your problem. I have no relatives in the government. Shake?'

Fernando sighed. 'Shake.'

The two men shook hands and the Dominican dealt a heap

of hundred-peso notes into Cunningham's upturned hat.

'Count the money,' he said.

'No, sir. I trust you implicitly. It will be fun to short-supply you if you've cheated.'

The two men hugged, tapped each other's backs, and Cunningham got into his car. He had just enough time to get down to the city to catch the American woman at the pool.

CHAPTER FOUR

■

The buzz was persistent and it woke her. She listened to it through two more cycles, then picked up the receiver and yawned into it.

'You spend too much time in bed, Marina,' Gerald was saying. 'You should be at the pool. There's hardly anyone there at this time.'

Of course there isn't, she thought. It's too hot to move. 'Will you join us there for tea?' she asked.

'Afraid not. Things are a bit sticky here. The man from Brazil is arriving this afternoon. That means I'm going to have to take them out for dinner, too. It may be best if I do that by myself. You know how these people are.'

'I know how you are,' she whispered. He did not hear. 'I'll see you when I see you,' she said out loud.

'Why don't you take the children for a dip? You can take them out for an early dinner after.'

'Why don't you stop telling me what to do?'

'It's quite safe, you know. Children stay up late in this part of the world.'

'All sorts of things happen in this part of the world.'

'Spare me your whining. You appreciate nothing. This is a great place.'

'To you, perhaps. Not me. All I get to do is sit in this room.'

'Don't start that again. I really must go now. There are five Brazilians in the other room.'

Five Brazilians. Five thousand Brazilians. Who cares? 'I'm sorry, Gerald,' she said. But he'd put the phone down.

She got up stiffly and moved over to the window that overlooked the sea. She was hating every minute of this. Then the telephone rang again. She thought it would be Gerald, with more instructions, and answered it sharply. But the voice on the other end of the line was not his, although it was both male and British. She couldn't identify it, or even remember the name Cunningham when he gave it to her.

'Who?'

'From the airport, remember? You were having problems with ...'

'Oh yes. Yes, of course. Mr Cunningham.' The vision of his attempt at elegance made her smile to herself.

'I'm downstairs, in the lobby. Been seeing some people here. Wondered if you and your husband might like to join me for a drink? Don't put yourself out,' he added hastily. 'If you're busy ...'

'My husband is out, but I was just coming down to the pool. I'll see you there presently.'

'If you'd rather make it some other time ...'

'No, no. I'll be down. But the girls can be a handful. Especially after a nap.'

'As I recall, you handle them beautifully. See you in just a few minutes, yes?'

He went to the men's room and checked himself in the mirror. He combed his hair and wiped the dust off his jacket. Life was looking better than it had for some time. He had had a good day at the plantation. Last night his numbers had come up and his luck was holding. A winning streak had appeared over his horizon after a long absence. If it were to last he could soon move out of his room into a better place. A few more rolls like this and he wouldn't need any more trips across the border. He was weary of these excursions and they were becoming dangerous. This woman was certainly a little young and the young were always in a hurry. His mother had not been much older when she left.

He saw her enter the pool area and pause. She looked around and he smiled. The barman, the gardener and the pool attendant smiled at her too, as did the two Americans in the water. Did she see him? Did she remember him? He couldn't see her eyes behind her dark glasses. And then she spotted him and waved with gusto and walked towards him. Her legs were long and the thin dress clung to a pair of shapely hips that danced as she walked. Cunningham ruffled his hair. She was not as skinny as he had thought.

'Hi,' she said, her mouth curving into a generous smile. 'Good to see you. Did I keep you waiting?'

'Good heavens, no. I have all the time in the world this afternoon. Must be tough on you, though, with your two sweethearts so close in age.' He pointed at a table in the shade. 'How about over there?' he asked. 'Would that suit you?'

'You bet it would,' she said. 'You lead.'

'Ladies first,' he said.

The gods were good to him and the sun was shining and Haiti was far away still. The woman smiled again and he took the bag from her and followed her to the table. He pulled the chair out and waited for her to sit.

'I just love the afternoons here,' she said. 'Don't you?'

CHAPTER FIVE

He always knew when the morning was about to come. Long before the golden stripe crowned the mountains around the village. Ti Allain knew and the knowledge had woken him up at the same time every day. He would roll off his cot and walk to the door of the whitewashed hut, touch the tail of the dead lizard that hung above the entrance, and stretch, taking the cool air in.

This was the hour of the spirits, and Ti Allain took a deep breath just in case the spirits had determined that it was to be his last. He had lived there by himself since his father died. He had never known his mother; his grandmother had been his mother too, and had looked after him when he was a boy. She had loved little children, especially him, and because she had been close to the black witch Monique during her lifetime she had powers. His father did not inherit her powers, as might have been the case, but that was because he did not spend as much time with her as Ti Allain had. He would, perhaps, not have been blessed with that privilege because he was fond of rum. He was mostly drunk by the time the sun came down and would curse the old lady and beat Ti Allain, then sink into a heavy-breathing sleep. He got involved in every village brawl.

That was long, long ago when grass, the elders said, still grew in plenty. The curse that took the water away from under the ground came after. But that, too, was long, long ago.

His grandmother fed him and took him everywhere and he listened to her talk to the spirits about Monique the black witch. His grandmother was fond of gossiping with the spirits about Monique. About how she had been when they were both little girls together and what she did and how she rose to become an important witch whose influence extended far beyond the village. How she died young and appeared after her death with her left leg that of a goat and her right leg that of a chicken. There were those in the village who said that Monique's legs had changed their form while she was still a person, but no one knew how or why that happened, and Ti Allain's grandmother never told him. He followed the old lady to many places near and far and ran errands for her and fulfilled her every wish. He watched her collect dry roots and flowers and insects and herbs. He saw how she brewed plants into teas that had powers to cure ailments and how she saved

61

the insects that had power for the future and protected against evil.

She hugged him a lot and always told him how she wished he would remain her little boy for ever. That was, people said, why Ti Allain stopped growing once he reached the age of ten. He was born with a different, bigger person's name, but people called him Ti Allain just as his grandmother did, and that was when he knew for sure that the spirits had noticed him. He was earmarked for greater things.

And then came the day when his grandmother was taken ill and lay inside the hut on her dried grass mat. She could not go out to the field and said it was because she was tired. Her face was pale, like a white person's face, and she looked at him with love and asked him to fill her clay pipe with tobacco and light it so that she might smoke.

'I will die soon,' she said, 'but one day you will join me where I am to go.'

'Talk some more,' Ti Allain had said.

'I will say one more thing. Then I will be silent until I die.'

'Why won't you talk to me more?'

'Because the next time you hear my voice, Ti Allain, will be the day you will die too. Join me up in heaven with Monique and all the spirits. We shall all go to that big mountain over Africa. Just as I have told you before.' She smoked some more and did not speak and then the pipe fell from her hand and she was gone.

Today was the day for the migrants to assemble. Ti Allain washed his face in the darkness and poured a handful of the precious water for his grandmother. She was fond of washing her face just before the morning came. It was, she used to say, good to cleanse the skin. That way the day's events would turn towards the powers of cleanliness and plenty which came from the good corner of the sky.

For many years now, Ti Allain had led the people to the market place at Petionville where the signal would be given. He would then take them to the small wooden church at

Diquini, below Port-au-Prince, where the fat city woman called La Grande Marie-Christine would choose the good from the bad. The good would be the lucky ones who would be allowed to cross the border to Saint Domingue, where they would work and eat and, if they were lucky, stay for ever.

Ti Allain was much sought after and popular in the village and beyond. Life had been hard for people in the mountains, where only a few grew old and children died of starvation. Ti Allain held the key to a better future. The people who went across would send money to their families, even if it didn't last for ever. Sometimes they came back pretending they were old men and died in peace where they were born.

He went to the door and searched for the lizard. He knew for sure he had hung it there the night before, after having chased it and killed it, but now it was gone. A sure sign that something was going to happen. That somewhere along the line the plan would change. Maybe not for the worse, maybe not for the better. Just change.

Certainly there was no point, now, in searching for another lizard. It could not possibly alter the course of events. The other lizard had already done that. Ti Allain put some earth on his head and danced quietly in front of his house. He hoped some of the earth would slip into his eye, to indicate that the spirits were unable to see what had befallen the lizard. Perhaps it had come back to life and crawled away. Or maybe it had been snatched by a bird, which was a good omen because from the air it could see the hills and what lay beyond them. Pictures of what it saw would surely come to Ti Allain. If not already, some other time. Knowing the future was important to a man in his position.

He danced quietly and then vigorously, but not a speck of earth came into his eye. Then the pink line appeared along the horizon to tell him that the sun was about to enter the village. From all corners, people started to make their way towards Ti Allain's hut. They stood stiff and still and waited for the small man to end his dance. No one knew for sure exactly what Ti

Allain was dancing for today, but they knew he was asking something of the spirits. This day it could only be something on their behalf, and they were grateful. They had already said their farewells, and, forming a half-moon shape, they waited for him to complete his ritual.

Soon, they knew, he would take his little sack and pass out things to them. They never knew what these things meant. The dead flies or the dried watermelon seeds. But they knew by hearsay that they were to keep whatever was given to them until after the choosing, and that was at least two days away. One thing was certain. Whatever Ti Allain gave them would bring them luck. They all needed luck, or else they wouldn't be there waiting for Ti Allain.

There was little luck to be found in the village these days. Their fathers and grandfathers had all talked about the old days of rain and greenery and plenty. Now they would have to go and find those good days elsewhere. Far away from here. Beyond the mountains and the dry rivers they would find it. In the land of light they called Saint Domingue. On large fertile lands the gods had given that country and its people because they were good and obedient. And the man Ti Allain could take them there.

He was ready now. He bent and scraped up a few handfuls of earth, more than usual this time, and stuffed them into his pockets. He never left the village without taking some earth with him. Cursed or blessed, it was the earth he was born into and it was connected to his grandmother's bones. He would carry it in a piece of cloth, if he could find such a thing. In the city perhaps, where the people were less poor and would sometimes throw away valuable things like that. It would be heavy and weigh him down, but he would take more anyway. He did not know why, but he knew the weight of his village earth would always keep him close to it.

By the time the sun truly reigned over the whole village, the little assembly was gone, led by Ti Allain, on its way to Petionville and beyond.

CHAPTER SIX

■

Port-au-Prince stretched far below them like a magic carpet. White and gold and green and red threads of houses and roofs and trees. In between snaked grey, winding roads that seemed to lead nowhere. There were boulevards and mansions. There were shanty towns on the edge of the city, crowded open-air markets and narrow alleys. But everything drew the eye to the breathtaking, blue-green miracle of the bay. Its waters, calm and wide and generous, extended all the way to the horizon where they kissed a distant heaven.

In the centre of town, surrounded by extensive, pampered tropical gardens, the white Presidential Palace loomed amidst unseen barbed wire and machine-guns. From where they stood, it all looked clean and beautiful and splashed by a myriad of colours, like a postcard designed by God. The sound and smell of poverty, the painful face of hunger, the filth and the pot-holes were all lost to the eye with the innocent bliss of distance.

She looked about her and tried to take it all in while behind, giant mist-wrapped mountains offered a fortress of reassurance.

'Poetry,' she said, panting, 'sheer poetry.'

'They used to call this city the Pearl of the Antilles,' Cunningham said. 'They had a night-life here to rival anything Paris could offer.'

They were watched by street sellers and painters whose canvases sang of make-believe jungles and animals and flowers and rivers and lakes. In the shade there were performing monkeys whose owners waited for a taker with a camera and a few gourdes to spend. There were royal palms and empty tourist buses and lime-juice vendors. Cunningham talked of the history of the country. She watched him. It seemed that his fiery words had the power to summon past inhabitants to return and hover above the precipice and listen.

'The Europeans were all here in their time,' he said. 'The Spaniards and the French and even the English. Imagine their tall ships entering this splendid harbour, sails rolling down the masts, guns spitting death towards the shore. It was a prize colony in those days. Saint Domingue, the French called it. It grew coffee and sugar and tobacco for them. Napoleon's sister lived here and the crops made the conquerors rich. In fact, it was so important to their economy that the French staged a great campaign to recover it.

'They came back in force and found thirst and hunger and disease lurking beyond the shore. This is the only place in the world where black slaves, any slaves, revolted against Europeans and succeeded. Their spirited liberation proved resistant to subjugation by any expeditionary force from Europe, and they all tried.

'There is an old Haitian song. I believe it goes something like this: "I was French in the morning, at noon I was English, in between I was a Spaniard, but at night I was free."

'After the liberation, the Haitians started to imitate the way in which their French masters had lived. By the end of the nineteenth century they had the whole thing off perfectly, including the old class system. The mulatto élite, clad in the latest Paris fashions, spouted French philosophy. They kept liberty, equality and fraternity to themselves. They kept everything else, too. The enslaved became slavers. Their masters have convinced them white is best. They're getting paler every twenty years, bringing back European brides to improve the blood. They prosper and some have become immensely rich while the rest of the population starve to death.

'Stupid, though. They had a paradise and they used it as a cash crop. Then they couldn't figure out what had gone wrong. They cut down all the trees for firewood and the rains, when they came, washed the topsoil into the sea because there were no roots to hold it. Now most of the land is barren and what fertile spots there are belong to the rich.'

'Isn't anyone helping these people?'

He looked at her and put his arm around her waist. He held her close for a second and then he said, 'I try to, in my own little way.' It was the first time he had touched her.

Marina had accepted Cunningham's invitation on the spur of the moment, driven as much as anything by Gerald's sudden departure for Brazil. It was not the sort of thing one did where she came from, but then none of her friends was ever left alone in the sweltering heat of a strange city with two little girls to look after. Gerald had given her only a few hours' notice, using the arrival of her cousin from New York as a smokescreen. She hadn't forgiven him for his past indiscretion in Rio, and his sudden departure for that city aroused her suspicions. She sulked her way through the rest of the week while her cousin tried to look after the children. Then came Cunningham's invitation.

It must have been anger which prompted her to accept. Anger that had been simmering inside her for weeks. And a feeling of trust towards the older man, who seemed harmless enough. Her cousin, who had lived on her own in the big city for years and had started a small but troublesome women's rights club there, was considered a rebel by the rest of the family. Having met Cunningham, she had laughed at her hesitations and told her to jump at the chance.

While she was packing there were doubts. Perhaps Gerald couldn't help being curt with her. Perhaps she was a spoilt bitch. Perhaps she should have stayed and entertained her guest and waited. But much to the other woman's delight she accepted.

'Consider it', Cunningham had said, 'an outing with an old uncle. We all need to come up for air sometimes.'

He had found her an experienced girl to help look after the children, and the hotel manager promised he would supervise. Yet still she was not quite sure.

'We will be staying in separate rooms,' he had said. 'Separate hotels if you like. Even separate cities if we can find any.'

What the hell. Whatever it was that had finally decided her, here she was. He had been the perfect gentleman. He stayed with her during the day and took her sight-seeing, and only attended to his business after she had gone to bed. He was polite and attentive and correct and he was fascinating. He never told her what to do. She was loving every minute of it.

Was her cousin right? Was Gerald trying to prove something to himself? Was she becoming less important in his life? This man Cunningham made her feel that she was interesting and capable, and he laughed at her jokes. Why couldn't Gerald see how starved she was of adult, intelligent conversation and company? He had always expected the girls to be clean and well behaved. He expected her to be responsive and attentive when he was around. Where was all that energy supposed to come from?

Cunningham was safely middle-aged. He did not evoke any romantic response in her. And now he was touching her waist. Perhaps he was not aware of it. She looked at him and saw his tanned face, his strong chin and his straw-coloured hair as it fell on his forehead, just above his eyes. He looked down at her, said something and laughed, but she didn't hear. God, how different he looked when he smiled. True, he wasn't young, but surely he was still interested in women. She'd noticed him watch them. His eyes lingering along their legs. Not her, though. Even her cousin had said that. Why not her?

Her eyes searched for his. She could not find them. He seemed miles away, then suddenly he bent down and planted a soft kiss full on her lips. There was a moment of silence that seemed to stretch before it finally broke. His head recoiled.

'Sorry,' he murmured. 'Don't know what came over me.'

What was he talking about? 'Is there anything wrong with me?'

'Now, now, young lady.'

'Don't "now, now" me, Cunningham.'

'I was quite out of order. You may slap my face.' His lips smiled, but his eyes were misty. He removed his arm and stepped away from her. The feel of her thigh played games with his imagination. He tried to regain his self-control. She might discover the intensity his detachment concealed.

He's got to be in his forties, she thought, and yet he has an ageless face. Maybe she bored him, just like she must have bored her husband. Doubt seized her. Did she have the strength to force it out into the light? It was all in her imagination. He didn't even notice her. Not as a woman. Provoke him. Make a joke of it, if it fails. 'Don't you like me, Cunningham?'

'Of course I do, dear girl.'

How she hated this 'dear girl' crap. 'I am a woman. I have a husband and two daughters to prove it.'

'Of course you're a woman,' he said, and his voice caressed her. He was interested, but why was he hanging back? Couldn't he sense the mounting excitement between them? She felt flushed.

'I've seen the way you look at women, Cunningham. Like a local. You look. I know you look.'

'It's only natural.'

'So what's wrong with me?'

The direct question startled him. What's wrong? Every time she said goodnight to him by her door, her lovely eyes trustingly fixed on his, every time he heard her key being turned, his heart sank to the bottom of the world. Should he tell her that? Should he tell her of his fantasies? His wild dreams of them taking cool showers together. His lips that would travel every inch of her body. The sounds and scents of her when they were doing it. He could not tell her any of this. She was too vulnerable. It would be wrong. Like snatching a sweet from a child's mouth. And yet. Yet what? She was no child. She must have some idea of his desire for her. Maybe she did, but he knew her self-assurance was crumbling and he must hide this knowledge. Next to go would be her smile, and after that the laughter would die and with it the happy-go-lucky atmosphere that had reigned between them. What was happening to him? he wondered. You are getting old and sentimental, he told himself as he motioned the driver to bring the car over.

'Turn the air-conditioning on, Guy,' he said as they approached the Renault. 'The lady is hot.'

Freudian slip, she thought.

CHAPTER SEVEN

'Would you like to go to a voodoo show tonight?'

She shook her head. 'Uh uh. We've been to one, remember? The guy ate the chicken's head.'

'This one is different. Especially designed for grumpy American ladies escorted by elderly English expats. This time the chicken eats the man's head. It then stands up on her thin feet, climbs a ladder to the roof of the house and the whole assembly sings "America the Beautiful" in Creole. It sounds okay. Almost as good as the original. I can sing it for you if you like. Anyway, at the end, as a special treat for good behaviour, the chicken lays an egg and everybody gets a bite of the omelette and a goodnight kiss and the assembly is packed off home happy.'

He mimicked and she laughed out loud as she put her head on his shoulder. He pinched her snub nose. Peace had returned and all was well. Perhaps he had been wrong about her vibes. Outside, an orange ball of fire was racing to catch the sea.

'In England the sun stays up until nine o'clock in summer. You can read out in the garden for hours and hours after dinner.'

'I didn't know there was a sun in England.'

'We haven't sold everything to the Americans.'

They laughed. A poor joke, but perhaps the tension had

been defused. What on earth was he so worried about? He hadn't taken her to Haiti for the view. Their being together like this felt so natural. What had he brought her here for? Yes, yes, but this one was special. Could be dangerous. Could linger if he wasn't careful. He couldn't possibly get involved now. There was too much to do. If this transaction went well, he could sit back for a bit. Not depend on others too much. No more risks.

He had had his highs and his lows. His fortunes and disasters had swung like the price of sugar. Things were going well. He must not get emotional just because this last long stint of poverty was over. He had even bought himself a new American car. Paid down almost half. And there was something else.

The note from the Israeli Embassy in Santo Domingo had been brief, almost to the point of rudeness. Over the years the South African woman's husband had kept in touch. He had followed their fortunes and he knew that to these people curtness was a facet of security. The better they thought of you, the more security they would try to maintain. 'Call Amos,' the note had said. Nothing more.

He did not know an Amos. That was not the colonel's name, but it did not matter in the slightest. Once he'd made the call, someone answering to that name would certainly know him. There had been notes like that before. For them to contact him like this meant they either wanted to warn him of something or else they wanted a favour. He preferred the second. Of course he would be happy to render them whatever service they might require. More than happy ... as soon as he got back. After all, they had been good to him.

On this trip he was going to make some real money. He would be in a position to relax for two, maybe three whole months. He wouldn't walk in there cap in hand. He'd be generous with the Israelis, like an equal.

The sides of the road were crowded now with perambulating human hedges. Lines of slow-moving people, most of them women, each carrying a basket or a bundle, or dragging a reluctant pig or a goat or calf. Children loaded with produce or chickens or eggs. He patted Marina's shoulder and pointed them out to her.

'What is it? Where are they all going?'

'These are the lucky ones. They have something to sell and they are on their way to Port-au-Prince market. They'll walk for miles and miles, often for days and nights, to get there. On the way they huddle together with the animals and their neighbours in fields and on pavements. Some sleep while others watch the fruits and the vegetables. Then, in the morning, the customers turn up. Mostly, what they carry is all they possess in this world. And when everything has been sold they turn and walk back the way they came, to their villages.'

She had a schoolgirlish admiration in her eyes as she listened to him in the approaching twilight. What was he doing here with this woman? There were people to see and talk to. There were workers to inspect and prices to be negotiated if the trip was going to be a success. And yet he could not concentrate on that. All he could think of was the picture of her emerging out of the pool that afternoon, not too long ago, her pubic hair pushing towards the nylon. He must put such thoughts out of his mind.

'The peasants have an impossible life here. The earth is dry and harsh. They grow what poor crops they can, and if no one burns them or steals them between planting time and harvest, or later cheats them at market, they can eat. Between the reluctant earth and the Tonton Macoute ...'

'The Tonton what?'

'The Tonton Macoute. The secret police. If the poor earth does not succeed in making their life a misery, the Tonton Macoute will. That's why they lean on the supernatural powers of voodoo. Or swim or sail or walk away from this country if they can. You've surely seen it all on television.'

He could see, or was it his imagination, the darkness of her nipples pressing through her blouse. He had to look away. 'That's the other reason for doing what I do. It's not just the money.'

'I don't really know what you do.'

He did not answer. There was so much to say and not to say. He wondered how long he could keep his hands off her. Good thing he was going to be busy later on. Later on belonged to another woman, Marie-Christine. The locals called her La Grande Marie. The plump, once-beautiful mulatto would receive him in her large walled house for dinner. It was a business dinner in which he would settle her commission for finding the labour force. Some of her income came from a small coffee plantation and some from renting out her dead husband's surgery, but most came from the never-ending supply of migrant workers she found for Cunningham.

Like most of the women he worked with, Marie-Christine had been Cunningham's lover once, long ago. After her husband died, their affair fizzled out. It became a friendship born of interests shared. It was a relationship of mutual usefulness now, but there was much affection. She always cooked for him herself, entertained him and often, when he was down on his luck, she helped him out.

She was still a handsome woman, whose large green eyes shone against her *café au lait* skin. Her beautifully contoured body had gone to fat and she had taken to wearing a ridiculous wig, but that did not detract from her enormous sensuality. She still walked like a swan and the low chords of her laid-back voice still painted bedroom scenes of long, lazy afternoons.

She had no men friends these days. She had once confided in him that there was no one to take revenge on once her husband had passed away. And yet she was jealous of his women and he took great care not to talk about them to her.

The car came to a squeaky halt. They had arrived at the El Rancho Hotel. It was an imposing white colonial edifice with large rooms and columns and its extensive gardens hovered high over the city and the bay.

'I'm afraid we won't be able to have dinner together tonight,' he said as they got out of the car. 'We can have a drink later if you like. It may be our last night here.' Her face fell and he pinched her cheek. 'Why don't you have a swim, Marina? It's the best time of the day for that.'

'Don't tell me what to do.'

He didn't answer. He walked away and disappeared through the marble-floored gallery into the garden. He took a short-cut to his room and did not notice the two policemen at the reception desk. They were chatting to the porter and moved away as Marina came into the lobby. The porter greeted her and handed her key over.

The fatter policeman saluted and then he smiled. 'Have you seen Monsieur Cunningham, madame?'

The porter was doing an odd dance in the background, trying to catch her eye. She was about to give an honest answer when she noticed his gesticulations. He was waving his arms and shaking his head wildly. The other policeman watched her closely, his hand resting on the butt of his pistol.

'Well, madame?'

'Yes,' she said. The porter shot a desperate glance at her, but she did not hesitate. 'Yes, I have, as a matter of fact. We spent the day together at Petionville. I have just this minute arrived back. Monsieur Cunningham stayed on up there. He should be back within an hour or two. I think the driver, Guy, has just set off to fetch him.' How easy it was to tell a lie. Mother would faint. How exhilarating.

The policeman saluted her again. '*Merci*,' he said, his golden teeth grinning. 'We'll find him there.'

'May I ask what the trouble is, Captain?'

The man was a sergeant and his promotion from the lips of the young woman did not displease him. 'He was supposed to see a lady tonight, a very important lady. Madame Marie-Christine Pinot. He was, we believe, to have had dinner with her tonight. At her house.'

Her heart sank. So that was it. All this talk of business deals. And the truth was he was to have dinner with his whore. She was impatient for him. She even sent the local sheriff to get

74

him. To make sure he turned up. That was rich. He had been playing a game with her. And she thought she was protecting him. Her cousin was right. All men were shits. What a child she was to think ... To think what?

'The lady was found dead in her bed early this morning. Shot through the head with a pistol. We think Monsieur Cunningham has something to do with it.'

'You can forget that. I've been with him all day.'

'What about last night?'

'And last night,' she lied. 'We were together all last night.'

'You are registered in separate rooms, Madame Buckmaster.'

Her stomach turned over, but she managed to wink at him. 'You know how it is, Captain.'

His smug, disgusting smile said he knew exactly how it was. The porter placed two bottles of beer on the desk.

'We might as well wait for him here,' the policeman said. 'We do need to talk to him. He was the only appointment in her book for this evening.'

'I do not believe Monsieur Cunningham has a gun, Captain. There must be some mistake. Would you do me a little service?'

'Of course, madame.'

'Would you please call me as soon as he returns? I'll be in my room. I would like to be present when you talk to him.'

'Of course, madame. We'll call you.'

'Thank you, Captain.' She waved and the policeman saluted. She turned and started to walk, her pace measured and slow down the steps towards the garden. It was going to be pitch dark any time now. The lights were coming on as the steel-band drummers took their places near the barbecue. She turned the corner out of sight of the desk and the lobby then ran like the wind for the stairs.

CHAPTER EIGHT

—■—

Cunningham opened the door in his underwear. His hair was wet. An embarrassed expression appeared on his face. 'Sorry,' he said as he took a step backwards, letting her into the room. 'I thought it was the maid. Someone's made a mess of my room. I can't find a thing.'

Her eyes travelled down his body. Just below the right knee there was a sort of garter belt which rested on the slight swell of the calf muscle, and attached to it was the prosthesis that replaced his own foot. He'd never said anything about why he limped the way he did. She remembered finding it attractive. She had assumed some sort of injury, but nothing like this. This was why he'd never swum, never taken his clothes off to lie by the pool. Oh my God, you poor man, she thought, as she tore her eyes away with an effort. She slipped inside the door and closed it behind her. She was still panting for breath after her mad dash up the stairs.

'You are in trouble,' she said as calmly as she could. 'The lady you were going to see tonight, Marie-Christine? She is dead and the police think you killed her. They are waiting for you down in the lobby. They do not know you are up here. I said you'd stayed at Petionville and wouldn't be back for a couple of hours. They've looked at her diary and they know you were going to see her tonight. You've got to get out of here, Cunningham. You must run. You must ... we must think of something. You'd better come and stay in my room for now.'

His jaw dropped. His eyes clouded then screwed tight shut in pain and disbelief. His mouth contorted as he fought to control himself. He lowered his head, turned and limped over to his bed and sat down. 'My God,' he whispered. 'Dear God. Not Marie-Christine. Why?'

'Cunningham, will you please get some clothes on and get

76

out of here. I'm not sure they believed me. I wasn't very convincing. If they see the car, they'll know I was lying.'

'You don't think I did it, do you?'

'Of course not. Will you get some clothes on?' She went over to him, took his hand and pulled him to his feet. She felt her excitement mounting. Suddenly, all her doubts evaporated. Here was a man suspected of murder. He was in real-life trouble and she was right there. His face looked appealingly helpless. His age didn't matter. Nor hers. Bogie was older than Bacall. Could he have killed? He pulled on slacks and a shirt and sat down again.

'Cunningham!' Her urgency was real and he knew it, but he had to think. Without Marie-Christine there would be delays. The whole plan could fall apart. Must organize someone else. Gain time. How could he think of that now? His friend was dead.

'Cunningham, will you get out of here?' She took him by the arm again and jerked it hard. He stuffed a few things into a bag and then motioned her to open the door. The corridor outside was empty. Still holding him by the hand, she stepped into the passage.

Once in her room, he slumped onto her bed then straightened up and ran his fingers through his hair. His eyes held a haunted look she had not seen before.

'Not much of a voodoo evening, what?'

The room seemed larger than she had remembered. She looked about and then saw her suitcase on the floor. The cupboard was open and her things were strewn all over the place. The book she had been reading lay open by the bathroom door.

'I see you had visitors too,' he said. The colour was returning to his face. He smiled. 'Would you get on the phone and book me a call to the Dominican Republic? Don't mention my name. I want to speak to Francisco Martinez. Give them both these numbers ...' He scribbled them for her on the room service menu. 'Tell them it's urgent, would you, please?'

He did not need to be so formal now. He and she were inmates in the same prison. This admirably clever man needed her. She would do anything for him now.

'We'll be safe here for a while,' she said after she had made the booking.

They sat together in silence. He contemplated his instructions for Francisco while she struggled to control her adrenalin-charged system. Outside, the steel band started playing and the light on her verandah came on. The large off-white bulb looked like the full moon. The phone rang. He picked it up and listened. Relief flashed across his eyes.

'Good to hear you at last, Francisco,' he said. 'Whatever happens, don't ask for me by name when you call back. They don't know I'm at the hotel. Ask for Mrs Buckmaster.'

He went on to tell Francisco about Marie-Christine's death and the police. 'I have no one to help me here in Port-au-Prince. You'll have to do something your end.'

'What can I do?'

'You know Monsieur Dubuffet at the Haitian Embassy? Tell him what happened and get him to help. He's got big connections over here. Make a deal with him, Francisco. It'll cost money, but get him moving. Go and see him right away.'

'It's late, Cunningham. He won't be at his office. He's a diplomat. They don't even work during office hours. And why should he help you?'

'Because he's in with us on this transaction.'

'I am your partner, but you never tell me a thing.'

'Because you talk too much. After hours he plays the casino in Naco.'

'I hope he's not spending our money already.'

'You tell him I must be free to move about. As long as I'm stuck here no one crosses the border and no one gets a single peso.'

'Do you want me to come out to Haiti?'

'I've just told you what to do, Francisco. I know it's late. I know you're having problems with your wife, but *por Dios*,

78

hombre, get going. They're after me here and they're not joking. They could ruin the whole thing ... She's dead. Imagine, Marie-Christine is dead.'

'Can I use your new car, Cunningham?'

'Yes, you can.'

'I have some bad news for you, Cunningham ... but it'll wait.'

'Don't spare the blows. Shoot, Francisco.'

'Can I keep the car until you get back?'

'Yes. Now tell me.'

'The gringo police in Puerto Rico have issued a new warrant for your arrest. They have officially asked the Chief of Police to arrest you. They say they let you out of jail by mistake.'

'What have you done about it? Did you contact the Chief of Police? He should deal with that. We pay him enough, don't we? You did make the pay-off last week?'

'Sure I did. I went to see him today, but he's out of town. He's in the mountains at Jarabacoa. At his brother's house.'

'Get someone out there to him. He'll listen. His brother ordered twenty-five labourers himself. They need to get me out of this badly.'

'What are friends for? I have already sent my kid brother to Jarabacoa. That's why I have no car, *compadre*.'

'Well, then, have you heard anything?'

'That's the bad news. The chief is delighted you are out of the country. Says you must stay in Port-au-Prince while they clear things up. If you come back now, they'll be obliged to arrest you.'

'I'd rather be in jail over there. In Haiti they throw the key away for ever. Right now I can't even leave this bloody hotel. You'd better get going.'

'I'm on my way.'

'One more thing. Send someone to the Hispaniola Hotel to check on Mrs Buckmaster's children. Make sure they're all right.'

'Of course they are all right. Didn't I get Chiquito's

daughter to help look after them? She's good. She's got a child herself, but Chiquito doesn't know about it. She's a very good mother. If you ever tell Chiquito he's a grandfather, he'll kill her. She says the other gringo woman is good with them too. Now, will you stop talking and let me get on?'

Cunningham wanted to laugh, but he couldn't. '*Vaya con Dios*, Francisco. And thanks. Here's a big *abrazo* for you.'

She sat there and listened and wondered at him. She did not understand it all but she understood most, and especially the bit about her children. He actually cared. He looked so attractive sitting there lost in thought, his eyes downcast over that face.

'You are leaving first thing in the morning, Marina,' he said. He did not call her 'dear girl'. He said her name tenderly. 'Things could became quite unpleasant.'

'Are you kidding?'

'Absolutely not. I'll arrange something. You must go back to the Republic.'

She took his hand and held it against her cheek. 'Sorry, Cunningham. No can do. This stuff is too riveting.'

'Marina, someone is trying to frighten me out of the country. At the very least. They've killed a very good friend, perhaps just to make that point. This is not a game. I won't have you involved in this.'

'What do you mean?'

'Just what I said. Someone wants me out of the way. You should leave before something else happens.'

'I wouldn't dream of it.'

He was serious. He cared. He worried about her. Perhaps she should worry, too. But the sense of peril engulfed her with a wave of sweet tension. A sensation she did not recognize and could not control. He looked a little lost and yet he knew what he was doing. He was a real man. But even so, she could do anything she wanted with him. Just then he looked at her and radiated a reassuring smile in her direction. Could it be she wanted him that way? She came closer and stretched her arm to touch his cheek.

'Not now,' he said.

CHAPTER NINE

Her face was flushed. The curtains were open and the air-conditioning whined at full blast. Outside, the night was greeted
by the chiming tones of the steel band. Soft, sensuous Creole
music. Into his nostrils came the smell of her sweat and fading
perfume. A sharp scent of woman that made his heart pound.
She pulled at his collar and he tried to tell her to stop but did
not. She kicked her shoes off and got onto the bed behind him
and kissed the nape of his neck. Her breasts were heavy on his
shoulders. He stooped to get away. Not now, his brain said as
her youthful passion flooded over him. The moistness of her
lips set him on fire.

'Do you want me, Cunningham?'

He said nothing. She slid a hand down his stomach and
touched him there and knew that he did. Perhaps he had been
a killer, but now he was no more than a man. The air was
charged. He was imprisoned here in the hotel room, but she
was freer than ever. This man was no match for her. He was
too shocked by the unexpected. Too immersed in his
thoughts to resist. She could do whatever she wanted to him.

She came around and rode his knees and touched him and
kissed his lips and probed and felt him harden through the
thin cotton of his slacks.

'You want me, don't you? You do too,' she heard herself
say. Unbelievable, she thought, but then everything was.

Cunningham tried to find something to say. To think of his
predicament. Of what he must do. But her womanhood came
at him through tantalizing scents of perfume and the taste of
dainty drops of sweat. His arms found the soft material that

caressed her hips and his knee touched the mound of her crotch. He must stop now. She pulled him closer and buried his head between her breasts. To hell with it. She had made her mind up. She knew what she was doing. Her inhibitions were gone. She was taking him. He bit at her nipples through the dress. She talked no more. Her hands were everywhere trying to unbutton something. She was forcing the issue and loving it.

Outside, the music danced with the night. She kissed his neck, his shoulder. All the while she held him in her hand. She felt the bulge and squeezed it as it grew and she wanted it to throb inside her and calm that delicious itch. She moved closer and locked her legs around him, only thin fabric between her and him.

'I must have you now,' she shouted as the sweet, sweet tickle intensified. She looked at his face and tore and unzipped and opened and pulled. Neither of them smiled. Suddenly she was free. She felt him rubbing close and her body rose and arched and fell back onto him as his hardness slipped into her. She twisted and turned and groaned and cursed and felt it everywhere. From the back of her neck down her spine and across her body into her loins.

She heard herself shout as her body danced and the sweet salvation came closer and closer and she screamed one more time and then the explosion hit her and she shuddered down on him where she rested, panting.

Cunningham lay still. On his mind played Marie-Christine and the police outside and the landowners across the border to whom he had given his word. But then he had done what he could. Francisco was on his way to the Haitian Embassy. This would sort itself out. It always did. *Mañana otro dia*. But how? No, he must not brood now. She might misunderstand. He sat up and looked into her eyes.

'What is it?' she asked.

A smile appeared across his face. 'Taking advantage of a man in my position,' he said. 'Shame on you.'

'You wanted me,' she said defensively, 'but you didn't enjoy it, did you?'

He planted a kiss on her forehead. His face exuded pain mixed with pleasure. An expression she had once seen on someone. Yes. A movie about Paganini.

'You didn't come,' she said, unabashed. He didn't answer. He got up and went to the bathroom. Perhaps he hadn't heard her. She hoped he hadn't. He would have hated it. She used to hate it when Gerald complained about the same thing. He walked very slowly, his limp pronounced. She heard him in the shower and watched as he came out of the door with a towel in his hand. He sat by her side and started wiping her down. Her brow, her back. Her eyes opened slightly as her lips parted. Her skin was soft to his touch. He wanted her. The fire that had eluded him before now urgently burned his insides. He climbed on top of her and parted her knees.

'You horny bastard ...' she said, and her words died with the sudden thrust of him into her body, and she looked at his chin and his mouth and he said, 'Move with me.' He sighed and gyrated and groaned and soon they were moving together and then he whispered something and kissed her ear with relief and she felt him pummel her once more before all went limp. She pulled the sheet over their interlocked bodies.

They slept. It had all been too beautiful and peaceful and they did not hear the knock on the door. Gentle at first, then impatient, finally aggressive and demanding. There seemed to be a whole congregation out in the corridor. They were talking and demanding and their fists hit her door incessantly. She opened her eyes and shook him, but he only grimaced and turned away and slept on. She heard a hammer and then saw the knob being turned from the outside. She kicked him and said, 'Sorry, darling,' and at last he awoke. She pointed at the door. The lock was now open and a small hand slipped in, trying to undo the safety chain.

Cunningham flew out of bed, a sheet wrapped around his body. He sprinted out to the verandah and climbed over the dividing rail. The occupants of the next room were out. He opened the large glass door and went inside. Through the thin walls he heard them burst into Marina's room. He waited.

CHAPTER TEN

—■—

'Talk me into another beer,' Francisco Martinez said to Antonio the barman. 'I've had a terrible day. The heat is killing me.'

'I think you've had enough, maybe.'

Francisco sighed. An argument with one's wife can mess up the whole day. Especially when it concerns another woman. She actually woke him up at ten o'clock in the morning just because she had found that letter in his jacket pocket. She had no business looking through his things, and why such a fuss? She knew he was only having a bit of fun. She had screamed at him and cried and threatened. He had not been able to think straight all day. With Cunningham in trouble he needed all his wits, if he was to be of some use.

'*Que va*,' he said. 'There's time for one more.'

Antonio's face showed concern. 'Why do other woman write to you at home? This address not good any more?'

Why indeed? Foolishness. It was just as foolish of him to carry the cursed letter around. To make matters worse, the woman had written to say she was expecting a baby and that the baby was his. Francisco did not believe that for one moment, but his wife did, and that was why she had woken him up and given him a telling-off. She said she was leaving. He must not try and look for her. Well, she had gone off to her father's before and he could do with a few mornings of unmolested sleep. The maid did the cooking anyway, and his wife never stayed at her father's house for more than a few days. His father-in-law had picked up these modern gringo ideas about the rights of women. God alone knew where it might all lead. The man backed his daughter regardless of who was right.

He shook his head and sipped his beer. Nothing like a cool beer to straighten one's head. He couldn't even talk to Cunningham about it because he was in the shit. In any case, Cunningham would only have taken his wife's side. He grunted.

'I know what you mean,' Antonio said. 'Life's a bitch sometimes.' He refused payment. 'Pay next time, Francisco.'

'You always say that, but I have no time to argue with you today. My car is badly parked. Here. There's a pencil and paper.'

'What is this for?'

'I'll be back in an hour or so. People may ring, so just take notes for me, that's all ... and *por Dios*, Antonio, get the names right.'

The Haitian Embassy was closed by the time Francisco rolled up at the gate. He didn't much care for automatic gear shifts. Why did Cunningham insist on buying these big *Yanqui* cars as soon as he'd got a few pesos in his pocket? You could never park them, you needed gas every minute, and they never fetched a penny when you needed quick cash. The guard told him to come back tomorrow. There was no one there. Only Monsieur Dubuffet. Good, Francisco said, that was the man he wanted. Would the guard call and tell him he had a visitor? The telephone at the gate was out of order, but with a prod of two pesos the guard agreed to walk up the stairs to the office.

'Would you watch the gate while I'm gone?' he asked.

'With pleasure.'

Francisco entered the cubicle and sat down. What a day, what a day. Everyone was making money and was happy. If this didn't work out he would have to drive all the way to the mountains himself. Visit the Chief of Police and plead Cunningham's case with him. More money. His wife had no idea how lucky she was to have a husband who wasn't greedy.

Women. Let her go to her father. Let her listen to his revolutionary crap, the old drunkard. She'd soon see.

'Monsieur Dubuffet would be pleased to see you,' the guard said from the shadows. Francisco got up and slipped into the garden. The Embassy door was open.

The Haitian diplomat was distressed. He had already heard that the Americans had issued a warrant for Cunningham's arrest. 'That could really cause problems,' he sighed.

'It would. But we can settle this as soon as our Chief of Police gets back to town. Where did you hear about it?'

'This is a small town.'

'Don't I know it. Anyway, Monsieur Dubuffet, right now we have a more pressing problem. Cunningham is locked in his hotel room in Port-au-Prince, hiding from your police. You'll have to pull a few strings. I'll be happy to cover any expenses this might cause you.'

'How happy?'

'Five hundred pesos. Maybe a thousand. The final figure depends on speed. The money belongs to Cunningham, you see? He will need his freedom to pay.'

'I see. I may need some up front.'

'Well, I do have a bit of cash on me.'

'How much?'

'That depends on how far your influence extends. I can't tell before you call.'

'I'll have to go home and call from there.'

'I will drive you there myself.'

'You couldn't give me some of that money now, could you? I keep my safe here. Can't trust my housekeeper. I have been robbed twice this month.'

'You book the call from here. They will connect it at your house in half an hour. Meantime I'll go to the car to collect the money. I keep it there.'

'We'd better go together. I have nothing more to do here. I don't like making private calls from the Embassy. Not even local calls. We are a poor country.'

'Honesty is the best policy,' Francisco said.

The Haitian diplomat lived in rented splendour on the fashionable estate of Arroyo Hondo, on the hills overlooking the city. All the beautiful people had houses up there. The cars parked in this neighbourhood were pure Hollywood. The house was ultra-modern, with a large landscaped garden sprawled in front. Monsieur Dubuffet was certainly living beyond his means. His salary had to be helped along in order for him to afford his rich neighbours. He was not married and at Antonio's Bar they said he was a *maricón* even though no one had ever seen him in the gay haunts.

He opened the gate for Francisco, whose car jerked forward, scraping the side panel. Damn the transmission. The house was clearly empty, dark inside, with only the garden lights switched on. Garden lights. Every child knew that trick. No wonder he was robbed.

'I would offer you a coffee, but the maid goes off at six.'

'I hate coffee. I used to serve it a million times a day when I was young.'

'Were you a waiter? I thought you were always in business.'

'In my time only the rich were in business. Where is the telephone?'

'Why?'

'You're going to call Port-au-Prince, no?'

'We have a minute for a drink, *n'est ce pas*?'

'Here, you'd better take the five hundred now,' Francisco said firmly. He looked menacing as his thick eyebrows contracted. '*Voilaga le téléphone*,' Dubuffet said. He booked the call and the two men settled down to wait for it to come through.

CHAPTER ELEVEN

■

The raid on Mrs Buckmaster's room at the El Rancho Hotel produced no results. All they managed to do was frighten the yawning young woman. They must have woken her when they burst in. The maintenance man struggled to repair the broken safety chain and the police, the reception man and Marina stood in the corridor apologizing to each other. Through the main partition board, Cunningham heard it all. When the proceedings were over, he slipped back the same way he had left.

Her eyes were bright and large with excitement. 'That was a close one,' she said. 'I loved it.' She turned the room lights off.

'You're quite mad,' he said, and sat down.

'I am making memories. Private moments to chuckle over when I slam the Sunday roast into the oven.'

She knows, he thought. She knows there's no tomorrow for us. What is keeping that son of a bitch Francisco? He should have done something by now. If Dubuffet delivered. And then there was still the problem of getting back into the Dominican Republic. With the police there after him and every informer on the look-out, he wouldn't get far. If the Americans really wanted him extradited, the government would have to hand him over. Quota negotiations for sugar, tobacco and beans were at stake. The Chief of Police would only be able to fend them off for a day or two, and only if someone made him risk his position for doing so. Very doubtful. After all, Cunningham was foreign, insignificant, and very dispensable. He looked up and saw her by the window. She sat there immersed in the night, calmly smoking a cigarette. Ignorance is bliss, he thought.

The Caribbean moon drifted into the room with the scent of frangipani. The music floated up with the song of the crickets. This is romance. Any minute now he'd get up and bow and offer her his arm and ask her to dance. White gloves. Ashley Wilkes and more besides. What shit. Was she ever going to grow up? Yes, yes, but not yet. Please, sweet Jesus, not yet.

The phone rang, jerking her out of her dreams. She picked it up and listened and handed it over to Cunningham.

'I have scratched your car a little,' Francisco said. 'It drove into Dubuffet's house and hit the gate all by itself. Nothing much. Enrique the painter says he'll fix it like new or better. Your car is too big, Cunningham.'

'What is happening?'

'That is what I'm trying to tell you. The heat in Port-au-Prince will be off any minute now.'

'When can I return?'

'You'd better stay in Haiti until the Chief comes down from Jarabacoa. He can't do a thing up there and Puerto Rico is American and out of his jurisdiction. The Chief is powerless because this is political. Maybe the Minister ...'

'Yes, but the Chief can make sure no one stops me at the border. We'll find someone who knows the Minister when I get back.'

'You'd better wait there. Don't you have to check the workforce?'

'Yes, yes, yes ...'

'You owe me five hundred pesos.'

'Great to have trusting partners. How are Mrs Buckmaster's children?'

'They are well.'

'How do you know? Did you check with Chiquito's daughter?'

'Check with her? She's not talking to me now. The other Englishman, Mrs Buckmaster's husband, is back from his travels. And what is the first thing he does? He kicks Chiquito's daughter out and the other gringo lady moves in disgust to another hotel. He is looking after the children himself now. Serves him right, the ungrateful *cabrón*. Didn't even pay the girl. She's sore as hell at me for getting her the job. By the way, can you buy a bottle of Barbancourt rum for me? Fifteen years old. Best rum in the world. For my father-in-law. I don't like him, but he's family, right?'

'When did Mr Buckmaster get back?'

'About an hour ago. Two maybe.'

'Are you sure?'

'Of course I'm sure. I spoke to him myself when I rang to speak to Chiquito's daughter. He speaks Spanish well.'

'You could have told me that before.'

'You had other problems. I didn't think it was important.'

CHAPTER TWELVE

— ■ —

His return had been one hell of a let-down. He'd done everything wrong. Not only was Marina nowhere to be seen, but that New York weirdo cousin of hers he'd never liked was looking after his daughters, assisted by a local nanny he did not trust. All right, the room was clean and the beds were made and there were fresh flowers on the table, but that was nothing to do with them. The hotel did that. Fucking impersonal hotel for a home and no wife in sight for miles. God alone knew what had gotten into her this time. The porter could not give him any information and all the little girl could tell him was 'Mummy's not here.' The stupid woman could have left a note. Perhaps she had and the maid had thrown it away. Come to think of it, Marina's crazy cousin had said something, but he hadn't paid much attention to her, except to tell her to mind her own business, so the bitch had left in a huff. Good riddance. The so-called nanny simply ignored his question. The baby's cot was dirty and Gerald unceremoniously discharged her without listening to her excuses. Marina could have chosen someone a little more forthcoming.

He had actually returned a week early. The business in Brazil had been concluded sooner than he had expected. He took two days off on his way back on the Dutch island of Curaçao. It was a duty-free territory and he had bought Marina some perfume and a little pearl necklace. He had enjoyed that orderly, civilized mini-Holland which survived untouched by its haphazard Latin neighbours. Marina would have liked it. Perhaps not. Perhaps he should have come straight back. He should have called her.

She must have gone out for the day. Good for her. She deserved it, of course. It could not have been easy for her to face the exuberance of Santa Domingo from the inside of a hotel room. He had hardly taken her out. And now he had been rude to her cousin too, but then everyone in the family was. Still, she had never done this sort of thing before. Maybe her cousin got on her nerves?

There was that odd local chap who called to ask about the children. Didn't have the decency to leave his name. Bloody insolent bastard. Gerald had told him so before putting the phone down on him. The little girl had started crying for no apparent reason and the baby was in urgent need of a nappy change. What a welcome after his success in Brazil. Oh, he would have loved to have told Marina all about that, but she wasn't there and the baby stank to high heaven.

He took the dirty nappy off and carried the wriggling body to the bathroom and washed the mess off into the basin. The water was either too hot or too cold and the baby let out a loud hriek. God, how tough little problems were when you'd just scored a big coup. Perhaps he should have kept the local girl. No. He'd manage. Come, come, little darling. Daddy will sing you a pretty song. Baa, baa, black sheep, have you any wool? The baby kept on screaming and Gerald dried her and wrapped her up and carried her into the big room. There, there. He put her on the bed and sat down beside her and suddenly her angry little face lit up into a broad smile. Wide cheeks and bright wet eyes. He got up and took a biscuit out of the can. The older girl came running to him and he put it in her hand. 'Thank you,' she said. There was a bowl of baby food on the table with a spoon inside. Wash it first, then feed the baby and get hamburgers and french fries for her older sister. Marina would be proud of him.

A cup of tea. They had a kettle and cups and they were clean. The girls looked on in silence. He must have looked like a stranger, lost in a quiet domestic scene. Only the night before he had been standing by the roulette table at the Curaçao Hilton, his tuxedo freshly ironed, watching the dollar chips changing hands while a bored woman eyed him lasciviously from across the room. He had not reacted. He was no angel. A lot of available pleasure floated about in this part of the world. Local business friends had often offered, but there was too much gossip and too much clap. Not worth it.

The only time he had accepted an invitation was in Brazil. A long way from teacups and baby food. Marina was pregnant with their first child and he was on an exhausting trip through South America. Stopovers in Miami, Caracas, Bogotá, Lima, and finally Brazil. The agent in Rio had to more or less carry him into the car. Why think about that now? Because he felt guilty about it. And he remembered, every tantalizing bit of it.

His Brazilian agent was very understanding. 'You are tired,' he had said. 'You have had one hell of a long journey. You should relax. We do not need to go to the office. People do not do business in the office anyway. Business is done in restaurants, bars or on the beach, watching backsides. We have the most beautiful girls in the world right here in Rio. The Copacabana beach sweeps along seven miles of white sands and coconut trees and high surfing waves. You gringos never relax. You should enjoy the heat and the sights while you're here. You'll be as good as new in the morning.'

He had slept in the car all the way from the airport and woke as it stopped at the hotel. Would you like to walk to the restaurant? It's only a block away. Oh yes, he would. It would do him good.

They walked along the shore. Across the blue bay, pointing at the sky, rose the stark conical shape of Sugar Loaf Mountain. People were smiling and women walked as if to music. They sat sipping their beers and ordered their lunch and then the agent said, 'We have a diversion for you, Mr Buckmaster.' That is how it had started. 'The afternoon is the perfect time for it,' the agent said. 'Nights are for dancing and for being with one's wife at home.'

Gerald said he was not interested in whoring around. The man protested. 'This is only a bit of fun among friends.' The women in the place they had in mind were not whores. Some were bored housewives, others needed pocket money, but mostly they came to meet people. Secretaries, housewives, even students. 'This is a big city. No, not whores.' Why not, he thought, and he went.

It was a modern apartment block. Expensive, wallpapered lobby, uniformed porters, and valet parking. Elegant little street off the centre of Copacabana, with a gilded, ornamental elevator that stopped in front of a highly polished mahogany door. The agent rang. A small window opened, revealing a pair of long eyelashes. The agent showed her a small golden key and the window closed. James Cagney in a speakeasy, Gerald thought. Prohibition time.

The door opened. Two well-dressed women ushered them into the apartment. A party atmosphere prevailed as they sat down at one of the tables and he strained his tired eyes to look about him in the dark. There were candles and soft, piped forties music filled the cool air. Drinks were served in champagne glasses. There were women everywhere. 'A lunchtime Moonlight Serenade,' his agent said. 'This is male paradise. You can choose anyone you like.' There were smiles and scents and shapely lips and long, crossed stockinged legs.

He took an embarrassed stroll around the room. It was a large place and he felt tall and awkward. Like buying a condom for the first time. Then he saw her. She was young, perhaps twenty. She had streaks in her short hair. A darkish Kim Novak who looked at him out of the corner of her eye as she chatted to another girl. That one, he said, and the Rio agent snapped his fingers. Before he knew what was happening, Gerald found himself being led out by someone. He floated out of the room on a cloud of anticipation.

They entered a blue bedroom through a door he had not noticed before. He was left alone. He should leave now, he thought, and then the girl walked in and his remorse evaporated. She said she had hoped he would choose her. 'We don't need to go with anyone unless we like them.' Would he like a drink? Yes. Yes to everything.

She was wearing a wedding ring. He took her hand and kissed it and then he took his own ring off. She shook her head. Her ring stayed on. He got up to undo his tie. No, she said. No. She touched his shoulder, gently easing him back. She unzipped her dress and it fell to the carpet. She took the rest off and stood naked. Strong, scented, tanned body. White stripes of skin over her breasts and down.

He had never been undressed by a woman before. She took her time and Gerald stole a hurried deep breath to calm himself. She hung over him and unbuttoned his shirt as a large golden crucifix dangled down her cleavage. He remembered it all, and then the baby started to cry. Rio was a long time ago and best forgotten. The plastic bottle was empty and a pair of eyes stared at him with rage.

'Now, now,' he said soothingly, 'we can soon fix that.' That was what Marina used to say and it worked for him, too. The baby stopped crying as he poured lukewarm sweet tea into the bottle and fitted the teat. 'Give me a chance, young lady,' he said, but she was hungry and her eyes dried as soon as she was allowed to attach herself to the bottle and suck. The reverie was over. He would tell the Rio story to himself some other time.

The telephone rang and the older girl picked it up. She had

made a mess of the biscuit he had given her. Holding the baby in one arm, Gerald battled with his elder daughter for the receiver. She was not keen on giving it up and when he took it forcibly she started crying. The baby stopped drinking and joined in. Gerald gave the girl another biscuit and stuck the teat into the baby's pouting mouth and all went quiet.

'Hello,' he said.

'Hello, Gerald,' Marina said.

He was going to ask her where the hell she was and when she was coming back, but he sulked. 'I'm rather busy at the moment, dear. Can't it wait?'

There was silence and then she said she'd call back in an hour. She sounded close by. She couldn't be very far from the hotel.

'He doesn't give a damn,' Marina said. 'He sounded stand-offish. The baby was crying in the background. I hope he isn't starving her. A bit of domestic responsibility won't hurt him.'

'As long as he knows you're all right.'

'He didn't even ask.'

'This is your children's father.'

'Don't lecture me, Cunningham.'

'Okay ... let's drop it for now.'

Time was fast running out on him. The workers had to be selected, inspected and taken across the border before the cutting season. He would have to move in two days. Three at the most. He could not afford to horse around with the land-owners. Cheap Haitian labour made their sugar-cane crop viable. And they had all paid in advance, in good faith. He'd have to start all over again and that was impossible. He had had enough of being poor and his marketplace was a village. And the Chief of Police would have it in for him too. His brother the farmer was waiting for his Haitians. He might turn nasty and shut the gates on him for ever. And now he could not leave his hotel room or delegate because Marie-Christine was dead.

'Is there anything I can do?' Marina asked.

'Yes. You can get the first plane out of here.'

'Not on your life, buddy.'

'Take the Pan Am tomorrow evening.'

'Forget it.'

'Come down to earth.'

'We can fly out together the way we came.'

'Your people are after me. If I am caught on an American plane, I'm done for.'

'They have no right to hold you on board.'

'Not here, they don't. But the plane might go straight to Miami or Puerto Rico and then they'll have me by the balls.'

'The flight goes to Santo Domingo first.'

'This is the hurricane season. Airports close. Especially small ones. The plane might be diverted. Then what? Besides, I've got things to do here.'

'I'm not leaving without you.'

He was going to say something rude when the phone came to life. She picked it up.

'Ah, Madame Buckmaster, good evening. Can I talk to Monsieur Cunningham, please?'

'He's not here. Who are you?'

'Kinet. Marcel Kinet.'

Marina repeated his name out loud and Cunningham nodded. She passed the receiver to him.

'Is that you, Marcel?'

'The nobody from Jacmel in person. What did you do to get the police so stirred up?'

'It's no joke, old friend.'

'These are sad times, it's true, but we can afford a little jest. You are free to go. They just found a suicide note on Marie-Christine's body. Do you believe she killed herself?'

'Not for a moment. One day we'll find out. Who is taking over from Marie-Christine?'

'I am.'

'When can you have the people ready?'

'Tomorrow night. We have almost eighty here in town now.'

'No one older than thirty, right? And make sure there is a doctor around tomorrow.'

'Leave it to me, Cunningham. I'll come for you at six. We might as well have a bite to eat before we go down there.'

'Thank you for getting me out.'

'It's Dubuffet's doing. Not mine. I'll see you tomorrow.'

'I'll look forward to that.'

He put the phone down and sighed. He could move about in Haiti. But there was trouble brewing across the border. Marcel Kinet was a trusted friend, but he was going to miss Marie-Christine. Her soft, caring voice, her generous smile. Quiet evenings on the terrace of her white colonial house. He'd miss sipping dark sweet coffee amidst bursts of harmless gossip and a million laughs. A mulatto aristocrat, that's what she had been. A lover turned friend.

The phone rang again. It was Francisco Martinez. He sounded agitated. 'My kid brother has just returned from Jarabacoa.'

'Well?'

'The Chief says he wants his brother's Haitians delivered first. He won't return to the capital or speak to the Minister or move his arse to help you before this happens. He is playing it safe. Blood is thicker than loyalty. He says if you show up you'll be arrested.'

'You'll have to change his mind. Without the Chief's protection there's no chance. You do have some money left, don't you? Promise the bastard whatever he wants. I'll have to go with them myself, and if they grab me at the border the Chief's brother won't get one man. You can imagine what will happen to these Haitians if they are left on their own. You remember how many of them have been butchered. Let me think. Now, just in case I can't make it, you'd better come up to Ferrier. That's where I'll have them cross the border.'

'What about my share, Cunningham?'

'Twenty-five per cent, as usual.'

'Fifty. I've got more responsibility this time. And more work. And expenses.'

'That's what I call kicking a man when he's down. Thirty-five per cent.'

'Okay. I'll see what I can do about the Chief.'

'Another thing. Mr Buckmaster may get desperate. You send Chiquito's daughter back there today.'

'That *hijo de puta*? What are you worrying about him for?'

'Do it anyway. We'll talk tomorrow.'

'*Sí. Mañana otro dia.* Leave messages with Antonio at the bar.'

There was still Marina to sort out. He'd have to get her to see the gravity of the situation. He had been in tight corners before, but this was different. There were too many coincidences piling up. In too many places. Francisco had said it. Tomorrow was another day.

CHAPTER THIRTEEN

'There's no way I'm going to see my bed before dawn,' Francisco mumbled as Antonio tried to coax him into staying a little longer. 'You know I don't mind late nights, but fighting hairpin mountain curves on the lonely road to Jarabacoa is no fun. Let me see. It's eight o'clock now. The drive will take at least three hours. I tell you, Antonio, life was simpler in the old days.'

Still, there was a challenge in it. By the time he'd arrived the Chief would be playing dominoes with his brother the farmer. He would be slightly drunk for sure and with luck he would be winning, and much more amenable.

A few street boys habitually hung around the bar and Francisco sent one to buy him a toothbrush and some shaving gear. He could not go home in case his wife was there. She might have decided not to go to her father's and meeting him at home would make her lose face. If she didn't see him that night she could safely say she had truly left him and had only returned because his absence from the house had worried her.

The beer tasted exceptionally good that evening and Francisco, against all odds, managed to persuade his kid brother to come along for the ride. It was not an easy task, since the boy had only just got back from the mountains, but the promise of being allowed to drive Cunningham's big American car was irresistible. The alternative was a little robbery to which he had been invited, but he had seen a few ex-convicts at the Chief's brother's house and one had talked to him. To know the Chief personally made no difference if you were caught stealing. Bribery or smuggling was okay, but robbery made the police look stupid. The Chief was all for law and order, clean uniforms and empty jails. Drugs or labour crossing borders was fine, as long as it was kept quiet and did not obstruct the traffic. Stealing was risky, and if you were caught you were lucky to go to jail. Working without pay for the Chief's brother on the farm was much worse, the ex-con had said. Even the Haitians were treated better.

That was why he did not go and Francisco wholeheartedly agreed. 'Crime only pays when they don't catch you. The *cabrón* in charge of your robbery is a beginner. You should join me in the family business. That's much safer.'

'Safe? How many times has Cunningham been inside?'

'Yes, but not one Martinez has. Cunningham gets into trouble for other reasons. Anyway, he's a friend and you'd better talk of him with respect.'

'What's his story, Francisco? How did you meet him?'

'We've got plenty of time to talk on the way to Jarabacoa.'

Francisco borrowed a spare shirt from Antonio and the brothers got into the car, with the younger at the wheel. They took the coast road towards San Cristóbal. The brightly lit bars and restaurants soon gave way to the dark span of the countryside. Francisco's kid brother kept the accelerator down and Cunningham's eight cylinders propelled the car forward eagerly. They sped onto the Santiago road within minutes. Other than the odd truck there was nothing to be seen along the black asphalt.

'What's Cunningham got on you?'

'Cunningham is a partner and an old friend. It's a matter of honour.'

'Bullshit. You wouldn't do this for your own brother.'

'I will not leave a business associate in the lurch.'

The car was slowing down. 'What's the matter with you, kid? We've got a long way to go.'

'If you don't tell me about Cunningham, I'm going back.'

The car stopped. The kid looked over his shoulder, slapped the shift into reverse and started to make a three-point turn.

'Don't be a punk, little brother. Drive on.'

'Not until you tell me.'

Francisco did not have the energy to start another argument. 'Okay, drive on. I'll tell you the story.'

The kid started forward again. The sparse lights of El Rancho la Cumbre marked the hills on their right. He was tired. He needed to sleep. Talking about Cunningham would engage his emotions and would revive him. It would take time. No one could talk of that man in five minutes.

'Next time you see Cunningham, little brother, you bow your head with respect. He is a very educated man. He has been to schools and universities in England, in Egypt, in the Holy Land and, yes, even in America, I think. When we first met he was a diplomat here in Santo Domingo. He was with the Nicaraguan Embassy and had a house in town and a CD plate on his car.'

'Was that when you worked for the customs at the port?'

'Yes, it was. At that time you were still wetting your bed. Cunningham was one of the most charming people this city has ever known. Even with his plastic leg, he was a fine horseman and, for a gringo, the best domino player you could hope to meet. The likes of us would never have had the chance to talk to him then. Trujillo himself was interested in him. There was talk of one of the presidential mistresses falling for Cunningham, but fortunately they were never caught. After he was through with her, Trujillo married her off to some general as a reward for her services. The general was made an ambassador and they were packed off somewhere. Cunningham always had something the ladies liked. They came to him as though they were flocking to mass. He was living in that house with a mistress, a cat and a dog, but he lived everywhere else, too. He was quite slim in those days and always dressed in white. I think he had a moustache, but I can't swear to that. He certainly had a dog. He used to take the animal for walks along the Malecon, while the women in the bars swooned over him. The country belonged to the Trujillos and they ran it like a private farm. But the Malecon belonged to Cunningham. Ask Antonio. Ask anyone.

'Anyway, one day an enormous crate arrived on board an Argentinian freighter, addressed to the Nicaraguan Embassy. No one knew what was in it. Cargo consigned to diplomats was not supposed to be opened, you see. All we had to do was get someone from the Embassy to sign for it and that was the end of the story as far as customs were concerned. The boss always received an envelope from the Embassy. A sort of duty payment, you could call it. The amount in the envelope depended on how badly the stuff in the shipment was needed. That is why an official had to come down to the port to sign for it.'

'Did you boys ever see any of that money?'

'Don't be stupid. The money went to the boss in the office. Perhaps even to Trujillo himself. One of his friends was always head of customs. Or maybe an ex-general or a cousin. I don't remember who he was. All I know is that the envelope had to be delivered to the boss's office. In my position one never saw the man, let alone knew him. That's why I don't remember who the boss was. Anyway, the crate, I can see it now, was gigantic. Big enough for two elephants or a tank or ten pianos. It was lowered off the ship into my section. I was given the papers and told to fetch someone from the Nicaraguan Embassy and make sure he had the envelope on him, make him sign for the crate and take it and then hand the envelope to the guard outside the boss's office. You see, the boss was hardly ever at the port, but he still had the biggest office there, with air-conditioning and running iced water. Those bastards knew how to live, believe me, little brother.

'As luck would have it, the man the Embassy sent for the crate was none other than our friend Cunningham. He was no more than twenty-five then. Yes, he did have a moustache. I remember it now. He looked like a blond version of Clark Gable.'

'Who is Clark Gable?'

'How dare you ask me who Clark Gable was. They did not teach you much at school. All that money for nothing. Clark Gable was a famous *Yanqui* king and cowboy and lover from Hollywood. Fought in all the wars and screwed all the women. Shame on you.'

'Was this Clark Gable working with Cunningham too?'

'Good God, kid. I said Cunningham looked like ... never mind. Cunningham came from the Nicaraguan Embassy and told me to join him in the car with the CD plates. I sat in the back with him, would you believe. Not in the front. His clothes were freshly pressed and he had some strong aftershaving cologne on. His fingernails were manicured and his moustache was trimmed like in the movies. You don't have to take the bus back, he told me, and that was when I first saw his smile. Did you ever see him smile, kid?'

'I can't remember.'

'Well, next time he does, watch him closely. Heaven opens and all the holy angels come rushing down when he smiles. Storms disappear and the sun rises even if it's midnight. You forget all the shit you are in and the world becomes a place of peace and plenty and you know you're important because

Cunningham's eyes tell you so.

'He offered me a real American cigarette, no imitation, a Camel, I think it was, and talked to me as if we were equals. He asked about my work and my house and my family and he really listened to what I said. On the way to the port we stopped at a very fashionable coffee house and he invited me to accompany him, shabbily dressed as I was in an ill-fitting uniform. But he did not notice or did not mind, and he introduced me to all the smart people who were there as if we were bosom friends. As if I was a real señor.

'When we got to the port he signed the papers and gave me the envelope. That would have been the end of the matter, but he gave me five whole pesos as a tip. The guard outside the office was not there, so I decided to take my lunch-hour then, and go to La Capita – yes, the very same La Capita – and spend some of that money on a decent lunch. In those days you could feed a whole family on five pesos for almost a month, but I felt hungry and selfish and important all at the same time and I had never been inside La Capita before. I should have given the money to Mother as I always did, but five pesos was a fortune and I became big-headed and Cunningham's treatment of me as an equal had confused me. Yes, confused me.

'To cut a long story short, by the time I left La Capita I had only three pesos left in my pocket, my stomach was bloated, and my head swam in a lake of imported beer and gringo whisky. To my shock I discovered that the envelope with the Embassy money was missing. I went back to the restaurant, but they kicked me out. "You don't think, young scum, that one of these distinguished people here have stolen your stinking envelope, do you?" the maître d' said. "Money, you say? Where would a jerk like you get money from?"

'To tell you the truth, I didn't know what I thought. They forgot I had just spent two whole pesos in there and that bought plenty in those days. I wasn't seeing too clearly, but one thing I did see. The envelope was gone and with it the boss's money. I was in terrible trouble. It was a very hot day, and when the maître d' pushed me out of the door I was as sober as a priest should be. I prayed and I looked and I cried, but the envelope was nowhere to be found.

'They would not miss me at the port until three o'clock, so I took a taxi and went back to the Nicaraguan Embassy. Cunningham was not there, and the guard directed me back to the Malecon, to some elegant coffee house which is no longer there. Cunningham was there playing dominoes with some other gentleman. He saw me as soon as I approached his table and gave me that smile again.

'"If it isn't our old friend from the customs," he said. Old friend, he had said, and all the others smiled at me as if I were the Prince of America, and he asked, "What can I do for you, Francisco?"

'There is no point going into details now, but Cunningham, after listening to my story, took me back to the Embassy in the car and gave me a new envelope.

'"There is a little less in there," he said, "but those *cojones* at the port won't know the difference. They didn't know how much there was in the first, *verdad*?"

'That, kid, was how I first met Cunningham, and we've been friends ever since. He's had his troubles and his successes as we all do, but by all the saints I believe in, and those I should believe in, there is nothing I wouldn't do for him or he for me. If you are not happy with this story, tough luck. I am going to sleep now. Stay on the road and don't talk to me until we get to the Chief's house. I'll need all my wits for that.'

Francisco climbed over to the back seat, gently stroking his brother's head. The car purred on, swaying gently from side to side as it negotiated the winding road. Cunningham's story had taken them as far as the foot of the mountains. It had brought memories back. Things he had forgotten or had not paused to think about for years. If only he could have convinced the Englishman to stick to one trade, they would all be rich now. Cunningham didn't really need to get involved with the drug pushers in Puerto Rico. He probably thought he was helping someone, but it landed him in jail. No one could persuade Cunningham to relax and enjoy the fruits of his rare encounters with cash. He had to get involved with everybody, have a finger in every pie. And those women with their tough-luck stories. Maybe he was looking for excitement or love or Christ knows what. And all that money he lost gambling? The business in Haiti was strange. It was as if the impossible had happened. As if someone hated Cunningham personally and wanted him locked up for ever.

But surely that could not be, Francisco thought to himself, and his mind eased. No one could hate Cunningham. Not if they knew him, and everybody knew him. That thought relaxed him and he lay on his back and stretched his legs out on the wide seat. He always slept on his back. He could see the stars better that way.

CHAPTER FOURTEEN

The familiar tickle of hopeful expectation started to throb under Cunningham's skin as soon as they entered the casino. He hoped a spell at the tables would inject some calm into his edgy system. The tin and jute shacks, the dusty roads, the empty wooden stalls and the hungry children provided an eerie setting for a place there just for people to throw money away in, Marina observed.

It was a quiet night and most of the players were locals. Offers of sympathy and enthusiastic congratulations followed the changing fortunes of the wheel. Immaculate in his black tuxedo, Cunningham settled down at the table. Within a short time there was a growing pile of plastic chips in front of him. Everybody looked at Marina. She knew how much he needed to succeed and several times she was on the point of urging him to collect his winnings and run. But the childlike excitement on his face kept her silent. She put her hand on his shoulder and he turned and read the concern on her face.

'You always feed a winning number at least once,' he said. 'You never stop when you're on a winning streak.' His eyes were wide and his lips were dry. The skin on his face was on fire.

'Give me some of that to keep. Just in case.'

'Take it. Take it all. There will be plenty more. Tonight is mine. I can feel it.'

It was him against the house. The croupiers and the inspectors watched in awe as he drained the table. Other players were joining him and by midnight the management had to bring a fresh supply of plastic money to his table. Someone touched his shoulder. He did not turn. He was watching the wheel. The little white ball rattled across the numbered slots. The hand touched his arm again, and he vaguely heard his name, but it was bad luck to take your eye off the wheel. He was still winning, and nothing could disturb his concentration. Bad luck lurked outside the casino, all over town, all over both parts of the island of Hispaniola. Here he seemed invincible. The ball teased him. It took its time. It hopped from the black thirteen into the red nineteen and then towards the zero. It flew past the seven and was slowing down. Everybody held their breath. Cunningham stared at the little white money-maker and willed it to continue. It ploughed on, and with what seemed its last bit of energy it landed in the red fourteen where it rested, quivering as if to say stop pushing your luck.

The others applauded. More chips were raked in his direction and suddenly he felt tired. He left one chip on the fourteen and another on seven and scooped up the rest. His tension gone, he turned around. The tiny figure of Marcel Kinet greeted him with a huge smile.

'I've been watching you, Cunningham. Good thing I have no shares in the house. I should have with what I have given them this evening. Are you going to introduce me to your companion?'

The man was eloquent, his small hands and face perfectly shaped. His immaculate white evening suit fitted his dapper body like a glove.

'I'm sorry. Mrs Buckmaster, this is Monsieur Kinet.'

'*Enchantée,*' Marina said. 'That's about all the French I can manage.'

Marcel Kinet's face lit up. '*Charmant, mon ami, charmant.*'

'You're not so bad yourself, Monsieur Kinet,' Marina said.

'Quite right,' Cunningham agreed. To have counted Marie-Christine as a friend and own three pharmacies and a travel agency was no mean feat for a nobody from Jacmel, as Kinet often styled himself. He was a self-taught man who had started as a fisherman in a country that respected only class and money. He had never been to school but spoke French, English and Spanish perfectly. He could quote Latin proverbs and French poetry and was an expert on naïve art.

'Why don't you watch the numbers for me, Marina, while I talk to Marcel for a minute.'

'What do I have to do?'

'If one wins, take the profits out and leave one on each again. If both lose, bet twenty dollars on twenty-seven. I'll be back very shortly.' She nodded.

He took Kinet by the arm. 'We could have our meeting now.'

'Perhaps not, Cunningham. There is nothing we can talk about or do before the rest of the workers arrive. That won't happen before tomorrow. I think we should stay right here at the table. I would like to win some of my money back.'

'Don't try it, Marcel. You can never get lost money back. Every time you sit down it's a new beginning. Forget what happened earlier on.'

'I know. I know. But I have to do something. Talk about – you know ... I was here with her only last week. She adored to gamble. We both won. Did you know I was in love with Marie-Christine? ...'

'Everybody was. Marie-Christine was special.'

'No, Cunningham. I mean really in love with her. For years. Even when you and she were going together, while her husband was alive, I loved her. I was going to wait for her to grow old ... But you know she never did. She became younger and more beautiful each year. Of course, she was society. I could never hope ... you know ... she was too far beyond my reach. But I loved her with all the vitality of a young Romeo.'

'You're as good as anyone, Marcel. Look where you were born and where you are now. She admired you greatly, you know. Talked about you often. Trusted you ... Look at that wheel, Marcel ... look at the beautiful white ball. It just landed on twenty-seven.'

Marcel's moist eyes were pleading. 'Can't we just talk, for a while, Cunningham? About the old days?'

'Tonight the old days are far away and sad, Marcel. Nothing to remember, not here. There is suspicion all around the place. And somewhere, someone who killed our friend is walking scot free. Hell, the old days were no better. We were all younger, that's all. Leave the past alone, Marcel. You must live for the present and plan for the future.'

'You may be right. I'm going to play. Maybe some of your luck will rub off on me.'

'Don't, Marcel. Your mind isn't on it and your heart isn't in it. You want to punish yourself. You want to lose.'

'I'm going to play.'

'It's your money. But let me get off the table first. We can't both win.'

Kinet spread his chips all over the table. There was panic in his movement. The first roll was lost. Then the second. And the third.

'Poor little fellow,' Marina said as they moved from the table.

'Don't be silly. He's loving it. Look at the enthusiasm in his eyes. Bless the wheel – it can do wonders for you, even if it won't bring loved ones back. Marie-Christine, how she performed around this very table.'

'What do we do now?' she asked.

'I am thirty thousand dollars up. Soon we'll be able to charter our own plane. Have a party somewhere far away. Blow some of this, what?'

'How long is soon?'

'If the lady wishes, soon is now,' he said. He took her hand and looked into her eyes and she felt the heat pouring out of him into her and she melted. He recognized her signals and said, 'We'll cash in now.' The local gamblers huddled around his table, trying his numbers, but the house was winning. Cunningham handed fifty dollars to the red-jacketed dwarf by the door and they stepped into the night.

There were only a few cars on the road and occasional bursts of music shot out of little rum shops by the roadside. It had rained earlier and as there was no dust they kept the car windows open. Port-au-Prince had cooled down. His mind wandered back to Marie-Christine and her killer. Could it have been money? She was a wealthy woman by Haitian standards. She had been married to a local heart specialist who numbered most foreign residents and diplomats among his patients. He was a shrewd investor and owned a lot of real estate in town. He had died of a stroke right after a New Year's Eve dance.

She might have been rich, but she was a lovable, kind woman. He could not think who would have wanted to harm her or how the police hoped to sell the suicide story to anyone who had known her. How long was Dubuffet's guarantee good for? He had to stay in Haiti for another twenty-four hours, and then, if Francisco failed to deliver, even if he did manage to get the Haitians across, where could he go himself?

The means of transport and the route could all be sorted out now that Marcel was in the saddle. But the girl had to go. Or did she? Of course she did. Her husband was back. So what? Was his optimism caused by the thick wad of bills in his pocket?

When they arrived at the El Rancho, he made no effort to sneak in unobserved. He walked in with her, arm in arm. The reception clerk welcomed him with a knowing smile and a big *bon soir*. The rumours about the state of Marina's bedroom must have reached the front desk. What the hell.

'Send some chicken and rice up to Mrs Buckmaster's room,' he said. 'For two.'

'There was a call from the Dominican Republic. The caller did not leave a name.'

'He'll probably call back.'

A large bunch of flowers welcomed her by the door. The note said, 'The lodger thanks you.' She threw her arms around him and hugged him close. Later, the waiter wheeled their food in and they sat down to eat. Outside, the night and its whispers sailed by. She looked lovely and childlike and happy. He must make her leave even if it took him until dawn.

Much later, the phone rang. It was the reception clerk. 'The police are here again, Monsieur Cunningham,' he said. 'A man has been shot dead outside the casino. A Monsieur Marcel Kinet. Will you please come down and talk to them?'

The police were apologetic. They hoped Monsieur Cunningham would understand. No one thought for a moment that he had anything to do with it. Everybody saw him leave long before Monsieur Kinet did. It was just that he was the last man to talk to Monsieur Kinet before he was killed. Right in his car outside the casino. Everybody heard the shot. What was it Monsieur Cunningham and Monsieur Kinet talked about? Perhaps Monsieur Cunningham could shed some light on the mâtter? Suggest some motive for the murder. Was Monsieur Kinet afraid of someone? Had he confided any such fears to him? No? Well, what did Monsieur Cunningham think? Yes, they understood Monsieur Cunningham was tired because it was late, but surely he had some ideas. A theory perhaps. That's all. Nothing personal. Nothing personal, Cunningham thought as he listened in silence.

'You knew both Madame Marie-Christine and Monsieur

Kinet, did you not, monsieur?'

'I did. Haiti is a beautiful country and her people are talented and friendly. That is why I come here so often. I have many friends here.'

'Not for business?'

'No. Just friendship. I was going to have dinner with Monsieur Kinet later today. We were talking about that at the casino. He had a bad time at the table and I did extremely well, but you would have heard all about that.'

'Well, if you get any ideas, please contact us.'

'Of course. Thank you for your trust.'

'Not at all. We apologize, but you were friendly with both the victims. It must worry you.'

'You don't expect all my Haitian friends to drop dead, do you, Captain?'

The officer gave an ugly laugh. 'I hope not, monsieur. That would keep us very busy. I know you have a lot of friends here.'

The grey morning glare had begun its crawl up from the sea and the porter switched the night lights off. Only the splashes of two early swimmers disturbed the silence in the gardens below.

'Would you like to join me for some breakfast?'

'No, thank you. I'm sure you could do with a few hours without the police.'

CHAPTER FIFTEEN

■

The crowded room sizzled with excitement as the domino game progressed through the night. Shouts of joy for points scored were flung across guttural curses that echoed losses. Three empty whisky bottles lay discarded on the floor along with scores of squashed beer cans. A cloud of cigar smoke hung over the room and through it all Francisco's kid brother slept unperturbed on the davenport. He had been told to sit there and keep quiet as soon as they had arrived, while Francisco was invited to join in. It was cold in the mountains and a huge log fire that blazed in the hearth did little to lift the temperature in the room.

'You should install some radiators,' the Chief of Police told his brother the farmer. 'The fires look good, but it's useless. My arse is frozen.'

'I like it cold. That's why I live here. Let's see, now. You owe me four hundred and twenty-seven pesos.'

'The game isn't over yet.'

The Chief was in a pleasant frame of mind. It would have been the right time for Francisco to have said something to him, but there were other farmers in the room, most of them Cunningham's clients. The Chief would not take kindly to discussing police business in front of them. Besides, it was not good for them to know that Cunningham was having problems getting back into the country. The harvest was close. They would surely panic.

'Francisquito,' the Chief said, 'you have been quiet all night. Are you unwell?'

'With what your brother is winning from me, you can't expect me to joke.'

'This is no social call, is it? We can talk if you like. We're both losing money to the farmers. Come on, what is it you want?'

'It's not urgent, Chief. We can talk later.'

'You're not fooling me, Francisco. If it wasn't urgent you wouldn't be back here so soon after your little brother. You can talk in front of our neighbours here. They know.'

'About Cunningham, you mean?'

'Sure they do. And they all hope he will deliver in time for the harvest or everybody is in real shit. Especially Cunningham.'

The game continued sluggishly. No one spoke, but all listened. The tension in the smoky room was almost painful.

'He'd better deliver,' someone said. 'Who does he think he is dealing with?'

'He'll come through. He has never let anyone down yet.'

'There is always the first time,' the Chief barked.

'Yes,' Francisco said, 'and unless you let him into the country unmolested, this may be it. Cunningham wants to deliver the people himself, but how do you expect him to do that if you're going to arrest him the minute he sets foot on Dominican soil, eh? How?'

The domino game stopped dead. The farmers looked up in total surprise. The Chief was no diplomat, Francisco thought. What was he playing at? The farmers knew nothing. The Chief calmly peeled the cellophane off another cigar. He bit off the end as three flamed matches raced to it from all corners.

'Thank you,' he murmured. 'I cannot do much about that, Francisco. The gringos want your friend Cunningham and I cannot stall the Minister any longer. This could land me in serious trouble. It's not just the sugar and coffee agreements. There is also the question of aid. I have done what I can, but it's way over my head now.'

'What has he done?' asked one farmer.

The Chief wasn't going to answer that, Francisco prayed. Surely not here and now. He should never have come.

'You've got to let him in, Chief,' another farmer ventured.

'Impossible.'

'What has he done?'

The Chief sat back, lifting one booted foot onto the table. Christ, he's about to hold court, Francisco thought. He needs to remind the rich farmers in the room who is boss. He will have to bury Cunningham to do that. He mustn't be given the chance.

'Let's forget it, Chief,' Francisco said in desperation. 'We'll think of something.'

It was too late. The Chief inhaled a mouthful of smoke into

his lungs and started declaiming with authority. His brother the farmer sat back, his face beaming with pride. The Chief was out to impress his audience, like a sheriff up for re-election. He must have waited all night for someone to give him an excuse. He wasn't going to let the moment pass. He would not stop until he'd finished. Cunningham, Francisco knew, would then be worse off than ever.

The gringo police in Puerto Rico wanted to see him about the murder of a hotel receptionist who had apparently been rude to him. The body of the victim had only just been discovered and Cunningham was required at the inquest. A girl croupier from the Americana Casino had been raped and robbed by a man answering his description. The woman produced Cunningham's Playboy Club membership card as evidence.

There was another charge concerning a light aircraft that had crashed into the old city's sea wall. Fifty kilos of cocaine were found in the wreckage. The pilot was not traced, but the plane had been chartered by Cunningham. Two gringo policemen had been shot by a local terrorist during a demonstration for independence from the United States. Cunningham was alleged to have been involved.

And that was not all. There was the sad case of Estella Carasco, married to one Peter Cunningham five years ago to help him obtain the coveted green American resident's card. He left her without a penny of the five hundred dollars he'd promised her, unable to get a divorce, and reduced to prostitution and begging as a result. He then married another lady for the same purpose, but the Chief did not have her name.

With charges of such magnitude, asked the Chief, how could he possibly turn a blind eye to Cunningham's possible return to the country? Justice, he said in a stentorian voice, must prevail. Francisco laughed it off.

'It's all a load of trumped-up rubbish and you know it,' he said. 'You don't seriously believe it, do you?'

'With your friend Cunningham, anything is possible,' said

one farmer.

Your friend. Two weeks ago, they were all his friends. Now they believed anything. The trouble was the Chief believed it too.

'I always knew there was some reason why Cunningham could never go back to England,' the Chief of Police declared. 'Only God knows what crimes he committed there, but as a policeman I believe the truth comes out in the end. On that day we'll know.'

We'll wait and see what happens to you then, Francisco thought bitterly.

'What makes you so sure this is true, Chief?' he asked.

'I got it all from a contact in the police department in San Juan. A professional, like me. We're not politicians. We don't need to invent stories to win votes. If a fellow policeman tells you something, you believe it. And in Puerto Rico, they are all American-trained.'

'He is no rapist. You all know that. I know women who would pay him for that. It's all a trick to get him back onto American soil.'

'If they want him so badly, he must have done something. Anyway, I have already told you, it's out of my hands.'

'But, Chief, how are we going to get the Haitians into the fields in time? Cunningham must be allowed in or your brother and his friends will lose their shirts.'

'Justice must be done,' the Chief barked.

Little do you know of other people's greed, Francisco thought as he watched the landowners' faces. The Chief had finally gone too far. The farmers came to Cunningham's defence to a man. As far as they were concerned, justice could wait, but not the harvest.

'There's a lot of cane out there this year,' one said.

'Let the bastard in, arrest him later,' said another.

'We'll pass some more Haitians to your brother for free if you can help. It'll only delay shipping him over there by a few days.'

The rest nodded in agreement and all eyes turned on the Chief. He yawned, then stretched his arms above his head. Cigar ash fell on his spotless white shirt.

'Perhaps I could find a way to delay the orders to the border posts until Francisco calls me to say they are safely across, but make sure Cunningham does not show his face in the capital, or there's big trouble. You hear?'

That was all Francisco needed to know. 'Don't worry, Chief,' he said, 'everything will be just the way you say. The Haitians will get here on time, and you won't see hide nor hair of Cunningham. You can count on me.'

He refused an invitation to stay for breakfast, thanked the farmers for their help, and woke his brother up. 'Let's go, kid.'

'We've only just got here. Can't we eat something first?'

'We'll get something on the way. You're just like my wife. All you think about is food. Now get out of here and let's get back. I need to catch up on some sleep.'

CHAPTER SIXTEEN

—■—

'Francisco had better have some decent answers after all this time,' Cunningham said. 'He's usually slow, but not this slow. With Marie-Christine and Marcel Kinet both dead I'm going to have to inspect the workers myself. I suppose this means they'll gun for me next. You really must leave, Marina.'

She took not the slightest notice. 'How do you tell the difference between a man who is healthy and a man who is not, in a country where everybody is emaciated?'

'Used to get a doctor for that. Not sure what'll happen now.'

'Some line of business you're in, Cunningham.'

'There's nothing wrong in what I'm doing.'

'Nothing wrong in buying and selling people?'

'Do you know what the alternative is for them? Nothing. Do you seriously think I drag them screaming from their beds in the night? There are no beds where they come from. They would pay me to get away from here if they had two coins to rub together.'

'Crap.' Why was she talking to him like that? Was she just mad at him because he wanted her to go?

'I am, you see, providing a service for society. These people are about to trade a country that treats them like dirt for regular work and food. They think themselves lucky, believe me. This is their one chance. Whatever the landowners pay is more than they get in a lifetime if they stay behind.'

He saw the 'who do you think I am' expression on her face, but he went right on. 'The other side of the old island of Hispaniola – the Dominican Republic – is larger than Haiti and infinitely more fertile. It is less populated. The division isn't quite fair. Either the politicians or God slipped up somewhere. All I do is tip the balance a bit.'

'What happens once they get through the harvest? You sell them off at bargain prices, like second-hand cars?'

That was downright rude. He'd have to answer back now. 'Most stay on in the Dominican Republic. Some start new families. Their children have a better chance. The whole show is better than the alternative. A lot of them sell everything they possess to buy a passage on some floating death-trap bound for Miami. I've told you. You've probably read about them sometimes, washed ashore or caught by the immigration authorities. Some never get there. Heaven knows how many drown or get thrown to the sharks by the pirates who sell these passages. I've never lost a soul. It wasn't always like that. Not too long ago Trujillo massacred thousands of them, yet they kept coming. Haiti is not a pretty postcard for everybody. To most it is hell.'

'How do those who stay behind live with it?'

'I've told you that, too. Most escape into the mystical world of voodoo. The real thing, not the parody you've seen at the shows for the tourists. Even the ones who make it, the one in ten thousand like poor Marcel Kinet, pull themselves up by their non-existent shoestrings and rise with optimism born of belief in magic.'

'I've got to see it. I want to be with you when you leave.'

'You're not going to. You have to leave here today.'

She looked at him defiantly and thought he might be right, but she sulked all the same.

He had yet to meet the man, Ti Allain, whom Marie-Christine had trusted to make the selection for her. Perhaps he was the man to watch. To be given some more responsibility. She had always said that he could not come to harm because he was protected by the spirits. Everyone he knew in Haiti believed in spirits. But the other side, whoever they were, believed in guns. They could have eliminated him at any time, if they had wanted to. Or Marina. Why hadn't they? It was wiser to get her out, before something did happen to her. And yet their intimacy was growing with the danger, and she was growing on him and constantly changing. She certainly had spirit.

She looked at him, smiled and said, 'I'm starving. Isn't life great?'

Confidence breeds optimism, he thought.

'You need me here,' she said, and then the phone rang.

'Cunningham,' Francisco Martinez said, 'you're in the shit.' He poured out all he had heard in the mountains. He told him of the charges and sounded serious, but Cunningham could not contain his amusement. He laughed out loud as a puzzled Marina watched.

'Things can't be that bad. These fabrications are childish.'

'Maybe in England they are.'

'Puerto Rico is American.'

'Not the police force, Cunningham. They are Indios, same as me. These charges are meant for Dominican consumption. In this country they'd believe anything. You should have seen those farmers up there. No one had any doubts, *amigo*. They forgot all about their friendship and you and they believed it all. You know how we love to gossip. Except that this time the gossip was hurting their pockets. Everybody up there understood what the gringos want. No one cares how the Chief does it, as long as they get you onto American soil. As long as they get what they have paid for first. Anyway, in the end the Chief agreed the cargo must come in. He will make sure no one stops you from coming in with the Haitians. No one will exert themselves looking for the point of entry, but as soon as delivery is made he'll have you arrested. Forget the old days.'

'Why is he being so generous?'

'He does not want to upset the landowners. They are his brother's neighbours. I saw them at Jarabacoa, sticking up for each other like cabinet ministers. A roomful of pigs, they were. A brotherhood of farmers.'

'Farmers? The Chief's brother has not planted one seed of shit in the ground in his life. He knows less about farming than the Pope. All the tobacco and the sugar and the beans growing on his land are put there by his neighbours. They do the planting, the Haitians do the reaping, and he collects the cash. It's been like that ever since the Chief got his job.'

'I thought the Chief's brother was an expert farmer. The farmers think the world of him.'

'He only got into farming after his brother got the job and could supply labour. He took them out of the prisons and shipped them to the farms. But then came the scandal. He was found out, but it was hushed up. I don't know how much money was spent to keep him in his job or who donated it. Anyway, when I started bringing the Haitians he was quick to get in on the act. All he needed to do was make sure I was not disturbed, and he got his cheap labour back. Cheaper. Without his cover, it would have been impossible. The farmers know that. That is why they tolerate his brother and help him run his farm.'

'If that is so, why is the Chief giving us such hassle?'

'Power corrupts, Francisco. Sometimes he needs to remind the world who God is. Do you know what the Chief's brother did before he became a gentleman farmer? Did he ever tell you where they got the money to buy all that land? You'll never believe it.'

'Try me. Trujillo? Were they close to him?'

'Not at all. They never got close enough. They used to run cinemas, Francisco. That is how I met them. I used to bring in Mexican, Spanish and Argentinian films for them duty free. New films every week, Francisco. And none about farming. They had the best films in the country and they made a fortune because everybody went to the cinema. That's where they got the money for the land. On my diplomatic back, Francisco. The Chief swore eternal loyalty to me long before he became Chief. He owned so much land in the mountains he could start his own country and he forgot. All the brother is good at is dominoes. He's got plenty of time to perfect his game up there.'

'You're right. He won a fortune off me. I forgot all about that. You owe me ...'

'Not now, Francisco. You go and get some sleep. Thank you for your help. I must think.'

He could not talk any more. A stream of facts and solutions shot into his mind and he needed to contemplate them. He was on the verge of a discovery. He said *adiós*, hung up and sat on the bed.

They all believed the Americans were after him. The Chief did. Even Francisco. But nowhere, nowhere along any corridor of his past, could he find a reason for it. He got up and walked across the room, and then back. Across and back. Patterns were beginning to emerge. Obscure, slow patterns that meant little and then more, and then suddenly it all came, clear as crystal. A picture gelled in his mind and he stopped and smiled. He should have seen it all before.

This was a whole new ball game. Much bigger than a vendetta against one man. If he hadn't been so busy feeling sorry for himself, so busy trying to figure out who would want to hurt him so badly and why, he might have seen it sooner. And if he had, poor Marcel Kinet would still be alive. Whoever was trying to stop the Haitians from coming into the country was not after him at all. This was big. Some sort of power struggle. Nothing to do with him. He was in no danger. At least not until they found the Haitians. They would never find them by themselves.

No one ever went to Diquini these days. They used to grow the best tobacco in the world in Diquini. The German Kaiser smoked it, and so had Marie-Christine's husband. What was left of the Diquini fields lay west of lower Port-au-Prince, surrounded by tin shacks and wooden structures, too poor and too dirty to be noticed. A place that seemed to be growing back into the earth. It was the safest place in the world to hide a Haitian, as safe as a forest is for a tree. No one would suspect a peaceful gathering at Diquini. Not even the Tonton Macoutes. There were no politics there. No danger to the regime. Only poverty that had gone beyond hunger.

CHAPTER SEVENTEEN

◆

The sun had arrived in the middle of the sky for the third time and hung there. Another day of waiting had reached the halfway mark. Ti Allain had brought the people down to wait for the tall foreigner who would take them away. But there was no sign of him yet. He was famous in the mountains; everyone knew about the golden corn colour of his hair and how he lost some of his leg fighting iron monsters far away in the land of Egypt where the great priest Mo was born before he became King of the Israelites. Marie-Christine had told Ti Allain of this and he passed it all on to the others.

The tall foreigner was famous, but no one except La Grande

Marie had ever seen him in the flesh. Not even Ti Allain, although he never admitted it. He was, it was rumoured, a good man who had sacrificed a part of his leg to foreign spirits far away from Haiti and had so achieved purity. That was why, it was said, the tall foreigner sometimes pretended to limp to show he understood the plight of those who lived among the tired, dry plants and starved there. He had come across many rough seas and tall mountains and fast rivers and spoke Creole. Sometimes he led the people into Saint Domingue himself, just like Mo the priest who led his people away from death in Egypt, where the foreigner's foot was buried.

No one really wanted to leave Haiti and its beautiful mountains. So few ever returned. Yet the people had lost their courage and could no longer face that slow, helpless death that stared them in the eye and laughed like the devil. It could have been the curse of Monique, the black witch who had come out of her mother's womb with chicken legs and who was burned by the villagers when Ti Allain's grandmother was a girl. None of the people by the little wooden church at Diquini were even born then, but they knew. Monique screamed before she died, but she was a witch so it was not pain that caused her to cry out. She screamed her curse upon the village and made the earth and the sky remain dry and that curse lingered until this very day. The spirits brought too many children into their huts and not enough food. When heaven did open it poured too much water down to remind the villagers of Monique's tears. The water washed away the seeds and the very soil into which they were pushed. But mostly it did not rain at all because the tall mountains stopped the clouds from coming close.

There were odd times when it was green enough for a goat to graze, but even then not a blade of grass grew in the place where the fire had sent Monique to hell. A sure sign that she was still watching. A man knows where he was born and a spirit remembers where the body it bore has died. Hers was marked by a dry stake, painted white to keep children away from it at night. Sometimes a dead lizard or a blood-soaked feather was affixed to it by someone.

Monique was dead. She could not hurt anyone directly. Not the way city people did when they came with their guns and taxes. Monique had the power to make death descend and take the children away by stopping the plants from growing tall enough to feed the chickens and the few cows that could have sustained them.

Ti Allain had never thought of crossing to the Spanish side himself. For several years now he had selected the right people to do that. With the money the fat city woman called La Grande Marie paid him he could support himself, but no one knew that because he lived like all the others and accepted the little bits of food they gave him. He was a small man and people thought he did not need more.

He never sired any children or married. He was the sort of headman-priest whose position and knowledge of the spirits and their world frightened women away. Some said he was a reincarnation of Monique and, as such, was not only dead, but really a woman. Nor did he grow to be as tall as his father or any of the other villagers for that matter, which is why they gave him his name. With all the food he ate at night he should have been the tallest man in all Haiti, but he was not, which was a sure sign that he was really dead.

His powers were famous nonetheless and people from far afield came to him to be healed. He was especially successful in curing barren women who came for short visits to his hut while their menfolk waited outside. The women never talked of how or why they were cured and his fame grew. That was why he could always find healthy workers for La Grande Marie's foreign friend. He was too powerful and too useful to be killed off by anyone who wanted his position. You would not kill a corpse, even if he did not possess the true look of a proper skin-and-bones, chalk-covered zombie.

Even Ti Allain's powers had stopped operating these last three days. No one had come to Diquini to see them. Not even the city lady Marie-Christine who sometimes gave them white pills to take the heat away from their heads. And without her he was helpless. In one more day there wouldn't be any money left for him to buy rice. They would have to steal some sugar cane to suck and when that happened some would cease believing in his powers altogether. And their unbelief would spread and his hold on the people would loosen, and maybe give way. Ti Allain was afraid.

There were almost one hundred mouths to feed. Most were the men who would make the journey, but some were their women, come to see the men off. Others were hangers-on who joined the assembly at Diquini in the hope of finding someone to feed them. During the first two days he still had some provisions which La Grande Marie had sent down with her man, Guy the driver. But now, with no sign of the tall foreigner and with hunger threatening, Ti Allain was becoming silent and morose. Had the others not known better, they might have thought something was worrying him. But worry is not something that could possibly bother the dead. He must have been tired or impatient or just talking to the spirits in silence. No one interrupted.

Ti Allain was afraid. For three days now there had been no sign of anyone. He was long overdue back at his village. More people squatted about the camp, either hoping to be selected or just to watch the next meal and share it with their eyes. He had been told in the market that morning that Marie-Christine was dead and that the foreigner himself was coming to lead them across the mountains, and he hoped it would come to pass. Without more food they could never walk back to the hills, let alone cross the border if they could find it. If the spirits had wanted Marie-Christine dead, he could be next. He did not want to die so far from his grandmother's grave.

Only smart people are afraid of living beings; the rest confine their fears to the unknown. Ti Allain, who had always lived by his wits without ever trying to work the land, was smart. La Grande Marie had told him so herself when she was alive. Her friend the foreigner had to come to them today or Ti Allain would be at the gates of trouble. The workers might lose their patience and their tempers and forget they believed he could not die again.

The sun was moving away from the centre of the sky when the little leader started to pray. No one was sure what he was praying for or whether he was only talking to the spirits the way he always did. It did not matter anyway. Ti Allain had already brought them this far, further than they had ever been before. They had seen white buildings and hard roads and trees and the sea and many, many people who talked and laughed and bought and sold. They had seen heaps of fruits and vegetables and animals on their way and the senseless miracle of water being wasted on grass in front of brick houses. They had seen cars and cycles and horses and could talk about it all without a lie. Their faith in him was greater than ever.

Ti Allain smeared mud on his hair and chalk on his face and began to dance. He danced silently, willing the sun to stop in the middle of the sky and keep the hours from racing away. The people looked on and wondered what was to come. The local children, sensing there would be no handouts today, drifted away in search of other things to hope for. The day got hotter and the mud on Ti Allain's face and hair dried and turned into dust and slowly fell back to the earth. Something was sure to happen once it had all fallen back to where it had been before. It would be well worth being there when it did.

CHAPTER EIGHTEEN

He thought he remembered the telephone during the night, but his whisky-stricken mind did not know for certain. Marina? No. Yes, of course. Marina. She had said she was in

Port-au-Prince. Or was it Puerto Rico? But it had gone from his head and he had woken up expecting her to be next to him, like she always was. His head was heavy and his mouth was dry and tasted foul. She had a thing about bad breath and often nagged him about brushing his teeth a million times before he came to bed. He was in no mood for lectures. The empty space in the bed goaded him in silence. Perhaps he was better off by himself.

He had never been alone with the children before. Not at breakfast time. The baby flatly refused to wait for him to shower or even shave. She wanted her food there and then and she badly needed a clean-up. He gave her slippery little body a good soaking in the basin and put her on his bed.

'You wait there, little lady,' he said, 'and let me find you some clothes.' While he was searching for a nappy, she managed to crawl to the edge of the bed and promptly fell off. She lay there on the floor, looking up at him, a worried look on her face. 'Naughty, naughty,' he said, mimicking Marina's voice. The little mouth curled downwards and she began to cry. 'Good girl,' he said, and smiled broadly. She went silent immediately, her eyes watching him intently, waiting for his next move. 'We'll get some lovely new diapers on and then we'll be comfortable, won't we?' The baby seemed to understand his every word.

The blessing of having been born a man touched him as he struggled to get a pin through the terry-towelling cloth. Marina had obviously fled to get away from all this. He couldn't blame her. How stupid he had been to kick the nanny out. The elder girl sat patiently in her cot, awaiting her turn. Her wide eyes stared at him with a disconcerting confidence. Well trained, he thought. He really should have called Marina to say he was going to be early. She would have been here and he could have showered and shaved in peace. He put the baby on the floor again to roam on all fours. He had just turned to the elder child when the phone rang.

'Two minutes,' he said to her, and picked up the receiver.

'Buckmaster here.'

'This is Francisco Martinez, señor. Is about the maid you throw outside.'

Gerald's face lit up. 'Oh, *Señor Martinez, usted puede hablar español.*'

'Is okay, señor. I like practise English better. Why you no happy with the daughter from Chiquito?'

'I didn't mean to be rude to her, Señor Martinez. I'd just come back from a long trip. I was expecting my wife to be here.'

'Is okay, señor. You like her come back?'

'Can you arrange that?'

'Is arrange already. When you want her?'

'Well ... I would be grateful if ...'

'She is in hotel reception. She come up now?'

'Oh, yes please! And, señor, where can I reach you?'

'I say goodbye now.'

The man hung up and Gerald said, 'Damn the man,' and apologized to his elder girl. 'Now let's see to you.'

The maid was let into the suite. She pushed past him and went straight over to the children. The little faces lit up in recognition. He smiled to himself. Now, at last, he could get on with his own morning ritual, unmolested. As he stood in front of the mirror, his face covered with soft white lather, the memory of the girl in Rio drifted back into his mind.

Oh, how pretty that girl had been. She'd said she was married to an engineer who was working in the interior. They couldn't really afford to live in Rio on his salary, but she was a born Carioca and what could she do? She wouldn't live anywhere else. Not for anything. Certainly not in the jungle without people and music and places to go. That's why she was doing this. Making a bit of extra money to buy clothes and go to the cinema. That way her husband could save his salary towards buying a place of their own one day. So she came here sometimes, but only went with someone she liked.

The perfume she wore was thick and pungent, and all the

while she talked she made love to him and he listened as if this was the most natural thing in the world. He looked at her in the dark and felt her skin against his. He listened as her narrative turned into noises that embarrassed him. Was he coming back again? Next day? she asked. He did not answer. He stayed with her all that afternoon.

He did return to the apartment the next day, but she was not there. Perhaps she had a cold or maybe her husband had come back unexpectedly. 'No hard feelings, Mr Buckmaster,' his Rio agent said. 'You don't fall in love in a place like this. You enjoy yourself and forget, that's all. If you see her in the street, remember you never saw her before. Just pick another, if you like.' He didn't like. He did not go back again. On his flight to Venezuela a week later, he worried he might have caught something horrendous from her and would require a course of injections.

Something pricked his face and he looked and saw a spot of blood dripping under his nose. How stupid he had been, some weeks later, to have told Marina what he'd done. It happened during a fierce argument they were having. He denied it all afterwards. Said he'd made it all up on the spur of the moment, just to hurt her. She never mentioned it again. Perhaps she did believe him. Perhaps she forgot.

He washed the lather off. He hoped she'd get back soon from wherever it was she'd gone. God, how empty the world was without her. He loved her and he needed her and he would tell her so.

CHAPTER NINETEEN

Three hundred miles of bad mountain roads separated him from the estates over the border. They could try and ambush him anywhere between Port-au-Prince and the crossing point, but unless they knew where he was leaving from and when, they would fail. To find a group of people up-country, along uncharted goat paths, was well nigh impossible. They would need an army for that.

Cunningham whistled happily as he got into the car. He was going to see the Haitians that morning. Marina had insisted on coming with him. She might as well. They wouldn't harm her. They were Latin. They wanted to frighten him, not upset a casual fling he was having with a woman out for a joyride. And just as long as they didn't suspect how important she'd become to him, she was safe.

It was eleven o'clock in the morning and Guy drove them past the white Presidential Palace onto the tatty coastal road. They were about to turn into Diquini when they saw the black Mercedes. It was parked, engine running, half blocking the intersection. Cunningham tapped Guy on the shoulder. 'Their engine is running. Let's wait here until they move off.'

But the big black car remained stationary. Two men, dressed in dark business suits, climbed out into the dust. Except for the bulges under their left arms, they looked like foreign businessmen who had lost their way. One moved towards them, the other stayed put, his lithe body leaning against the gleaming car.

'It seems,' Cunningham said, 'that someone knows every move I make in this town.'

The man's walk was purposeful. It lacked the dance of a Haitian. He reached the car and Cunningham lowered his window and looked at him. Under his dark glasses shone stained teeth studded with golden caps. He was a tall, powerfully built man. His swarthy looks seemed familiar.

'Can I help you in any way?' Cunningham asked in Spanish.

'Maybe,' the man said, and Cunningham knew he was a Dominican. He took a hard look at the face. He had seen it before. He tried to remember.

'What can I do for you, señores?'

'We are both going to the same place, but the road is too

narrow for two cars. We were here first, so you'll have to give way. Unless you are interested in doing business with us.'

'I am always interested in doing business, but I've got commitments.'

'Perhaps we can settle your commitment for you. Circumstances change.'

This was the opposition all right. 'Surely, señor, you would not like to deal with someone who breaks his word?'

'It would depend, señor, on who you had given your word to. If he's a thief and a liar you would be better off breaking your word to him, wouldn't you?'

'I have been working with the same people for a long time.'

'What if these people are working against you now, Señor Cunningham?'

'You know who I am, señor, but I don't know you.'

'I am Dominican.'

'There are three million people in the Dominican Republic, give or take a few thousand. I know. I live there.'

'We know that, señor. We know most things about you. We know the police are looking for you.'

'In this part of the world the police are always looking for somebody.'

'Perhaps. But we can help you, señor, my friends and I.'

'That's nice.' He had certainly seen that face before. Another setting. Different clothes. Uniform. That was it. He had seen that man in uniform somewhere. 'You and your friends ... and you are?'

'Balthasar. They call me Balthasar.' Of course, Cunningham thought. Some call you that. But most call you El Carnicero, the Butcher. The man outside his car was Balthasar Fernandes, the former police chief. The man who lost his job when the government changed. That made sense. A personal vendetta against the current chief of police. But that could not be all. There had to be more.

'What would you like to talk about, Balthasar?'

'I told you. The road is too narrow for both of us.'

'You were here first. I'll follow you.'

Balthasar took a cigar out of his pocket and lit it slowly, watching the Englishman's face. 'You go first,' he said.

'Let's stop playing games, Balthasar. It's too hot. Why don't you just say what you've come to say? I have things to do.'

'I wouldn't go back into town, Cunningham. The air there could be bad for you.'

'We cannot talk here.'

'What do you suggest?'

'We could go to the casino. They serve a great smorgasbord there at this hour.'

'We'll follow you.'

Cunningham rolled up the window. He looked at Marina. 'When we get to the casino,' he said to Guy the driver, 'you go back to Diquini. Make sure they haven't got another car to follow you. You arrange to postpone the selection until this evening. We have to have electricity, *comprende*? Otherwise we won't be able to tell the sick from the healthy. They can run a cable from the overhead wire. Monsieur Kinet told me he'd done that before.'

'Why don't you have them arrested, Monsieur Cunningham? We'll go to the police station now. They won't follow us there. You must denounce them. They've killed Madame Marie-Christine and Monsieur Kinet. We can have them in jail inside an hour.'

'Go to the casino, Guy. Then do as I've said.'

'*Oui, monsieur*. You are the *patron*.'

Bless Marie-Christine. She always had the knack of finding the right people.

By the time they got to the casino, the Mercedes had disappeared from sight. They went inside and sat down by the window. As they waited for Balthasar to pull up, Cunningham was trying to persuade Marina to go back to the hotel. She flatly refused and remained adamant until the Mercedes came to a halt outside. There were no dramatic sounds of screeching brakes or slamming doors. The two Dominicans slid out, looking almost comical, stuffed as they were inside three-piece suits and white fedoras. There walked Hollywood's Chicago of the thirties. They came through the door and smiled broadly in their direction the way old friends would.

'Please,' Cunningham whispered, 'please go back to the hotel now. The show's over.'

The Dominicans approached their table, then sat down. There was a strong odour of cigar smoke and sweat in the air. Cunningham handed Marina a wad of bills. 'Go do some shopping, girl,' he said in a loud drawl, 'while we men talk.'

She got up with a flounce, her eyes shooting green anger at all three. 'Don't bother to see me out. I'll take a taxi.'

'Get something to eat in the room.'

'I'm not hungry.'

And then she was gone, but not before she'd faced the backs of the two Dominicans and treated Cunningham to an elaborate wink.

CHAPTER TWENTY

◼

Francisco Martinez was having a rare lunch with his wife and she did not need any prodding.

'I'll have the soup, Francisco, and the tostones and the spaghetti. Then the chicken looks good, and a little rice to go with it. Not too much. I'm on a diet, you know.'

Her husband looked sheepishly at the waiter. The fellow was hovering only feet away and would have heard every word. How could he show his face here again?

'And maybe a few fried shrimps, Francisco? They do them with garlic. I love garlic. It stimulates the appetite.'

'Are you sure that'll be enough for you, dear?' The waiter smiled. The bastard was listening. His wife was now addressing the waiter directly.

'I don't get out of the house that often, you know. My husband is never home.'

What was she going to tell the man next? 'Come back in five minutes, *camarero*,' Francisco said. 'We'll decide in peace.'

He turned to his wife and banged his fist on the table, causing the ice in his glass to rattle. 'Can't you behave like a lady for once? The news of your greed will be all over town in five minutes. I have a reputation to maintain.' He was just getting into his stride when a hand landed on his shoulder. 'I told you five minutes, waiter, didn't I?' he said.

'I am not a waiter,' a thin, high-pitched voice said. 'Are you Francisco Martinez?'

Francisco tried to turn his head, but the hand gripped his shoulder, squeezing. 'You are hurting me, señor.'

'Are you Francisco Martinez?'

'Yes I am, but that doesn't give you the right to hurt me. What do you want?'

'Some people want to talk to you. Please come with me. Your wife will have to eat by herself. She can easily manage your lunch too.'

That was funny, but the man had no right to joke about his wife. Everyone had heard her, including this fellow who was obviously no friend of his. His wife did not seem perturbed by his pained expression. The bitch could at least stop perusing the menu, *coño*. Make some fuss or something.

'Say goodbye to your wife, Señor Martinez,' the high-pitched voice commanded. 'We are leaving.'

'I'll be back,' Francisco said to her, but she paid no attention. 'I'll be back very soon,' he repeated louder. This time she heard and nodded and waved her hand without lifting her head.

'You don't deserve such a woman,' his new guardian remarked as they walked onto the terrace. 'Mine would have raised hell.' Francisco did not dare take a look at the man, but

133

he caught a quick glimpse of his large frame in the mirror by the cashier's desk.

People were sitting on the terrace: slim, handsome young men, suntanned and hairy-chested, gold chains and ornamental crosses swinging from their necks. Pretty women giggled with drinks in their hands, all chattering away without a worry in the world. How could anyone face such loaded plates and remain slim? And not one of them did he know. He walked faster, but the owner of the squeaky voice was in no hurry.

'Take it slow, Francisco. I'd hate to lose you in the crowd.'

'If you are from out of town, I can show you the way.'

'Shut your mouth and keep moving. I've got a gun in my pocket. Just walk down the pavement and smile. The car is a bit further on. A Mercedes.'

'I prefer American cars myself.'

'No one asked you.'

'There is no need to be rude, my friend. This is a classy place.' There was no answer. 'Carrying a gun is against the law.'

'So is the slave trade.'

'Only if you get caught. You're not with the police, are you?'

'You'll find out in good time.'

'You can't be with the police. They can't afford flashy cars.'

'Stop your blabber,' the man said. He was losing his grip. He was only a messenger.

'If you don't like my voice, just say so. I love yours. I could listen to you all day.'

The man walked faster. His steps were short and angry. A little brawl was all he needed. The Malecon was full of people and someone would intervene if the man got really aggressive. A painless little fight would give him the chance to get away.

'Move, Francisco.'

'I thought you wanted me to walk slowly. Make up your mind, *amigo*.'

The man did not take the bait. 'Okay, Francisco. That's

very funny. Now be a good boy and nothing will happen.'

'My poor wife ...'

'You'll be back in time to pay the bill. There it is.'

'The bill?'

'No. The car.'

The long, sleek Mercedes was parked ahead, its back door open to the sidewalk.

'Get in, Francisco. We're going for a little ride.'

How many times had he heard that sentence, first in the movies and then in his imagination? He was going to tell the man what an honour it was to hear it in real life, but a strong hand pushed him inside and the door slammed shut as the car shot off into the lunchtime traffic. Francisco barely felt the prick of the needle going into his arm. Just the coldness of the fluid as it was injected. He wondered what it was, then was suddenly too drowsy to care. *Caramba*, but these Mercedes are comfortable. Must tell Cunningham about that, he thought as his mind slipped away. What a rosy world it was. By the time the car turned up towards the Arroyo Hondo hills, he was slumped down on the seat, oblivious to everything.

CHAPTER TWENTY-ONE

Of course, they said, they had nothing against him. It was the Chief they were after, and they wanted Cunningham to join them. At first they were crude about it, then they tried coaxing, but he stuck to his guns. Why? he wondered. What did he owe the Chief? The Chief didn't really give a damn. Francisco had been right. All he wanted was to get his brother's beans and tobacco and sugar harvested. And his cut. Money, that's all.

This thing was much bigger than the settling of old scores,

they went on. Discrediting the Chief was to be just the beginning. They were going to bring down the whole government. No blood was going to be shed. A glorious revolution, Caribbean style.

'How', Cunningham asked, 'do you intend to accomplish that?'

'We represent the business community.'

'You must be joking.'

'No, we're not. And while we have nothing against the police or the army, too many generals are getting fat at the expense of business. You know that every businessman in this country is forced to share his profits with uniformed apes who have their hands in the till. Every import licence, every export permit, every fucking transaction must be authorized by some general or other.'

'You're not telling me anything new, Balthasar. It's been that way ever since Columbus, for Christ's sake. Every lucrative ministry was held by a general in Trujillo's day. How else could any president pay his officers for loyalty?'

'Yes, I know. Trujillo is dead and buried, but the generals still rob the country blind. The ministers let them because they are cowards and in the meantime the business community foots the bill. The generals will have to go, and since the President allows all this to happen at the expense of the only people in the land who pay any taxes, he will have to go too.'

'I see. And the first step down this road is to stop the Haitians crossing the border. That would make the landowners mad, because their crops are rotting in the fields. The tobacco generals and the coffee generals will be out of pocket. They will all take it out on the Chief, because they think it's his fault I'm not allowed to cross the border, right?'

Balthasar nodded.

'Not bad. They press for the Chief's dismissal. He'll have to go. He's gone, and the whole of the police department can be destabilized. Then the army is called in to manage the whorehouses and the traffic. Dominoes. The crops have failed and there's no money about. What next?'

'You are doing well, Cunningham. There is no money in the country to pay the generals. The all-powerful Chief is gone and that will give the landowners the courage they need. They will stop paying bribes altogether, and so will the business community. The city generals will be exposed for the blood-suckers they are. They will be taken off the boards and sent back to their barracks.'

'Big deal,' Cunningham said. 'And what would that achieve? They will still be there.'

'The generals will resign, Cunningham. That's what will happen. No general will stay in uniform for army pay alone. With their lifestyle, they can't afford to. Anyway, their power will be gone. The government will be controlled by the right people again. By those of us who pay tax. Our people will be in. That is what we are trying to achieve. We will achieve it, and all without bloodshed.'

'You believe that?'

Balthasar nodded. 'You join us,' he said.

'No, señor,' Cunningham said. 'You'll all be shot and if I join in, I'll be shot too. I'll probably be the first, and all for nothing. Not one peso for me. Thank you, but no.'

There was silence. Cunningham lifted his hand for the waiter.

'Hold on,' Balthasar said, 'You tell us what you want.'

'I'm not buying, Balthasar. You are selling. And you're going a damn strange way about it. You're stopping me from doing my business, and you've killed two people in the process. You said there would be no blood.'

'They were only Haitians.'

'They were my friends.'

'My associates want no bloodshed, but revolutions have casualties.'

'I don't believe you've got the power to swing it, Balthasar.'

'Oh, but we do.'

'Prove it. Show me.'

'Prove it? Prove it how? Show you what?'

'I want to take my girlfriend to Puerto Rico tonight. As things stand, I'll be picked up at immigration. You fix it.'

'You can go. You have my word on that. As soon as this is over. No one will arrest you there.'

'What did you involve the Puerto Rico police for?'

'We had to make sure the Chief of Police would act against you. It was the only way. No one can afford to ignore the gringos. Not even him. All that would upset the landowners. Good for the cause.'

'I want to go to Puerto Rico tonight. If you have that much influence, you can fix it ... if what you say is true.'

'Impossible. You'll have to wait until tomorrow. We need time.'

'You'd better hurry, Balthasar. The Pan Am leaves at seven. You have five hours.'

'What about your Haitians? Aren't they waiting for you somewhere in this city?'

'Puerto Rico is your problem. The Haitians are mine. If I join you, they will all have to go back to their villages. No one cares what happens to them, do they?'

'Great. Does that mean you accept?'

'Nothing of the kind. You have made no offers. I have made no decision. I am in business. Same as the people you represent. So far I see no profit in your offers. Nothing. What about compensating my losses, Balthasar? I suppose you may want to consult with your people about that. Ask for instructions. You do what you have to do. In the meantime, I shall be flying to Puerto Rico tonight and I want to see how you deal with the gringo police. Killing a receptionist ... flying in drugs ... really, Balthasar, you could have found better charges. A true revolution needs imagination, not gimmicks.'

'You are being unreasonable. This took three weeks to organize.'

'You are in a hurry, then, Balthasar, aren't you? I'll be on that plane tonight and if they arrest me there, the Chief will get all the credit. I'll say he convinced me to give myself up. Popularity is a tough enemy, Balthasar.'

'But with you in jail over there, the Haitians will not leave. That's the main thing ...'

'What makes you think they need me here to move them? You have killed Marie-Christine and Marcel Kinet, but there are others. You have not done your homework, *muchachos*. Would I be leaving tonight if I were needed here? I have been doing this business for years. The business is well organized. The people will leave and they will get there, I assure you. And as for me, if the Americans arrest me in Puerto Rico, not only will I make sure the Chief becomes a national hero, but I'll shout my head off about your little revolution and about how you framed me. With not a shred of evidence, I shall be released with one hell of an apology. You and your associates will be in the shit up to your necks. The only way you'll get my help is to get me to join you of my own free will. Or kill me.'

'Nobody wants you dead, Cunningham.'

'In that case you'd better pray the gringos don't arrest me. You should be calling the Puerto Rico police right now.'

The blood drained from Balthasar's face. The other man had said not a word so far. He looked hard at Cunningham, then turned to Balthasar.

'The gringo is right,' he said. 'We are wasting time. If he wants to go to Puerto Rico, we'd better make sure that he can.'

François Duvalier Airport in Port-au-Prince braced itself for the arrival of the Miami flight. There were always crowds there, some to meet returning passengers, others just to pass the time. Now that the sun was well down in its final drop into the sea, the glare was greatly reduced. They could sit outside and fill the terraces facing the runway and look, their eyes following every spot in the sky. Others looked down below and gazed at the sights on the tarmac, where a few private planes were parked alongside elderly Haitian Air Force Dakotas. There were guards marching up and down the apron offering the crowd some measure of excitement. The train-like luggage vehicles stood by, ready to unload the big plane. A group of beggars looked for someone to approach, while a home-made flute spread soft Creole music through the charged atmosphere.

Soon, the great attraction would appear. The big blue and white bird would land and people would descend. Interesting people, new people who had never seen Haiti before would come down the silver steps and look. Some would be recognized and would wave, their eyes searching for loved ones. All dressed like kings and queens as befitted sky travellers. There would be the smell of gasoline and engines would whine, while those who had arrived would change places with those who would leave. There would be much to see and hear. It would all make for interesting tales to recount on the long walk back to the shacks.

Cunningham took Marina's arm as they walked away from the counter. Their luggage had been checked in and he wanted to get through to the duty-free shop to buy a bottle of fifteen-year-old Barbancourt rum for Francisco. The telephone call he had expected from him all day had not come.

CHAPTER TWENTY-TWO

■

Recovering from the effect of the injection, Francisco Martinez pondered his situation. By the look of it, he was in one of the big houses of the rich in Arroyo Hondo. He had never in all his years set foot inside such a place. Not until he visited Monsieur Dubuffet. And now he was there a second time and against his will. Strange, he thought. He must have passed the place a thousand times, but had never been invited in.

They must have been watching him, for as soon as he could open his eyes and see, someone came and took him into another room. They sat him down on a couch and started to talk to him. It took him a while, but eventually he realized they were trying to get him to participate in some revolution. Big things, they said, were about to happen in Santo Domingo. They kept on using these big words that went right above his head and confused him. A great movement was being assembled to bring down the uniformed corruptors of the state, the military parasites, the bloodsuckers. Everybody. There was going to be a new order. The common people would be saved, they said – the women, the children and the old. Everybody would be saved. How everybody was going to be brought down and saved at the same time he did not understand, but they did not give him the chance to ask. There was little time left, he was informed, and he wondered why they were wasting it by talking so much. He could, they said, avoid a lot of bloodshed by co-operating with them.

Francisco was confused and half asleep, but even so he could see they were more confused than him. One moment they were telling him he could save the country and how important he could become, at least as important as the national hero, Duarte. The next they would tell him he was a good-for-nothing, a small-time thief, and his being alive or dead meant nothing. Something was very wrong. He decided to listen and humour them and try to make them out.

'You come in with us or you're dead. Even your wife won't miss you. She didn't even notice you being dragged away. Likes her food, no?'

'She does, but it's not for you to say that.' They did not know what to make of him.

From time to time, he knew, people would announce things. They would announce that it was time the government was overthrown, it was time for corruption to be exposed, time for the people to take power in their own hands. Time for everything. But he knew, too, that the people who announced these things were communists. Antonio the barman and Rafael the taxi driver confirmed it. But these people did not look like communists. They were well dressed in American suits and had educated accents. The servants who came in and out with food and drinks seemed to know them and treated them with respect. It was best to wait and see. They looked clean and harmless, but they kept calling him names, brandishing guns at him and threatening him with all sorts of terrible tortures, diseases and death.

'I don't mind you stripping the generals of their country houses and Cadillacs and making them ride on the bus. If they agree, I agree too, but what can I do about it?'

'You are either stupid or ignorant. Don't you understand we are trying to help you? This revolution is for the people. For you.'

'Look. Why don't you just go and make your revolution and let me get on with my business? I really appreciate you bringing me here and telling me all these things. I really like the bed and the food and the drinks, but enough is enough. What can I do when my head weighs a ton and I feel confused? The beer is almost as good as Antonio's and I know you mean well, but now that we all agree the generals must go back to their barracks and let us businessmen get on with making money, why don't you just let me go?'

The men must have been from out of town, if not from another country. He had never seen them before. They drank Scotch whisky and one even smoked a pipe. Not his sort of people at all. They were clean-shaven and he had been out cold in his street clothes and he felt itchy. They all talked at the same time and while they became angry at his pranks he watched them and he listened and began to understand what they were about. The educated classes had always scorned his kind. They repeated everything twice in a condescending way, but he didn't mind because it gave him time to digest it all.

Cunningham would have been proud of his performance.

He would have gone on with it had it not been for the impossible smell of roast pork and rice and black beans which drifted into the room.

'I am hungry and I need a change of clothes,' he said, 'but I still don't know what you want with me.'

'The protein might put some grey matter in his brain,' one of the young men said.

'Protein won't help this one,' said another. 'It's probably too late. Let's go and eat.'

Francisco did not understand all this talk of protein, but he understood the bit about eating.

Through the gap in the low cloud, she saw bright, wide streets and coloured neon signs and she held on to his arm while the plane approached San Juan. The anticipation of a new adventure drummed away within her as the wheels hit the long runway.

'You know,' Cunningham said, 'this island has got it all. It is Latin, it is Caribbean and, since Spain ceded it in 1898, it's American, too. My friend Francisco Martinez says that without the Stars and Stripes fluttering over the place it would have been as poor as Haiti. He's got a point. You know, they used to live on crops too, but the bananas and the coffee, the cocoa beans and the cattle ranches gave way to scores of casinos. Those, along with the sun-drenched beaches, attract thousands of frozen New Yorkers to the island each month. With the roulette wheels and crap tables came nightclubs and strip shows that would have delighted the conquistadors. After all, they did call it Puerto Rico. Now it is truly a rich port.'

Most of his Dominican friends would have heartily agreed with him. They often went there to do their shopping and some deposited their dollars in the local banks whenever the government enforced currency control. Within a few minutes' flying time from Santo Domingo, it was a different world. The American way of life had brought wide expressways which pushed the old cobblestone roads to the back of the old city. The proud Spanish horses had faded into the history books and the elegant carriages they had pulled in the old days had found their way into museums and hotel lobby decorations. Cadillacs and Chevies roamed the streets instead, while during the night Xavier Cugat and rock music reigned supreme in sumptuous clubs. There was order in the streets and supermarkets and Chesterfield cigarettes and soda fountains. Latins and gringos alike were made to feel at home in San Juan, where both cultures gained some of the other's merits.

The Clipper drew to a smooth halt. 'You'll be seeing this town all by yourself if Balthasar hasn't done his bit,' he said with a chuckle. 'I may yet be led out of here in a pair of shiny new handcuffs.'

'Don't be silly. He will have. He wouldn't have risked letting you get on the plane if he thought they'd arrest you.'

They sailed through immigration as if it hadn't been there and took a spacious, clean yellow cab to the hotel.

'Let's blow some of that money,' Cunningham said.

The servants fussing over the table were better dressed than he was, Francisco observed. The meal was every bit as magnificent as the house in which he was held. Some of them, he suspected, were secretly enjoying his humour. Had it not been for the never-ending stream of questions, he'd have been sorry to leave.

'How many slaves are you bringing in this time, Francisco?'

'Do you have to talk business all the time?'

'We've been patient with you, Martinez, but enough is enough.'

'That I agree with. You see, I'm not being difficult at all. Let's just eat in peace. If all we do over dinner is argue, you'll never invite me back again.'

'Just tell us where your friend means to cross the border. You can make things much more pleasant for yourself.'

'I am not complaining.'

'Are you trying to wear us out, Francisco? We are peaceful people, but there are those among us who will not hesitate to kill.'

'At least no one will say I died hungry.'

'There are many ways to inflict pain.'

That one seemed to work. Francisco's sneering face changed at last. He seemed, for the first time, a little perturbed. He stopped eating, shrugged his shoulders in resignation, and looked up. 'All right,' he said softly. 'Can I make a telephone call, please?'

There was no reason to deny him that. Perhaps he wanted to consult someone. From what they had heard earlier, Cunningham was nearing capitulation too.

While Francisco went to the library to make his call, two of his captors were sent out to find his kid brother.

Ten blocks to the west of Arroyo Hondo, Gerald Buckmaster struggled up the stairs to his room. After the heavy dinner he had eaten he needed the exercise. He'd had a little more than his usual dose of Scotch. He was feeling bitter about Marina. The lesson she was trying to teach him had gone on long enough.

He reached his floor and stumbled towards the door. Inside his suite the phone was ringing. The key refused to fit into place and Gerald began to pound on the door. It was late in the evening and Chiquito's daughter was a heavy sleeper. He knocked harder and a few doors opened along the corridor.

'*Un momento, por favor,*' he heard the girl say. She opened the door.

'Is it my wife?'

'No, señor. Is Francisco Martinez. He want talk to you.'

Gerald raced for the receiver. 'You again,' he shouted. 'What the fuck do you want?'

The voice on the other end had changed. It was harsh and urgent. The man was whispering. 'Speak up, man. I can't hear

145

a word you're saying.'

'Señor Buckmaster, you can please do me a favour?'

'What is it?'

'Please, you go to Antonio's Bar there on the Malecon and tell him to get off the line until he hear from me? I try reach him urgent urgent, but line busy for ever. For me is difficult. Where I am now I can no make the telephone easy. Okay?'

'I'll do what I can, Mr Martinez,' Gerald heard himself say.

He wasn't sure who he had said it to or why. He poured a glass of Scotch from the bottle by the bedside and gulped it down.

'I'm drinking too much,' he mumbled to himself. The receiver said something from the carpet. He replaced it and lay down. His thoughts became less coherent. Outside, the traffic hummed ceaselessly. These bastards never go to bed. He took one last sip and the glass rolled onto the floor. Peace came to him. His wife's absence did not worry him any longer. The children were in bed and quiet.

The phone rattled again. He shook. He picked it up to hear Marina's voice speaking to him from somewhere. He could see her quite clearly, naked with a golden crucifix dangling between her breasts. She was humming a song. Perhaps it was someone else's voice.

'Are you all right?' It was Marina.

'Since when have you become religious?' His hoarse voice seemed amused. 'I've never seen that cross on you before.'

'What are you talking about?'

He murmured an incomprehensible reply. He did not seem surprised or pleased to hear from her.

'Are the girls all right?'

'Oh, they're fine. And Francisco Martinez, he just called. Asked me to go down to some Antonio down the Malecon and tell him to get off the line. Said they didn't let him use the phone where he was. Marvellous guy, this Martinez. The maid left and he phoned and made her come back. Could you be a dear and go down there for me? I'm a little tired. No. Very tired. I was just falling off when you called.'

'I'm sorry, Gerald. I did call earlier, but the hotel operator said you were out. Your key was at reception.'

'I'm bored with the operator. I'm bored with this hotel. I've spent all day looking for a house. I'm tired. Don't wake me when you get back.'

'I'll call again in the morning.'

He did not answer. He was fast asleep. The receiver rested on his chest. She could hear his breathing clearly.

'I told you he'd be okay,' she said to Cunningham. 'Drunk, but it doesn't matter. Chiquito's daughter is there, so the girls are safe. He's not like this usually. I don't know what's got into him.'

'He misses you.'

She told him what Gerald had said about Francisco and his message.

'Someone must be holding him somewhere. This Balthasar is no fool. He's taken out an insurance policy. In case I decide to stay here. I'll have to make a couple of calls while you get dressed.'

No, Antonio the barman said. Francisco had not been seen in two days. Not since he'd gone up to the mountains with his kid brother.

'They won't hurt him, will they?' Marina asked.

'Not until they know which way I'm going. At least, I hope not. In any case, they won't find Francisco an easy man to manipulate. The fellow's got a way with him. He can be exasperating, tiring, maddening, but he's irresistible.'

'Where ... who could be holding him?'

'The same people who employ Balthasar.'

While she was in the bathroom, Cunningham called the concierge. 'Pablito,' he said quietly, 'could you do an old friend a service and find out where I can charter a plane for tomorrow? No. Not a jet. A single-engined Cessna will do me fine. Where? To Port-au-Prince, Haiti. Oh, around two o'clock tomorrow afternoon. You can leave me a message at reception. Tell them I'll pay cash, Pablito. You make the deal for me, would you?' Tonight he was going to paint the town red.

Much later, as they listened to the horses' hooves hitting the cemented road, she looked at the stars above the open carriage and smiled. She could not remember the last time she had laughed so much. A new Cunningham had unfolded before her very eyes. The considerate, preoccupied, middle-aged lover she thought she knew had become a light-hearted, fun-loving, devil-may-care youth. He told dirty jokes to the waiters and danced the orchestra into exhaustion. He made small-talk, spiced with local gossip, and roared with uncontrollable laughter at everything she said.

Their horse-drawn, small-hours excursion into the old city was followed by a walk on the hotel beach and a swim. He plunged into the water, oblivious of his tuxedo, his black tie and patent leather shoes. He crawled on all fours through the surf, pulling a magnum champagne bottle dog-fashion behind him in the shallow water. These last years of relative poverty, his recent anxieties and the turbulence of his fortunes exploded into a symphony of abandon. Marie-Christine's death had gone from his mind and with it all sense of responsibility. He craved for her to make him laugh and listened to the sound of the sea when she was silent.

The sun, rising from the horizon, found him building an elaborate sandcastle near the steps up to the hotel, with a seaweed forest to enhance it. Then, suddenly, the night was over and he knew that the heat of the ensuing day would bring the old pain back to his leg. Nothing had changed. He was still the same man inside the same body and this had to be his last day with her.

A red-eyed, yawning reception clerk handed him a cable. 'NOW YOU HAVE YOUR PROOF COME BACK AND DEAL.'

He was tired himself now. He knew how soon his scattered brain would recoup, and with it reality. Not yet. He took

Marina by the hand and together they sailed up in the lift to sleep his second childhood off.

CHAPTER TWENTY-THREE

Francisco Martinez slept in his clothes for the second night running. The injection they had given him after his telephone call would last until morning. They had placed his kid brother's bullet-riddled body on the floor nearby, where Francisco would see him when he woke.

They did not consider him to be much of a loss. The boy was no good. When they had found him, he was drunk out of his wits and driving a stolen car. Perhaps they should have tried to talk to him first, but after they gave chase he suddenly stopped. The girl in his car ran off screaming and the kid got out and pulled a gun on them.

Now he lay face up on the floor next to his brother's bed. Rigor mortis had set in long before morning. Francisco woke up at first light and saw his kid brother. The boy's dead eyes were open and they gazed blankly at Francisco's face. His mouth had a fixed, determined smile across the full lips, but there was fear elsewhere in the young, waxen face. He looked so lost, lying there, the healthy brown hair strewn across his forehead. That irresponsible little brother of his lay beside him just as he had when they were children. But the eyes that had admired him then were sightless and the ears that would rarely listen to advice were deaf for ever.

Francisco's body contracted into a numbness he had never known before. He floated, thinking of the poverty and the laughter they had known together. And then he thought of what might have been and the numbness turned inside out and he was burning. He fought to hold the eruption down as waves of frustrated rage churned inside him.

With his anger came sudden loneliness. He lay there oblivious to time. He heard sounds, but they were not of this world and meant nothing. They were serving lunch next door and they had called for him, but he did not move. No one came in. No one tried to prod him. There was a new, sinister expression on his good, open face.

He was going to tell the kid many things, but his voice stayed inside him. Everybody, all the people of the whole island of Hispaniola and throughout the world, were as dead as the kid. He needed to scream and rant and kick, but nothing happened. There was, he knew, a flame inside him that was making his blood boil in his veins, and still there was no eruption. In the hours that had passed since he woke and saw his brother's face, depression and paralysis had seized him. The kid lay there in his dirty khaki slacks and unkempt hair. The hungry look he had as a schoolboy had returned to him in death. Francisco heard his mother's voice telling him to wash the kid's face, as she had done so many times, and he tried to stretch and reach it, but inertia controlled him now and rendered him useless.

They came in and said they were going to take the body away. Francisco just looked at them and what they saw in his eyes chased them out. A tidal wave of tears swelled in his throat, but his menacing eyes were dry. He heard his own voice telling them he was going to stay right there with the kid. For ever. He fainted and then came to again and then he was out like a cold stone.

Next door they were serving coffee when Balthasar's call came through. 'Let them go,' he said. His words fell on incredulous ears. 'We've got a deal,' Balthasar added, but no one dared tell him what had happened. 'We don't need the Martinez brothers any more,' Balthasar said, and hung up.

Francisco's captors shared a similar background. Expensive schools and the corridors of illustrious universities. They shared the political conviction of freedom. They shared, too, an unadulterated fear of Balthasar. They would never have put him in charge of field operations, but he had been chosen by the leader himself. The man who was going to bring the revolution about. The Miner. They had all been told to follow Balthasar's instructions to the letter. And he had told them to bring the boy in, not kill him.

Much later, in the middle of the night, the sound of voices woke Francisco for the hundredth time. His brother's body was still there, and through the thin wall he heard the young men shoot each other down with abuse. He crawled out of his bed and reached the door. The animated conversation kept coming through. What they were saying alerted him. He and his dead brother had become a problem.

He looked through the keyhole and saw that they were all in there. No one was missing. No one was watching the front door or the garden. Even the man on the verandah, the law student, was inside and was shouting like the rest. Francisco came back to his brother and knelt by his side. 'Soon,' he whispered. 'I'll get you out of here, kid. I'll take you home.'

He went back to the door and listened. The discussion had become a fully fledged fight. They were throwing mugs and plates at each other. There was frustration and suspicion and there were bitter accusations. Those who had stayed in the house blamed the others for the killing, while the perpetrators insisted they had been tricked into it.

'Someone had to stay and watch Francisco.'

'Someone had to get the boy.'

'Did you expect him to come of his own free will? He fought like a tiger.'

'You keep changing the story.'

'We need a cool head,' the law student said. 'This isn't getting us anywhere.'

'You have to produce a corpse before you can accuse anyone of murder.'

'We can dump him out in the country. Up there he will not be found for a hundred years.'

It seemed like a brilliant idea, but no one volunteered to put it into practice. The killers insisted that their hands were already stained. Then others argued that this was not their line of business. Finally, they agreed to do it together. One and all. They would then all be equally involved. They would get him into one of the cars. Balthasar was not going to call before morning. There was plenty of time.

'To the revolution,' someone said.

'A shared guilt. Murder on the Orient Express,' said the literature student. They were all feeling light-headed. They called for more drinks.

Then, much later, when someone asked about Francisco, they all burst into the room. It was empty. Outside, the thug they had hired to stand guard by the pool lay at the gate with his throat slashed open and the law student's new Chevrolet was gone.

'Trujillo must be having a good laugh in hell,' the poetry student said. 'He never trusted the rich.'

'Or their sons,' said another. 'Revolutions need men of action. Not words.'

Now, more than ever, they would need the Martinez brothers, but they had vanished into an uncharted sea.

CHAPTER TWENTY-FOUR

◼

They waited, hollow-faced, by the little wooden church at Diquini. There were more people there than ever, and Ti Allain sensed their trust giving way to impatience. Soon, suspicion would creep into their hearts and then despair. These things had never happened to him before and he felt confused. He looked at the place of the sun in the sky. It would have to start its retreat into the sea before he could stop his prayers. He would then have to act, but he did not know what that action would be. The spirits never gave him answers while the sun was out. Soon, after it reached the tall palm at the edge of the clearing, darkness would fall. They would tell him what to do then.

Ti Allain spoke to them without words. He had sinned and he apologized. He had not gone out looking for the lizard when he saw that it was missing from Monique's pole. The missing lizard had meant that the plan was going to change, but he had not known the change would mean a delay this long. He would, as soon as he came back to his village, make a special sacrifice for them. Something rare and significant, like a fresh cob of corn or a fat breast of freshly killed chicken. And where was the one-legged foreigner? Surely, from where they were, the spirits could see him.

He asked, wordlessly, whether La Grande Marie was really dead. No one was dead until their body was seen by someone who could be trusted. How many times had he been told that someone had gone over to the other world and then seen them, in the field, looking for something like any other person. A bird landed in front of him. It snatched a tiny twig and took off again with a trilling song. The spirits were trying to tell him something, but he couldn't be sure what it was. It had something to do with the foreigner they were waiting for. He was coming to see them soon to take them across the border. Just like the bird that took the twig.

Ti Allain had delivered workers to Marie-Christine and the foreigner many times before and there had never been a hitch like this. It was a simple operation because there were plenty of willing workers. All he had to do was make the first choice, where people's age and strength counted most. The importance of years had always puzzled him. Washed-out, tired thirty-year-olds looking ancient were wanted while older men with youthful vigour in their bodies were rejected. But people knew that the best chance of success lay with Ti Allain and so they tried to please him.

That could mean many things. Small gifts of food or perhaps a young, comely wife. The latter always helped a man because Ti Allain could help a pretty spouse overcome her loneliness in the long nights that followed a husband's departure. Only the spirits knew of this because those lucky women were reluctant to spread such news. Having much food at night and a child with the small man who was rumoured really to be dead would create much jealousy in their starving villages where women ruled.

Ti Allain was discreet, confiding mainly in the spirits, and thus no one's reputation was ever soiled. Some of the women, when their men failed to return, often found themselves new husbands with his help. There were other ways of being shortlisted, such as the number of social invitations extended to him by prospective workers' families. Ti Allain's reputation as a job broker had spread as the years went by.

Once the necessary number was reached, he would start the trek to Port-au-Prince. This could take up to three days and two nights of marching through the mountain passes down to the capital. The meeting place was constantly changing and was only decided upon once the procession had arrived at the vegetable market in Petionville, above Port-au-Prince. It was there, in the cool, hilly suburb with its stone houses and new motor cars, that Ti Allain would meet Marie-Christine. She would place a cloth doll with a red face in the window of Kassim's grocery store to indicate that a new shipment was required. He had cause to go to Petionville many times in the year, mainly to make sure the village produce arrived there safely. That was not a task anyone had bestowed on him. It had simply happened years before, when it was found that he could be trusted not to sell it off and disappear.

As soon as the sign was given, Ti Allain would hang the blood-dripping head of a freshly caught wild bird on Monique's white pole. That way everybody knew it was time to go and see Ti Allain. It was no mean task to catch a wild bird in the mountains. They did not fly that far often because there was no food up there for them. But Ti Allain always found a bird when he needed one.

No one ever saw him prepare the sign, but somehow, by the time the head was reduced by the sun and the flies, another delegation was ready. And yet even coming all the way down to Petionville was no guarantee. The final decision was always made by the fat city woman. People were sure she was related to Monique, but no one dared tell Ti Allain this. She would wait for him outside Kassim's grocery store and he'd know she was there because her car was parked outside. She allowed her driver Guy to step outside while she stayed in the back.

This last time she was not there at all. Only Guy the driver was waiting for him and he told him quite rudely to go to Diquini and wait by the wooden church there. And now they were there and waiting. Three days had gone by and no one had come to see them. Ti Allain looked up into the sky as his lips moved and he saw the sun had not moved at all. Perhaps the day was waiting for him.

In the shade of the trees, the others pooled what was left of the food they had carried down on their backs. Water was fetched from the broken cast-iron pipe by the tobacco shop. There would be no need for a fire tonight. There was no rice or beans left for them to cook. Some of the younger men were sent to scavenge and they returned with a handful of discarded bananas and a few rotting watermelons.

They were hungry, but they all knew that Ti Allain was busy talking to the spirits about important matters and no one was going to bother him with trivialities. Sleep, they knew, would not come easy on an empty stomach, but the sun was taking her time crossing the heavens that afternoon. And such a thing could always produce a miracle.

CHAPTER TWENTY-FIVE

They were waiting at the end of the runway for the Iberia

flight to land. The pilot was revving the engine in anticipation of a clearance when they heard a voice from the control tower. 'The one-legged English bird is taking off,' it said in Spanish. 'Tell Port-au-Prince.'

The message would have been transmitted in English had it been routine. The San Juan tower could have made a slip, but then he knew they wanted him to hear this. That way he would know that Balthasar's connections on the island were as firm as ever.

Soon after they were airborne, the curving coastline of Hispaniola came into view. They flew over water most of the time, with the central peaks soaring out of the afternoon haze. Cunningham did not pay much attention to the familiar scenery that slipped past the side of the plane.

The pilot, a quiet young American, concentrated on his instruments. Relieved at not having to make small-talk, Cunningham pondered the fate of Francisco's kid brother. Antonio the barman had told him about the shooting before he left the hotel. It had been one of those frustrating mornings when no one was where they were supposed to be. Antonio did not tell him more since he was on his way to a cock fight out near Boca Chica. Francisco's wife had gone out and, worst of all, the Chief of Police refused to come to the phone.

There must have been a mistake somewhere. To take Francisco Martinez into custody while he was in Puerto Rico was prudent, but to have his kid brother killed while negotiations were on was downright stupid. And there was the short, cruel parting from Marina. But he couldn't afford to dwell on that now. They circumvented the coast and he thought of the landowners and Francisco and the elusive Chief of Police. He had planned to tell him all he had heard about the revolution, but would he be believed? They flew on into the afternoon.

Port-au-Prince lay wrapped around its bay, basking in the brilliant sunshine. The clouds that had covered the interior of the Dominican Republic were left far behind, trapped by the mountains of the Cadena Central. It was always hot in Haiti, even when it rained. And especially in the lower portion of the capital. The white vastness of the Presidential Palace stuck out in the centre of town. From the sky it made the rest of the city look insignificant.

Cunningham's eyes wandered towards Diquini. He couldn't find the little wooden church. Someone had to go there soon and make the final selection. If what Antonio the barman had said was true, the Dominicans meant business.

Haiti had always carried a special message for him. There was a peculiar hush in the local voices, a slow sensuality in the music, and a bright living colour in the local art. The language, too, was soft and warm and sounded like little feet dancing barefoot on a low-toned drum. In the local dialect one could still discern traces of the old idiomatic language the French colonizers had used, long ago, before Toussaint started the revolt that chased them away.

The food was appetizing and the rum, distilled in the mountains, better than any other. The coffee, the honey, and even the tap-tap buses did not possess the vulgar undertones of the other islands. Somehow, the Sorbonne and Beaux Arts and haute couture mingled with the marketplace and the pot-holes, extinguishing the stench and discomfort. It was the poorest country in the western hemisphere, but walking the streets was safer than in Miami or Kingston, and the people smiled as if they lived in a perfect world. They had time for laughter in their eyes and their songs were sad while their bodies moved to the rhythm of love.

The violence he had encountered did not originate here. A power game over on the other side of Hispaniola had killed Marie-Christine and Marcel Kinet. He had the power to bring this violence to an end. He could simply leave the Haitian workers right where they were, but he had given his word to the landowners.

He looked out and saw the runway dead ahead. A guttural English permission to land came over the radio and the serious-faced pilot checked all the instruments and eased the stick forward. Cunningham could not miss the black Mercedes as it entered through the main gate and moved towards the space allotted for them to park in. Not everyone was permitted to drive into the customs area. Balthasar's contacts held firm in Haiti too, it seemed.

His own life would be in danger as soon as the meeting place was found. He would no longer be needed. He fought an urge to order the pilot to swing the plane around and take off again. But there was nowhere left for him to go, little to do but meet the occupants of the Mercedes and talk business. He was not sure what he was going to say. He shrugged his shoulders and hoped luck would smile on him. The little plane crawled towards the space allocated to them. Then the engine slowed, coughed to a halt, and there was silence.

On her short flight across the narrow strip of sea that separated Puerto Rico from the Dominican Republic, Marina cried. Perhaps it was relief. Perhaps remorse. She was looking forward to seeing her daughters again. That morning, when she had rung Gerald, he had sounded quiet and a trifle subdued. He said he missed her and loved her and wanted her back. She told him she was in Puerto Rico and returning today. He was quiet and sober and she could hear the children cooing in the background. Gerald said he hoped she was enjoying her little trip. She deserved to, he said. She felt like a shit.

She had said goodbye to Cunningham over a coffee at San Juan airport. He looked a little tired and very old. His limp was pronounced and he sounded foreign and a bit sentimental.

'You won't miss me for a while,' he had said. 'Perhaps you'll have to force yourself to forget. Do what you have to do to get through the cooling-off period, but when you're over that, remember we have had an adventure together. It will always be there in the shadows.'

'It will be there for you,' he had said. 'For you alone.' Just who the hell did he think he was?

As the wheels of the great plane touched the uneven surface, she thought of Cunningham's little plane and where it was heading. It would be good to see Gerald again. Or would it? Of course it would. They were even now. The engines were being reversed and the plane began its long taxi along the bumpy runway.

Later, waiting in the arrival hall for her bag, she had to smile. It was by that same conveyor belt that she had first set eyes on Cunningham, long ago. Long ago? And then she thought she saw him. Handsome and warm and funny and larger than life, and she laughed. She could almost hear his voice.

Her bag arrived and she lifted it and swung it onto the desk in front of the customs man. She unzipped the top and looked the man straight in the eye the way Cunningham would have done and she smiled. The man smiled back at her and motioned her on. The automatic doors were out of order. The police forced them open and through the gap she saw her husband. His face was serious and he looked tall and slim and young in his shirtsleeves.

'Welcome back, Mrs Buckmaster,' he said, and rushed forward for her bag. 'Good to see you again.'

She noticed the sarcasm in his voice and took the flowers he handed her and pressed them to her face to hide her eyes. She asked about the children and where the car was and did it rain last night. His answers came fast and his voice was cold. The children were at the hotel, the car was parked right outside, and he had been too drunk last night to notice the weather. They got into the car.

She looked at the sky and barely noticed him. Gerald said something about having found a house and then it thundered and the rain started to fall and all she could think about was the little plane Cunningham was in and she fretted. 'The sooner we leave that stupid hotel the better,' Gerald said. The road was wet and slippery now, but for once she said nothing about his driving. She said nothing at all.

CHAPTER TWENTY-SIX

Cunningham opened the door. Outside, by the wing, two customs men and an immigration officer waited for him to descend. Behind them loomed Balthasar's large frame. Marie-Christine's car had pulled up beside the Mercedes and Guy climbed out. The formalities were concluded without a hitch. Cunningham introduced Guy to the serious-faced pilot, who managed a smile.

'You get into the car with him. He'll take you to the El Rancho Hotel. There's a room booked for you there. Would you wait there for me, please?'

Sure he would. He had been hoping Mr Cunningham would ask him to stay. No, he did not need any introductions or female company. All he wanted was a swim and a shower. Yes, he did have a change of clothes and a toothbrush. They did take dollars in Haiti, didn't they?

The pilot got into Guy's car and Cunningham got into the other. The two cars sped from the airport down the road to the city.

'I suppose you believe me now, Señor Cunningham. Did you enjoy Puerto Rico?'

'Oh yes, but I still prefer the Dominican Republic. I'd rather be able to go there.'

'But you can, you can go right now. Just take off and go there in your plane. Leave the Haitians to us.'

'Not so fast, Balthasar. I can't deal with you.'

'What do you mean?'

'I don't trust you any more.'

The ex-policeman gasped. 'What's wrong? Did you have any trouble in Puerto Rico?'

'No, but Francisco ran into trouble in Santo Domingo, didn't he? Trouble he couldn't handle?'

'*Por Dios*, Cunningham. You have to understand. That was

just insurance. He wasn't hurt, and they've turned him loose already.'

'Then why did you have his brother killed?'

'What? What are you talking about?' Balthasar's eyes had opened wide.

'Don't try to shit me, Balthasar. The kid's dead.'

'I never gave any such orders.'

'Then some of your gorillas back home have gone into business on their own. It's a dangerous game, that, when fools believe they can think for themselves.'

'Cunningham, I swear to you ...'

'I'd started to sympathize with your aims, but this changes everything. You shouldn't have killed the kid, Balthasar.'

'I tell you once again, I gave no such orders. I swear I didn't. Ask him.'

The other man nodded.

'I thought you were a gentleman,' Cunningham said.

'You're just trying to gain time. That won't wash with me.'

'The boy is dead and if your people didn't kill him, who did? Aren't you in charge?'

'I am. I'll prove it to you as soon as we get to your hotel.'

'I'd like to speak to my pilot.'

'Go ahead. As long as you don't try to run.'

'I won't go anywhere. This car is infinitely more comfortable than mine.' The Mercedes stopped and Cunningham rolled out. He flagged Guy's car to the kerb. 'Guy,' he said in French, 'go pray for my eternal soul.' He grinned at Balthasar who was watching his every move. 'You don't need to set the wooden church on fire, but pray anyway. Now that the poor Martinez boy is dead we'll all need God's help. Get some from your local spirits too, if you want. I'll be waiting for you at the hotel. You can take the pilot with you. He'd appreciate a bit of sightseeing. He'd like the voodoo bits, especially.' He winked at Guy and turned back. 'Let's go, Balthasar,' he said.

It seemed as though the city lights had been switched off and the stars themselves were dead. Francisco Martinez did not drive fast, nor did he look over his shoulder to see who might be behind him. He didn't pay much attention to the traffic. He was going towards the old city. No one would find him there. The old city was built between the port and the River Ozama, into which Columbus and his tall ships had once sailed. The houses, in the old Spanish style, still boasted wrought-iron balconies. They had now become warehouses and flats painted in different shades of pink and pastel green and mustard. Where Columbus once had his headquarters now lived a ragged mix of Dominicans. From these streets, proud sons of Spain had ruled their colonies while their womenfolk exchanged pleasantries on these same balconies.

Francisco knew the old city well. He had grown up there, and while good fortune had taken him away, most of his friends remained. It would take his captors for ever to find him, but he was not going to wait that long. He was going after them as soon as the kid was laid to rest. His first stop would be at a small paint shop in the middle of the barrio. By morning the car would be given a completely new identity; its owner wouldn't recognize it even if it were parked in his own drive. Before long he would find out who had killed his brother and send the bastards to hell. Now that he himself had killed a man, he knew he'd meet them in the next world. But he was going to see them one more time in this one. The Haitians, the Chief, his wife and even Cunningham were far away from his thoughts as he drove through the narrow streets. Little needed to be said to the people he had come to see. The look on his face and the body by his side would tell them all.

The owner of the little run-down grocery store was a friend from childhood and, like most of them, owed Francisco a favour. They lifted the kid's body out and carried him to the back of the shop. The car disappeared. Later, seated behind the open windows of the flat upstairs, Francisco said what he wanted done.

'The first thing you must do', he said, 'is to spread the news of my death around town. Tell everybody that I have been shot, too.'

It took Francisco a while to explain what he had in mind, and long before they had finished their meal the news of his demise reached the bars along the Malecon. It would take no more than an hour for the whole town to start mourning him.

CHAPTER TWENTY-SEVEN

Ti Allain cast one last look at the sky to thank the spirits for giving him a trusting nature. In the middle of the afternoon, a new face appeared by the little wooden church. A white foreign man accompanied by the Haitian named Guy, Marie-Christine's driver. It was the first time the Haitian Guy had spoken at length to him and in a friendly manner. He assured Ti Allain that his waiting was nearly over. The foreigner he had brought with him was not the one they were expecting, but he was sent along to prove he was serious. Not every Haitian could produce a young foreigner just like that. It was a sure sign that the Haitian Guy was telling the truth.

'We need food for the evening,' Ti Allain whispered, 'or else the people will be tempted to go out and steal it.'

The market next door was beginning to fold up for the day. They would need to hurry. Guy's English was not too good, but he managed to borrow twenty dollars from the pilot. He did not have to explain. A glance around the lean faces was enough. The pilot extracted another ten dollars from his billfold and handed it over. 'That's from me,' he said.

'*Merci,*' said Guy.

The large bills were unsuitable for the local tradeswomen and Guy planned to go into one of the bars to change the notes into sweaty single dollars people could recognize.

'Where is the tall foreigner?' Ti Allain asked. 'The one-footed man.'

'He will be here soon. Maybe tomorrow.'

'And La Grande Marie? Is she really dead?'

'Yes,' Guy said.

It was obvious that Monique the black witch was in town. She could have taken the form of a stray dog, a coconut tree, or even a stone. Perhaps she wanted to make sure no one escaped her clutches. Ti Allain did not share this knowledge with Guy, who kept looking over his shoulder for reasons Ti Allain could not make out. But the whispering added much to his own importance.

'You wait here for me,' Guy said.

Ti Allain scratched a large circle on the ground and told the others to clear it. Soon, he told them, they would all eat. There would be plenty for all as soon as the circle was cleaned up and he had consulted the spirits.

Guy and the foreigner got into the car, watching Ti Allain with fascination. The little man slumped to the ground, his ear affixed to a rock. His face contorted in concentration. The others watched. Something was happening at last. Suddenly he leapt to his feet.

'The spirits have spoken!' Ti Allain exulted. 'Two of the strongest men will come with me.'

Guy looked at the pilot and shrugged. He nudged the car into gear and drove away.

Ti Allain, the two strong men and a dozen more began their slow descent down the road to the market. Word of the new-comers' sudden fortune spread like lightning and stalls reopened in the hope of beating rivals for their custom. The others approached the circle to clear the ground of shrubs and rocks. Some of the former hangers-on returned from the shadows. If they waited long enough, there might be a meal around. In the late afternoon the world moves at a snail's pace. Most of them could easily wait all night. They had nothing else to do. Nowhere of interest to go to. By the wooden church at Diquini, Ti Allain looked at the sun. It could go now, he thought. The spirits had heard his prayer and he intended to thank them for it.

The Haitian called Guy had told him to clear the whole area by the church and have everybody ready for the inspection. He did not tell him when that would be, but the waiting was surely over. Guy had also ordered him to block the little dust road that led to the church to make sure no outsiders could enter. Ti Allain did not know why such an order was given, but he had had a rewarding afternoon and he had nodded and said he would do as Guy had asked. Now that there would be food for the people, the spirits were sure to allow the sun to descend.

The last glow of late afternoon cleansed the gardens at the El Rancho Hotel. The heat had lost its bite. Up in his room, Cunningham handed the phone to Balthasar. 'Antonio is still on the line, you murdering son of a bitch,' he shouted. 'You talk to him yourself.'

'You are all crazy,' Balthasar said as he grabbed the phone. He listened and said, '*No lo creo, Antonio. Eso no es posible.*'

Antonio said he didn't really care whether the señor believed him or not, but the fate of Francisco Martinez and his kid brother was all over the capital. Francisco never let a day pass without having at least one beer at his bar. He used it like an office, Antonio said. And he hadn't been seen for three whole days. Everybody knew he had been kidnapped and now he was dead.

'He'd rather be dead than thirsty,' Antonio the barman said, 'and no beer tastes as good as mine. Francisco told me so himself.'

'Why did you have to kill Francisco? Why anybody?' Cunningham asked quietly.

'That barman gossips like an old woman. So he hasn't seen Francisco for a day ...'

'What sort of man are you, Balthasar? How can I be sure

you haven't invented the whole revolution story yourself? What do you know about revolutions anyway? They have them in these parts every day, but no one bothers with little people. They shoot a general or two, and by morning there's a new picture in the papers with the caption "El Presidente".'

'That is different.'

'Oh, shut up, you stupid bastard. People go to work and screw their mistresses; they beat their wives and kiss their children the day after as if nothing had happened. The man in the street doesn't give a damn. So the generals kill each other, so what? Most of these generals have never seen a battle in their lives anyhow. Too many of them die in their beds of old age. Go and visit the cemeteries yourself. They grab the most expensive marble tombstones for themselves.'

'You are wrong. This time everything will change.'

'You're a joker, Balthasar. A miserable fool. Do you really believe you are going to change things? Only the faces change on coins and banknotes, nothing else. Why did you have to kill Francisco? Did you know him? What did he ever do to you?' He was screaming at the man, but he didn't care.

Balthasar's face fell. His voice was low. 'I'm telling you, this can't be true. Even if it is, I never gave the order.'

'Who gives a fuck about your orders?'

'He could have had an accident. Or been in a brawl. He and his brother. They are thugs.'

'Thugs? You're full of shit, Balthasar. Francisco wouldn't harm a fly. We have nothing to say to each other. Go on, fuck off, you hear? Get out of here and don't come back until you've got some answers. I'll give you until tomorrow and then I'll hand you over to the Haitian police. I have my contacts too, and you know how they love revolutionaries in this country. Here the police keep their jobs because the president never changes. He's in the palace for life and you'll rot in jail for just as long, Balthasar. Go and talk to your boss. He'll probably fire you anyway. Now piss off.'

Balthasar did not move a muscle. In spite of the blinding

anger that coursed through him, Cunningham sensed that the Dominican was as surprised as he was. The man was losing his grip. He would have shot him for a fraction of what he'd said.

'Get out of here. I don't deal with office boys,' Cunningham screamed, his voice raging with grief. And then he saw Francisco's broad, smiling face. His presence filled the room. Could his spirit have come over the Cadena Central to hold his hand? Voodoo.

Balthasar's eyes were telling him he was gaining the upper hand. He got up and put his hat on. His face was drawn, but he pushed his chest out and pouted his mouth and said with his old voice, 'I'll be back, Cunningham. And soon.' The door slammed angrily behind him.

Cunningham took his shoes off and lay on the bed. His stump hurt. Guy was coming back any minute now and there were things to be done. Then the telephone rang.

'There is a collect call for you, Monsieur Cunningham, from the Dominican Republic,' the operator said. 'A Monsieur Francisco Martinez is on the line. Will you accept the charges?'

'Yes,' he whispered as his heart missed a beat. 'Yes, I will.'

CHAPTER TWENTY-EIGHT

By the wooden church at Diquini they were preparing a feast fit for good old King Solomon himself. Twenty chickens, a thick paper sack full of rice and a tricycle-load of beans, fruits and vegetables were being transformed into a mouth-watering event. Five great earthenware pots sitting atop a slow open fire oozed exquisite odours into the star-studded sky. It was pitch dark, and the flames jumped again and again as their quivering reflection bounced off eager faces and hungry eyes. People were going to remember this meal for ever. Songs would be invented to perpetuate the occasion long after.

Ti Allain's head was covered with mud. He had tied ten chicken heads around his waist and had made himself a crown with the other ten. He poured white flour over the wet mud. He was almost ready for his dance. This was going to be a special dance because the spirits had to be rewarded for what they had bestowed on the people. Nothing on earth or above, Ti Allain knew, could move right or left or forwards or upwards without the knowledge and blessing of the spirits. A man was surrounded by them all his life. They were there and if he treated them with respect they would be fair with him. Especially when the man became a spirit himself.

Not every man could be sure he would become a spirit upon his death. That depended on his attitude to the universe and the spirits while doing time on earth. People who went through life on a full stomach did not have much of a chance. You had to suffer before being allowed immortality. After all, most of the spirits had been poor.

To become a spirit or a living-dead zombie offered a man a nibble at real powers. Fat city-dwellers who ran other people's lives and gorged on meat possessed power right here on earth where it did not count because it was too temporary. Most of them would surely miss their chance of power in the next, eternal world.

He was no wretch himself and he did hold much power over other people in his lifetime. That was why he often pacified the spirits to make them forget how seldom he had gone hungry himself. Did he not tell them again and again in his silent prayers and violent dances that whatever he owned was theirs? Did he not fast for days on end? He never forgot to offer them a share of the food on his table or the woman in his bed. If they never took advantage of these offerings he was not to blame.

The night reigned supreme. The flames had burned through the young wood under the pots and the magic of red-hot embers was glowing. And all the while, tired and hungry as he was, Ti Allain kept on dancing. There was new, fluorescent paint on his face, compounded of mud and chalk and sweat and blood. The others watched him with reverence, waiting for the food. He had a special language for the spirits. It was not Creole nor French nor even the ancient African tongue. He used words the white gods had taught his fore-fathers when they were slaves on their way to Haiti in large old sailing boats that flew across the seven seas. Only Ti Al-lain understood the meaning of the words and the songs and the secret signs because his grandmother had passed them on to him and she had learned them from Monique herself.

The spirits were good to him. They had brought the Hai-tian Guy and the food and now, after three long days of tense waiting, they were going to deliver the tall one-footed for-eigner. The good man who was going to take the lucky candi-dates to where they could work and eat for ever. Ti Allain was curious about the foreign man, although he already knew what he looked like.

All white foreigners looked the same and all of them were rich. Yet this one was different. He was good and he loved to help others. La Grande Marie had told him so. She always spoke of him with affection. She did not appear to Ti Allain in his dreams, not even once, and that was a sure sign that even though she was dead she had not become a spirit.

Into his dreams only living people or spirits could enter. They would enter with their voices and faces intact and revive their image while he dreamed and therefore they were immor-tal. Sometimes, very rarely, he would find people who loved him or hated him edging into his dreams, and even then only for a short moment. His father was neither alive nor a spirit. Nor did he love him or hate him. That was why Ti Allain could not remember his face. No dream of his father ever came to remind him of it.

The fire was now quite dead. None of its former glory remained. One of the women stood still in front of Ti Allain and looked down on him. She was tall and thin and quiet and respectful. She was going to wait until his ritual had ended before she told him the meal was ready. The others sat where they had been sitting or standing or sleeping these past few days. The years of hardship in the mountain villages had taught them patience. They looked at Ti Allain with respect, they stole loving glances at the food and the women, and they waited.

CHAPTER TWENTY-NINE

———■———

Francisco Martinez crouched in the back of Rafael's taxi. He took an occasional look at the house that had been his prison. It was a large property with a broad, sweeping drive that led to the front door. Every light in the place was on. The gate, tucked in between two ancient palms, had been left open. Rafael sat in front with a young girl from San Cristóbal they had picked up on the Malecon. She had just arrived in the capital and said she would only charge twenty pesos for both of them. Provided one left the car while she was doing it with the other, because she was new to it. Rafael was fondling her breasts while he kept an eye on the gate over his shoulder.

'Gently. You are tearing my blouse, *querido*.'

'Keep your voice down,' hissed Francisco from the back.

'I said one of you must leave the car. What do you think I am?'

'Shut up.'

'How long are you going to take?'

'As long as I like. Unless you want me to drop you in the middle of nowhere for the police to find you and throw you into jail.'

Francisco tried not to listen to them. He lay down and held his large pistol at the ready. Rafael would tell him as soon as someone left the house for the night. He watched Rafael's hand travel up and down the girl's body. Their breathing was getting heavier and she started to moan. That was not what they had agreed.

'Don't overdo it, Rafael. You are supposed to watch the door over there.'

Rafael said he was watching the place like a hawk, but he was tired and having a bit of fun was keeping him awake. He wasn't forgetting himself. Did Francisco think he was a child? Didn't they grow up together? Was he one to break an agreement?

Francisco shrugged his shoulders. Good thing the taxi was a large Impala and had plenty of room. The small Austins they used now were a disaster. The girl was groaning now and that pleased Rafael no end, but Francisco did not care. The anticipation was sweet. His gun felt like a crucifix.

'Get ready, Francisco,' Rafael whispered. 'Someone is coming.'

'How many?'

Rafael pushed the girl away from him to get a better view. 'Hold it, there are two of them. You'd better get out of the car now. The interior light won't come on. The bulb is dead.'

'You're a genius.'

Francisco pushed the wide door open and crept out. He lay on his side in the gutter, peering underneath the car. He heard footsteps and saw two pairs of wobbly, trousered legs moving towards the car.

'Taxi!' cried one of the cultured voices. Francisco recognized it instantly. 'Can you take us to the Mirador?'

'The lady has hired me for the night, señor. You'll have to ask her.'

He has a great brain, that Rafael, Francisco thought. The teachers had been dead wrong about him.

'What about it, señorita? We'll pay.'

'I only do one at a time.'

She must have been a little nervous, bless her, but Francisco knew that the others were too drunk to notice.

'It's nothing like that, señorita. We're both engaged to be married. We're not looking for a good time. We want to get home, that's all.'

'Then you'll have to find another taxi. I am here to do business. What's the matter, boys? Don't you like me?'

The two men went silent. One was scratching his ankle with his shoe. He then bent down sideways and lifted his trouser leg with his white hand.

'Come on, boys, I haven't got all night.'

'What do you think, Roberto?' asked one voice. 'Shall we?'

'There's no harm in a bit of that, but where do we do it?'

'Just decide which one of you loves me first. We'll get into the back seat and while the car drives around the park I'll show you where paradise is hidden.'

Poetry, Francisco thought. The girl deserved another ten pesos at least.

'Why can't we both come?'

'House rules.'

'But the driver. What about the driver?'

'The girl is new to the business, señor,' Rafael said. 'Shy. You know how it is. Don't worry about me. I'm a careful driver. Keep my eyes on the road. If you both come into the car I will have to talk to one of you and that makes me nervous. Screwing in the back is okay, but I can't concentrate when I'm talking. We might have an accident. It's best one comes along now and we'll come back for the other. He can wait by the gate there.'

The two were whispering now. The girl must have unbuttoned her blouse, Francisco thought when he heard a low whistle of admiration.

'Okay, you go first, Roberto. I'll wait by the gate. How long will it take, señorita?'

'That depends on how macho your friend is. Don't worry. There'll be plenty left for you.'

'And then we'll take him home,' Rafael said.

'Come on, Roberto, get in the back,' the girl said, 'and let

172

me touch you. Oh, what a man.'

There was a giggle from the other side of the car. 'How much will it be?'

'You are both handsome boys,' Rafael said. 'She only likes young men. She only does it because she can't get enough of it. Why, only an hour ago she refused a big rich gringo who came out of Vesuvio with a cigar. You are quite lucky, you know, but don't take too long deciding or we'll have to leave.'

'You wouldn't want to frustrate me, would you, *querido*? Your touch makes me tremble with passion. Get into the back and I'll show you. You can decide afterwards how much you want to give me. I must have you right now.'

Pure gold, Francisco thought. Twenty pesos extra for sure.

'You be sure to wait by the gate,' Roberto told his friend. 'We'll talk in my apartment later.'

Things started to move quickly. The door opened and one pair of legs stepped in while the other turned away to cross the road. Rafael started the engine, pushing a cloud of dust and fumes into Francisco's face. The car crawled down the road as the girl climbed over the top onto the young man's knees. She lifted her skirt and covered his face. He giggled in the dark.

With the two busy exploring each other, Rafael stopped the car and Francisco slipped in. They took off. The couple cooed and laughed at the top of their voices. Francisco watched them from the front seat. He wanted the young man to get a hard-on before blowing his brains out.

Later, he felt no pain, nor was he as elated as he'd expected. The time-bomb in his brain had been defused, not exploded. The first young man had been too giggly to recognize him as he pulled the trigger. The second had passed out as soon as Francisco appeared by Rafael's side with the gun in his hand and had to be dispatched while out cold. They did not even know why they were dying.

They brought the bodies back to the house and propped them upright by the gate facing each other. They looked like two stone lions guarding the entrance of some country estate.

Rafael drove along Avenida Abraham Lincoln and then down towards the sea. In the back of the car, the girl had tried to proposition Francisco as soon as the shooting was over, but he had declined. He didn't feel like it, he said. Cunningham had been right. That very afternoon he had tried to talk him out of it. Nothing, he said, was going to bring the kid back. Revenge could only put a noose around his neck.

'You're not a killer,' Cunningham had said. 'You should leave that to the others. Take a deep breath before you do something you might regret. It's an old English trick.'

He should have listened. He had done it all for nothing. He was useless. Not even a man. Francisco lay back on the girl's lap and cried. She stroked his hair. Only the Englishman would know what to do now. He was a real macho. Not a child like him. Cunningham would need him more than ever now to complete the operation. That would serve him better than any number of killings. To work with Cunningham again would restore his sanity. But would the Englishman want to touch him now?

'Let's get back to the shop, Rafael,' he said, 'I need a drink.'

They dropped the girl on the Malecon. Richer than she had ever been, she said they could count on her any time.

'Are you sure she won't talk?'

'You bet I am. While you were crying your eyes out back there I told her she was in it as much as you are. Besides, I found out she is related to my wife. I can never enjoy her now.'

As they drove past Antonio's bar, Rafael noticed how full it was. Antonio's trade was brisk as Francisco's friends gathered to mourn him. Rafael did not tell Francisco of this. In his state he might go crazy and get out of the car to buy them all drinks.

CHAPTER THIRTY

A long, lonely night lay ahead. He could hear Marina's breathing, feel her skin and smell her scent. Earlier, she had been friendly enough and did not contest his suggestion that they dine out. She did not argue with him when he ordered her food. Above all she did not protest when he said he had chosen the house without her.

'I have to live in this place,' she would have said. There would have been an argument. She would have thrown a tantrum. She would have reminded him of all the other times he had been an insensitive, selfish shit, before storming out to the spare room to sleep on her own.

That night she did not utter one word against him. He wished she had. Had she been angry, she would have taken her time in the bathroom. She would have told him she wanted to read or do her nails or rearrange the photo album. That night she undressed quickly and showered and came straight to bed. She lay beside him and was subdued, but did not object to his lovemaking. She did not talk before he came into her in his uncontrollable rush, or after.

Now he was lying on his side of the bed in the dark and she on hers. He had wanted to tell her how he was going to change things. How the house would make all the difference. How she would have a garden and a car and neighbours and a life. How he'd arrange things so that he wouldn't need to be away that often. He'd never treat any member of her family badly again. He was going to tell her that his next trip would be his last for a long while. He would miss her dreadfully and would come back as soon as he could. If she ever left him, he'd die. To hell with business.

Her head was turned the other way and she was awake, but he knew none of those things were going to be said that night. Because a cloud of indifference had settled on their bed and over their life. Marina prayed for sleep. It would take her to Haiti and Puerto Rico and wonderland. Of course her fling had to come to an end, but not yet, God, not yet. If she could not be with Cunningham, she could dream. Dream herself over the mountains to Port-au-Prince to be there and watch his plane land. Dream herself into the interior, hiking along beside him and the Haitians on their long trek across the border to a new life.

At the restaurant she had looked around for a familiar face from Cunningham's world. But she knew no one who lived in it. There were names, yes, and there was even Francisco's voice. But there was not a single face to go with any of them. No one to remind her of that freedom. Now, as she lay in the dark in her own private corner, she could do as she liked. She could give them names and faces and paint personalities for them and imagine conversations and laugh with them in silence.

Inside a sweating human circle, by the wooden church at Di-quini, Cunningham watched Ti Allain dance. His steps and his arm-swinging gyrations were begging the spirits to let every one of the people pass the tall foreigner's inspection. The spirits had brought them thus far and now, with the little prod his dance would give them, the spirits were sure to convince the foreigner to take them all. They were all fit for work because they needed it.

Ti Allain had expected the foreigner to be paler than he was, and larger. He should be sitting tall, on a par with the trees, yet he crouched with the crowd like any mortal. Marie-Christine had told him the foreigner was a giant. Perhaps the spirits made him appear small so as not to frighten the rest of the people. He talked like a man, in Creole, and laughed and drank the rum and even shook his upper body to the rhythm of the drums. Ti Allain did not take his eyes off the foreigner. He watched him pull a stalk of grass from the earth and chew it, a sure sign of nervousness. A state of mind of people, not of gods. Perhaps he was not sure how many people he wanted to take this time. Perhaps he was worried about something.

Ti Allain concentrated harder on his dance, moving faster now to the speeding drums. Some of the confidence of his pounding feet could surely be transmitted into the foreigner's heart if only he would stop pulling the grass out of the earth.

It was Cunningham's first inspection. Beyond some fuzzy notions of physical fitness, he had no idea what he was looking for. He had never worked closely with Guy before, but only he was left alive on this side of the border to help him.

No one could guess what Balthasar's next move would be. And then there was the change that seemed to have come over Francisco. The man he thought he knew so well. All this talk of vengeance would mar his judgement. He could hear it in the disturbed tone of his voice. Without Francisco on the other side of the border he was sunk. Could his friend have been hallucinating about revenge? Was it all in his imagination? He was too kind and soft to carry it out. He wouldn't do any of it. Of course he wouldn't.

He watched Ti Allain dance. Dead chicken eyes gazed at him from the small man's crown and girdle. Cunningham saw blood everywhere and then, suddenly, he was gripped by a notion that Francisco had meant what he said. He was going to carry out his threat. Do something terrible. Someone had to stop him before he killed them all. No police or government could afford to let Francisco get away with it. The young men involved came from important families and those would remain important for ever. Regardless of who would finally be installed in the Presidential Palace. He must be quick. Get out of there as soon as possible.

The drums roared their deafening blows. One of the heads fell off Ti Allain's waist. He halted in his tracks, picked it up and appeared to swallow it whole. The drums stopped. No one breathed. All eyes turned on him.

Cunningham cast a cautious look behind his shoulder. The market women had moved their stalls and wares from the alleys. The little dirt road that led to the wooden church had disappeared completely now. It had vanished under the lively clutter of the dealers who attracted a sizeable clientele from nowhere. No one could have followed him there. Nonetheless, he knew it was time to act. He leaned over and whispered to Guy.

The driver motioned to Ti Allain. The little man took his time. He walked slowly, then stopped. He then sprinted at speed around the assembly looking each man in the eyes, his hand touching their foreheads with a blood-stained feather. He walked to the centre of the circle, took his frightening crown and belt off and tossed them into the embers. The hissing was followed by flames that lit Ti Allain's face. He looked at the sky and let loose a long last scream before hopping towards Cunningham on one leg. He halted in front of him and fell on his knees to the ground. His face looked up into the Englishman's while his eyes remained fixed towards heaven. Silence reigned.

'I'll take them all, Ti Allain,' Cunningham said quietly in Creole. 'You too.'

It was the first time the tall foreigner had addressed him. His voice had the deep, rich quality Ti Allain had expected. His smile was warm and honest and it captured the world. The little man had his answer, but the shock contained in Cunningham's last two words had stung him. You too, he had said. He would have to digest it before he could tell the others what the spirits had decreed.

The foreigner had spoken clearly, in a language all the people knew and understood. He had said they were all to come and so was he. That was a cruel blow which could only mean that an error had been committed. The others could go, but he could not go anywhere. He would have to make clear to the tall foreigner once daylight came. Had his single-legged dance offended the foreigner? All he wanted to do was to comfort and encourage him. Identify with his pain and show him how well a one-legged man could dance.

The foreigner got up to take his leave. He told Guy to give Ti Allain some more money. At the sound of his name, the little man started towards them.

'Stay where you are,' Guy said. 'I'll be back tomorrow to tell you when we leave.'

Ti Allain watched helplessly as the tall foreigner turned and limped away. Unable to speak, he now recognized what had happened. Monique the black witch had caught up with him at last. Perhaps she did not approve of his way of life, his sins, his obesity, his constant trips to the city, neglecting the place where her body had died by fire. Taking her people to a new land, far from her influence. But there were things he could do to change her mind. Convince her he must stay. Without his presence in the village, her powers over the people would wane. And once over the mountains she could lose her control over his own destiny. His grandmother was her friend. She would never allow that.

He would not sleep tonight. He would look for her under every stone, behind every tree, and he would feed her and pray until dawn.

CHAPTER THIRTY-ONE

Some miles west of Diquini, at the Hotel la Résidence, Balthasar attempted to talk to his boss, the Miner. The ornamented room and the cannon that stood among the tropical plants in the garden, the old maps and artefacts along the corridors, were all lost on him. La Résidence, carved out of the palace Napoleon's sister had occupied when her husband was governor, was the Ministry of Tourism's pride. Old furniture and paintings of slavers and slaves and sculptures of long-dead European beauties lined the pink walls, and people from all over the world came to sample and breathe and admire the once-despised colonial atmosphere.

'Don't waste my time,' the Miner said in his soft voice. 'The boys at Arroyo Hondo are not following orders.'

'You keep bothering me with details.'

'All I am asking is, do I have authority over them?'

'You have been given a job to do, Balthasar. Just do it.'

Balthasar could well picture the big man, sitting as he must have been in his large study, surrounded by books and maps and glass jars of earth, and shelves full of metals and minerals. The Miner liked to fondle them and move them about while he talked. He did not talk much and not to many. He guarded his privacy and always described himself as a mining engineer. Over the years the Miner had acquired, under different names, exploitation rights to land all over the Republic. He did not drive large cars or take publicized trips overseas. He was not fond of gambling or fancy clothes or chasing after women. His picture never appeared in the gossip columns in spite of his having amassed a fortune.

The year before, a newly appointed general had appeared in the offices of a small steel-rolling plant outside the city. He asked to see the owner and in the Miner's absence one of the managers received him. The general came straight to the point. He had been assigned to the area and demanded to be put on the board of the company. It would help them, he said, to get import permits for equipment and obtain foreign currency. He would not interfere in the running of the business. He would expect a car, a fixed monthly pay cheque and funds for his telephone and restaurant expenses. He would expect his credit card bills to be paid. He also expected an immediate answer. If the owner was not there, someone should go and fetch him.

That was the first time the Miner was confronted with the reality of army power and it marked the end of his lifelong disinterest in politics. He did not meet the general in person, but an agreement was struck within an hour and the soldier reportedly left the office with a satisfied smirk across his face.

The Miner's scheme to end uniformed corruption was born. But he stayed firmly in the background. Except for Balthasar and three or four close friends, his part in the plot was a total secret. To his inner circle, the Miner was a formidable figure. His vicious temper, so well contained behind his soft-spoken manner, was a source of anxiety to those near to him. It was rumoured that neither his wife nor his children dared talk in his presence. He had a small group of friends with whom he would meet for a drink and a talk in his study. Balthasar, having been employed as an overseer for the Miner's farming land, had only been there twice. First when he was hired, soon after he lost his job as Chief of Police. The second time, recently, when he was brought into the plot and put in charge of field operations. And now he had called because Cunningham's anger had unnerved him.

'Have you given Arroyo Hondo permission to act independently of me?'

'I have not given anyone permission to do anything, Balthasar. I am not involved.'

'In that case ...'

'If you are not capable of doing what you went over to do, we'll find someone else. Just let me know when it's done.'

'These students are not following orders. I shall have to take steps.'

'You, of all people, should understand discipline. Do not call me again until you have done it.'

'Leave it to me,' said an uneasy Balthasar, and he heard the Miner hang up.

There was no one he could consult. Had things been different, he could have confided in Cunningham. Even asked his advice. The Englishman was experienced and would put him on the right track. He could make a deal with him. Ludicrous. He must be losing his head. Cunningham was firmly on the other side for now. Why should that be? They were of the same generation. They could have been friends. They knew the same people in the old days. Still, he had been put down by Cunningham, and the Miner, too, was losing patience.

He was lonely. He could suggest a ceasefire. He could go back to see him at his hotel. Offer him dinner or something. Cunningham liked women and Balthasar could always organize a few girls to make him feel at ease. He was not a real gringo any more. He could call and tell him frankly he was fed up with life and wanted a few hours of fun. He could go to the casino where he was sure to find him. He could take it from there. Playing at the same table was sure to form a bond between them, however temporary. Good thing he had had the sense to pack a tuxedo.

His spirits began to rise. A couple of light-hearted hours with the opposition and a few plastic chits were all he needed. But first he would relax. The ex-policeman went to the bathroom and ran the water. The black suit was a little creased and he hung it on the shower to let the steam pass through it. He got into the water and lay down. He stayed there a long time.

He was just coming out of the bath when the phone rang. He had not expected any calls and he ignored it as he sat on his bed towelling his hair dry. The prospect of a carefree evening was relaxing, but the relentless buzz refused to stop. It could be the reception desk. Perhaps he had forgotten to extend his stay. Not important, he told himself, as the incessant ring grew louder. Finally, compelled by lifelong force of habit, he picked the receiver up, if only to silence it.

It was the Miner. He did not introduce himself or say good evening. Within seconds, Balthasar knew he had fallen from favour. The Miner was shooting him down over the wires. He had never crossed swords with him before, and as the monologue and the threats progressed, Balthasar experienced the sinister side of his gentle-voiced employer.

'You have gone too far, Balthasar. You were going to discipline the boys at Arroyo Hondo, not massacre them. One of the boys you had shot was Roberto Arias, the son of my best friend. You'd better find a place to hide when this is over. In the meantime, just tell me who pulled the trigger for you.'

Balthasar pleaded innocence. He said he had nothing to do with any killing. It was the first he had heard of it. 'I have nothing to hide,' he said quietly. 'As soon as I've finished here I'll come straight back.'

'You are a dead man,' the Miner said, and slammed the phone down.

He would go see Cunningham all the same. If the Englishman was behind it, he'd soon know.

CHAPTER THIRTY-TWO

The dwarf, splendid in his red jacket and turban, opened the casino door with a smiling wink of recognition. Cunningham ushered the pilot through ahead of him and pressed a bill into the little hand. Ashen-faced, he exchanged a few hundred dollars for chips and handed some to the pilot. He wondered whether he wanted to play at all, but he placed a hundred-dollar bet on number seventeen and called the waiter. It had been a harassing day and he needed a stiff drink. He knew he should not bet that much or make decisions in his state, but there was little choice. The harvest was ready and his Haitians had to get going immediately. Guy had said they should go on the open road. He would look after the transport if Cunningham made sure no one was going to follow.

Seventeen came up. Cunningham would have let his bet ride, but the waiter came back to say there was a telephone call for him in the office. He pushed his winning pile outside the playing area and left the table. Having placed a bet on the same number, the pilot took all the chips off the table as soon as his client was gone. Number twenty-seven came up, but the pilot did not bet again.

There was only one winner this time, a sturdy-looking, swarthy, middle-aged man, dressed in a crease-ridden tuxedo.

He had just joined the table and one of the American ladies facing him uttered an envious 'Beginner's luck' under her breath. The remark remained unacknowledged as the man watched the croupier push the chips in his direction. The pilot did not recognize the groomed Balthasar, who wondered what the man and his flying machine were doing in Haiti still. Across the table, the pilot looked about him. More money than he had ever seen in his life was being won and lost in minutes.

Balthasar continued betting carefully on colours. The American lady was having an argument with the dealer and the game came to a stop. She claimed that a chip from her un-stacked pile which had slid off into the square marked nine-teen had been put there on purpose, and as the nineteen had come up, she insisted on being paid. Balthasar had watched the whole scene and knew she was lying. The croupier refused to pay and the assistant manager was called to the table. Balthasar lowered his head. The man listened, then ordered the croupier to pay out, and the game resumed with the lady losing it all on the next roll. She left in a hip-swaying huff. Not a real gambler, Balthasar thought, admiring her posterior.

In the office, Cunningham listened to Francisco's story. 'Of course I'm glad you're alive, but these killings could not have come at a worse time.'

'They killed the kid, Cunningham. The family name is at stake. You should have seen those *cojones*. They died like dogs.'

'I am just on the point of convincing the opposition that we're playing along with them. They're not going to believe me if they find out you did it.'

'You gringos are all alike. Business always comes before honour with you, doesn't it? Well, we are different. Anyway, it's all over now. I am back with you. There is just the matter of the kid's funeral. He must have a funeral, but how can he be buried without me at the graveside? My mother will never forgive me for allowing him to go alone. And he will tell her as soon as he sees her in heaven.'

'Why don't you go, then?'

'Have you forgotten I'm dead? What will people say? The kid will never forgive me either. Maybe I should tell the truth. Just turn up. What do you think?'

'Do as you wish, Francisco.'

'No, no. I think I'll keep things as they are. Being dead makes me invisible.'

'Fine.'

'All I wanted was to let you know where I am. You tell me when you're ready to cross and where. I'll be there.'

'All right. Does the Chief know about the revolution yet?'

'No. You want me to tell him?'

'Don't talk to anyone, do you hear? Get some rest. I'll call you as soon as things are set up.'

'Don't forget to buy the Barbancourt rum for my wife's father. He'll need it when I come back to life. Fifteen years old.'

'It's already done, Francisco. Mrs Buckmaster has got it. Don't move out of the shop, no matter what happens.'

'I heard you the first time,' Francisco said, and the line went dead.

It was stuffy in the little office and it was hot. He did not want to play the tables any longer. The long day and doubts about Francisco's reliability were crowding in on him. But he went back to the table and placed a hundred dollars on number seven. It came up. His energy returned with a whoop of exultation. People tapped his back in congratulation. Some applauded. Across the table, a nightmare in the shape of Balthasar punctured his elation. The ex-police chief had made a little win on the red.

'Using my luck to make some money on the side, Balthasar?' Cunningham said. 'Don't they pay you at all? You should have gone the whole hog and backed a number.'

'Working people can't take risks.'

'Working people shouldn't gamble.'

'What you can do, I can do.'

'Enjoy the game, office boy.'

Twenty-seven came up. The pilot was jubilant.

'I told you, you should back a number. You'd soon forget the revolution.'

'You are making a fortune in here. Outside you could lose more than money.'

'Don't make threats, Balthasar. Where Francisco is there are no casinos.'

'No. No casinos. Only eternal fire.'

They were changing dealers. The tourists were taken to their cruise ship. The pilot went to the men's room. They were alone.

'You should not have had those two boys shot, Cunningham. They came from influential families. We'll have a vendetta on our hands.'

He'd need time to work that one out. 'What are you talking about?'

The lights went out. Perhaps the house was losing too much money, Cunningham thought, as players on other tables were told to stop until the current was restored.

'We have to talk in private,' Balthasar said.

'Fine. Let's go to my hotel.'

'Not on your life.'

'You're not afraid of me, are you?'

'I know a place where we can talk freely. It's not far from here.'

Cunningham was just about to say he was not going anywhere when the lights came on. A swarm of gamblers rushed to the table to grab seats. Balthasar got up. His haggard eyes betrayed a hint of fear. Something was wrong. The menace had gone from his face.

'*Está bien*,' Cunningham said. 'Let's go.'

The Dominican reacted with a strained smile. 'Thank you,' he said. 'Thank you very much.'

In their tuxedos, the two men cut a strange sight in the little waterfront bar. It was a simple wooden structure built on stilts, its creaky dance-floor stretched over the water. The music was subdued; fishermen and their women embraced to its rhythm in the dark. Above, the pale quarter-moon etched itself on a cloudless sky. They found an empty table in the corner.

Balthasar's voice had weakened. His large hands shook as he raised the Cuba Libre in a toast. He dropped the glass on the table. It shot a splash of liquid onto Cunningham's trousers. Balthasar apologized and bent over to wipe it off with his velvet sleeve.

'Don't worry about it, man. It'll soon evaporate. You wanted to talk, didn't you? Talk, then.'

The waiter came back with another drink on his tray. Balthasar held on to it with both hands. He took a long, pensive sip. His shoulders sagged. He looked pitiful. He lifted his head and looked at Cunningham. He wasn't sure how to start. The smell of stale fish distracted him. The gringo seemed impatient.

'You made a terrible mistake.'

'I've made many.'

'You should never have touched the boys.'

'What are you talking about? What boys?'

'You don't need to lie. This meeting is private. It's off the record.'

'Oh, go to hell, Balthasar. Either tell me what you're talking about or let me go to bed.'

Balthasar took a gulp and Cunningham summoned the waiter to fetch another drink. Balthasar talked. He told him of the carnage at Arroyo Hondo. This was supposed to be a quiet little bloodless coup. There would be a major scandal. Now heads would roll. Yes, he knew the Martinez brothers had been killed, but that was not his doing. Perhaps they had tried to escape. He was still trying to find out what had happened. He was telling the truth, he kept saying. He had little to lose now that the Miner was after his blood.

The Miner? Cunningham knew who the Miner was. He looked at the sky and feigned a yawn to hide his surprise. Balthasar must have been telling him the truth. He would never have divulged the Miner's name otherwise. The Miner mounting a coup? It was too incredible to be a lie.

'We could have settled the whole thing between the two of us, you know,' Balthasar said. 'I am not the head man. I follow orders. It's all too late now. You, you run your own show. You can make decisions. You should never have ordered your people to shoot the students. This is a catastrophe.'

'What about Francisco and his brother?'

'Oh, come on, they were garbage. How can you compare them with society?'

Cunningham slammed his fist on the table. 'What sort of creep are you?' he shouted. 'Francisco was my friend.'

'I had nothing to do with that. Believe me. Look, I trust you, Cunningham. Otherwise I would not have asked for this meeting. I could have shot you a dozen times. All right, if you say you had nothing to do with the shooting, I am prepared to believe you. You did not have them killed? Okay. I wish I knew who did.'

'Oh, I can tell you that, Balthasar. Your society friends did that all by themselves.'

'You are crazy. Why should they do that? What for?'

'To get you out of the way,' Cunningham said quietly. 'You must have trodden on someone's toes. Top families, my arse. Can't you see what's going on around you? Whose revolution is it anyway? The rich against the generals, that's whose. And who are the generals, if not peasants like you and poor Francisco? Peasants in uniforms with money and Cadillacs. You made Chief of Police, but you had no chance of joining society. Do you honestly believe any of those rich bookworms have any time for you? They simply jumped the gun, that's all. They thought you had me under control, Balthasar. When you told them to let Francisco go, they were sure we two had come to an agreement. So they decided it would be better if

Francisco couldn't talk to anyone ever again. God knows what he might have seen them do in the house. The Miner wanted a bloodless revolution, yes? Do you think they're going to tell him they got rid of Francisco and his brother? That would have been that, but then someone comes into the house and shoots two of the bastards. What do your expect? Francisco had many friends. But never you fear, Balthasar. They'll hang it all on you. They're clever, Balthasar. They'd chew you up before breakfast. They're doctors and lawyers and they'll find a way.

'You've no future. You never had a future with those people. They were going to use you to get rid of me. I should know. I'd have been one of them if I'd been born a Dominican. You think about it, Balthasar. Your rich society friends have used you. Now that they think you and me are together, they'll have you buried without having to do it themselves. Where do you get your information, Balthasar? The Vatican? Whose side are you really on? It's this dog-loyalty of yours that makes the fuckers rich. Who cares if some of that money goes to the generals? Your friends' sons would only waste it on women and fast cars and grass anyway. You know that. The poor never see a drop of it either way.'

The music must have stopped or else something was wrong with his hearing. The world went numb. Balthasar shuddered. All he could see was Cunningham's face. What the man had said was shocking, but it made sense. Every word of it was true. They wanted to hang it on him. He was being blamed. The Miner had said so himself. During their last talk the Miner had said he was a dead man. He meant it. It was a class war. He had been betrayed. Money sticks to money.

'What should I do now?' He didn't mean to say that. Yet he did. He was right to trust Cunningham. The man told him what he had known all his life, but refused to accept.

'It's not what you should do, Balthasar. It's what we two should do. You said we could have settled this together. You were right. We still can.'

'Oh yes, Cunningham? What do you think we should do? Tell me. I'll do anything you say.'

'I won't make any deals with you now, Balthasar. You're drunk and tired and the Miner has upset you. You don't really believe what I'm telling you. When you wake up tomorrow, you'll forget everything I've said. You'll come up with some new scheme to help your masters. A slave is always a slave. I shouldn't have said anything. You don't understand. All you can see is the bone they throw at you. You smile and wag your tail and you nibble at it while they dig a hole for you.'

Balthasar had tears in his eyes. He should tell him off some more. Make him suck salt. For Marie-Christine. Marcel Kinet. The kid. The man was going to pieces. He should enjoy the spectacle, but he did not.

'I am not drunk or tired, Cunningham. I have heard it all. I agree with it all. But what can we do? Do you know what you are up against? Do you know what those families control? This is a Latin country. Things don't change here. The poor remain poor, but the rich get more powerful every day.'

'I know. I'm local. I've lived here for ever. You're right it will never change. The least we can do is stick together. Instead you kill my best friends.'

'It's all over, Cunningham.' The man's voice had steadied. 'What is it you want us to do? I'll do anything. I won't ask any questions.'

'Take me back to my hotel,' Cunningham said, and Balthasar jumped to his feet. 'Then go and get some sleep. Meet me at the airport at noon. If you don't, it's your funeral. We're going to the Dominican Republic.'

'What for?'

'To pay the Chief of Police a visit.'

CHAPTER THIRTY-THREE

A shadow slipped past, cutting the sunlight that warmed his face, and it startled him. The man had made no sound; his feet brushed the earth like an alighting bird. But the split-second darkening of the glare woke Ti Allain and he opened his eyes.

He was accustomed to waking with the sun, clear-headed, long before the others. Back in his village in the mountains he drank no alcohol and only slept late when he had a visit from a woman. No woman had come to his side last night because they were mostly local and knew nothing of his powers, but he had drunk because the chosen men, in gratitude, kept pouring rivers of white rum down his throat. Now his head was heavy and several moments passed before he recognized Guy's face, staring at him with a sneer.

There is always something behind a man's face to reveal who he truly is. You have to live with someone and look into their eyes and listen to them laugh or cry or scream before you can recognize what their other face says. In the case of the man Guy, who lived in the big city and had never known the hardship of village life, it was his voice that gave him away. He had a way of changing it whenever he was left on his own. Ti Allain had seen him talking down to people whenever Marie-Christine was not about. Now Marie-Christine was dead and the tall foreigner was gone. Guy looked at him and could see he was not awake yet and still he shouted at him and said, 'Get up, little man. We are leaving.'

'What about the selection?' asked Ti Allain. The spirits had given the answer last night, but he needed an earthly confirmation of the news. Events often took a long time to come to pass, even after the spirits had decided.

'Did you drink that much last night, you lazy dwarf? It's all done. Everybody is going. You too.'

There it was. Monique the black witch was no longer there

to change the order of things. Perhaps the spirits had whisked her back to the mountains in the night.

The people were up and about, packing the little bundles they carried on their backs, slowly moving towards the steps of the wooden church. Ti Allain got up. Save the clothes he stood up in, he had nothing at all. He would leave his own land empty-handed, and that could only be a bad sign. It could mean he wanted no part of the place he was born in, no memory of his heritage. It could mean he would never return.

He bent and scooped up large handfuls of earth. Together with a few blades of dry grass, he stuffed it into his pockets. He still hoped the tall foreigner would come and tell him it was all a mistake. Pay him his money and let him go back to his village. Just like Marie-Christine had always done. Surely he still needed him here for the next time.

Ti Allain was pleased to see that all the people were going this time. There had always been those who had failed the inspection and those he had to feed and take back to the mountains at his own expense. He was particularly pleased that the tall, bald Jean-Hercule was going. He had a bad cough and had failed two previous inspections in a row. Jean-Hercule had a pretty wife back in the village and had extracted a promise from Ti Allain that he would keep an eye on her if he passed the inspection. Ti Allain had looked forward to that and now it would never happen because he himself was going. And yet the spirits had been kinder than ever. How confusing all this was going to be.

The people were assembling by the wooden church. Some were saying their goodbyes to the locals they had befriended during their stay. There were a few laughs and a lot of tears. Children scoured the area for any small thing the passers-by might have left behind. The rest of them just stood there looking on. The diversion the travellers had brought into their midst was passing on.

Down the road, a line of brightly decorated tap-tap buses waited, their stainless-steel sides painted with pictures from the Bible and animals and people long gone and others still alive among trees and lakes and spirits. The men started for the tap-taps, led by Guy. Ti Allain followed close behind.

There is no end to the power of the spirits, the little man thought. This time, instead of a long, arduous walk, they were going across the border on wheels. The tall foreigner really must be a giant. The little mistake he had made in telling him to come along too could be forgiven. It was surely going to be corrected as soon as they met again.

Cunningham had been trying to reach the Chief all morning. His office in Santo Domingo said he was still out of town. He might be at his brother's house in Jarabacoa, but they could not give him a telephone number. Anyway, they told him, it was constantly changing. Security.

He tried Fernando Bogard. The landowner answered the call with a torrent of abuse before he even said good morning.

'You were a lot more cordial last time we met.'

'The cane's going mouldy in the field and you, sitting in some whorehouse in Port-au-Prince gambling my money away, you want me to be nice?'

'I have run into some problems, Fernando.'

'We all have problems. All I want is my money's worth. If you don't deliver, I'll see to it you never set foot in this country again. And as for Francisco Martinez, we'll have him sell his house to repay our money and let him rot in jail until the sea reaches Santiago.'

'Francisco is dead. He and his brother have been murdered.'

'I am sorry to hear that. Haven't seen the papers yet. What happened?'

'Can't talk about that now. I need to talk to the Chief urgently. I need his number.'

'He won't do a thing for you. Everybody knows that. In any case, I don't have it.'

'For Christ's sake, there must be somebody who knows how to get him.'

'Try police headquarters. After all, he is the Chief of Police.'

'Very funny.'

'Okay, okay. Try El Gordo. He was there, playing dominoes last night with the Chief. He'll know. He knows everything.'

'I'll try him. And Fernando, don't worry. In two or three days you'll get what you paid for. There's plenty for everyone this time.'

El Gordo was his usual jovial self when he answered the phone. He owned huge estates, but could always be found at home. He was the fattest farmer in the Republic, Francisco Martinez once said, but he could steal horses without upsetting their owners. No one knew for sure where his ancestors or his money came from. His only claim to a name was a vague connection, by marriage, with the Trujillo family. It was rumoured that some of the slain dictator's money had found its way into El Gordo's coffers. Having invested in farmland afforded him that air of permanence associated with people who live on the land. He was successful at it. His cattle kept winning awards for their milk. And even the stuck-up farming community had accepted him, if only for his larger-than-life personality. They were quite happy to forget his connections with the hated Trujillos.

Cunningham had known him for years, since his days in the Embassy when he had sold him imported cars at duty-free prices. He'd always enjoyed doing business with El Gordo.

'So who can we rob this time, Cunningham?' El Gordo asked.

'I thought there was no one left worth the trouble, considering how little I hear from you these days. Actually, I am trying to find the Chief, Gordito. Do you know where he might be?'

'You can walk into any police station in town.'

'That would be difficult. I'm in Haiti.'

'Well ...' There was silence.

'Oh, by the way,' said Cunningham, 'do you need a few more than you've paid for? I hear the harvest will be good this year.'

'You are one smart son of a bitch, Cunningham,' the fat man said, and laughed. 'All right, I'll take a few more. But you make sure you come up here yourself for a drink one of these days.'

'You've got a nerve, Cunningham,' the Chief shouted. 'Everybody is screaming for their Haitians and blaming me for the delay. Where the hell are they?'

'I'm coming to see you this afternoon, Chief.'

'This afternoon? You really are something. How did you get into the country?'

'I didn't. I'm still in Haiti.'

'Where are the Haitians?'

'That is being taken care of. What I'm coming to see you about is more important. If you want to keep your job, and maybe your head, and anything else you've got, you'll be waiting for me.'

'What are you talking about?'

'I've said too much over the phone already. I'll be at your brother's farm at six this evening. Just you be there, too. And Chief, I'll have an old friend of yours with me.'

'And just who might that be?'

'Remember El Carnicero?'

'The ex-policeman?'

'The ex-police chief. The man whose job they gave you,' Cunningham said, and hung up.

The telephone operator called. There was another collect call from Señor Francisco Martinez. Would Monsieur Cunningham accept it? He would.

'Are you sure we are backing the right horse?'

'No, Francisco. One never is. Why?'

'I hear Balthasar swore he'd kill the Chief one day. He is dangerous and if his side wins we will find out we've been playing a double game. You know how losers talk. What are we going to do then? What do you think, Cunningham? Should we, perhaps, join the revolution?'

'Don't worry about him. Right now Balthasar thinks I'm the best thing since rum. What news, otherwise?'

'It seems Chiquito's daughter is now part of the family,' Francisco said. 'Señor Buckmaster thinks the world of her.'

'How do you know? Did you talk to Chiquito?'

'You must be joking. Chiquito has got a mouth so big he could bite the peak off Mount Duarte without straining his lips. It was him we chose to spread the rumours about me being dead. He's better than a newspaper and people believe what he says. No, I didn't talk to him. He told Rafael. That's how I know.'

'Would you call Mrs Buckmaster and ask her to wait for me at the hotel from four o'clock this afternoon? You can tell her. She knows you're not dead.'

'Thank you for that. If I don't talk to someone soon, I'll die for real. I hear my wife has been to see the insurance company today. That's loyalty for you.'

It was good to hear the old Francisco again. He had a talent for lifting spirits. 'Don't call me again, Francisco. I'm going to be very busy for a few days. Okay?' They said goodbye.

Down the valley, outside the entrance to the airport, Balthasar sat in the back of his taxicab, waiting. He had slept well the night before. The Miner was far away from his thoughts. He felt refreshed and alert. He had given his gunman the day off and left the hotel without paying his bill. He took the key with him and his pistol. No one had noticed him. As he waited for Cunningham to appear, he went over the situation in his mind. He had been treated unfairly, just like he'd been when they'd dismissed him. He was a free agent now and he'd keep an open mind until he knew for certain who could be trusted.

CHAPTER THIRTY-FOUR

The small convoy wound up the hill through Petionville on its way to the mountains and beyond. Tap-tap buses were a familiar sight in Port-au-Prince. No one gave them a second glance. But for the people who rode on the hard wooden benches, the journey was strange and different. Not one of them had ever ridden in a vehicle of any sort. The excitement and elation were shared by everyone except Ti Allain. He had been on tap-taps before, but that was only when he was in town and could spend his money without being seen.

He thought of Monique the black witch and how no one would remain in the village to attend to her grave. The people would now have to face the spirits by themselves and not one of them was ordained to do so. Having reached his middle years, Ti Allain should by now have had a son or a disciple to follow him in his craft. But he had no one. And since he was still very far from death, he waited for the sign that would identify his pupil to him. Two nights before they had set out from the village, Ti Allain had dreamed of the market. It was a short dream, which was significant. Long dreams were never important; they had little to do with other people's fate. They were just poor reflections of the dreamer's own thoughts and hopes and memories and were, therefore, initiated by himself. But short dreams were put in a man's head by the spirits or even the gods. A short dream that had to do with earthly matters could be a very lucky dream indeed.

Ti Allain's short dream had been about the market. He saw himself walking up to a very old lady who was selling honey. He saw her pouring the thick golden liquid from a metal container into used rum bottles. It was flowing very slowly and some had escaped down the outside of the bottles, but Ti Allain saw no flies. That in itself was an important detail because flies were sometimes a sign of sickness, an evil sign. The highlight of his dream was the boy he noticed watching the old lady as she dispensed the honey. She dropped one of the bottles onto the ground and it broke in two. The honey flowed out onto the asphalt. The boy fell on his knees and, while carefully collecting the broken glass, he licked some of the honey off the larger pieces of glass.

There was no blood to be seen, which meant that someone was protecting the boy from harm. He then turned to Ti Allain and smiled and bowed respectfully. At that point the dream ended, leaving Ti Allain to ponder its meaning for the rest of the night. He had wondered where he had seen the boy before. His face was familiar and he could have been a son of the village. And then again he could have possessed a face Ti Allain had seen in one of his other lives.

The boy was sure to materialize one of these days and Ti Allain would recognize him instantly. He saw him once more, in another short dream, one day later. On that occasion the boy was helping him out of his hut. The dream was very clear. As they walked out, Ti Allain saw a face in the mirror that hung by the door. The face he saw was an older version of himself.

He had promised himself he would look for the boy as soon as he got back to the village. It was only because the expedition was delayed and more eventful than usual that the dream had faded from his memory. Now that the spirits had settled things, he could start his search for the boy. If he was meant to find him, he would find him wherever he went.

The tall foreigner did not come to bid them farewell the way Marie-Christine had always done. The small convoy laboured through the countryside, climbing slowly through the mounting heat of the morning, and Ti Allain dozed off. Perhaps sleep would bring him some new sign.

They watched Port-au-Prince disappear below as the plane reached five, then six, seven and eight thousand feet. The land stretched out beneath them and for a while they flew along the coast. The sands and the rocks and the surf played a symphony of colour atop the sparkling, sunlit water. There was not a cloud in sight.

'Perfect day,' said the serious pilot.

The comment was lost in the roar of the engine. His passengers seemed too taken by the view to have listened. Considering that he had only been in Puerto Rico for two months and his knowledge of Spanish was close to zero, the airman was doing well. He had come a long way from Phoenix, Arizona, flying tourists up and down the Grand Canyon. He'd had a craving for the blue vision of water ever since he could remember. And one day, thumbing through the latest issue of an aviation magazine, it had got the better of him.

The small ad for the air taxi service in San Juan had said only Spanish speakers need apply. But his love of flying and his business-like demeanour had won the owners over. There had been only one other candidate for the job and he had a drink problem. Another point in his favour was the fact that he was not considered particularly good-looking. A serious young man, he would not be given to flirting with the female customers whose shopping trips made up a good part of the work. Both his clients and his employers appreciated his discretion, and within a few short weeks he was much in demand. He was not a big spender and was able to save a little money. With a thirty per cent commission on all takings, he stood to make a hefty sum out of this job. Cunningham had told him he was on indefinite hire, all expenses paid.

Cunningham had asked him to search the chart for an airstrip close to Jarabacoa, but he could not make one out. That, he had told the Englishman, did not matter too much. The little Cessna could set down in a field or a straight stretch of road if it had to. Cunningham would have preferred to have someone else with them to guard the plane once they landed. With the market for marijuana growing daily, a light aircraft was always a temptation.

The weather was clear enough that morning for them to cut

through the mountains. It would have taken longer to fly along the coast. Except for the odd up-draught, they were having a smooth ride. They did not talk much. All there was to say had been said the night before. The two passengers sat quietly, their eyes fixed on the terrain. Thick bush soon gave way to royal palms and sugar-cane and huts and houses and animals and roads.

Balthasar was looking for the town of Ferrier, the town that marked the border. Thoughts whirled through his troubled mind. The uneasy thoughts of a convicted man. What if all this was a trick, designed to deliver him up to an old enemy, trussed and oven-ready? Once in the Chief's hands, there would be little he could do. They could listen to him and use him as a witness to bring the plot to an end before it had started. They could kill him.

There was nothing to connect him with the seizure and murder of the Martinez brothers, but that did not matter. If the plane was to land in an unauthorized area, Balthasar could be held for entering the country illegally. Or something. They could always rustle up something at police headquarters. He knew. He had seen it done often enough when he was Chief. His thoughts made terrifying sense, and as they circled the peak of Mount Duarte he became more and more apprehensive.

He turned to study his travelling companion. Cunningham's eyes were closed. He was fast asleep. His face did not betray the menace of a double dealer. What he had said in Haiti was not without foundation. The two rich youngsters had been in his charge and he was accused of sending them to meet Jesus long before their time. The Miner was not going to give him a chance to prove his innocence. What was there for him to lose? The Miner's people were going to use him, then throw him to the dogs. They were educated, they had money, and they were not going to share power with the likes of him. They were going to remove the generals for just that. He was not indispensable. There were others like him where he came from.

But what was there to gain? The Chief was not going to give his job up for him. With his own people out of the force, what possible position could he be offered? The generals to whose side he was about to defect would not remember his help. It would be the Englishman who would reap the fruit. Not him. The Chief of Police would listen and then get rid of him. He would never be allowed to leave Jarabacoa alive. How could he have been so stupid?

An air current woke Cunningham. The short, deep sleep he had sunk into had replaced his weariness with optimistic energy. He was coming back without the Haitians, but the fish in his net was just as big. No one was going to quibble about the price from now on. He would have saved their necks. The police would send a reception committee for the Haitians from now on. He would be established for ever. On top of all that there was the prospect of seeing Marina again. She was waiting for his call and she would come to him tonight. His numbers had been coming up constantly. There were good years ahead. His good fortune just might last.

Sosua and Santiago crawled past below them. The ground seemed closer. 'We'll be near Jarabacoa in about fifteen minutes,' the pilot said. 'Shall I start looking for a suitable place?'

Cunningham turned to Balthasar, about to translate what the man had just said. He looked confused. In his hand, pointing at the pilot's head, the ex-policeman held his old service pistol.

'I think we'd better go back, Cunningham. I don't want the young man to get a fright. Just tell him there has been a change of plan. If we land and go through with this mad scheme, I won't see tomorrow. Look, I didn't mean to make a speech, but I owe you that much. I made a big mistake. So tell him. Tell him now.'

The pilot, concentrating on the ground, was oblivious to the drama playing out behind him. Cunningham's face expressed the shock of complete surprise.

'Don't panic,' Balthasar said. 'The fellow doesn't need to know a thing. Just tell him to go back. I've made a mistake, that's all.'

His matter-of-fact voice steadied Cunningham's nerves. 'You hadn't made a mistake, Balthasar, but you're making one now.'

'I don't expect you to see things my way. It's not the revolution. You're right about that. It's the Chief. He's going to kill me. You know that.'

'Think, Balthasar. Think.'

The pilot turned his head. He did not see the gun. 'There are a couple of straight stretches of black-top road down there. Shall we take her down?'

'No,' Cunningham said. 'Just circle for a bit. Tell me if you see any large trucks. I'll let you know.'

The serious-faced man turned back to his controls. They were flying over El Gordo's land. Balthasar's agitation increased. 'What did you say to him?'

'I told him to circle. I want you to be absolutely sure of what you're doing.' He looked the Dominican square in the face. 'Why don't you put that thing away. I'll forget this ever happened. Let's just get on with it, as we've discussed.'

'So you can hit me over the head and deliver me unconscious? Think of something else.'

'You're reading me wrong. You're reading the whole thing wrong. If you kill the pilot, we both die. You'll have done the Miner's errand for him again. The Haitians will get through anyway.'

'I can shoot you.'

'You're pointing the gun at the wrong head. Anyway, if you kill me, you'll have my people after you, too. Where will you hide then? A man must have a safe house in times of war. You can't fight everybody.'

Balthasar sat back. He pointed the gun at Cunningham, then back at the pilot's neck. 'There is nothing left to say,

Cunningham. I've made up my mind. You have five minutes, then I ...'

'It's not me who's got five minutes, Balthasar, it's you. This is your future we're talking about. You'll get all the credit for this, you know. Not me. The Chief knows how to look after his friends. I've nothing to gain from your downfall, but the Chief could lose an awful lot if I get into trouble. Remember, you've got blood on your hands already. Both here and in Haiti. They were all my friends, yet I was willing to listen to you and co-operate. Above all, I was willing to forgive you. Take you in with me. Say I become stubborn and ignore your threat. You won't kill me because either way you need me. You won't shoot the pilot because that will be your end, too. No one wants to die. Not even you. I'm holding all the cards and yet I'm still talking to you, trying to make you see sense. I don't need to talk at all. I can relax. Why am I still talking, Balthasar?'

'Because you are scared.'

'No, Balthasar. I'm not scared. Your local gun games are not serious. I lost my foot in a real war. You could have killed me back in Haiti. I have no gun. Do you want to go to hell with another name on your list? The only way you can hope to survive this doomed plot is to come with me. Your people don't want you.'

'I trust you. I'd go with you, Cunningham. But I don't trust the Chief. He has a grudge against me.'

'He has what? Are you mad? It's you who have a grudge against him. Wasn't it your job he took? He'd jump at a chance to make it up to you. Think about it. He owes you his job. Now he might owe you his life. You get all the credit and no one will dare prosecute you for the killings.'

'I did not kill the students.'

'No, but your people won't believe that. Even your own boss thinks you did. Anyway, you did have Francisco and his brother shot.'

'That was a misunderstanding.'

'We've been through that before. You were in charge, right?'

'I don't know. I don't know what to think. You confuse me.'

'Look, Balthasar. I'm tired of this ping-pong game. I'm trying to help you and all I get is a gun pointing at me. You win. I'll tell the pilot to turn back. Your presence in Haiti is useless anyway. As soon as we get back, you won't see me for dust. The Haitians are on their way. And you – if the Haitian police don't get you, the Miner's people will. What do I care? It's your head.'

Cunningham tapped the pilot's shoulder and told him in Spanish to turn around. Below, there was a fine stretch of straight, hard-surfaced road with not a vehicle in sight. The pilot did not hear what was said, but he nodded. 'It's better laid than the runway at Port-au-Prince,' Cunningham said.

Balthasar heard the casual mention of the Haitian capital and assumed that Cunningham had given the order to return there. The Englishman was not bluffing. He seemed to relax visibly. He'd been right yet again. Balthasar thrust the pistol into the waistband of his trousers.

'*Está bien*, Cunningham. I have nothing to lose. Tell him to land here, but God help you if they try anything. If I must die, I swear we'll go to hell together.'

'Put us down there,' Cunningham pointed. The pilot nodded again and started altering the power settings and lining them up for an approach. He eased the stick forward as he reduced power. 'Fasten your seat belts please, gentlemen,' he said.

'I'll guarantee your safety myself, Balthasar,' Cunningham said. 'You know you can rely on me.'

'I am just a little confused.'

'I'm not surprised. In your position, I would be too.'

The pilot was concentrating hard, making sure they stayed on the glide-path. The thin mountain air was still. The plane descended, its wings as steady as a rock. The pilot reduced the power some more. On both sides of the plane, green mountains and cultivated fields and palms raced backwards to the rhythmic clatter of the engine. And then, as the plane touched down on the road with hardly a bump, they became part of the earth again.

There was little left for Cunningham to do. Get Balthasar to the Chief's house and leave. Let the guest tell his host of the Miner's plot. He was out of it now. In his mind, he was already walking the magic path through the enchanted garden that was the American woman. He would hold her hand and look into her endless blue eyes and forget everything else.

CHAPTER THIRTY-FIVE

God, how he missed it all being stuck there, out of circulation, away from the delicious gossip at Antonio's Bar, away from the action. The people around him were nice enough and he had known them since they were children together, but he had moved on and they hadn't. He'd seen greener pastures and they'd just grown older and duller. It was especially bad in the afternoons, like now. It was time for a beer and a discussion, but here no one dared contradict him. Here everybody treated him like a king. With not an argument in sight, he began to miss his wife.

The only contact he had with the outside world was the dusty old telephone. It stood there, on top of a broken-down piano no one had played for years, provoking him. Teasing his fingers. Come on, Francisco, the instrument said, use me. Dial. Call someone. The American woman. She might have heard something. Even if her Spanish was bad, it would be a breath of fresh air.

Marina picked up the phone at the first hint of a sound. 'Cunningham,' she said softly, 'at last.'

'No, lady. Is no Cunningham. Is Francisco Martinez.'

She hadn't heard yet from his friend, she said. She uttered a few nervous sentences, but Francisco could not understand any of it. He told her that Rafael, the taxi driver, was standing by outside her hotel in case she needed any transportation. He repeated that until she understood. She said she was going to meet Cunningham, but did not know where. She was sure to hear soon.

Did she like Chiquito's daughter? he asked. No, he did not want to speak to her. He only wanted to know if she liked her. That's all. She went on talking for a bit and then, as she waited for him to reply, he said he had to go. Someone was coming in, but he'd call her again as soon as he could. They brought him the first beer of the afternoon. Speaking to the lady was all the tonic he needed. His brain started simmering again and his depression lifted.

Marina had kissed her husband goodbye an hour before. She would see to the house, she had assured him. They would move in as soon as he was back. He could leave it all to her. He had nothing to worry about. She was going through a bad patch, that's all. Not his fault. Nothing to do with him. It would all be better when he came back. It was good for him to get away from her. She knew she hadn't been much of a wife these past few days.

He said he'd call her as soon as he knew when he'd be able to get back. She wished him luck and a safe journey, and then he was gone. Chiquito's daughter had taken the children down to the pool and at last she was alone. In the quiet of her bedroom, Marina settled down to wait for Cunningham's call. Just one more time, and then it would all be over and her life could resume its course. It was three o'clock in the afternoon and soon, in an hour, the telephone would ring.

Francisco's call was confusing. She had been nervous, but it reassured her. She had not been dreaming. There was a man called Cunningham in her life. And she would see him again. Just one more time. Please God, make sure he calls. Just one more time with him before it settled in her mind and turned into the sweetest memory. He would ask her to join him. Of course he would. He must.

She had laid her plans. Gerald would be out of town. Chiquito's daughter was on hand to look after the girls. She could easily take off. Just one more fling. She had no right to expect any more. Just to see how she felt. Perhaps she'd gotten over this strange obsession; she might not even want him any more. She might not feel a thing. But she had to find out. And for that she'd need to see him. Just once more.

Guy changed down into second gear. Just what in hell was holding them up? he wondered, as he looked in the rear-view mirror. At this rate they would never make the distillery in time for Cunningham's call. It wasn't as if the road was particularly steep. Where the tap-taps had slowed to a crawl there was hardly a hill at all. He should have made the lazy bastards walk, he cursed. He watched the whole convoy grind to a halt. The lead vehicle had broken down. Guy turned the car and set off back to the stalled column.

'Didn't I tell you to have the bus checked before we left?' he shouted.

'I'm sorry,' said the driver with an embarrassed smile. 'The water in the radiator is boiling. There are twenty people in the back and it is a hot day.'

Guy told the man roughly to lift the bonnet and looked at the ticking engine himself. 'Well,' he said, 'you'll have to wait until it cools down. We might as well let the men stretch their legs.'

'What about me?' asked Ti Allain. 'Can I go back to the village now?'

'Stop whining, will you? The *patron* said he wanted everybody. You stay where you are.'

'I am not meant to go to the other country. I have never been there and there's much to be done here. How will you find more men, next time, if I'm not here?'

'Just shut up and do what you're told.'

Ti Allain was not in the least surprised that the tap-tap had broken down. He had been sitting in the front with the lead driver and had had hours to examine him thoroughly. He had the face of a bird with shifty eyes and a hooked nose. He moved erratically and had the strange habit of wiping the sweat from his rounded forehead upwards instead of sideways. Then he would rub it into his thinning hair. He had told Ti Allain that sweat was good for hair. He expected, he said, his hair to come back soon. Ti Allain said nothing. He wasn't fooled for a moment. He knew the driver was not really a man at all, but a bird that tried to conceal its identity behind human vanity.

Every man has his origins, which come from his parents' blood and his destiny, which is his own. A man's destiny can always be determined from his face, his expressions and movements and the shape of his head. A man's looks often decide his character. He learns to react to the way people react to him, and thus he sets his own course and therefore his fate.

Once, when Ti Allain was younger and even smaller in stature, he saw a strange man walking through his village. He had the face of a dog and the eyes and the tongue of a dog. He was pulling a small cart, laden with boxes full of live rats. He was on his way to the market at Petionville where there was a customer waiting for his vermin. Ti Allain had emerged at that moment to place a garland of lizard tails at the foot of Monique's white pole, and the man stopped right next to him. He was breathing heavily, the air entering and leaving his mouth in quick, windy gasps. His tongue hung far out between his brown teeth, almost touching his chin. He was lost, he said. Could Ti Allain tell him the way to Petionville?

It was two weeks later when Ti Allain heard that the man had been torn to pieces by dogs at the gate of a big, iron-fenced house close by the market. The rats had gone, scattered all over Petionville, evading the buyer. Ti Allain could not imagine who would have wanted the rats, but he had known the dogs well enough. Had they not been outside the big house in the first place, the spirits would have put them there for the occasion. No man can ever escape his destiny. He can only pretend, but few can pretend long enough to fool the spirits.

On the ride from Diquini, Ti Allain had been watching the man preen while pretending to push the sweat off his forehead into his hair. He knew that when the man was satisfied, he would make the bus stop. He didn't really want to be a driver, or roam the countryside on rubber wheels. He wanted to be a bird, to take to the sky and be with the birds. Ti Allain knew that the man would find his way up there somehow, just like the dog man had found his way to be with other dogs.

Ti Allain watched all this and said nothing. A man must never know about his own destiny. It could be dangerous. He might, if it was good, lose all desire to improve himself; if it was bad, he might become a danger to others since he knew he was going to come to a bad end anyway. If you knew where and how to look, you could see other people's destiny written in their face and manners, but most mortals were too busy to do that. Especially in a land of hunger and poverty like Haiti.

The buses had all stopped. Ti Allain did not join the milling flock of people on the road. He did not need to go out because he had all the comfort of the bird man's cabin. There was no call to tempt the spirits further. The sun was right up in the sky and he could not communicate with them now unless it was urgent, and it was not. Perhaps the bus stopped to give him a chance to get away, but that was a man-made sign and he needed something much more substantial.

The tall foreigner should have come to see them off. La Grande Marie had said he was a generous man, but where was his generosity now? He hadn't even given Ti Allain his usual fee. Of course, it could have been the Haitian Guy who kept him away. Guy had never been as important before and as long as the foreigner was absent, he could remain important. He had ignored Ti Allain completely since the last, short interchange, had not even looked in his direction. He was driving Marie-Christine's car and sat in it splendidly, all by himself. Perhaps, Ti Allain thought, he had not even told the tall foreigner who Ti Allain was or about his prominent place in society. Perhaps he would have to cross the border with the others.

Should he pretend he wanted to go over to Saint Domingue? What was it like there? What would they make him do? Ti Allain's anxiety was fast turning into fear and he wished night would come and pull the sun into the sea. But darkness was a long way away and it seemed to him that the spirits were too.

CHAPTER THIRTY-SIX

The pilot stood by the Cessna's port wingtip, looking around at the countryside. He had never been in the Dominican Republic before. It was a place of soft hills and order. There were flowers and, to mark where the fields began and ended, the farmers had planted stakes of *framboyan*, which sprouted new leaves, forming themselves into strangely symmetrical hedges. There were no houses or people to be seen and pine trees grew in dark shadows cast by royal palms and tall coconut trees. There were many trees, dark green and pastel green and some with ruby-red leaves. They had landed in a cool, snowless alpine valley not fifty miles from the Caribbean Sea. A long, long way from parched Phoenix.

They had man-handled the plane off the road and now they waited for someone to pass by. It was nearly four o'clock in the afternoon and the heat had gone from the fields. The air was crisp and clean and the eye could travel for ever.

'We could use the radio,' the pilot said.

Cunningham shook his head. 'No need for that,' he said.

'This land belongs to a friend of mine. And I can promise you he knows everything that moves on it.'

'Is he expecting us?'

'No. That's why we cannot call him. He would be offended if we paid him a visit without giving him notice in advance. In these parts, people really like to spread the red carpet for guests. Any excuse for a party. They don't have much of a social life here, but they are sticklers for protocol.'

'What are you going to tell him?' asked Balthasar.

'Just that we had a small problem with the engine and had to land to clear it up. Of course, we've fixed it now, but when I found out we were on his land, well, of course, I couldn't go on without saying hello to an old friend.'

In the distance, they heard the sound of an engine. Moments later a small car materialized, speeding in their direction. It bumped over a little bridge, then pulled up a respectful distance away from the plane. A burly young man jumped out. He looked at the machine and the people who had come down with it and he asked if they needed any help.

'Not any more,' Cunningham said, focusing a disarming smile on the youth. 'We had a little trouble with the magneto, but it's all right now. Could you perhaps tell us where we are?'

'You are about ten miles from Jarabacoa, señor. This is El Gordo's ranch. He owns everything you can see from here to that mountain up there.'

'El Gordo? But he is an old friend of mine. I thought we were nearer to Constanza, where they grow flowers.'

'That belongs to the Japanese, señor. Here we raise cattle for beef and milk. Coffee too. And beans and tobacco.'

'Do you work for El Gordo?'

'Everybody in these parts works for El Gordo, señor. You really know him? In person?'

'Oh yes, I know him, and Señora Teresa, too. And his daughter Pilar. Still winning prizes on her horses, is she?' Cunningham turned to Balthasar and winked. 'El Gordo likes nothing better than hanging those trophies on the stone walls of his study. He wouldn't mount a horse these days. He'd tell you himself the animal's back would break if he did. Three years ago, El Gordo fell off Pilar's horse and made a hole in the ground, dislocating his foot into the bargain.'

'That's true.' The young man nodded with great gusto. 'Would you like me to take you to the house, señor?'

'We can't leave the plane here, young man.'

'Nothing will happen to it on Señor El Gordo's land.'

'Sadly, it's against the law to leave an aircraft unattended. What a shame. El Gordo will be mad when he hears we've been here without calling on him. Well, you'll have to explain for us. Tell him I said not to blow his top with you. It wasn't your fault we couldn't pay him a visit. Tell him Cunningham was here, all right?'

'Please, señor, I beg you, you can trust me. I will stay here with your aeroplane while you take my car and visit with the *Jefe*.'

'No, no. I couldn't. You know what El Gordo's like. He'll offer us a drink and then dinner and a game of dominoes. We couldn't do that to you. You'll be here all night. Your wife and family will worry about you.'

'I am not married, señor. And I would be proud to watch your aeroplane. I drive the big tractor and tomorrow is Sunday. Please let me stay.'

'I must tell El Gordo about you. What is your name?'

'Montoya, señor. Carlos Montoya.'

'I'll remember that. Carlos Montoya, the tractor man. Won't you be hungry later, Carlos?'

'Oh no, señor. I was on my way to the cock fight when I saw your aeroplane. I have some food in the car. I will be all right, señor. Please, you take my car. I will just sit in the aeroplane, watch out for it and be sure not to touch anything. There will be another cock fight next Saturday. You take the car, señor.'

'Well, if you're sure ... thank you very much, Carlos.'

'It is for me to thank you, señor.'

Later, as they sat in El Gordo's spacious living room, Cunningham began to wonder how they would ever get to see the Chief on time. Their host couldn't have been more attentive, constantly calling for more and different snacks and drinks. Perhaps the visit was a mistake. Now the fat man threatened he might throw a party for them that evening. Cunningham protested, but more trays appeared. Rice and peas. Roast lamb and chicken. Heaps of beans.

'May I use your telephone, Gordito?'

'Cunningham, please don't offend me by asking. This house and all that's in it are yours.'

Cunningham slipped across the hallway to the office. It was nearly five o'clock and he got through to Marina in seconds. He told her he couldn't talk, but would she like to come to Santiago and meet him at the Hotel Matun that evening? Yes, she said. 'Would you wait there for the driver? He'll know where to meet Francisco. I'm sorry to be short, but you understand. You always understand. It may be late before I get there, but I'll be there. I'm longing to see you.'

'Yes, Cunningham,' she said simply. 'Yes.'

He called Francisco.

'Thank God, Cunningham. I am going mad here. Can't you do something?'

'Yes. That's why I'm calling you. Get hold of Rafael, tell him to go to the hotel and pick up Mrs Buckmaster.'

'He's there already. He's been waiting outside the Hispaniola since three o'clock.'

'Good. Tell him to pick you up along the way. You're coming to Santiago. I don't want the lady traipsing around the countryside on her own and the change of air will do you good, too. Get her some flowers, please, but make sure someone else goes out to get them. And bring your gun.'

'You might have told me you're back in the country, Cunningham. You have no idea what it's been like cooped up here, unable to go anywhere. Unable to ...'

'If you hadn't killed those two students there would have

been no need for any of this. Because of it your usefulness to this operation is strictly limited now. So don't start complaining to me. Just get yourself going. I want you to be on the road to Santiago within the hour.' He put the phone down.

Back in the main living room, Balthasar and El Gordo were engrossed in a conversation about beef cattle. Pilar, with the pilot in tow, was on her way out of the door. 'Just going to see the horses,' said the young man, reddening slightly. Balthasar, comfortably settled on the chesterfield with a cigar in his mouth, was on his third beer. He was getting on famously with the rich landowner. He had to hand it to Cunningham. He certainly had classy friends. He could get on with the others too, if they were anything like this one. A sensible man, who knew how to listen. If this was the kind of relationship Cunningham had with the Chief, why, it would be clear sailing from here on.

El Gordo was more than happy to have his old friend Cunningham in the house, but Balthasar's presence puzzled and disturbed him. The reason for his anxiety was his own ace in the hole, his part in the Miner's conspiracy. Because of his close relationship with the Chief's brother in Jarabacoa, his involvement with the planned revolution had never been revealed to any of the others. El Gordo spent much time up with the Chief, listening to conversations the policeman had with his army friends. As a close neighbour, his cover was perfect. The information he passed to the Miner was invaluable.

El Gordo had joined the Miner because of his instinct for survival. He was not searching for a better world. He was a businessman who did not believe in backing the losing side. His loyalties were strictly reserved for his family and the people on his estate. The sheer strength behind the Miner and his friends had convinced him that they had a fair chance of success. Besides, his known family ties with the deposed Trujillos did not endear him to the current regime. He'd had to play the good chap for a long, long while before they'd even started to accept him.

In truth, El Gordo did not care either way. He was playing a waiting game with his cards close to his chest and his loyalties lay firmly with the winning side. Whoever that might be, El Gordo would be safe. Of the revolutionaries, only the Miner knew the truth and he would never survive if things went wrong. If that happened, El Gordo would be above suspicion. The Chief and the generals would be convinced he had always been one of them.

He was, therefore, seized by trepidation when Cunningham showed up with the Miner's hit-man by his side. He was not too worried about the Englishman. They had no intention of putting him out of business for good. As soon as the revolution was over, they'd let him bring in his Haitians again. When the subject had been raised, El Gordo had been happy enough with the plan. Stopping this season's immigration and making it look like the Chief's doing had seemed straightforward. His only concern had been for Cunningham himself, but the Miner had promised him he would come to no harm. Being a foreigner, he was in no one's way.

It could have been an accident. The two might have reached an agreement. Cunningham might have consented to join the Miner, but why were they both here, so close to Jarabacoa and the Chief? El Gordo had not forgotten Cunningham's call from Haiti. He had asked him for the Chief's number. There was more to it. Either Balthasar had defected or else he had been sent by the Miner into the lion's den. To eliminate the Chief? The Miner had said it was going to be a peaceful revolution. To spy? He would have been told, El Gordo reassured himself. The Miner had given him his word that no one would operate inside the Chief's camp without his knowledge. Balthasar must have gone over to the other side. Or was about to.

This information had to be passed on to the Miner without delay. He was hoping the Englishman would say they were going somewhere else. But Cunningham had made his telephone calls and sat with them, staring into space as if he had all the time in the world. Balthasar was steadily rendering himself immobile with all the alcohol he was consuming. He wasn't going to kill anyone.

El Gordo turned to Cunningham. 'I bet you were talking to some woman back there. I've seen that lecherous expression before.'

'Cunningham is a ladies' man,' Balthasar said, his eyes shining.

'Who is the lucky one, eh? You have always stuck to one at a time. Always married to someone else. A real romantic.'

'As it happens, you're right,' Cunningham said. 'The problem is, I've got to be in Sosua. I haven't got a car.'

'But of course you have a car. You can use the one you arrived in. I told you. This house and everything in it are yours. I hope she's pretty.'

'Oh, that she is. And she's got a sister, too.'

'Thank you. That's very nice of you.'

'Not this time, Gordo. She's spoken for. I've promised Balthasar a good time. I'm really grateful for the car, though. It's getting late. By the time we get back to the plane ... Talking of the plane, where's that pilot?'

'He's looking over the place with my daughter.'

'Well, he must have seen it all by now. Let me go and get him.'

That must not happen, El Gordo thought. He'd have to make sure the two could not leave the country until he knew what they were there for. 'Unless you need to carry dead weight to Sosua,' El Gordo said with a smile, 'you should leave him here with us. Pilar's English needs improving.'

'We'd better go now, if that's okay with you,' Cunningham said. 'Let me ask the young man if he wants to stay.'

'Nonsense,' El Gordo said. 'Leave him be. We'll look after him. You two run along and have a good time. We'll have a party for you when you get back.'

One could always count on El Gordo, Cunningham thought as they got up to take their leave. It was only a few miles to the Chief's place. They were going to be there on time.

CHAPTER THIRTY-SEVEN

The cool mountain air cast a hostile spell on the royal palms. Only a handful of tropical plants survived within the pine forests around Jarabacoa. The slanted roofs, wooden walls and painted windows reminded Cunningham of the Swiss chalets he had known long ago on his holidays with his father. Outside the houses and along the window sills, flower pots burst with pink and red geraniums. Up above, the chimney pots puffed white smoke into the evening sky.

This was the first time Cunningham had been up here, to the Chief's hide-out. It was a small, exclusive place where the rich escaped from the heat of the cities below. Many of them, Balthasar had said, were associates of the Miner, and as they entered the village he crouched down in the back of the car. They were, he said, in enemy territory.

The Chief was waiting for them outside the gateway of his house. Tall and thin, and dressed simply in a heavy sweater, he wore thick-rimmed glasses and sported a pipe. He could have been a schoolteacher or a clerk and only the presence of two armed men with attack dogs on short leashes reminded Cunningham of who it was they had come to see.

'Come in, come in,' the Chief said with a broad smile. 'You must be freezing, dressed like that. Leave the car right there. One of my men will park it for you. There's a fire inside, *amigos*, and some drinks to warm your insides.' He and Cunningham embraced, each tapping the other's back. He then extended his hand to the other man.

'It's good to see you again, Balthasar,' he said. He'd never called him by his Christian name before, but now he had been Chief for almost five years and could afford the familiarity.

'Nice to see you too, *Jefe*,' Balthasar said with a solemn face. 'Circumstances change and men must change with them, no?'

The Chief turned to lead them into his house. He looked puzzled, as if he didn't quite know what to make of his predecessor's remark. Well, he shrugged mentally, he's welcome to come inside with Cunningham. But whether he leaves here dead or alive depends entirely on what he has to say. He could hardly wait to hear it.

'We must talk,' the Chief said as soon as they were all seated.

'Do you get any preferential treatment from the telephone company?'

'Certainly, Cunningham. What do you need?'

'I have to make a call to a small town in Haiti. Perhaps you two can talk things over in the meantime.'

'Let the sergeant book the call for you. He is in the kitchen.'

The two police chiefs, past and present, walked into the domino room where a log fire burned. The Chief took a chair by the table and motioned Balthasar to another. He selected a cigar from the humidor, pushed the matches towards his guest and accepted a light from him.

'Take one yourself, Balthasar,' he said sternly, 'then tell me your story.'

In the kitchen, Cunningham got through to the distillery. Guy answered the telephone himself. He sounded alert. 'We are short of one bus. It had a faulty water pump. But we'll manage. I can squeeze seven of them in my car. The rest will have to manage as best they can in the other buses.'

'No other problems?'

'A little bother with the man Ti Allain, but that can wait until we cross.'

'Good. Stay the night at the distillery. It is close enough to Ferrier. You should easily reach it by tomorrow afternoon. Go into Gautier's Pharmacy. It's right in the centre. Tell him Marcel Kinet sent you and give him fifty dollars.'

'But Monsieur Kinet is dead!'

'It doesn't matter. Marcel was the contact, that's all. Just do as I say. Gautier will take you to his mango orchard. It's about ten minutes away from the town. It straddles the border. Do you remember Francisco Martinez?'

'Of course, monsieur.'

'In case I can't be there myself, Francisco Martinez will be. He'll give you the rest of the money due to you after you hand the people over to him.'

'Thank you, Monsieur Cunningham. *Au revoir.*'

That was a man to watch, Cunningham thought as he replaced the receiver. The end was close now. Soon, Francisco would arrive in Santiago with Marina. The thought of seeing her again elated him. He tapped the sergeant's shoulder and pushed a ten-peso bill into his hand. He entered the smoke-filled domino room. The other two men were hunched, facing each other across the table, locked in hushed conversation. The Chief broke off and turned to Cunningham.

'You can't trust anybody, can you?' he lamented. 'I have helped every one of these bastards out of one sort of jam or another ever since I took over. They are supposed to be my friends. Have I not helped them over stupid tickets? And their fat children? How many dope-smoking charges have I burned to keep the brats out of jail, eh? That's gratitude for you.'

'It's nothing personal, Chief,' Cunningham said. 'All they want is to get the generals away from their cash. You must admit they've been overdoing it. They know you've hardly ever taken a thing for yourself, Chief. The generals should have taken a leaf out of your book. It's a class thing really, that's all. Not all the bigwigs are behind the Miner. Only the old families.'

'El Gordo is as rich as any of them. Is he in it too?'

'No,' Balthasar said.

'And what about Fernando Bogard?'

Balthasar shook his head.

219

'There's no logic in it, Cunningham,' the Chief said. 'It's a war without rules.'

'There never are any rules in war, Chief,' Cunningham said, and looked at his watch.

'Are you in a hurry?'

'Yes, I am. I've got to see to the Haitians. But you, instead of worrying over rules and families, just worry about the facts. Balthasar and I are on your side. The Haitians are being delivered on time, the cane will be cut and the farmers will have no excuse to hold a grudge against you. The Miner will have to think of some other pretext to start his revolution. They might even forget about throwing you out. It's the army they're after anyway. I hope you appreciate what Balthasar has done for you, telling you all this, Chief. If the other side find out, he's in deep trouble.'

'Don't you worry about that, Cunningham. I know how to look after my friends. Should we bring the Miner in?'

'On what charge, Chief? He hasn't done a thing.'

'He's done plenty.'

'Chief, officially he's done nothing. Officially, you know nothing. You can't bring Balthasar forward as a witness without signing his death warrant, and once they get to him you can't prove a thing. It's all just a plan at this stage, and you know all about it. What could be better? All you need do is just sit tight and wait.'

'That's right,' Balthasar said eagerly. 'It's an advantage to have your enemy believe you are ignorant.'

'All right, all right,' the Chief said. 'Don't you worry, Balthasar, my old friend. The Miner won't be able to touch you. If the police say you've had nothing to do with the killings, he might even believe it himself. But those others, would you believe those ungrateful bastards?'

'I've got to get going,' Cunningham said, but between the Chief's fit of self-pity and Balthasar slurping his beer down with optimistic zest, no one heard.

The telephone rang and the Chief picked it up himself. He

listened for a few minutes and his face brightened. The caller was making him laugh.

'This couldn't have come at a better time,' he said with a broad smile. 'Tonight? Yes of course we'll be there, thank you. Who would miss an El Gordo party? Yes, sure. Balthasar and Cunningham will be coming too.'

'I can't make it,' Cunningham said. 'I've got to go to Santiago to meet a certain lady. Are you sure Balthasar should be seen in this country?'

'It's only El Gordo and his family. Balthasar will come with me. What better way to celebrate this reunion? If Cunningham wants to go chasing skirt, we won't stop him. Anyway, even Cunningham can't keep it up all night. He can join us later. El Gordo's parties go on until dawn.'

They stood together by the gate to wave Cunningham off. He thought they looked incongruous there, like an old married couple. He started the car and watched the Chief take Balthasar by the arm to lead him back to the house for more beer and cigars. He whistled a happy tune as the headlamps danced down the road. And Marina would be there, waiting. It would take him an hour to reach Santiago and he would lose himself in Marina's arms while Francisco went to the border to take care of the Haitians. He'd averted a revolution and that meant this was his country now. There was nothing left for him in England. There never would be.

If women had ruled the world, he thought, there would be no need to overthrow anybody. They would bicker and argue and envy each other's diamonds and lovers, but there would be no generals and no guns and no revolutions. Women hate uniforms. They would never wear the same thing day in and day out.

Chapter Thirty-Eight

He hadn't been sleeping too well lately. The prospect of an upheaval was upsetting him. El Gordo knew only too well that ultimately it was the man in the street who provided him with his livelihood. And when, after a revolution, a new ruler mounted the steps of the Presidential Palace, that man stayed at home. Neither buying, nor selling, he would wait, holding on to what he had, ignoring what he did not have.

El Gordo had survived the trauma of change after the fall of Trujillo. The dictator had ruled the country for so long, it had seemed as if, like God, he had always been there. He had left his mark on coins, statues and manhole covers alike. There was some comfort in the order, harsh as it was, that prevailed during his lifetime. When Trujillo was killed, El Gordo had to start all over again. The last thing he wanted was a revolution, but the Miner had talked him round. The man in the street, the Miner had argued, would not know a change was taking place because this time there would be no bloodshed. And to succeed, El Gordo would have to be on the winning side.

As soon as Cunningham and Balthasar had left his house, El Gordo was on the phone to the Miner. He told him, in terse phrases, of the visit he'd just had. He then asked just one question: had the Miner sent Balthasar to see the Chief?

'No way,' the Miner said softly. 'Let me look into this. Tell me, Gordito, could you get Cunningham and Balthasar back into your house, later tonight?'

'I could try,' El Gordo said. 'Would it matter if the Chief came along too?'

'It would not,' the Miner said. 'Just make sure Balthasar is there.'

El Gordo said he would invite the three men over for a party. The Miner thanked him and said he'd let him know what the next move was to be. Now the Miner was on the phone again. He was as calm as ever. He was pleased to hear that El Gordo's plan for a party had worked.

'I want you', he ordered the fat man, 'to get Balthasar to spend the night in your house. We'll have to liquidate him.'

'Are you mad? Didn't you say there would be no blood this time? And anyway, am I not supposed to be a silent partner in this deal? If you kill Balthasar at my house, my cover will be blown wide open. Where will my usefulness be then?'

'We'll think of something. It will have to be done before he goes back to Haiti.'

'If he's got to get back to Haiti, why don't you have it done there?'

'Can't get anyone there in time. The other man is Balthasar's own choice. His pal. He'd never touch him. I could have someone there by tomorrow, but that would give him time to escape.'

'Escape? Why should he escape? As far as he's concerned, you think he's still in Haiti, stopping Cunningham's workers from leaving. You could hire a professional. Send him to meet Balthasar in Haiti on some pretext.'

'Balthasar knows every hit-man in the country. He used to be Chief of Police, remember?'

'Send a friend, then. Someone dedicated. Surely, if he knew the man had come from you ...'

'That wouldn't work. We had harsh words. I threatened him. Lost control.'

'Perhaps that made him go over.'

'Perhaps it did. The fact is, we have to get rid of him. It will have to look like the Englishman's people did it. They have plenty of reasons. Balthasar's killed four of his people. Two were close friends. You just make sure Balthasar and Cunningham stay in your house tonight.'

'You'll have to find some other way to discredit the Chief.'

'We might still stop the Haitians. We could get rid of Cunningham, too.'

'Killing Cunningham won't stop them,' El Gordo said.

'They are already on their way. The man is a good organizer. The best. He used to be a British officer. He won't have left anything to chance. I believe someone is managing it for him. I know the man well, Miner. I only wish you did, too. He'd never have promised to let me have them in time otherwise. Anyway, you are killing the wrong people. I thought we only wanted to get rid of the generals. You could make it look like it was Cunningham himself who killed Balthasar. On the way to Haiti or something. You said he's got plenty of reasons for doing it. He'd be locked up and out of the way. As effective as killing him, no?'

'Could be. I'll be in touch,' the Miner said quietly, and hung up.

Pilar and the pilot came in from the stables to have drinks. The fat man hoped Cunningham would turn up at the party or at least call. Otherwise he would not get the chance to warn him. He had promised to bring the car back later that night and had always kept his word.

Make it tonight, dear God, later tonight. Or sooner if it pleases you. And thank you, Lord, El Gordo thought, for making me keep the pilot in the house. At least, with the plane on my land, the rascal will come back here for it. El Gordo was not a religious man, but for his friend's sake he hoped the Almighty was tuned in. Just in case he was there, El Gordo looked up at the sky and his lips whispered a little prayer.

CHAPTER THIRTY-NINE

There were lots of empty rum casks strewn outside the distillery and the one that was meant for him lay by the old moss-covered wall. It seemed larger than the others and Ti Allain lined its rounded wooden floor with the soft green grass that grew up there in abundance. He lay down on his back, facing the stars, and began talking to the spirits. Quietly, gently, he whispered of his discontent.

He had placed a little ball of steamed rice on his forehead, right between the eyes, to feed them if they were hungry. It was always safer to offer food to the spirits. As with men, food would put them in a more amiable listening mood. They had all been people once and they knew about steamed rice even if they couldn't eat it.

Things were bad, he told them. He did not want to complain, but shouldn't they have brought him back to the village by now, to attend to Monique the black witch? Her stake had not been painted afresh for six days and grass might have grown around it. No one had hung any fresh lizards or bird tails on it and he begged them to make sure she forgave him.

She must surely have known that he was where he should not have been. Without being paid he could not leave, even if he could find the way back. He had hoped that Guy the black driver would pay him and take him back himself. But Guy did not appear to understand, hard as he had tried to explain it all to him. He just kept on saying that they would be paid once they were across the border cutting cane. No one expected them to work for nothing, he'd said, and he had money only for food and fuel and bribes, not to pay workers who hadn't even begun to work yet. Ti Allain had wanted to tell Guy he was not a worker. But Guy was a man who could talk to tap-tap bus engines and to telephones. He was the man who was taking them to Saint Domingue. No one could upset him. That was why Ti Allain needed the spirits to intervene. He would not have imposed himself on them otherwise.

Surely, he whispered, the spirits knew that Guy was only pretending to be a great leader. Was he not just following the orders given to him by the one-legged foreigner? He knew the spirits could make the one-legged foreigner tell Guy that Ti Allain was not like the others. The people themselves could have told him that. But Guy would not have listened to them because they were from the country and he was a city man and better than them. That was why Ti Allain had to appeal to the spirits and he apologized for doing it so often, as if he thought only of himself. The man Guy had always addressed the people through Ti Allain, and that surely meant that Guy knew he was special. But the day had gone away, the evening had passed, and then the night brought the stars and still he was there, not paid for his efforts.

Only the spirits knew how generous Ti Allain had been with the money he had received from La Grande Marie in the past. How he had helped the others in the village. How often he had led those who had failed to pass the inspection back to the village and fed them all out of his own pocket. Could they not see their way to helping him out of his plight now?

If only he could find a rat with which to please Monique and the others. Steamed rice was good, but not the best, and as his situation became desperate, Ti Allain needed the best. He closed his eyes to hide his soul from the spirits and he thought of what had happened earlier in the day. Just after they had arrived at the distillery, Ti Allain had tried to catch Guy's attention and had failed. He had tried to talk to Guy with words, but those had fallen on deaf ears. Now he chose to talk to him with the rabbit-in-cage dance because it spoke clearly of his feelings. But people from the great city of Port-au-Prince did not understand the special meaning of a dance. And Guy had never seen a rabbit-in-cage dance before, which was regrettable since Ti Allain had always enjoyed it and his performance of it was famous.

He had whirled and moaned and waved his arms and his face had shown the rabbit's suffering and his yearning to roam free in the distant green field that was his home. His feet climbed imaginary steps to show how the rabbit tried to get out of the cage and he licked his hands to ease the injuries the rabbit had suffered in the process. Ti Allain put his whole soul into the dance, but as he watched Guy out of the corner of his eye he saw plainly that the man did not understand what the dance meant. He wore a bored expression right up to the point where the rabbit gave up and settled in the corner of the cage to await his executioners. When that dramatic climax arrived, Guy had actually yawned, and Ti Allain spoke to him in Creole, using simple words as he would to a child. But Guy had lost patience with him and dismissed him with a loud, humiliating curse.

To enhance the effect of those harsh words, Ti Allain was obliged to wash his ears with muddy water. He had spent the rest of the daylight hours making a cloth doll in the shape of Guy. That was quite a good way of drawing people to oneself, especially when one pricked the doll's head with a pin dipped in one's own spittle or blood. He pulled the pin out of his collar, lifted Guy's cloth image and looked at it. He took great care not to prick the doll's heart since that might have killed the Haitian Guy, which was something he had to avoid. The spirits would do that if he deserved to die, but surely not before the people crossed the border and he was paid in full.

And so it came about that Ti Allain, in the dark of night, lay inside an empty rum barrel, far from his village, talking gently to the spirits with a ball of rice between his eyes. He would have preferred to have a living being, such as a rat, in his right hand while looking at the stars. That would surely have drawn the spirits' attention to him earlier. But then again, at that hour of the night, when most people were asleep, time did not matter so much. The spirits were bound to turn their attention to him eventually, even without a living being in his right hand. They would notice him because they were everywhere. They owned eternity. It was late in the day for man, but early enough for them, and so he waited.

At the Hotel Matun in the Dominican city of Santiago, Francisco Martinez was listening to Cunningham's instructions. Now that Francisco was taking charge of the operation, there was much to discuss and plan. Once the Haitians had crossed Gautier's mango plantation into the Republic, Francisco was to assemble them all into trucks that would discreetly wait for them a little distance away. Francisco would then deliver the workers to Fernando Bogard, El Gordo, the Chief's brother and the others.

There were, Cunningham said, more Haitians than he had contracted for, and he left it to Francisco to place them. He could keep all that money to himself, after paying for the transport. It was, Cunningham said, to be a bonus of appreciation for his suffering and his efforts. It would be best if Francisco and Rafael could set out for the border quickly, under cover of darkness, to wait for Guy.

Marina sat quietly on the bed while they talked. She did not say a word. It seemed that eternity, not just two days, had gone by since their madness in Puerto Rico. He would now, she hoped, keep his promise and take her to the coast. There they would walk on the sand again and watch the water. A different stretch of land, beautiful beaches and palm forests, would wait for them up north. The coconut-water vendors, the fish fryers, the oysters and lime boys and, most of all, those haunting nights with their crickets would be the canopy of their love, their last refuge. Yet for all her expectations, a feeling of finality was creeping into her bones. Or perhaps she was just tired.

He had not said much to her. Perhaps it was because Francisco was there. By the time the two men ended their deliberations' and Francisco was gone, she had fallen asleep. Cunningham turned the light off, pulled the cover over her body, and sat beside her watching her face as the moon looked in.

That night the clouds had gathered over the city of Caracas in Venezuela, obscuring the moon from view. There was only harsh, artificial light in Gerald Buckmaster's room. Earlier in the day, he had booked a call to his agent in Peru and had dozed off while waiting for it to be connected. When it finally came through, Gerald opened his eyes and for a few seconds forgot where he was.

'I am worry about you,' his Peruvian agent said. 'I am happy you call. All day I wait at Lima airport and see all the planes from Caracas, but you not come. So of course I wait for you tomorrow and take you straight to the city.'

'Would you mind', Gerald said, 'if we had our meeting at the airport? I must go straight on to Rio. I have urgent business there.'

'Could you do favour for me and buy a carton of Kents? We have no imported cigarettes here no more. The customers very very pleased with your machine. We sell mountains of them if left-wing government lose next elections. Then we get permits to import more.'

There would be, he had reasoned, little point in going to Lima now. He wasn't going to get any new orders and there were plenty of direct flights to Rio from Caracas. He could cut short his trip that way and be home much earlier. It would do his marriage a lot of good. But the man had been waiting for him all day. He could stay the night in Lima. What did one day more matter? So long as he got to Brazil before the licence his agent had negotiated ran out.

What a prospect. Less than six hours' sleep before flying another two thousand miles, just to do it all over again. His brother-in-law, the banker, thought his life was one big party, swanning around the world, all expenses paid. If he could only see him now, dog-tired in a crappy hotel, hungry and confused and alone, he would change his mind.

'I'll stay the day with you,' he told his Peruvian agent.

'You no imagine how happy I am to see you again,' the man said.

'See you tomorrow,' Gerald said. 'Goodnight and sorry you had a wasted day.'

He called reception and asked them to wake him at 4.30. He did not have much time to sleep. He must make himself drop off without whisky. One day, when his daughters grew up, he would take them to all the places he had been to and never seen. Gerald lay awake on his bed and tried to imagine his girls as grown-ups. Teenage people he could converse with. He heard voices, but they were Marina's. He felt the urge to call her, but resisted. She'd be in bed, and to wake her would only remind her that she was alone.

All this was going to change once they moved into the house. They would do so as soon as he returned. All the papers were signed and the hotel had been informed that they were leaving. How sick he was of hotel rooms, of elevators and reception desks and telephone operators who kept him up all night. The children could play in a decent garden and learn to swim in their own pool. Marina might develop an interest in gardening. Her mother had. Maybe they could get a dog. Children should have a dog to grow up with. Oh no. He was not going to stay one more night in a hotel. They would move as soon as he got back. She could pack the stuff while he was away. He could call Marina and tell her that. It would make her happy. God, how he missed her. No, no. It was late. She would be asleep. He'd do it the day after tomorrow, in Brazil. By that time he would know exactly when he was coming back.

CHAPTER FORTY

The serious-faced pilot had become very friendly with El Gordo's daughter Pilar. The two were huddled together in the corner of the large room, deep in conversation. She laughed a lot and El Gordo kept despatching nervous glances in their direction. He could not hear what they were saying for the music; he couldn't concentrate on reading their lips. Not with the Chief and Balthasar sitting there with him and the party in full swing.

The Miner had ordered him to listen to every word the traitor uttered. So far Balthasar had said little. It was the Chief who did all the talking. He appeared to be particularly pleased with himself that night. And with all the alcohol he had consumed, what he said was of little use to El Gordo.

He could not relax. He was never comfortable with any kind of tension. Right now, he would have given a lot just to behave normally. Enjoy his own party, be the centre of attention, tell jokes and watch people's faces as they laughed. He looked at Balthasar's contented face and cringed at the thought of what the Miner had in store for him. Thank God he didn't know the details.

The Miner had called him earlier, just before his guests had started to arrive. He wanted to know about Cunningham. Was he there yet?

'No,' El Gordo had said. 'He should be here soon, though.'

'I knew I could count on you, Gordito. Balthasar's killers are on their way now.'

'Christ,' El Gordo had gasped, 'you promised nothing would happen in my house.'

'Trust me. They will wait until Cunningham and Balthasar are seen leaving the house together. With the Chief himself as a witness, it will be easy to accuse Cunningham of Balthasar's murder. Wasn't that your idea, Gordito?'

'Yes,' El Gordo had said, 'but nothing must happen to the Englishman.'

'Don't worry yourself. He'll only be put away for a while, that's all. But remember, Gordito, Balthasar is a different kettle of fish. He failed to stop Cunningham in Haiti and yet he killed two of his friends. Then he turned on our own people and had two of them mercilessly shot. They were sons of important families, Gordito, families who backed the revolution right from the very start. Balthasar must have gone over to the other side a long time ago, long before he went to Haiti. God knows how much he's told them.'

'He doesn't know about me, does he, Miner? I mean ... you didn't tell him, did you?'

'Of course not, Gordito. What's the matter with you? I

haven't told anyone about you. Balthasar would have shot you on sight if he had known. He's that sort of man, Gordito. A killer. He didn't try too hard to stop Cunningham over there in Haiti, but as I've told you, that didn't stop him from killing two of the Englishman's best friends. One was a woman, you know ... Balthasar's got to die, and you must not feel sorry for the bastard, Gordito. We're not murdering him. He's merely being executed for desertion. These are hard moments for us, but unless our own ranks are secure, we cannot proceed. You understand, don't you?'

El Gordo understood every word. He had never heard the Miner talk that much, but he had heard that sort of talk before. A self-searching, self-cleansing, long-winded excuse for failure. The fat man looked about him. The party was in full swing and his guests were enjoying themselves, but his own brain was too lucid with worry for him to have fun.

Clearly, Cunningham knew far too much about the operation. Having charmed Balthasar into changing sides, he would certainly have known who the leader was. The Miner, regardless of what he had said, would never allow him to survive. Both he and Balthasar had to be eliminated. Without them the Chief would have no proof of the Miner's involvement. Without them there would be no direct evidence against him. No case at all.

El Gordo understood these things and through the evening, as the party tinkled and carried on around him, he fretted. The Miner must, by now, have abandoned any thought of revolution. All he was doing was trying to save his own neck. God alone knew how far he would go in that cause. He must have become desperate. El Gordo sighed and looked at his daughter and the pilot. A new spark seemed to have ignited between them and that did not appeal to him at all.

The Miner joined his arms behind his head and stretched. Had the fat man noticed his anxiety? Perhaps not. There had been much fear in El Gordo's voice. He was far too concerned with his own safety to sense anything else. And that, in the Miner's mind, made El Gordo just as guilty as Balthasar. After all, the man had been the bearer of news that had caused him to abort the plot. And even while he had been reporting, he seemed to be holding back. His one-time confidant had changed. Perhaps he didn't tell him everything. He was nervous and unreliable and could cross over to the Chief's side at any time. The Miner picked up the telephone and dialled his chief engineer.

'I need the best explosives man you've got,' he said softly.

'At this time of night?'

'I don't care how late it is. I need to make a little mess in the silver mine we bought last year. Just a little roof-fall in one of the shafts. It's got to be done tonight, before tomorrow's inspection. A remote-control mechanism with a thirty-second fuse.'

'But, Miner, all the work we've done down there ...'

'Precisely. Do you want the government inspector to discover what we've found there? If they do, they'll tax the shit out of us. A small charge. I don't want to collapse the whole tunnel.'

'Yes, sir. I'll put it together myself. Four ounces should do it.'

'If you say so. Make two, just in case one fails. Use those new radio-controlled detonators. I'm going to set it off myself, and I don't want to be too close, you understand?'

'Yes, sir. Shall I bring them to you?'

'Yes. Within the hour,' the Miner said, and broke the connection.

He played with a jar of zinc as he dialled his schoolfriend Pepe Arias. 'I am sorry to disturb you in this hour of grief, Pepe. But there's some comfort in what I have to tell you. It concerns the family's honour.'

'There is no family now that Roberto is dead. God curse Arroyo Hondo.'

'I'm going to give you a chance to avenge Roberto's blood.'

'I'll never forget you for that. What do I have to do?'

'Get your pistol and come over to the house. You and I are going on a little trip.'

'You and I? This is my affair. Mine alone.'

'So it is. I will only take you there. You'll do it on your own.'

'Thank you. I'm on my way.'

The Miner sat back. He lifted the jar to the light. It's all quite simple, really, he thought. He felt a craving for a stiff drink, but denied it. It wasn't necessary. He wasn't buying any trouble. Pepe Arias would never talk. He pulled the telephone towards him again and dialled the airport. He asked them to get his Piper Cub ready. He then called his site manager up in the mountains and told him to light up the runway markers and get the jeep out. The Scotch would have to wait. He never drank when piloting the little plane himself.

Forty-five minutes later, on El Gordo's land, the tractor man Carlos Montoya woke to the sound of a jeep engine purring by the side of the plane. He opened the door and climbed out. His face stretched into a smile of welcome as he waited for the gringos to come towards him, but it was not his car and the man who climbed out of it was a total stranger.

The moonlight spilled onto the road as both men faced each other. 'Can I help you?' Carlos Montoya asked. He was tired and a little hungry and suddenly the other man looked familiar. He thought he had seen him somewhere before when he heard the shot that hit him in the chest. He fell on the asphalt. He did not hear the second shot which blew his head open.

CHAPTER FORTY-ONE

His daughter and the pilot were no longer where he had seen them, but El Gordo could not go looking for them. He had

234

been forced to watch the wench very closely ever since she had come back from Miami with all those bad habits. The smell of stale cigarette smoke in her bathroom was one thing, but the diaphragm he had found hidden in her underwear drawer was another. She was no longer that young, and unless a suitable husband was found for her pretty soon he could never hope to be a legitimate grandfather. The way she and that gringo flyboy had behaved in front of his guests was scandalous.

He thought he heard her sports car starting up outside. He got up to go to the door, but at that moment the telephone rang again and stopped him. He shrugged his shoulders, hoping no one else had seen the pair leave. He couldn't risk anyone else picking the phone up in case it was the Miner, but it was not.

'I wanted to thank you for the loan of the car, Gordito,' said the unmistakable voice of Peter Cunningham.

El Gordo's heart sank. If he was to choose between his integrity and his life, he'd have to do something right now. He should tell the Englishman to run as far as he could from wherever he was. But hadn't the Miner said he'd set Cunningham up for Balthasar's murder? Have him held in prison until the coup was over? If he could believe that, the Englishman's presence in the house was imperative. Was the Miner telling him the truth? Should he follow the plan or warn his friend instead? He hesitated.

Pathetic, El Gordo thought bitterly. He, the man who could sell salt to the gods of the sea, was short of words now. No guts, he thought, as rivers of sweat poured down his neck.

'Do you mind if I keep the car a little longer? I was thinking of having a couple of days in Sosua. Driving along the coast for a bit. Puerto Plata and that. The lady has never seen that part of the country.'

The decision had been taken out of his hands, El Gordo thought with relief. Or was it? Cunningham was safe enough roaming the countryside, but what if the revolution was still on? What if it succeeded? The Miner would find out.

'Go ahead,' he said. 'You know you don't have to ask. Why don't you take my Camaro? It's a lot more comfortable and your ladyfriend will be happier with air-conditioning. Just get yourself over here and take it.'

Sensible, Cunningham thought. It would be murder driving up the coast in that broken-down old heap. Marina was still asleep and he could nip up to the ranch and back in less than an hour. She wouldn't even know he'd been gone.

'It's a deal, Gordito,' Cunningham said. 'Keep a few slices of beef in the oven for me. I'll be up there very soon. I won't be needing the pilot any more, but he might still have to fly to Haiti if Balthasar wants to go back there. So make sure the young man doesn't drink a thing. And thanks again, old friend. I'm on my way.'

The pilot had offered to take El Gordo's daughter for a flight and she jumped at the chance. Pilar had been surrounded by friends of her father who were too old, or young farmhands who were out of bounds. This man was eligible and she was enjoying his company. Behind his serious face she found a kaleidoscope of fun. His native Arizona meant ranch-houses and cowboys and romance. Could they fly to the big city of Santo Domingo and be back by breakfast? Sure, he had said.

El Gordo stood outside his house looking for the young couple, but there was no sign of them. Two ancient women sitting by the outside kitchen plucking a turkey looked up at their employer with an affectionate smile.

'Have you seen my daughter?'

'Se han ido al cielo,' one said. They have gone to the sky. Everybody knows what is going on in this house, he thought to himself. Everybody except him. He was going to give his daughter and that pilot a piece of his mind. He'd show her who was boss. No more shopping trips for a year. She'd see. He clenched his fists and went inside. He smiled at his guests and walked through the living room to his office. The sooner this was over the better. He'd neglected his own family long enough. He poured himself a large Scotch and sat down. The phone rang. It was the Miner. His voice was as soft and as calm as ever.

'Is Cunningham there yet?'

'He'll be here in half an hour. What do you want me to do?'

'Get him and Balthasar back to their aircraft as soon as he arrives.'

'Cunningham's not planning to go anywhere. He's got a ladyfriend with him. He's taking her for a trip down the coast.'

'Isn't someone looking after the plane?'

'Yes. Carlos Montoya. One of my hands. He's watching it.'

'Then tell Cunningham you've had a message from Montoya. Tell him you're not sure what it was, but make it sound important. Say something's come up. You're good at that sort of thing, Gordito. Tell him he ought to check it out ... you know ...'

'What if Balthasar insists on staying behind? He's having a good time here.'

'That's easy. Tell him I have just called you. Say I have invited myself to the party. Balthasar will take off all by himself when you tell him that. Tell him anything. Just make them go to the plane and take off for Haiti.'

El Gordo did not answer. God, he hoped the pilot would come down soon. Maybe they had not reached the plane yet. And if they had, they couldn't stay up there all night. No shopping trips for ten years.

'How you know they will head for Haiti?'

'It doesn't matter where they go.'

'Come on, Miner. We're not dealing with children.'

'Don't worry about it. You get those two out there to the plane. Take them yourself if need be. Trust me, Gordito. I told you, nothing is going to happen in your house.'

They said goodbye. El Gordo took a swig directly from the bottle. The phone rang again. It was Cunningham.

'I thought you were on your way here?'

'I've changed my mind. I'm going to the plane first. See if everything is in order. I need to thank young Montoya. He's a good man, Gordito. Do you mind if I give him a hundred pesos for his trouble?'

'Sure. Tell you what ... why don't I meet you there? It would buck Montoya up no end if I'm present when you thank him. I'll bring the Camaro and you won't have to waste your time coming here at all, unless you want to.'

'That's very good of you. Something else – is the pilot about?'

'Of course.'

'Would you mind bringing him back to the plane? I've no further use for it. He can go back to Puerto Rico in the morning. Tell him I'd like to settle with him tonight.'

'I'll bring him over myself. Or get Pilar to do it.'

Things couldn't have worked out better, El Gordo thought. The gods had listened. His nightmare was coming to an end. Nothing was going to happen in the house. He hoped the plane had landed by the time Cunningham arrived at the spot. If they had to wait, he could make excuses for them. They had taken a joyride or something.

'Fine,' Cunningham said. 'What do we do about Balthasar?'

'Leave him where he is. He's having a whale of a time in there. The Chief will take him to his house later. They're so chummy you wouldn't believe a word of all those rumours about revenge and that ...'

'I'll do that. See you by the plane.'

El Gordo consulted his watch. The couple had only been gone five or ten minutes. If he got there quickly enough, he might catch them before they took off. Perhaps they liked each other well enough to have a little cuddle in the car first. He could always force the gringo bastard to marry the wench. If the boy had any balls he might try to do something before showing her how planes fly. The thought, annoying as it was, made El Gordo laugh out loud as he walked back into the living room.

The Chief was slumped on the chesterfield, floating on an ocean of whisky. His glasses had dropped down on his nose, his eyes were open, his lips parted in an inane smile. He stared at El Gordo.

'Great party,' he mumbled with a slurred voice. 'Great, great party.'

'The best,' Balthasar said. He was erect, looking dignified with a cigar in one hand and a drink in the other. The man held his alcohol well. He looked much more like a chief of police than the other man.

'Cunningham just called,' El Gordo said. 'He wants to meet you out by the plane.'

Balthasar was elated. How could he ever have doubted the Englishman? No matter what the next step in the plan was, he was game for anything. The Chief's eyes hardened.

'Cunningham called? Isn't he here yet?'

'He wants to meet Balthasar over there, by the plane. I'll give him a lift. Would you like to come along?'

'Cunningham wants to meet Balthasar over there, by the plane?' the Chief repeated. His voice cracked. 'He doesn't want to bring his woman here?'

'Are you coming with us?'

'No, you go along. I might have myself a little sleep.' The Chief managed a slow wink. 'Tell me what Cunningham's woman looks like.' His spectacles dropped off the end of his nose as his head fell on his chest. The glass slipped onto the carpet.

'I don't want to know your business, Balthasar, but I think it's urgent. I'm going to take you there myself. You go on outside. Go sit in my Camaro. It's right by the door. I'll be with you in a moment. Take your drink with you.'

Balthasar obeyed. It didn't matter what Cunningham wanted him for. He was at his disposal. El Gordo walked him to the door and showed him where the car was.

The sound of a low-flying plane interrupted his swift walk

back to the house. The bastard had better come down soon. The two old ladies pointed at the sky. '*Se han ido al cielo,*' one said again. He ran back to his office and dialled the Miner's number. The phone rang for a long time before someone picked it up.

'All is well,' El Gordo panted into the receiver. 'Cunningham is on his way. I'm just about to bring Balthasar to the plane.'

'Who is this?' a woman's voice asked. It was the Miner's wife.

'May I speak to your husband?'

'The Miner is not here,' the woman said.

'I don't understand,' El Gordo said. The receiver dropped onto the table and he raced out of his office with all the vigour of his long-gone youth.

Cunningham saw the plane's lights, low over the valley, as soon as he crossed El Gordo's boundary. Just what the hell is going on, he thought. Why would the aircraft have taken off without his permission? There might have been some development that he was unaware of, but it looked to him as if the Cessna was going nowhere in particular. The plane was just flying around, as if someone was trying to show off their skills. It was flying dangerously low, at barely three hundred feet, he figured. It had turned now and was coming along the road towards him. The roar of the engine grew louder. In a few seconds it would be overhead. Cunningham stopped the car. The moon shone brightly over the land. The hills and fields and the trees were clearly visible as if it were daytime, he thought as he looked up. The little machine took off into the star-laden sky, banked towards the mountains, then burst into a pineapple of fire.

CHAPTER FORTY-TWO

From the other side of the valley, El Gordo and Balthasar saw the spectacle. The plane had died in an instant. The fat man stopped the car and gazed at the burning fragments of the man-made bird as they floated slowly to the ground. He was breathing hard. To him, the awesome drama belonged to another world, far, far away from this one. The panorama in front of him was not real. It was a distorted, three-dimensional cinema screen, playing out a story of violent death. An imaginary nightmare in the lives of make-believe, celluloid people, one of whom was made up to be his daughter. His sweet, sweet Pilar could not be dead. She was only twenty-three. She was stupid, yes, and she had a will of her own and she was careless and irresponsible and indiscreet. But she was not dead.

Balthasar's voice sounded hard and calculated and sober. 'So that was what Cunningham wanted me for, Gordo, yes? To blow me out of the sky like a meteor. The bastard Chief must have known that. They were in this together.'

Balthasar pulled out his old service pistol and pointed it at El Gordo. 'And you, fat man, what about you? Were you going to be paid for delivering me to the gallows up there in heaven? Are you the Judas in this game? Talk, Gordo, talk now. I will kill you anyway.'

El Gordo did not answer. He had been troubled by thoughts of death for a long time now. Dark, momentary fears of suffocating with no one around. There was no God in his mind, or any belief in heaven or hell. He would dream of dying in the car or with a strange woman who would dump his body for fear of complications. He would wake up in a sweat and scream and turn the light on and then fall asleep again. But that happened rarely and only at night.

Now death was close. It pushed itself into his side in the

form of a dark barrel. He was quiet. He did not sweat. Pilar, his podgy little Pilar who sat astride his shoulders as he rode, who had laughed wildly as she'd surprised him in his bed of a Sunday morning. Pilar, who would rush into his arms at the end of the day, had crossed the far barrier. But her burned, broken body was close. It lay somewhere on his own land. The land that would have been hers one day.

It was the Miner who had put her there. And the gringo Cunningham and all the others and their stupid revolution. And now Balthasar's pistol was pressing against his flesh. He did not want the man's pity. Anyone's pity. He had none for himself. 'Shoot, Balthasar. What is there to live for?'

Balthasar pushed the long barrel into El Gordo's side and pulled back the hammer. He twisted the gun savagely. He had shot people before. Everyone must die. But the guilty made excuses. Asked for time. Begged for mercy. Offered fortunes. Not this one. The fat man did not move a muscle to stop him. No matter. He hated them all. The whole fat, rich clan of better ones. They hired him and then tired of him and now they had tried to kill him. Cold sweat had drained the beer and the rum and the whisky away. Balthasar was now totally sober.

The fat man coughed noisily. His enormous body shook in all directions. Balthasar pulled the trigger. The thump pushed El Gordo sideways. The smell of burning flesh came into his nostrils. The fat man was very much alive. He stretched his head to look at the sky and he smiled. Balthasar shot him twice more. How long was he going to take about it?

El Gordo turned to him. 'She said Pilar had gone to heaven,' he said with a faint, bitter-sweet smile. 'That woman knew, Balthasar, but she did not know I was going there too. Heaven. Can you imagine me flying through the air with little wings attached to all this flab? Funny, huh, Balthasar? El Gordo the cherub. I almost wish I could live to see that ...'

'You won't live to see anything, Gordo. Not even the Miner's victory. I promise you, he'll win.'

'There's another joke, Balthasar. I was with him too. From the start.'

'Like hell you were. I knew them all.'

El Gordo didn't speak again. He tried to laugh.

'Go fly,' Balthasar said in a rage, and raised his pistol and shot the other man once more. El Gordo slumped forward, his head falling on his chest. Balthasar slipped out of the car. He walked around and opened the driver's door. He pulled the large body out of the seat and onto the grass verge. Blood gushed out of the body in all directions. He seemed lighter than Balthasar had expected. He rolled El Gordo over and searched the pockets of his muddy jacket. There was a wallet. It bulged with notes. Balthasar removed it and tucked it under his arm. He could use every peso he could lay his hands on if he were to find Cunningham. The fat man did not need his money any more. On his own land everything would be free. Even his burial. Balthasar wondered why he had money on him at all.

Had El Gordo been telling the truth? Had he really been part of the Miner's faction? If he had, why did he attempt to deliver him to his death? Ah yes. The Miner must have ordered him to do it. No. That couldn't be so. The Miner did not know he was there. Or maybe he did. El Gordo might have told him. But then why the plane? El Gordo could have killed him in his own house a dozen times. No he couldn't. Not while the Chief was there. It was all too confusing. He had been surrounded by liars and cheats. Only one clear truth stared him in the face. The real villain. Cunningham. Balthasar's troubles started and ended with him. He was behind it all. Oh, how he would enjoy killing that foreign scum. He'd leave that for the end. Like a sweet dessert after a good meal.

He put the empty wallet back into the dead man's pocket. If all else failed, it would look like a robbery. His mind was as sharp as a whip. He would redeem himself. Go and shoot the Chief himself. Prove his loyalty in a big way. They were sure to take him back into the fold without question after that.

They might even give him his old job back. And then it would be Cunningham's turn. He would then have all the time in the world. Years if need be. He would follow the double-crossing gringo to the ends of the earth.

There was a lot of room in the car now that he had it all to himself. He would drive slowly up to the house and park outside. No. Everyone knew El Gordo's Camaro. He was seen leaving with him. He'd better leave the car outside and sneak up the garden. Wait in the shadows. The Chief would have to come out of the house at some stage and he would get him then. He would make an easy target, right by the door, his silhouette showing up clearly against the light. Or park outside the gate and let the Chief pass. They were certain to stop at the sight of the Camaro to thank El Gordo for his hospitality. He'd shoot him then. Easy.

Balthasar hummed a little merengue to himself. He started the engine and doubled back onto the road. If his luck held, the Chief would leave the house before first light. He could always hang El Gordo's death on Cunningham. And the Chief's. The revolution would surely succeed and he would emerge as its real hero. A man of the people. Someone with mass appeal during the next elections. Who knows?

His craving for water was painfully sharp, but there were things to be done, he thought. Far more important than any earthly needs. He drove slowly.

CHAPTER FORTY-THREE

———■———

The rice ball slipped down Ti Allain's forehead and came to rest on his nose. It was a sure sign that the spirits were aware of his vigil. He had fallen asleep and the dream that had come to him was vivid in his memory now. It was daylight in his dream, which meant that it was a true prediction of the future.

He had seen the one-footed foreigner kneeling before Monique's white stake as if he were in church. His white face, shining with sweat, was tense and frightened. He was breathing hard as if he had been running. He looked over his shoulder as if someone were chasing him.

It was very unlucky to kneel before Monique's white stake. Especially without an offering to repay her for sitting on the very place where she had died. It was worse than dancing on a grave. Every child in the village knew that.

Could the foreigner have been attempting to apologize for taking her custodian away from her? Ti Allain remembered that the man was speaking in a strange tongue. Spanish, perhaps, or the thick, clicking language the Anglais used. She would not have understood either. He thought he might have heard footsteps behind the foreigner's back, but at that moment he had woken to the touch of the rice ball on his nose. The dream had stopped there.

If the tall man was in danger, he would not know it yet. If the threat to him came from some human source, Ti Allain would be able to warn him. And if he had heard right, the threat was surely human, for spirits have no footsteps at all. They make no sounds even when dancing on a drum, as they did sometimes for messages or for summons.

In the big, black mountain of Africa, where all Haitians came from, drums were used to send people to war. His grandmother had told him that legend once. It was a hard story to believe because only white people went to war. Because they had everything, but still wanted more. There were some black people like that too, but then they were only pretending to be Haitians. Like the man Guy, who so wanted to be a foreigner and most probably was.

How fast the spirits had chased this night away. Already, a pink line had appeared along the horizon and become a stripe of pure fire. The whole night had lasted less time than it took to boil cassava, but the spirits were the real rulers and they could ask the king of the world to do anything for them. Even move the moon and the stars back to the sea and bring the sun to splash the sky with light instead.

Outside his barrel, the first stripes of gold hit the grass and filled it with diamonds. Why did they make rum here, those people behind the fence? Goats would live well here by the distillery. Maybe even cattle. They could move his whole village here, Ti Allain thought. No one would need to go to Saint Domingue then, but places can change, too. Once, long ago, there had been plenty of water under his own village, but the people drank it all. The people up here might have to go across the border themselves one day, if the spirits wished them to.

A coarse sentence cut abruptly across his deliberations.

'You're awake, then, little man,' the Haitian Guy said with a sneer, out of the dawn. His face looked dry and there was no happiness in his eyes. His voice, attempting to resound with authority, sounded weak and hoarse, as if he had been drinking all night. 'Get your people on the tap-taps. We are leaving now.'

The man was obviously demented. He walked from bus to bus, kicking the wheels, trying to put life into his feet. Drinking new rum can give people a heavy foot in the morning. Ti Allain thought. Especially after such a short night. He would not bother to ask Guy about his fate now. The spirits would do that for him just before they arrived in Saint Domingue.

They might want him to go there if he was chosen to warn the tall foreigner. If that was decreed, he was sure to meet the foreigner again wherever he was. Even in Saint Domingue. Perhaps he was now chosen to worship and keep house for bigger powers, bigger than Monique the black witch, who had chicken legs and could never venture that far into the mountains. Unless she was allowed to fly, and that was not possible now that no one offered her anything to sustain and increase her power.

Ti Allain crawled out of the barrel and looked at the mountainous horizon. His hand touched the wet grass. He licked the cool dew off his fingers and the rice started to roll off his nose. He caught the white ball in mid-air and weighed it. He knew there was more rice in his hand now than there had been last night. That meant he should eat it before it got too big and made him fat like Marie-Christine. He had always cherished a desire to collect some flab around his waist, but that would only show the others how well he had fared.

In his own way, Ti Allain had grown quite rich. It was a secret between him and his grandmother. Not even Monique knew about the money he kept hidden in an old ruin of a sugar mill on the way to Petionville. He had placed it in an old lead-lined tin his grandmother had left him. Monique could not see through lead.

Slowly, the people climbed onto the hard wooden benches at the back of the tap-tap buses. During the night, someone had started a rumour that soon they would be working and eating. Very soon. Maybe today. No one spoke, but there was excitement in their eyes.

The bird-like driver had come back. During the dark hours he had acquired a repaired bus and Ti Allain climbed in beside him. When the man offered him a cigarette, Ti Allain shook his head politely and declined. Those made him cough and his grandmother had told him he would have bad teeth and would suffer if he used them. It was cool still, but the driver who was really a bird was already sweating and pushing the drops of salty water up into his thin hair.

Somewhere, far along the road, the tall foreigner was waiting. The bird man could have flown ahead and might have seen him there. But bird people, like any other people, never knew what lay around the corner because no one had told them they could fly.

The little convoy moved through the clear morning, following Marie-Christine's car. Behind them, the sun rose, bringing vivid colour to the bright paintings that adorned the tap-tap buses. There were more trees and taller grass and birds. And if there were people living in this enchanted land, they did not come out to watch the city machines that spat black smoke into their clean air.

CHAPTER FORTY-FOUR

He did not want to know what had happened. Not now. Not yet. Whatever it was, news of it would reach him soon enough. Cunningham sat in the car in front of the Hotel Matun in Santiago and gazed at the deserted entrance. He had no memory of how or when he got back there. His nerves were shattered. Fear lurked in the morning air. He was numbed. He could not get out of the car. It must have been the thought of Marina which had drawn him back to Santiago, but he did not know what he wanted of her. Of anybody.

He had lived for forty-three years inside his body and he knew himself well. Well enough to recognize that finally he was facing the onslaught of a breakdown. He was not too sure whether he was scared or angry. None of these feelings materialized and sluggishness began to spread through him. Someone, he did not know who, had died in the plane with the pilot. The good-humoured Latin patch he had lived in for so long had exploded in his face. Whoever caused the plane to explode had him in mind and must have hated him more than death. He was too tired to wonder who. The old pain of Marie-Christine's death came back to haunt him. If he was the real target, why did they keep missing?

He was alone again. As he had always been. As he had felt that Christmas before his eighth birthday when his father came into his room with breakfast. Where is Mother? he remembered asking. She had gone. He knew she had, and later he had found out where and with whom, but often he was convinced she had gone because he had been bad.

His reaction to that was always the same. First he was hurt, then puzzled and sad, and in the end he would get angry, but he never showed it. Did that anger make him sin against his homeland and become a traitor and be lost in this God-forsaken country? There was nothing exotic or exciting or homely about the view of the Hotel Matun. His life had been wasted. He could have ... What? He could have nothing. His soul was being eroded. He was sinking again.

That black void couldn't last for ever. It never had. There were other problems now. Other pains to bear. And then anger came and forced his tired mind into action. He must call the Chief and tell him what had happened. The Chief would know who had perished in the plane.

He got out of the car, walked into the hotel and called El Gordo's ranch-house from the lobby. The party was still on, he was told by a servant. No, he was not lying. Yes, of course he knew who was speaking. The Chief was asleep on the couch. The other man, Balthasar, had gone out with El Gordo.

'Out with El Gordo? Are you sure about that?'

'Of course I am sure. I was serving Señor Balthasar a drink at the time. El Gordo came up and told Señor Balthasar that you had just called. He said you wanted Señor Balthasar to come and meet you at the plane. Right away, he said. And I remember that very well because Señor Balthasar got up immediately and handed me his drink, but El Gordo said he could take the glass with him. It was still full, you see, señor. Anyway, Señor Balthasar went out to the car and El Gordo went to his study. I was frankly surprised to see that as he had said you were in such a hurry that he was going to drive Señor Balthasar to you himself. But he wasn't there long. I saw him go out to the car soon after.'

'Where is he now?'

'I just told you. He's taken Señor Balthasar to the plane. He said he was coming back in five minutes. Asked me to make sure everyone had drinks.'

'What about the young pilot? Did El Gordo take him too?'

'No. He only took Señor Balthasar. I have not seen the pilot all evening. I suppose he went to the plane earlier.'

'Let me speak to the sergeant, will you?'

'I'll get him for you, señor.'

He must speak to the Chief right away. He could tell him with certainty that El Gordo had been against them all the time. He had never asked El Gordo to bring Balthasar to the plane. He hadn't even asked him to go there himself. That was El Gordo's suggestion. That could only mean he had planned it all. Could El Gordo have hated him that much? No, he did not hate him. This had nothing to do with hate. El Gordo was following orders. The sergeant came on the line. 'Where is the Chief of Police?'

'Asleep, señor.'

'Get him out of the house and into the car right away.'

'The Chief is asleep, señor. It is nearly morning. He needs to sleep at least until lunch. He will kill me if I wake him.'

'Someone will kill him if you don't,' Cunningham said. 'Get him out of there this minute. Blame it on me if you get into trouble. Tell him I called and said what I said. A question of life and death. Say anything. Just get him out.'

Balthasar waited outside El Gordo's gate. He had been waiting for what seemed to be an eternity. He was just about to drive up to the house when the Chief's official car came racing down the drive. Someone had left the interior light on and to his horror Balthasar saw the sergeant at the wheel. The Chief himself was not visible. Balthasar jumped out of the Camaro, his pistol at the ready. The sergeant slowed down as he came closer. He recognized Balthasar instantly and stopped by his side.

'I've got to run, señor,' the sergeant said. 'Cunningham just called. He said the Chief must be taken out of the house right away. There is danger.'

The sight of the gun cut him short. Balthasar raised his pistol and pointed it towards the recumbent figure of the Chief in the back of the car. He fired once, then again. The sergeant put his foot down and took off into the night, his tyres screeching.

Francisco Martinez, his humour and confidence restored, was bubbling over. Cunningham had taken him back into the fold. He had entrusted him with closing the deal. And he was going to make more money now that there were more Haitians than contracted for. He was going to be rich.

They were driving south-west across the hills. He was too excited to feel sleepy. He had taken two lives for the kid and there would be more. Once the revolution failed, they were sure to squabble and shop each other like the whores they were.

'I don't miss my wife at all, Rafael,' Francisco said. 'Sad, huh? I haven't seen her in a week. I don't even remember what she looks like. Only how much she eats. God, you have no idea how she sweats when there's a power cut. And even when we have electricity she turns the air-conditioning off to save energy. She buys shoes instead and she sweats. Are there any women in these villages up here?'

'I think we should finish the job first.'

'It wouldn't take long, Rafael. Your wife is from these parts. She must know someone. A widow or a divorcee. Anyone. You know how long I've been dead. What's the use being alive without a woman? You tell me.'

The road was becoming too narrow for comfort. Big cars were all right as long as the roads were wide. There was nothing like an American engine. Rafael wanted to tell Francisco about American engines, but the man did not know a carburettor from a gearbox. He was really quite a useless son of a bitch when he had women on his mind. But they had known each other all their lives. A friend is better than a relative any time.

'I don't know any women here. Neither does my wife. And if she did, she wouldn't tell me.'

Rafael hoped they would find a place to sleep some time soon. He did not want to sleep in the car. It was cold in the hills and the upholstery might get scratched. He would never listen to Francisco again. The bastard never paid him anyway. He should have stayed behind. There was plenty of work in Santo Domingo and the roads were wide and well laid. Good thing he had a new set of tyres on his wheels. This time he was going to get paid or he would make Francisco walk all the way back from the border. The sun was coming up over the mountains.

The first light touched Marina's face and she woke. By her side, fully clothed, Cunningham lay asleep on his back. His pale face was drawn, the stubble on his chin ashen. He mumbled something and she strained to make the words out. Soon he would wake and look at her and his face would give birth to a smile and all would be just as it had been. She stroked his hair. He opened his eyes, his face contracting sternly. He did not smile. 'What time is it?' he asked. He did not say her name.

'It's eight o'clock. Why don't you go back to sleep? You look beat.'

'I've got things to do. Phone calls to make.' His hoarse voice did not sound the way she remembered it.

'Would you like some breakfast?'

'No, thank you. Did you have a good night?'

'Yes.'

'Splendid. Splendid,' he said, a distant look in his eyes.

'You need a change of clothes.'

'I've got a bag somewhere.'

She did not comment. Nothing they said seemed to require an answer. There was nothing to say. How she had been looking forward to this. To seeing him again. She looked at him and she searched for that magic. Perhaps she was tired too.

Gerald was away and she was right where she had longed to be. With the man she wanted. But he was not the same man. There was no music in the air. No moonlight. Across the street there were houses. The bay of Port-au-Prince was far away. On the other side of time. Perhaps she had been expecting too much. Nothing is ever the same. Such a lot had happened since she had seen him. They had found a house. Chiquito's daughter had settled down and the children adored her. Maybe she was just confused. Over-reacting. Had she done it all for nothing?

She had been remote with her husband. Without words, she had asked him to bear with her a little longer. Wait until the glitter of adventure and freedom and music had faded. Wait until those drums of love and faraway places had stilled. If only she could have the thrill of it again. Just one more time. Then Cunningham and all that went with him would become a memory. Just like the graduation ball that once meant everything and was now a forgotten photograph. Like the trip to Europe, like the wedding.

This must be it, she thought as Cunningham hogged the telephone. Her last fling was dying before it had begun. That marvellous intensity of danger, the music, had gone as if it had never been. Pictures to bore her children with. All she had now was grey reality. No carnival. Nothing.

Guilt? No way. None of this had hurt Gerald or the children. It had saved her when she was down and given her a new insight into herself. Maybe she did not like herself. Too late. Too late. Too late. That's all it was. Too late.

Cunningham's brain raced and his face contorted. Nothing was working out. He had been trying to get through to the Chief's house, but the number was constantly engaged.

She looked at him. Why was he so distant? Who was this man? He looked small and tired and frail and old. What was she doing here with him? Home. She must go home this minute. Before the memory turned sour. Before the dream was lost.

'Cunningham,' she said, and he turned towards her and for a split second it was all there again. She thought she had him. But then the Chief picked up the phone and began to scream at him and his eyes went blank.

She must leave. She was of no use here. She had things to do in the city. He did not take any notice of her as she got up and went to the bathroom. She showered and dressed, and all the while Cunningham listened to the barrage the Chief was directing at him. He told him of El Gordo's death and Balthasar's shots and the plane that had crashed. She knew things were going badly for him. But he was no longer hers.

'It's all one big misunderstanding,' she heard Cunningham say. His voice was faint and weak and too servile. That way he wouldn't reassure anyone. Not even her.

'Misunderstanding? You must be mad. You are a double-crossing gringo son of a bitch. It was you all the time. You dragged me out of El Gordo's house to have your friend Balthasar shoot at me. You hoped he'd get rid of me, then take off in your booby-trapped plane and die and leave you free and clean. But why did you have to kill El Gordo? Maybe you didn't, but the evidence points at you as sure as hell. I am confused, Cunningham. I have known you for years, but you are trouble. No wonder they don't want you in England.'

There was a pause, but it did not last long enough for him to recover from the shock. Then the Chief's voice came back. It was calmer. 'I have just heard that Balthasar is alive and looking for you. We think he has killed El Gordo and stolen his car. It was your idea to bring El Carnicero here in the first place. You should have stayed in Haiti as I advised you. You should never have brought Balthasar over. El Gordo would have been with us still. I don't know what to do with you, Cunningham. You have the Miner and Balthasar after you. The police can't save you. Nothing can save you now.'

'You're wrong, Chief. You're terribly wrong.'

'Let me finish. Just make sure the Haitians are delivered, do you hear? We will start looking for Balthasar after that, so be on your guard. He was never in my house, do you understand? Never. And don't call me again, *chico. Adiós.*'

Waves of nausea rolled into his chest. He needed to be alone now. In the protective boundary of his body he would find his old courage. What use was courage now? There was nowhere to go. He was not armed. He was not going to ask anyone for help. He was beyond help. The Chief had said so. His own home ground was being swept away from under his feet. He must not feel sorry for himself now. He must do things. He must make sure the landowners got every hand they'd ordered. He'd been paid in full. No one would ever say he'd been a crook. Francisco would finish the job. He should by right have all the money, but he had no use for it any more.

Marina? He saw the way she looked at him. She felt pity. She must not feel that. She must not remember him downcast. He'd be better off alone.

'Marina,' he said softly, 'I have a lot to tell you, but I can't tell you now.' He took a thick wad of notes out of his pocket. He peeled off a few hundred pesos and held out the rest to her. 'Would you give this to Francisco when you see him?' She nodded. Not one tender word had passed between them since she had arrived. She looked at him. The lines around his mouth were deep. There was no need to say it was all over. She knew.

'Don't you need more money?' she asked. 'I can ...'

'No,' he said.

He looked shabby and hungry and so very tired and she tried to insist, but he said he wouldn't take money from a woman. Somehow, somewhere, if they ever met again, he would explain it to her, he said. But he did not tell her it had all been impossible right from the start because a man in his position cannot afford to dream.

He said none of this as they sat close together on the bed while he waited for Francisco to call. There was no tension, no excitement. She did not want him to kiss her. They were friends. An outing with an uncle. She took his arm and at last he smiled. He was yesterday's lover. He was safe.

'You must go soon, young lady,' he said. 'Once you've given the money to Francisco, you'd better forget all about the likes of him and me. Pick up your life where you left it.'

He did not need to tell her that. They got up and embraced. He held her and they started for the door. Then the phone rang and he looked at her once more before she disappeared down the hall.

Francisco's voice was clear and full of bounce. Cunningham couldn't bear to listen to him. He cut him short. He told him, in a few terse sentences, what he was to do.

'I always get the tough jobs. You slept in a bed last night, didn't you, Cunningham? You had a woman last night, too. And now you expect me to collect the Haitians and deliver them all over the place while you ...'

'Just make sure the job is finished.'

'While you sit there on the beach, Cunningham, just think of poor Francisco whose sweat and honest labour enables you to live like a gringo lord.'

'You're in charge, Francisco. The business is yours.'

'What? What do you mean?'

'Exactly that. The business is yours. You're the boss. Go see Mrs Buckmaster when you get back to Santo Domingo. She has money for you.'

'You talk like you're not coming back ...'

'*Adiós*, Francisco,' Cunningham said with a measure of finality, and put the phone down. All he needed was a few hours' sleep. Then he could face people and walk tall. He had decided to go directly to the Miner's house and meet Balthasar there. Whatever was to happen, would happen. He had no gun. He hadn't held a gun in his hand since Palestine. Sleep the day through, then drive at night. A rested mind can perform miracles. He would die poor. So what? He wasn't leaving any debts behind.

'He's talking funny,' Francisco said to Rafael. 'He worries me.'

'Who is?'

'None of your business. Drive on. That's what I pay you for.'

'What's come over you?'

'Just drive on, Rafael. I'm in charge now. Just shut up and drive.'

Balthasar's valley came alive with the sun. The morning brought doubts. What if El Gordo had really been working for the revolution? The fat man had said something like that, but his own mind had been too full of frustration and hatred to listen. He should have done. He had failed to kill the Chief and his last chance of reconciliation with the Miner was up the spout. Worse. The sergeant had recognized him and had gotten away. He saw him shooting his gun off in the glare of the headlights. Half the police force would be after him now. The Camaro was known to everybody. He must not be seen in daylight. He was safe enough now, he thought, and smiled.

He had driven into the hills in the last hours of darkness and was now inside an empty straw shed, once used for drying tobacco. The car had burst through one of the walls and as he got out to inspect the damage he found he had stumbled on an unexpected hiding place. The car would not be seen from the road and he could sleep unmolested all day. Sleep was all he needed now.

He would go and see the Miner later, in the cool of the evening. He'd explain. He might have made the odd mistake, but then he was a human being. The Miner would know he'd only been trying to do his best. But all that could wait. Right now he was tired, confused and lonely. He did not know how to act on his own any more. He had been following other people and their orders for too long.

CHAPTER FORTY-FIVE

◆

Some sixty miles away from Rafael's American car, across

mountains and valleys, the tap-tap buses came to a halt. They had arrived in the small town of Ferrier with a little time to spare. Two punctured tyres and a broken windshield had slowed them down. Guy parked his car outside Gautier's Pharmacy and sprinted towards the glass door as he shouted at the others to stay put.

Achille Gautier, a huge, grey-haired individual, was pounding a mixture of white tablets on a small metal plate. He raised his distinguished face. A pair of clear blue eyes stared at Guy through gold-rimmed glasses.

'You came for the penicillin?'

'No, sir, Maître Gautier. I come from Monsieur Cunningham.'

'Never heard of him. And who are you?'

'I am Guy. Madame Marie-Christine's chauffeur. You would not remember me because I stayed outside last time Madame came in to see you.'

'Ah yes, Marie-Christine. Very sad. The shipment is going through today?'

'Yes, Maître. I would like to see the mango plantation.'

'It's not a plantation. Just a grove. Have you any other message?'

'No, Maître. Just to ask you to take us there. We pay when you get us there.'

'I understand. Wait while I finish this preparation. I'll lock the place up. I have a motorcycle outside. You can follow me.'

Outside, Ti Allain did not sulk about not being told why they had stopped. He did not want to ask Guy about it because the man looked nervous and would have shouted at him in front of the people. In any case, he now knew that Guy, the man who wanted to be a foreigner and a leader, was no more than a little mouse aspiring to be a cat. Real leaders did not need to scream at people or humiliate them. Everyone knew that irritation came mostly from a bad stomach, so an irritated man should really be pitied.

Ti Allain wanted to pray, but he was not sure who to pray

to. He knew there was a new master to serve now that Monique was out of range. He had his suspicions, but he did not utter them even to himself because Monique might just have managed to follow him either by herself or through someone else. In any case, it was bad luck to guess, and whoever was in charge of things now would soon make himself known. A few general prayers would not go amiss. Someone up there would hear them and he could sneak his grandmother's name in, just in case.

He bit into a green onion he had carried with him from Diquini and sucked the biting juice. That would show he no longer cared about the pain he had suffered having to pretend he was going over the border. If he ever got there, the spirits would not let him be treated like the others or make him work hard. In time, they would guide him back.

The tall one-footed foreigner was not going to show himself before they reached Saint Domingue, of that he was now sure. Otherwise Guy the Haitian would never have been so domineering and disrespectful to him. The tall foreigner spoke Creole, and once Ti Allain could warn him of the dangers he was facing, he would gratefully send him back to his village where he would enjoy bald Jean-Hercule's wife.

The bird-man driver had lost his tongue during the drive from the distillery. Ti Allain had always felt disdain for quiet people because they were for ever trying to hide something. The bird man had been quiet because he had recognized Guy's powers and was afraid he would tell him what his destiny might be.

People enjoyed their ignorance. They got used to a way of life, a partner and a corner to sleep in. If destiny decreed that their lot, bad as it could often be, was about to change, they would rather not know of it. The bird man had eaten too much of the rice he concealed in the little metal pot under his seat and the food had made him tired. When a man was hungry, Ti Allain reasoned, he talked more and moved faster. But the bird man was driving the tap-tap bus and could not move.

That meant he must have been afraid to find out what lay ahead.

Guy came out of the pharmacy. There was a smile on his face. They were now close to the border and Francisco Martinez would be waiting for them on the other side of the mango grove. Guy liked Francisco. He was a funny man and the anticipation of seeing him again made him happy. He would ask Francisco what to do with Ti Allain. The driver shut the pharmacy's doors and walked back to his car to wait for Monsieur Gautier.

That smile was not lost on Ti Allain, who kept his eyes on Guy even while he prayed. Someone, up above or down below, was listening to him. From now on he would stick to green onions. The new master was clearly partial to humans who could stand a little pain. Perhaps, when the new master was alive, he had been a medicine man like Marie-Christine's husband.

He could stop praying now and rest. He had surely made his wishes crystal clear. No one would force him to cut cane in the fields of Saint Domingue. If the spirits that had known him before had heard him, or felt his anxiety, they would stop him from crossing over just in time. A motorcycle engine was kicked into life outside and the bird man started the car. Ti Allain put the rest of his onion in his pocket and waited for events to unfold.

CHAPTER FORTY-SIX

◼

All sorts of women came into his bar, but Antonio did not understand them all. There were those who came with their men and stayed in the background while the *muchachos* talked of important things. There were others who came to sit and sip a beer in search of company. He could always make those out because they looked the men over and examined the quality of their clothes and often asked for the time to see whether they were wearing expensive watches. Sometimes they came straight up to a man and talked to him and Antonio knew it was because they had noticed the car the prospective client had arrived in. He could point these women out to boys who were looking for diversion and often booked them into one of the hot-pillow hotels down the road if a deal was struck.

Otherwise his life had been easy. Because of his discretion, his bar had stayed popular while others had failed. Here, patrons could do business without being overheard. They could keep cash safely out of sight, or buy and sell American dollars without the authorities knowing. Most of the people who frequented his bar had long ago become his friends.

But the gringo woman was different. He did not know what to make of the way she sat there, all by herself. She hardly touched her beer and looked at the sea with downcast eyes. She did not present any problems because she did not talk to him or anyone else. She never came into the bar during the busy afternoon and evening hours. She never asked to use the telephone.

She was an American and had been coming in frequently these past few days. Other than reducing a perfectly good bottle of beer to stale piss-coloured water, she looked innocent enough. She would say *buenos dias* when she arrived and *adiós* when she was going and always left him a generous tip.

Antonio knew he did not deserve such a gratuity. This morning he would talk to her because he had found out she had been Cunningham's woman and because Francisco had told him the night before to let him know when she came in. No one knew how shy Antonio the barman really was. It was not easy to ask a married gringo woman to call another man at his house. Nor could he guarantee that Francisco would be polite with her, since he hated being woken up. This was the hour of the siesta.

Antonio didn't want to get involved in Francisco's business. He was still very cross with him for not really being dead. He had a reputation to maintain and Francisco could have let him in on the secret. Worse, being the main source of gossip along the Malecon, he had become used to spreading the story around. Worse still, when the truth finally got out, he couldn't even say he knew it all along. People laughed at him. That was why he hesitated to talk to the gringo woman and tell her to call Francisco. This could be another hoax.

Marina was about to leave when the barman spoke to her. The hesitant words came out slowly. 'You likes another beer, señora? No cost. Antonio me pay.'

She looked at him and tried to smile, but her lips did not obey. There was nothing to smile about. Cunningham had been gone for days and they had moved to the new house. Gerald was back with more success stories and there was talk of a trip to England later in the year. To visit his sister and that boring banker husband of hers.

Sitting in the bar like this was the closest she could get to Cunningham. Antonio had been his friend. Here she had the time and the space to think of him with no interruption. This had been Cunningham's world and he had told her to come here. He had left her Francisco's money, but she did not know where to find him or how to ask for him. She could only come here at this time. In the afternoon she was busy in the garden and the evenings belonged to Gerald and the girls. Chiquito's daughter came to the house every morning and Gerald had found a Spanish teacher. She was meant to start her lessons in a week.

All she was left with was an out-of-focus fairy tale of love and flowers and moonlight music. A pink, romantic story of two people she used to know. A schoolgirl and a matinee idol. There was order in her life now and soon the precious moments she possessed in which to dream over a glass of beer would be traded for Spanish lessons. Francisco's money was buried at the bottom of her shoulder-bag and she kept coming to the bar to look for him. And now Antonio was talking to her. She could ask him about Cunningham. No. She wouldn't ask Antonio. He might tell her things she didn't want to hear. This was her chance. She must make a move mow. He must have noticed her, day in, day out. He must have wondered what she was doing, a woman alone in a bar. A foreign woman at that. Was that why he had offered her a beer?

'Thank you,' she said. 'Next time.'

No one had ever refused a free drink in his bar. 'Please take another,' he said, perplexed. 'This one sure cold like ice.'

'Thank you, but no. Do you know where I could find Francisco Martinez?'

Antonio did not believe his luck. It was no hoax. 'Francisco Martinez? For why?'

'I have a parcel for him. *Dinero*. Money. Do you understand?'

'I can give him *dinero* for you, señora,' Antonio said in his barman's English. '*Cuando viene*. When he comes to bar tonight. He sleep now, *comprende*? *Dormir*. He likes to sleep in sun time, *comprende*?'

She smiled. Gerald would have told her to ask Antonio for a receipt. She pulled the paper-wrapped wad out of her bag. She could almost hear tired old bills hug up against crisp new ones. The money Cunningham had won at the casino in Port-au-Prince the night his numbers came up. The money the landowners had paid him for taking the Haitians over the border. She handed the parcel over. The last tangible remains of her time with Cunningham had gone. Antonio put the package above the bar between two bottles of smuggled Chivas Regal Scotch he kept for special customers.

'Will it be safe there?' she asked. 'It's *mucho dinero*.'

'Is all right,' he assured her. 'More better than Banco Nacional. If you want, we call Francisco, tell him now. Sorry, no good English speak. Only gin and tonic or whisky sour speak good. Me *teléfono* Francisco after five o'clock, señora. You come back?'

He assumed a serene, cashier-like expression and she smiled. 'I trust you,' she said, and asked him to call her a cab. It seemed to have pulled up by the kerb before the phone was put down. *'Adiós,'* she said as she got into the car.

'Bibi,' Antonio answered proudly, and wiped an invisible spot off the counter.

In the car, she thought of the evening ahead. It would be like old times. There would be roast beef and potatoes. Gerald's favourite meal might alleviate his doubts. She would make it all up to him. She could only cut Cunningham off completely once she knew what had happened to him. Haiti and their time together were light-years away. Minutes had become hours and days stretched to weeks and years. Tonight, her husband would carve the roast, but Cunningham's presence would still be there. She was confused, yes. But not as confused as she had been this morning and much less so than yesterday. Gerald's reserve and patience would help her to pull through. She would be grateful and show it and one day, when she truly woke up, she hoped she would wish it had all been just a dream.

Chapter Forty-Seven

∎

Hunched and out of sight behind Antonio's bar, Francisco counted his windfall. No one would have robbed him there, but he did not want his friends to see his wealth and allow the deadly sin of envy to enter their hearts. He had only come back to life a few days earlier and that took some getting used to. And now all this money. Thousands and thousands of mind-boggling, genuine gringo dollars and eight thousand pesos, all in large denominations, and some brand new. Better than what the street money-changers had. Better even than the bank.

The beer he could now buy could sink a battleship. There was more to come once he had placed the remaining six Haitians. He was now a gentleman of means. A señor. He must think of his future and learn to smoke a pipe or cigars like all señores. Buy the bar perhaps. A new apartment on the Mirador. It wasn't fair on the Englishman. He had given him the lot. Why unfair? The money was no good to Cunningham. He would only spend it on married women or give it to the casinos or buy yet another big *Yanqui* car. He could buy a little store. Or a garage and a petrol station. The kid would have liked that. He loved looking at the expensive canned food on the shelves and was crazy about cars. Especially *Yanqui* cars. Cunningham's *Yanqui* car was in the family now, but the kid was not and he would never come back.

No. He might as well keep the money in cash. Not spend it all in one go. Cunningham might come back and ask for his share. Best to take his expenses and Rafael's money out, then divide the rest by two in case Cunningham surfaced. He could keep Cunningham's money with Antonio. Lots of people kept money there. It was sitting all over the place, piled up in little boxes. Gambling debts and lending money and protection money and more. The bar had never been robbed because the whole town knew it was there and who came to the bar.

Francisco drank his beer and another and thought of his money. Maybe he should have given Cunningham a bigger share because he was the real boss, but what the hell. He had worked hard for it. It had been no picnic. No, señor. Not even counting the long drive to Santiago to drop the American woman. On the way to the border he couldn't sleep because he had to watch Rafael, and once they got there? He had to wait a hell of a long time before the Haitians came out of the mango trees. That *hijo de puta* Rafael snuggled in the luxury of his Chevrolet taxi like a new-born baby in a cot while he kept watch. Kept watch for ever. Fighting hunger and thirst and heavy eyelids. It was almost dawn when he saw the small fire on the other side of the grove.

He stood there, tired and hungry and wet. As usual, when one was out of town and unprepared, it had started to rain. How it rained. Perhaps God was angry with him for telling everybody he had died, but no one can help upsetting God from time to time. Especially when you're trying to make an honest peso. Let people think he was lazy; he knew better. Take Rafael. That man never got further than that one miserable taxi because he was a true good-for-nothing lazy son of a bitch who hated work. All he could strive for and boast about was a new Impala now and then; and that was only possible because he had a cousin in the customs and got away with paying no import duty. With his connections, Rafael could have had a whole fleet of Impalas by now, but he was too lazy to grab passengers. That was why he was always available. Only God knew how Francisco had tried to get Rafael to mend his ways, but the stupid *cabrón* wouldn't listen. All he cared about was his stomach and his bed. He wasn't even interested in women. Certainly not in work.

Later, when the Haitians started coming out of the mango grove, things didn't improve. Francisco had tried to wake Rafael, but the man refused to leave his dreams and come out to help him. The trucks they had hired were parked a mile away from the taxi, and he had to walk with the Haitians all the way there. The strange herd that had followed him seemed hungry and frightened. They walked barefoot through the mud. He was to take them straight to the estates where they would be put to work upon arrival. The harvest was overdue and they would be driven bitch hard. They must have been dog-tired and cold, yet they were eager and light on their feet. Everyone smiled as if they were going to a dance. Life must have been worse than shit where they had come from.

'My heart bled for them,' Francisco said to Antonio. 'It wasn't easy, believe me.'

Antonio nodded in silence and Francisco told him about the little man. He hadn't noticed him at first. He had kept himself apart from the others. As the people passed by to mount the trucks, all glanced respectfully in his direction. Some bowed and others crossed themselves with reverence. He stood erect and proud, like a miniature emperor. Shabby as he was, the man acknowledged the gestures individually with a grand, if reserved, nod of approval. He didn't look much physically and his face was childlike and without blemish. Only a close look betrayed the wisdom of his expression. He was in no hurry to join the others and remained standing there, his eyes sternly watching the proceedings. Francisco motioned the little man to come with him. Followed by his new friend, he started his slow, tiring ascent to Rafael's taxi.

'Oh no,' Francisco said to Antonio as the other man handed him his beer, 'don't you ever kid yourself. Being rich isn't easy.'

Ti Allain liked the look of the new foreigner as soon as he set eyes on him. It was a dark morning and heavy drops of water were falling from the sky. That made the earth sticky and difficult to walk on, but he could taste the clean rainwater and he spat a good measure of it out for the spirits who had brought him this far. He touched the onion in his pocket and followed the man up the slippery road. This foreigner was plump like a rich city man, but he had smiling eyes. Above all, he had recognized Ti Allain's powers because he had singled him out from the start.

When at last they got to the car and woke the driver up, Ti Allain knew he had won. He stood outside for a little while and looked at the sky and prayed. He wiped his feet clean with his shirt until the plump foreigner laughed out loud, touched his shoulder, and flicked his head sideways, motioning him to come inside. There was something about the plump foreigner that reminded Ti Allain of the tall, one-footed foreigner. This one was younger and not as clever, but he had a kind face and soft, chubby hands, and his movements were slow. He was most probably the other half of the man he had come to save.

All people come in two parts, but most spend their time on

earth denied that knowledge. Vainly, they search for something, not knowing what it is they are looking for. They try many things, many places, many kinds of work. Some try many wives. They do not know why. They are, of course, looking for perfection in the form of their other half. Very few people ever realize they are meant to have one, let alone succeed in finding him. Or her.

This is why no one can ever die. One half can die, and is eased into the earth. As soon as that happens, the remaining half begins a search for a new half. Only that will make him whole again. His grandmother used to call them mirror images and had told him every person had a mirror image somewhere on this earth. So it went on and on, his grandmother had told him, and no one ever expired for ever without leaving something of himself with his mirror image. Most people did not know about this, and that was why they were so afraid to die.

Ever since he had first heard of the tall foreigner, Ti Allain had secretly hoped that he was the mirror image. That was why he decided not to run away before he had a chance to warn him of the danger he was in. Now that he had met the plump man and had been bidden to join him in the car, he knew that one of them would have to die. Only then would he be allowed to become the mirror image, because there are never more than two halves to any one man.

Of course, ambitious men like Guy the Haitian knew all about mirror images, but these men always barked up the wrong tree. If a man admired another and wanted to be like him, he could often mistake the subject of his admiration for his other half. Ti Allain knew this was no more than an illusion. A mirror image is not someone a man can imitate or try to emulate. It is the other half of him; it lacks precisely those qualities he has. Thus a good man has a bad man as his mirror image. A short man has a tall man. Ambition like Guy's had nothing to do with the serious matter of finding your other half.

But then, perhaps it had. Ti Allain could not be sure whether he had allowed his personal grudge against Guy to cloud his judgement. After all, Guy was not the master of his own destiny. No one was. Destiny was in the hands of the spirits, which was a lucky thing. Had Guy done what he had wanted at first, Ti Allain would not have crossed the border and would not be on his way to see the tall foreigner and warn him of the danger he was in. If Guy had listened to his plea at Diquini, he would have left him there. He would never have met the plump man who was the tall foreigner's other half.

The plump foreigner, Francisco, did not leave Ti Allain in any of the work places they passed. He was not included in the inspections and haggling that went on at every estate they visited. No one tried to get him out of the car and he stayed there in comfort all through the day. Eventually, all but a handful of the workers were handed over to their new masters. The plump man, Francisco, got into the car beside the driver. Ti Allain knew he was watching him where he sat in the back of the car, chewing on a piece of bread he had been given earlier.

'*Vamos al capital,*' Francisco said to the driver, and yawned. Soon they were on a smooth, black road as wide as a river, speeding silently through the afternoon. Ti Allain was not afraid. His eyes were closed, but he was not asleep. One of his hands rested across his face. Behind it, right between his eyes where no one could see, he held a ball of the soft, chewed bread. Silently, Ti Allain was calling on the spirits to notice him and see that he was safe.

Chapter Forty-Eight

'Of course Balthasar will listen to reason,' Cunningham mumbled as he ate the last piece of cassava bread. 'The goat's cheese is all gone. If he doesn't show this evening, I'll have to go back to the village for more supplies. I must be a sight, all dressed up for a party, with three days' worth of stubble on my dirty face. Nails are filthy. Haven't combed my hair. Bloody foot hurts like ...' He trailed off, suddenly aware he was talking to himself. Am I losing my marbles? he thought, taking great care not to vocalize any more.

He had been scrabbling in the unaccustomed filth of the bush for three days. This sort of country was a temporary diversion for him, not a way of life. He needed the running water, the restaurants, the bars and the casinos. Above all, he needed people. Now the country had hit him with its loneliness. Not since the Egyptian desert had he been surrounded by so many enemies. Sure, there had been people who did not agree with him or were jealous of his charm, but that was just clean competition. They hadn't been out to kill him.

The web of coincidence in which he'd become enmeshed seemed endless. The shock had started in Haiti, when Marie-Christine was killed. Then Marcel Kinet and the kid. His share of responsibility for that had vaguely dawned on him then, but he'd been with Marina and in love. He'd been winning and able to contain and postpone his guilt. He was now living in the car, in the middle of nowhere, waiting for Balthasar to find him and kill him. Perhaps he deserved to die. Many of his friends had been killed because of him. Had he been in a different trade, they would still be alive. The strain of his conscience was consuming him.

Wrong, wrong, wrong. Not his fault. The Chief, the generals, the landowners and the tycoons had caused all this. They were smug in their lavish houses, leaving Balthasar and him to play a deadly game of hide and seek in a mucky battle-field. Surely Balthasar would see this was not of his making. It was the cursed greed of the system. Balthasar would listen. Together they would make the killing stop. Not in a million years. Why not? He was right. It didn't matter. He'd been right before. That was why Balthasar had come with him in the first place. It had all gone too far.

He felt old. Too old to suddenly turn aggressor. The tension that had gnawed inside him ever since he saw the plane explode in mid-air had weakened him. Life was not for this. People were there to talk to and women to be loved. He couldn't live like this, constantly having to look over his shoulder. Not now. Not ever. He must get out of there this minute.

Cunningham started the engine. He'd drive to the village. If he met Balthasar, he would soon talk him out of it. If he did not meet him, he would go and seek him out. He had no gun. Balthasar knew that. If he didn't, he could easily prove it to him. He would get out of the car and raise his hands. The man wouldn't just shoot.

A telephone, that's what he needed now. Talk to someone. Reassure himself that there were still people out there. Not just mud and trees and bushes and flies. And food. And a place to clean himself up in. That's what he must find.

He entered the little crossroads store. From behind the counter, a wrinkled Chinese lady offered him a toothless smile. He bought a few packages of cassava biscuits and some cheese, a bottle of milk and a quart of whisky. He apologized for his clothes. The old lady looked back at him blankly. He did not look any worse than her usual customers.

'May I use the telephone please? I can pay for it.'

'Of course, but you'll have to guess how much it costs.'

He tried Francisco Martinez, but there was no one at home. Antonio's Bar was engaged. He dialled Fernando Bogard. The landowner's wife answered. 'Fernando loves your Haitians. Why didn't you come over with them? Is it true you're in trouble?'

'No more than usual.'

'Stop chasing women, Cunningham. One day some husband will kill you.'

'It's not that sort of trouble.'

'We're all getting old.'

He agreed and said *adiós*. He dialled the Chief's number in Jarabacoa. The Chief's brother answered. 'I don't think my brother wants to talk to you, Cunningham. He can't talk to anyone. It's all to do with you. The Minister's giving him a hard time about those two rich kids shot in Arroyo Hondo. Why don't you stick to business, Cunningham? Or chasing women or something less dangerous.'

'I was only trying to help your brother. We're old friends. Remember the cinema?'

'This is a peaceful place. Always has been. Why don't you leave the Republic, Cunningham? Everybody knows you can't go back to England, but *por Dios*, there must be somewhere that would take you. In any case, we all thought you were dead by now. Balthasar is after you. When he was Chief of Police, the saying went "Balthasar always gets his man".'

The man had been drinking, but his voice became softer. 'Balthasar is dangerous, you know. He shot El Gordo and now he's roaming the countryside looking for you. My brother told me yesterday they are trying to find him, but you should be careful. They know he is driving El Gordo's Camaro. He's rumoured to be somewhere near the Miner's estate. He is hoping he can hide there, I suppose. Shoot first, *comprende*?'

'Give my regards to your brother.'

They said goodbye and he dialled Antonio's Bar again. Francisco answered the phone. 'You there full time now?'

'I am thinking of buying the place. The gringo woman gave me the parcel. I've left your share with Antonio. Don't give it all to the casino.'

'You don't need to leave a thing for me, Francisco. I've got enough. Buy your wife a car or something. Use it.'

'You don't have a penny and I know it. Did you hear what happened to the flower woman, the one outside Vesuvio's? She won the big prize in the lottery. Half the town is telling her how to invest the money. One hundred thousand pesos. And all she wants to do is sell flowers like she always did. She doesn't want to be rich. She wants to keep her friends.'

'Look after Mrs Buckmaster, Francisco.'

'She was very correct with me. Gave me everything the way you said.'

'Be good, my friend,' Cunningham said and replaced the receiver.

Francisco always made him feel good, Cunningham thought. He knew what he must do now. He'd go to the Miner's ranch. See Balthasar. Clear the whole thing up. He might get to see the big man himself. Now that they all knew the revolution was over, they could talk. Even Balthasar would listen.

He took the little package and left ten pesos on the counter. He walked towards the door. Behind him, the old lady was fast asleep on her rocking chair. Nothing seemed to disturb the distant smile that stretched across her face.

The Camaro's petrol gauge had been knocking on empty for the last ten miles or more, and Balthasar noticed the petrol station with a sigh of relief. He turned in, stopped the engine and got out of the car. It was then that he saw the young policeman leaning against the station's wall. The attendant was busy handing out change to a truck driver in front of him and Balthasar lifted the Camaro's bonnet. The young policeman approached.

'Are you going to Santiago, señor?'

'No, officer. I've just come from there.'

'Shit. I'm missing all the fun.'

'What's happening in Santiago?'

'Dangerous criminal on the run. We're on general alert. Can you imagine, we've orders not to try and arrest him, but shoot him on sight. Have you ever heard of such a thing? Shoot him on sight ... and I'm stuck here with no way to get back to my station.'

'Who is he, then?'

'I can't tell you that, señor. I've been on leave for three days.

I phoned the station to find out what shift I could report for and they just told me to get back there as fast as I could to join in the manhunt. I can't wait to get back.'

'Shoot on sight, you said?'

'Yes. Shoot on sight. The order comes from the Chief himself. That's all I got. The telephone is out of order up there. I can't even call them. Must get there as soon as possible.'

'I am truly sorry ...'

'It's not far, señor. I'm willing to pay you if you take me. Taxi rate, say five pesos?'

He must have looked like he needed the money, Balthasar thought to himself. That's what being on the run does for you. 'I wish I could, young man. Such dedication should not go unnoticed. You will go far in the police.'

He had been eating in small roadside cafés, always making sure the ostentatious Camaro was parked out of sight. His luck had been holding. Even now, he thought, it was still working for him. He had intended to go to Santiago. Cunningham might be hanging about there somewhere. But Santiago was out of the question now.

The young policeman walked off slowly, glancing back at Balthasar, as if willing him to change his mind. He reached the road. There were no other cars in sight. Balthasar waited for the attendant to come. He had tried to reach the Miner on several occasions during the past few days, but without success. That English bastard who had got him into all this mess was still alive. He was going to lay Cunningham's body before the Miner's feet. He'd call the Miner and tell him about it. There was no one else he could call.

Years before, Balthasar had friends. There was the police force and a few cousins. The latter had either died off or refused to talk to him after his fall. One emigrated to the United States. The only person who had meant anything to him since then was the Miner, who had given him a job in spite of his disgrace. All his disciplined energy had been directed towards the Miner's wishes. He would call him and assure him that his loyalty was still intact. He would tell him of the momentary madness that had made him listen to Cunningham. A weakness brought about by the understandable rage the Miner had felt after the killing at Arroyo Hondo.

The young policeman sat on a white stone marker by the roadside. He'd better leave soon, Balthasar thought. But he'd try the Miner first. He walked over to the telephone booth. His heart was full of remorse. He was sure to convince the Miner of his sincere support. The whole police force was after him just for that support. The Miner had represented the old law and order Balthasar was raised to respect. He had given him a chance before. He was bound to do it again. He dialled the Miner's number. He'd make it up to him. He'd serve him for ever. In any capacity.

This time Balthasar struck gold. The Miner, the housekeeper said, was at home now. He had just arrived. Could the señor wait for a moment while she fetched him? Of course he could, Balthasar said, and a warm feeling of humility overcame him. He had tears in his eyes. He would drive the young policeman right into the station and give himself up if the Miner ordered him to do so.

Outside, his luck seemed to hold firm. Down the road, the young policeman got into an empty taxicab. Then the Miner came on the line. Balthasar smiled as he announced himself, half expecting the soft voice to embrace him. But the words that blasted at him were poison. It was Haiti all over again.

'What are you calling me for? Just shoot yourself, Balthasar, and be done with it. Francisco Martinez, who the boys you shot supposedly killed, is alive and well and drinking beer in the Malecon. Yes, you've probably known that all along. You keep killing our own people. Why did you shoot El Gordo, you stupid bastard? Why weren't you on the plane, like you were supposed to be, instead of Pilar? You don't know what you've cost me, Balthasar, but you're going to pay for it. If I knew where you were, I'd phone the police myself and turn you in. Perhaps the Chief should stay where he is.

We'd all be in trouble if castrated shits like you were allowed to run the police. You've killed one of my best supporters and the man whose death might have done some good, that Englishman Cunningham, you let him live. I'm told he is somewhere here, around my estate. I shouldn't be surprised if he decides to pay me a visit. And do you know, you scumbag, if he did drop in, I'd give him a drink. He managed to see through your dumb thick skin and used us all to his advantage. I respect a good opponent. We'd drink to you, Balthasar, and your failures. All your failures. And to my failure, too, Balthasar. I planned to have you blown up, but you're still here. I only hope you die somewhere far away, where no one will have to buy your incompetent body and mess their hands up while lowering you into a hole.'

The Miner was stammering badly. Balthasar was too shocked to speak, too tired to listen to more. 'Just go away and die, Balthasar. Burn in hell for ever.'

The Miner was still screaming into the phone when Balthasar hung up. His strength was sapping away. Could the Miner really have planned to blow him out of the sky? He must have heard wrong. The Miner was not a man he could ever hate. He hated no one. Only Cunningham.

Rage assaulted him as he started the Camaro. Where should he go? He was a leper. An outcast. An enemy of all he ever believed in, and the man who had charmed him into that position was still alive. The Miner had told him where Cunningham could be found. He was not going to wait until dark. Face the gringo bastard in broad daylight. Shoot and stab and kick him and watch him agonize in slow, excruciating pain. Scream. Then die. After that, nothing would matter.

CHAPTER FORTY-NINE

■

A world full of Franciscos would be a good place, Cunningham thought, as he approached the wood. The trees were tall and well maintained. Down the hill stood the Miner's house, its thick stone walls half hidden behind a vertical sea of bougainvillea. Francisco, he thought, would knock on the door and ask if Balthasar was there.

A bird passed overhead and it sang, dropping a freshly caught worm on the ground just in front of him. He would laugh again and love again, he thought, but Marina was not on his mind. One day soon, he would find a lasting relationship with a woman. Oh, he was in love with Marina, but his love was no longer any good for her. The bird came back again. It dived towards him. He ducked. The worm tried to dig itself back into the safety of the earth, but the bird landed and pulled it out again. Some never escape, Cunningham sighed, and then he noticed the Camaro crawl up to the Miner's gate. Its window was open. Balthasar was at the wheel.

Balthasar parked the car by the gate and got out. He held his large pistol in his hand and looked about him. The bird, undisturbed, nibbled ferociously at the worm. It swallowed the remains and went on digging. Balthasar looked up towards the wood, then crossed the road.

The Chief's brother had told him to shoot first. He had nothing to shoot with. He should go down the dirt road leading to the house and hug Balthasar around the shoulders the way he had before. Oh, how easy it would all be. He could explain.

The man reached the dirt road. He started the climb for the woods.

Cunningham got back into the car and started the engine. Slowly he drove out of the wood towards Balthasar. He stuck his head out of the window. 'Balthasar,' he shouted, 'wait!'

The ex-policeman stopped and looked up. He recognized the car. He raised his hand, took aim and shot. The windscreen shattered. Splinters scattered over Cunningham's lap. The afternoon glare made them look like gems.

'Don't be a fool,' Cunningham cried. But Balthasar doggedly continued towards him, swaying in a drunken fashion. The pistol went off again and something grazed Cunningham's shoulder. There was surprise, then fear, then anger. Balthasar stopped in the middle of the path and took careful aim. Cunningham stepped on the accelerator and the car shot forward. Balthasar got one more shot into the radiator before the car hit him and threw him to the ground. Cunningham did not stop. The wheels thumped over the thick-set body as the engine roared in a cloud of hissing steam.

He could almost hear the sickening sound of bones cracking under the wheels. The engine had stalled, but the car continued to roll down the dirt road. It came to a halt by the Miner's fence. The manicured front garden looked deserted.

Cunningham got out of the car. The windscreen was gone and steam gushed out from under the bonnet. His shoulder was bleeding as if to remind him that this was no dream. He turned round and looked. Balthasar was lying where he had fallen, his face looking at the sky. There was a spade in the back of his car. He would put the man in the ground among the trees. It was the least he could do for the poor blighter.

How he had come to be sitting in El Gordo's Camaro he did not remember. He did not feel any different for having deliberately killed a man. His father was wrong, or the Bible, or whoever invented the idea that life was sacred.

The wide empty road from Santiago to the capital stretched under the late afternoon haze. He was speeding past tobacco plantations and pink mountains and valleys of thick sugarcane. The wind embraced his face and somewhere, not far away, there was a fire. He could not see it, but the mild, intoxicating scent of burning grass entered his open window. He knew the police were looking for the Camaro, but not on the open road. The Chief's brother had told him that when he warned him about Balthasar.

He was listening to the radio. There was, amid martial music, constant talk of an aborted coup. The plotters had fled the country and some were under arrest. Not all had been identified yet and the public were advised to be on the alert. The radio kept alternating between music and short staccato announcements. The Chief was the hero of the hour. He was going to be decorated for valour by the President of the Republic. Other people were involved in uncovering the coup, but their names could not be released until all the rebels were safely behind bars. Be alert, the radio advised its listeners. Balthasar was not mentioned.

There was a new roadside complex a few miles ahead. Petrol stations and shops and hot showers. Hot food and telephones. Closing in on the place, on the edge of Rancho La Cumbre, Cunningham slowed down. He watched the sun perform a sinking dance into a sea of sugar-cane. He saw the last stripes of light quiver on the horizon over a multitude of shapes and colours. Then a final flash of gold raced into the sky and the valley went dark.

A neon palm tree welcomed him to the station. He could stop there until night fell. No one would recognize him. And even if they did, it wouldn't matter. He had been running long enough. He was going to call the Israeli Embassy and talk to the colonel. He knew the man was in town. There was a picture of him in the social column of the paper he had seen in the Chief's house not four days before. A cocktail party of sorts. His South African wife was not mentioned, but Cunningham remembered the old glow of her presence.

The oil company's electric arrows guided him into the parking lot and his spirits rose. Telephone the colonel first. Then shower and shave and eat. He was free at last. Poor, but alive. Any minute now he would take off. Load some wench on the back of his horse and ride away. Marina? Not after Santiago. She had a life to lead. Now he had one too. One day he would find someone who would last. Someone all of his own.

He parked the Camaro and looked about him as he locked it. No one gave him a second glance. Two Harley-Davidsoned policemen thundered into the station. They clattered past the Camaro and one looked nonchalantly back, but his gleaming machine roared on. Nothing has changed, he chuckled to himself with relief. The Chief's orders have not reached everyone in the force yet. Some didn't even know about Balthasar. Shower first. No, call the colonel first. He had been meaning to do that ever since he had received the message weeks ago.

'At last, you scarlet pimpernel,' the colonel said. 'We thought you had disappeared to avoid publicity. Any minute now you'll be a hero.'

'What are you talking about?'

'It looks like you've saved a few important bulls in this ring, boychick. But we can talk about that when we meet. This little adventure of yours could not have come at a better time.'

'You must be joking. Better time? For whom?'

'For us, boychick. For all of us.'

Boychick. That was the name the South African woman had called him years ago.

'When are you coming into town, Samson?'

'Tonight. I have to get rid of the car I'm driving.'

'Is it hot?'

'It's on fire.'

'Are you into stolen cars nowadays?' They both laughed. 'We can collect you if you need to be invisible.'

'No. Thank you, my friend. I'll get to you tonight.'

'Dinner?'

'No thanks. I'll get something on the way. See you in a couple of hours.'

'I'll wait for you at the Embassy. I'm staying here this time. There's a lot to talk about. *Shalom*.'

The word brought long-gone memories back to him and he

repeated it and hung up. He was not sure what the Israelis were after. He had learned something about their single-mindedness. They had kept in touch with him over the years and he saw the colonel whenever he passed through. They had asked him to call just before he had left for Port-au-Prince. That trip had now taken a back seat in his mind. It seemed to have happened long, long ago. Before Egypt and Palestine. Before everything. He was at a crossroads now. To survive having killed Balthasar he would have to look for a change. Perhaps he could go on an extended trip somewhere far away.

Someone told him once that the old remember things that happened in their childhood and forget what occurred the day before. Perhaps, he thought as he got into the shower, age was catching up with him.

He sat at the long wooden bar. The chef's special was *sancocho*, a local stew of beef, pork and chicken cooked with corn and other vegetables. It was thickened with red beans and was very peppery, and the first spoonful that ran down his throat numbed him. The Israelis were up to something. They had never sounded that keen before. But they had helped him once. His mood swung between elation and anxiety. He must not be pushed into any decisions now.

As he paid the bill and tipped the pretty waitress, it occurred to him that there might still be a long life ahead of him. Anything could happen. Outside, it was pitch dark. The parking lot was filling up. People from the surrounding towns and villages were streaming out of their cars for an evening out.

On the road, the air was cool under a clear, moonless night. The sign he flew past said 'Santo Domingo 60 kilometres'. The oxygen-hungry engine that had once worked for El Gordo would whisk him there in less than an hour.

CHAPTER FIFTY

─ ■ ─

The guard at the gate had been told to expect him. Cunningham drove the Camaro into the Embassy's drive. Must remember to inform the police, he thought as he mounted the stairs to the door. His body felt heavy. He didn't use his walking stick that often these days. Vanity, the colonel had told him the last time they met. The doctor he had visited in Miami a few months before had warned him about that. If you go on bullshitting yourself you are twenty years old, you'll end up having to use it all the time, the man had said. But that was not so. Only when he was tired or under strain would the pain remind him he was different. His right shoe did not crease with use as the left one did. Only the sole wore out. He sometimes thought about collecting his right shoes, but always dismissed the idea as macabre.

'Come in, Cunningham,' the colonel said as the door opened. 'You look like a real shmuck in that outfit. Still in tuxedo. We'll have to get you something.'

Later, wrapped up in the colonel's kimono, Cunningham sat on the sofa. They were using the First Secretary's flat above the Chancery. The flesh at the end of his stump was tender.

'You've earned yourself a medal,' the colonel said. 'They're going to pin it on your chest as soon as they find you.'

'I don't know what you're talking about.'

'You've saved the whole fucking government, boychick. Mama will be proud of you. She always said you had something.'

His face flushed. The old guilt would hit him whenever he met the man. Mama. The South African woman. The train all those years ago. Perhaps he called her that because they had no children. 'How is Mama?'

'Up and down, boychick. Up and down. She's not been too

well these past few months. We're all getting old.'

'I'm sorry to hear that.'

'You don't look so hot yourself.'

'I know what you mean. I'm going to take a long rest.'

'We have other plans for you, Cunningham.'

'What do you mean, other plans? I've just told you what's been happening in my life.'

'Things are happening all over the world. We must grab the opportunity. It's going to be good for you, too. I won't mince words with you. You and I are going on a trip.'

'When?'

'Tomorrow morning, Cunningham. Latest the day after. We're going to start with the small republics in Central America, then work our way down south. A few weeks. Months maybe. That's all. A few months that will make you rich.'

'I don't want to be rich. I need a rest.'

'We're looking for new markets, Cunningham. We have spare production capacity. This is the time and the place and you are the right person.'

The man couldn't be serious, yet his strong eyes were firmly fixed on his own, the face taut and eager. Then the mouth softened into a faint smile. 'What do you say, eh, boychick?'

'What are you selling?'

'Sub-machine guns, grenades, ammunition. Reconditioned tanks. Surveillance electronics. That sort of stuff.'

'You're selling arms? I thought you were buying.'

'You've been here for a long time, boychick. You've not been following our fortunes. We've been self-sufficient for years.'

'What makes you think there's a market for that sort of junk over here?'

'We have our sources.'

The conceited bastard would say that. 'There are no wars here, Colonel.'

'These countries are shit scared of revolutions. Not all of them are blessed with mad Englishmen like you to save them. They are arming their police and their militia to fight the reds. Everyone sells here, but we offer after-sales service.'

'What do you mean?'

'We train people. We set up repair shops. Field hospitals. We build runways in jungles. Oh, all in a small way, but then we are a small country. We can't sell a morsel to our neighbours so we have to look further afield. To survive we need markets, boychick. People to work them. We need someone over here. Someone we trust. Well, we trust you, Cunningham. You know we do. You have lived here for many years. You know the generals ... you know their price.'

'It's not my scene.'

'You've done all this before. That's why you've been hiding here, remember?'

'That was different. That was self-defence. You were fighting for your life then. What you're asking me to do is a bitch. I can tell you who will get their heads blown off with the shells you want me to sell here. These banana republics have nothing to fear from the outside. Not one of their neighbours will ever invade anyone. It's all on the inside. Prop up the bloody army to frighten the hungry masses into submission. Execute a few starving miserables and make sure no one gets any ideas. Keep the goodies where they've always been, the big families. Fuck the rest. That's what your deal is about. Don't tell me.'

'My God, Cunningham. Have you become a revolutionary in your old age? Haven't you just saved the generals and the big families right here?'

'You're full of shit. You know nothing. This so-called plot was hatched by the big families. It was a class thing, that's all, and I got involved by chance, while I was looking after my own business. I'm no revolutionary. The generals here are not British generals. They come from nothing. Nowhere. And if they make a few pennies, so what? Oh shit, I don't know. I don't really care. I've killed a man today. Self-defence, I know, but he wasn't really my enemy. He was just a slave who thought he could become king. It's all so bloody confusing. *Mierda*, I wish I could go back to civilization. Spain. Europe maybe ...'

'I was just coming to that. We may be able to help you on this one. You want to go home?'

'England? Don't be funny. I'm a deserter. Deserters are never forgiven.'

'You're not listening.'

'The Provost Marshal is waiting for me, Colonel. The list I'm on goes on for ever. Like the banks.'

'We know all about that, Cunningham, but there are ways.'

'Get me cleared? Not a chance. I am surprised at you, Colonel. I mean, maybe I've become naïve, but you, a military man, you know they'll try me as soon as they get their hands on me.'

'Oh, shut up, will you? I'm trying to tell you something. We may be able to work something out with the Ministry of Defence in London. We may have a few bits and pieces they might want to buy.'

'Equipment? From Israel? Your head has grown big.'

'Information, boychick. Information. Our secret service is one of the best. Horse-trading, you know. Stuff we know might interest MI5 or MI6. Irish stuff, IRA.'

'I don't know what you're talking about.'

'You're better off not knowing, believe me. Sometimes, Cunningham, you're so naïve it's a wonder you've survived. Maybe it's part of your charm. Anyhow, you listen to me now and listen good. All I'm going to say is this: we could, perhaps, help you to go back to England. You never know your luck. We'll deal for you.'

'Would you really do that for me?'

'Before we get on to that, I must have your answer. We've got it all worked out. We need you. I don't need to remind you we know how to look after our friends. We have never let you down, Cunningham. We won't start now. I hope you say yes. You may get back to England. You will certainly make a fortune.'

'Do I have a choice?'

'That's hitting below the belt. Shame on you, boychick.'

'There you go again. Stop making me feel guilty.'

'No one is forcing you.'

'Yes, I'll do it, I will do it. What more do you want me to say?'

'I knew we could count on you. You don't have to shout. Here's what we want you to do. The local Minister of Defence here is preparing a document for you. It will recommend you to his opposite number in every country in the region. It will say you are a national hero and a staunch conservative son of a bitch. You know what I mean. That will open every door for you. Simple, no? It's going to be fun, Cunningham. The Jews are turning their spades into swords. And you will get a ten per cent commission on all sales that follow. This commission will be paid to you until you leave this job. After that, it goes to five per cent and will be paid for all the business we do by ourselves for an agreed period of time. We won't screw you, boychick. You know that. We're talking big numbers here. The opportunities are here if we hit it now. The big boys are only interested in warships and planes. Later they'll kick us out anyway. But there's a lot we can do in the meantime.'

Cunningham's face dropped.

'What's the matter with you?'

'I'm exhausted.'

'Of course you are. Things will look much better in the morning.'

'Don't be condescending. I'm not a child. I know what's wrong with me. I've already told you I'll do it. But you and I have known each other long enough for me to be able to tell you I don't like your deal. I'll only do it because I owe you and because it might get me back to England. I need to get away from here and I'll need money. Peace and quiet. That's what I want now.'

'With what you're going to make, you'll be able to buy a lot of peace and quiet. Acres and acres of it.'

'I know. But I don't need to pretend that I'm some sort of saint. Not to you. I'm a mercenary. That's all.'

'We're all mercenaries, boychick,' the colonel said, his eyes downcast. 'Every one of us. The saints died a long time ago. Ideals are for the young. That's why they are made to pay for them with their lives.'

Cunningham sat back. He poured himself another whisky. He took a deep breath and looked at the Israeli. 'I'm sorry about that. Life is heavy sometimes.'

'Happens to all of us.'

'The Camaro. Would one of your people get it to the police? No, no ... better not. Anyone seen in that car will be shot on sight. You mustn't get involved in this. I'll see to it myself. When did you say we were leaving?'

'Lunchtime tomorrow. The letter from the Minister should be here first thing.'

'Fine. Could I keep the car inside the compound until I can make arrangements for someone to pick it up? I'd better be off now. Pack a few things. In this part of the world people dress to kill. We do want to succeed, right?'

'You said it, boychick.'

'Would someone drop me at my flat?'

'You're on your way.'

He saw the Camaro in the courtyard as he got into the Embassy car. He was tired. The colonel said it was best to leave tomorrow. Good. That way he'd save himself the embarrassment of congratulations, ceremonies and shoulder-tapping he did not deserve.

CHAPTER FIFTY-ONE

◼

The afternoon sun reached the terrace. Sweat ran down his

face. He watched, fascinated, as the little gardener worked on the flower beds.

'Shall I pour you another?' Marina asked. 'You look hot.'

'Yes, please,' Gerald said. He pointed out into the garden. 'Doesn't your little friend ever get tired?'

She smiled and took his glass. She chipped some ice from the little tray, dropped it in, and poured the golden Scotch on top. He nodded. He's a weird little creature, Gerald thought. Had he not been given to them by Francisco Martinez, he'd have sacked him after the first week. He'd shown no interest in the flowers or the plants. Not even the lawn. Marina enjoyed gardening herself and would have been quite happy to do it all, yet for some strange reason she begged him to keep the Haitian. He wasn't lazy, she said. Just shy and weak and frightened. Judging from his hands, he'd never worked in the field before. Anything to keep her happy, Gerald thought, and this afternoon he looked at the man and had to agree she was right.

She handed him the whisky and he said *gracias*. She bent to kiss him on the cheek. His eyes followed her to the door and she waved. He had planned to take her out that night, but she said she had cooked and anyway it was Chiquito's daughter's day off. He had suggested they take the girls out to the Malecon, local-fashion. Walk along the sea after dinner. Watch the people like everyone else. She preferred to stay in. Just the two of them. And now she was inside, turning the roast.

She had not been back to Antonio's Bar for a long while. She felt lazy and safe in this kingdom of hers, surrounded by walls and grass and coconut tree boundaries. The outside world was still uncertain. If she kept herself calm, she would recover. Gerald need never know about Cunningham. Still, in bad moments, there were times when she could hear Cunningham's voice and see his smile and the present just floated away. Then the gossamer of guilt that surrounded what had happened would return, and she did not dare think of him by name. He'd been in the papers after the aborted revolution, but there was no more personal news of him, even though Francisco Martinez was now a regular visitor to the house.

Gerald liked Francisco. He talked a lot about him. He thought him amusing. He knew everybody and everything and had taken pains to teach him the local dialect. He had been good to them. He had provided them with Chiquito's daughter. He was a superb judge of character and knew the back-street marketplace better than anyone in the Ministry of Finance. Had the man been a little less allergic to work and keeping office hours, Gerald would have employed him.

She opened the small oven door and slipped the knife into the tender meat. She lowered the flame and started peeling the potatoes. Through the kitchen window she looked at her husband. He was hers and the little girls were hers and they loved her and depended on her and were all waiting for her to call and say dinner was ready. Everything was as it should be. Where it should be. Including the Haitian.

'Use him as a gardener,' Francisco had said the day he brought the little man. 'I have tried everything else. The *cabrón* is hopeless. He must be good at something.'

He was no taller than a boy of ten. He had a well-shaped head and a pair of beautiful hands. He could not speak any Spanish, Francisco said, so Gerald asked her to try to communicate with him in that school French of hers. The gardener had a soft, melodious voice. His powerful, searching eyes pierced the air with sadness yet never lost their contentment. He said his name was Ti Allain and that was all he said. He did not look unhappy about his sleeping quarters at the back of the garage. When they first gave him a spade he looked at it as if he had never seen one before. He was not a big eater and was fascinated by lizards and other vermin which he caught and kept in an old label-covered cardboard suitcase someone had left behind. P & O Lines. Cairo. Firenze. Rio. British Imperial Airways. Saigon.

At first he just sat about doing nothing. One morning she saw him pick the daisies off the lawn. He sorted them and washed them and spread them in the sun to dry. She asked him what they were for and he did not answer. Two days later, when Chiquito's daughter complained of stomach pains, Ti Allain brewed her a tisane that worked almost immediately. It must have had other ingredients, but it had the unmistakable scent of daisies.

He could tell the advent of rain, too. Suddenly, he would stop watering the flower beds and stand still and point at the dry blue sky without a word. He would ignore her protests and smile and just say *attendez*. He would repeat that word again and again and then, invariably, the sky would turn black and explode.

He often looked at the sky, like a believer, yet he never asked where the church was. Nor did he want to go with Chiquito's daughter when she dressed up to go there of a Sunday morning. Marina knew he was a good man who would not harm a soul, and she wanted to know more about his village and his people. She wanted him to stay.

His simple, detached, accepting nature relaxed her. The peace in his eyes seemed contagious. She became dependent on him. She needed to see him every day or hear his voice whispering as he stood and looked towards heaven. She needed to know he was there, outside somewhere, on the grass or under the old mahogany tree. She thought she saw him talk to it once, but she was not certain. Somehow, to make her world complete, she needed his presence close by. It was madness, of course it was madness. But slowly her anxiety and restlessness fell away and she stayed in the house and began to feel it was home.

Ti Allain flicked the last morsel of earth from the root of the plant and looked at the house. He saw the foreign woman's face smile at him through the window, and he remembered the days that had passed. Until the plump foreigner they called Francisco brought him to her house, Ti Allain had thought the spirits had forgotten all about him. Otherwise he would surely have been taken to the house where the tall foreigner lived. The one whose mirror image he so longed to be. At first he shut himself off from the family he was forced to live with. They tried to show him how to cut the grass and kill the herbs and give water to the flowers. They seemed intent on finding him wasteful, cruel things to do.

Life in Saint Domingue had been different. No one knew or respected him there. The family he had come to live with certainly did not understand the ways of the world. They drank beer and pampered their children and the man was never in the house. When he was, he just sat about on the terrace reading the papers.

If the spirits wanted the flowers to die, they merely closed the sky to stop the water from coming down. Some flowers were not meant to remain alive at all. Like the spirits, they were much more important when they were dead. One could keep them for a long time that way and in their leaves hid medicines for many ailments. The big trees, under which a man could escape the heat, stayed green because of the deep water that God had hidden under the ground. He and the trees knew man would only waste the water as his own people did back in the village. The grass patch the people had in the front of their house was useless because neither cows nor goats were allowed to graze on it. Ti Allain did not understand why they wasted so much water keeping it growing only to have it cut down again.

When he had first crossed into Saint Domingue, Ti Allain still hoped he would be reunited with the tall one-footed foreigner. When the plump foreigner Francisco tried to amuse him by attempting to find an occupation for him, he feared it was not to be. No one understood that Ti Allain, ordained by the spirits and one-time custodian of Monique the black witch, needed no one to tell him what to do. He was guided by the spirits, and when he was not he was happy to be alone and meditate.

The plump foreigner taught him how to polish shoes and

wash other people's clothes, but that did not fool him. It was Monique trying to trap him by pointing him in the wrong direction. She was trying to confuse the real reason for his coming to Saint Domingue with foolishness. She must have transferred her powers over the border to one of the others who lived and worked with the plump foreigner. She would catch him that way, hoping to become his mistress again, but Ti Allain knew her game. He spent two nights and a day looking for Monique's local source of power.

It turned out to be not a man but a small brass spoon which one of the people had carried with him all the way from the village. It was only when the spoon was in sight that the plump foreigner found Ti Allain some work to do. When he discovered that, Ti Allain buried the spoon in the ground and sat on top of it one whole day, looking at his feet, not uttering one word. After that vigil, the plump foreigner shrugged his shoulders and left him alone, and Ti Allain knew he had beaten Monique for as long as he stayed in Saint Domingue.

He had sincerely wished to stay there with the plump foreigner who was the tall foreigner's mirror image. The one-footed foreigner knew that Ti Allain had come to warn him and was sure to come and seek him out one day.

When Francisco took him in the big car to this other house to live with the tall thin man and his woman and the two pampered little girl children he was filled with despair. He feared that his masters had left him to float without direction on an endless sea. But he took the spoon with him and hid it in a tin can just in case.

It was not until he had the chance to look at the foreign woman's face that Ti Allain realized that the big guiding hand had finally brought him ashore. The foreign woman was telling him in her halting French that the beds in which the flowers lived had to be kept clean. That was done so that they could keep all the water and all the food in the earth for themselves and grow strong. At first, Ti Allain did not know why she was telling him all this. It had nothing to do with him, and if the woman wanted her flowers to be strong, she could keep the beds clean all by herself. She must have thought he did not understand what she was telling him because she clipped one of the flowers off with her scissors and held it up in the air to show him what she meant.

At that moment, the sun was in the middle of the sky and it caught the flower in the full flush of its light. The hour was ripe for the spirits to show themselves with the glow. If they were to speak to him he had to concentrate on the last thing he had seen before the sun hit the flower. The last thing he had looked at was the foreign woman's face. And with the sun and the flower and the midday glare he thought of her face and watched and saw it all.

She did not speak, but her lips were moving just like the one-legged foreigner's had when he'd seen him, in his dream, praying at the place where Monique had burned. The wind in the trees died. There was no sound at all. Even the little girl playing on the grass stopped her high-pitched song. In the silence, Ti Allain heard the footsteps again, but this time they were receding. The foreigner had stopped running. He was now limping away. In the wrong direction.

On the surface, the woman in the garden with him seemed to belong to the tall man who lived in the house with her. But there was something in her face and about her eyes which made Ti Allain think of the one-legged foreigner. There was, as sure as there were mountains in Haiti, some bond between her and the one-legged man. The spirits were telling him that the one-legged man wanted to come to see this woman. And that she wanted it too. Perhaps neither of them knew of it, but his own vision was painfully clear. He could not possibly have been wrong about that.

The one-legged man had made all the people come to work and eat in Saint Domingue, leaving no one behind. Now he wanted to come himself. Come all the way to where he was living and see the very face Ti Allain was looking at. Ti Allain was brought here to guide him. Work for the woman the man wanted to see. Perhaps she herself did not know it, but her eyes were searching for the one-legged man. Not her outer eyes, but those in the soul behind her face. She needed the one-legged man, and Ti Allain was the only one who knew it. Only he could help her. It was then that he made up his mind to stay where he was and pretend he was a gardener. To clean the beds and water the flowers and learn to cut the grass even if it was a waste of effort.

That day had started badly for her and she was sad that morning, but only until the sun had reached the middle of the sky. What happened next she could not explain. That day, in the garden, the little man stood behind her motionless. Then, as if prompted by some sudden decision, he sat down at the edge of the lawn to do just what she'd tried to show him for days. He started to pull the weeds out of the earth with great expertise. He smiled. And then he smiled again. It was a smile she knew. On someone else's face. It gave her peace and it made her happy.

When Gerald came home that afternoon, he was amazed to see the little man working industriously in the garden. Marina's face had assumed an expression of dreamy contentment that he had long forgotten. She said a broad 'hi' and held him close. She straightened his hair and his tie the way she had when they'd first been married. He said, 'Why don't we go out tonight?', and she said his favourite dinner was in the oven. Life had been good ever since.

CHAPTER FIFTY-TWO

He liked Geraldo Buckmaster well enough. True, the man was a gringo and was married to Cunningham's woman, but for all that he wasn't such a bad fellow. Always had a cold beer waiting for him when he came to the house. Outside of Antonio's Bar, Buckmaster's beer was the best in the Republic.

Out in the garden, the little Haitian was hacking away at the edge of the lawn. The heavy spade towered high above his head. The ground was dry and hard, but the little man sliced the earth as if it was butter. The lady of the house knelt by his side, holding a straight edge to guide him.

'Why don't you go inside,' Buckmaster said. 'Get yourself another beer. My wife is going to be hours. She's in the garden from morning to night helping Ti Allain.'

'He is the laziest man in the Caribbean when he live in my house. With you he work like *un diablo*. What you do to him?'

'Nothing. He was the same, to start with. Wouldn't do a thing. Then something happened to him. I can't think what. Suddenly, he started to work like this and, you know, he won't take a centavo in wages. Won't even talk about it, Marina says. Would you settle that for me? He says someone else is paying him. Not you, is it?'

'You be sure is no me, *palabra de honor*. No worry, Geraldo. When he ready, he come ask for money quick as my wife. No one works *por nada*.'

'I suppose so.'

Stranger things have happened, Francisco told himself. He'd have to ask Cunningham about that. Cunningham had all the answers. But the ungrateful *cabrón* had been very silent these past few weeks. There were rumours in the Malecon about him, but nothing was certain. He had been seen in Managua, in Honduras and Panama all at the same time. God alone knew where the bastard really was, and Francisco did not care. Well, maybe he did just a bit, but why did Cunningham get all the credit? They put his picture in the papers, gave him medals and made him an honorary consul or ambassador or something. Soon they'd make him President. All he did was look after his business like anyone else. And who did all the work? Who got Cunningham out of the shit in Haiti, if not Francisco? Was it not him who suffered at the hands of the rebels, and killed the killers and everything? He was rich, but he deserved praise too. Much more than Cunningham. Life was not fair.

He stood on the terrace, drinking Buckmaster's beer and thinking. Even today he was made to work. The Chief's brother had called about the Haitians. One of them had lost his head. Didn't want to work. Could Francisco come up and collect him and find him another? That was a tall order, but he promised to see what he could do. The Chief's brother was as lazy as the police. And as useless. They were still looking for Balthasar, the Chief's brother had told him. Night and day they were looking for him, and when they found him he would be dead. Balthasar must have left the country long ago, Francisco thought, but he did not say so. Life was really boring now, without Cunningham.

He'd heard from him just once, weeks ago. The connection had been bad, but he did make out what was wanted of him. Cunningham had phoned for a favour, what else? That was why he'd done nothing about it. The Englishman had asked him to go to the Israeli Embassy and collect El Gordo's Camaro there. He was to bring it to the Chief himself. He said Francisco should be careful. Francisco had wanted to tell him off for not bothering to visit him any more now that he was big and famous. But the line had died before he'd managed to do that.

Who did Cunningham think he was anyway? Careful bringing the car to the Chief? He had known the Chief for as long as Cunningham. Well, maybe not, but wasn't it him who dealt with the Chief personally all the time and paid him off and everything? Careful? Didn't Cunningham know he was a careful driver? Didn't he trust him with his own *Yanqui* car to look after?

He delayed it as long as he could. At the time, the Chief wasn't in his office anyway. He was in Jarabacoa having a rest. No one ever works in this town, he thought, no one except Francisco. Everyone was filthy rich. Everyone was lucky.

Even this gringo Buckmaster was lucky. The little Haitian did nothing when he was at his own house. Now he was working like crazy for Buckmaster.

He couldn't discuss his troubles with Buckmaster. Not with his wife having been Cunningham's woman and that. Nor with Rafael. Not even with Antonio. Ever since he'd become rich, Antonio treated him with too much respect. But today he could go to the mountains and see the Chief's brother. He'd take the Haitian away and get him another and they would owe him a favour. He'd take the car up to the Chief at the same time. Like Cunningham had asked him.

He would talk to the Chief that night. See if they could find some business or something. He would drive the Camaro up there as soon as he had finished his beer. He had collected the Camaro that day from the Israeli Embassy. A little later than Cunningham would have expected, but so what? Even at the Embassy they knew all about Cunningham. They treated Francisco with great honour as soon as they heard he was the friend who'd come to collect the car. Cunningham was a bastard. But he was a lucky bastard.

'*Tengo que irme,*' Francisco said to Gerald. 'I go work.'

'Why so soon? It's too hot to work now.'

'No hot in mountains. But must go work there too,' Francisco said with a sigh. He took a last sip and pumped Buckmaster's hand and went to the gate. Outside, the Camaro was waiting for him. They had cleaned it and polished it up at the Embassy and there it stood, gleaming proudly in a splash of afternoon sun. The woman was still in the garden pretending not to notice a thing. Francisco waved at Buckmaster and shut the gate behind him. He'd drive straight to the mountains now. He had nothing else to do. Cunningham had not left any other instructions.

Later, the lights burst out along the Malecon. They'd been turned on a little early. It wasn't dark enough for the bright reflections to reach the water. Moths danced around the lightbulbs. The evening traffic moved slowly. The newspaper boys did brisk business, screaming shattering headlines at the customers. This time it was real blood, they shrieked. Cops and robbers and everything.

The papers told of death. Of some dangerous murderer cut down in a hail of police bullets miles from the city. The red Camaro he was driving was riddled with bullets and it caught fire. Its charred frame was spread in full colour on the front page. The police gave the man's name as one Balthasar Fernandes. Used to be in the police a long time ago, before he became a killer and an outlaw. Not much had been left of the body and there was no picture of it because it was too gruesome, the paper said. But they printed a picture of the Chief of Police with his foot proudly resting on the wreck. He was congratulating his men for protecting the public. The paper said the Chief had come down especially for the occasion. Interrupted an important assignment in the mountains at Jarabacoa. He had come to lead his men. He had come down to make sure that law and order had been restored and the citizens were safe. That was his job, he said with great humility.

Ti Allain, protected from evil at the back of the garage, was decorating his head to face the spirits. Tonight they would have to wait a little longer for his words. As he painted chalk paste across his forehead, he noticed grains of dry wheat on his mattress. The head of the little doll he had made in the likeness of the plump foreigner had split open, spilling all the grains that had filled it. Of course he was not going to remove them because they were going to make him itch. A sure sign that a new soul was about to join his own. He was happy about that because a new soul was always a good sign.

A man with two souls could live anywhere and never be alone. Not even if the sea reached the mountains and flushed away the village and Monique's grave. This was surely going to happen one day, but for now he had his mission. He would have to look after the foreign woman and make sure she ended each day with a smile. She was his master until he was called elsewhere. From now on, perhaps for the rest of his life, Ti Allain would have to pretend he was a gardener. The spirits knew he was not really a working man and that was all that mattered.

One soul had gone. He dared not say whose, for this was not the time. The doll's head had only recently split, and sudden death was no stranger to the spirits. He would not grieve now, perhaps not at all. One man's misery was often another's fortune.

He now belonged to that rare breed of people whose bodies contained not one soul but two. He had replaced someone and was now firmly established as the one-footed foreigner's mirror image. He would represent him in this house by the side of this woman until he came. That was what he had crossed the mountains for.

The woman could look at him and smile and think how well he tended her flowers. And no one would ever tell her who he was or why he was there or who had sent him.

BOOK THREE
NOW

CHAPTER ONE

■

SUNDAY 22 JULY, 1984, 2 A.M.

Ti Allain listened to the night. The dance was over and he was ready to follow the voice he had heard. It was his grandmother's voice and she was in the sky, near the moon. She had told him to go up to the house and see about the explosion. He had made no mistake because it was the first time he had heard her voice since she passed on, years before. And it was clear and loving. He had not heard a word of love directed at him for many years. Not since he'd left his village long ago, on his voyage of adventure.

He did not often think of that or of how he had finally become the one-footed foreigner's mirror image. It was ordained that the plump foreigner Francisco would die a violent death as his doll-head predicted. It was all in the hand of the spirits then. He had pretended to be a gardener in the foreign woman's garden in Saint Domingue for a long time, and then one day a heavy-set woman came to the house and said he belonged to her because her husband, the plump foreigner Francisco, had disappeared without a trace. She had a piece of paper to prove it. His master, the foreign woman's husband, was forced to let him go, to many tears and sadness on the part of his wife. He said a gentle goodbye to her and he took his brass spoon and packed his handful of Haitian earth and followed his new mistress out of the gate. He did not know how long it was he had lived with the plump foreigner's wife, but it was not long.

Things had much changed for him because he was no longer a gardener. His new mistress had tried to teach him how to cook, but a big fire had destroyed her kitchen that same day and after that he quickly buried the spoon in the ground and from then on he was left alone. He just sat outside the house and was given food sometimes and lived under the big tree until the day his mirror image, the one-footed foreigner who had taken them all across the border to Saint Domingue, came to the house. The visit did not surprise Ti Allain, who quickly unearthed Monique's spoon from where he had buried it, pressed it close to his forehead, and prayed to Monique and the spirits and anyone who was listening to make his mirror image take him away.

The plump foreigner's wife and the one-footed Englishman had words. He knew they were talking about him and he heard the plump foreigner's wife say he was the laziest man in the whole world. He was not sure how long the conversation lasted because he was concentrating on the spoon and only had eyes and ears for the spirits. Then the conversation stopped and the tall foreigner came to see him under the tree.

Ti Allain pretended not to notice him, but the tall one-footed foreigner tapped him on his shoulder and spoke to him in Creole. 'Come with me,' the one-footed foreigner said. 'We are going away from here.'

Ti Allain had expected something like that to happen because if two mirror images meet, they need to be together as long as they can so as to learn as much as possible about each other and protect each other from evil. To make sure he was not imagining it, he pretended he did not hear and the one-footed foreigner said it all again.

Ti Allain looked up and saw the man's face. He was smiling, and in his eyes Ti Allain saw how much the one-footed foreigner needed him. His eyes spoke in a language Ti Allain did not know, but understood. Come with me, they said, because beside you I have no one left and I must have you near me so that you can look at the road ahead and warn me of what may befall me.

The eyes said, 'I am lonely and you are lonely and, now that we have accomplished what we have come here to do, we must leave.' The eyes said, 'I will die if you do not come with me.' And then the sadness disappeared and the one-footed foreigner smiled and the heat of the day disappeared and a feeling of great well-being engulfed Ti Allain and he got up and followed the one-footed man out into the street. All he took with him was his little sack of Haitian earth and Monique's brass spoon. He left all his potions and his dead lizards and his dolls at the back of the garage in the foreign woman's garden because he was forced to leave in a hurry. Of course that was not the real reason. The real reason was that the foreign woman needed it all to represent him and his other half and keep her company once they were gone from Saint Domingue.

And that was how it came about that Ti Allain, the one-footed foreigner's true mirror image, left Saint Domingue in a small machine that flew like a bird without waggling its wings. They flew to another island nearby. The tall foreigner told him in Creole that he would leave him on that island, but soon they would meet again. It had all been like in a dream, because like in his dreams, Ti Allain was never put to work. He was sleeping in a bed in a room that had cloth grass on the floor. They brought him food and there for the first time he saw a picture box with people in it. They took him out into the streets and they flashed a bright light at him which burned his eye, but he did not fret. They gave him clothes and papers with a small image of himself affixed to them and he waited.

And then he was brought to a big building the shape and size of Jonah's whale. Inside, there were rows and rows of strange chairs. A foreign woman led him to one, sat him down and tied him like a prisoner with a wide belt. There were many people there and they were all tied up into their chairs with wide belts. Then the building that had the shape of a whale took off into the air with all the people. It stayed there for a very, very long time and he was given food he did not touch because he was in the sky and when a man reaches the sky he need no longer eat. He clutched his spoon and his Haitian earth and hoped Monique was watching over him because up there where he was he must have been close to the spirits. High enough almost to be one of them.

The punishment for that thought came as soon as the whale-bird came back to earth. The place they arrived in was cloudy and grey and the air was so cold that Ti Allain thought he had arrived at the land of the dead. The people were all tall, like the one-footed foreigner. Many had golden hair and most were darkly attired and sullen and nobody smiled when they saw him. He was too tired even to think of approaching the spirits and he fell asleep in the back of the big car that had come to collect him from the house of the whale-bird.

When he woke, he saw that they were driving up a long road that led to a big house that looked as white and almost as big as the President's Palace in Port-au-Prince. At the door he saw the tall foreigner with the one foot who was his other half. Ti Allain got out of the car and performed the rabbit-in-cage dance and the one-footed foreigner did not mock him or shout at him. A lady who was there took him by the arm and led him to the back of the house where he was shown to his shed.

The very same shed he stood in front of now, wearing his crown in the dark of the night, having completed his dance. The air was silent and the echoes of the explosion he'd seen before he'd started to dance, before he'd heard his grandmother's voice, were dead and gone. There was no light in the house and Ti Allain started across the grass towards the window of the room where the one-footed foreigner usually sat. He had been his master for many, many days now. He used to like watching the foreigner's back as he sat by his desk talking to himself, holding the black thing that looked like a calf's foot and shone like an eggplant.

He approached carefully and to his nostrils came the smell of fire and burnt flesh. Perhaps the one-footed foreigner had made a sacrifice. Perhaps that was the reason why his grandmother's voice had come to him. A sacrifice made by your mirror image often reached God faster because it did not suffer from the same greed or fears, or carry the same hopes you suffer or cherish yourself.

He arrived at the window and his foot stumbled on a man. He was a young man who lay dead on the grass by the wall. His half-face looked at the sky. His one eye was open and Ti Allain thought he saw an expression of pain in it. By the side of the body lay a large gun like the one he had often seen in his master's picture box. From the pictures he had seen, Ti Allain knew that this gun was mean and could kill many good people at the same time.

Now the gun lay on the grass, as dead as its master. Ti Allain looked in. The full moon shone into the room and he saw his one-footed master lying upon the floor. He fretted. No dead, his grandmother whispered, and with that came relief. If the man was dead, he would be left alone to look for another mirror image. He was not as young as he used to be, and he now lived in a world he did not know. He had never been away from the garden since he had arrived many, many days ago.

Half lying on the window sill, he watched and listened closely and he heard his master breathe. The tall man's face seemed full of happy thoughts. He had come out one moment too early, Ti Allain thought, and he climbed down and pulled the half-faced man and his gun across the grass, all the way to his shed. The earth in the beds around his shed was always soft. For all the time he had been there, Ti Allain had used this place as a burial ground for countless dead creatures – mice and cats and dogs from the house. Only one bed in which nothing had been buried was left. He picked up his shovel and started digging.

He knew they were watching him. Monique and the spirits and his grandmother were there. And they were proud of what he was doing, protecting his mirror image from the half-faced man he was going to put into the ground. Tie him up well, Ti Allain heard his grandmother say, and he remembered how they had to tie his father up when he came back from the village in a belligerent mood, having filled himself with rum.

He took a length of rope from his shed and he tied the half-faced man's hands and feet and covered his face with a sack. Then he surveyed the large hole he had dug and with his feet he rolled the half-faced man into the hole. He went back to the place where the man had died and picked up what other pieces of him he could find, and also the gun, and threw them into the hole, too.

The sun began to show itself behind the trees just as Ti Allain finished. The hole was covered up and he spread leaves all over it to confuse the half-faced man's spirit. He then danced over it because his one-footed master was safe and therefore he was safe too. He brought more leaves and twigs and pressed them on top of the others. If the sun shone all day, it would dry the whole bale. Then he would start a fire over the half-faced man and that would be a sign for the good spirits to carry his soul into hell and have it burn there for all eternity.

Ti Allain recited the prayers he had heard in church when they mourned people. The half-faced man must have had, among his family and friends, someone who was good and deserving, and Ti Allain prayed with great concentration.

He was tired now and, as the sun brought the diamonds onto the grass, the way it did at dawn in the mountains of Haiti, Ti Allain went into his shed and lay down, holding his spoon, and slept.

Later, much later, Ti Allain got up. He took the spoon and the bag of Haitian earth he always carried with him and went to the front of the house. The one-footed man's big car was not there. He would be coming back when the sun reached the other side of the large tree by the gate of the house. It meant the day was Sunday.

On the step, in front of the door, Ti Allain poured the precious earth of his homeland in a small pile. He spread it thinly until it covered the step from end to end. At the very centre, he placed the brass spoon where Monique the black witch lived. When his master touched the earth, he would be safe no matter what his enemies did. As long as the one-footed foreigner stepped on the earth of Haiti, nothing could happen to him. But if he did not, the danger would double. And Ti Allain himself would be in great peril, having used the holy earth in vain.

CHAPTER TWO

—◼—

SUNDAY 22 JULY, 1984, 8 A.M.

Cunningham sits up in bed and rubs his eyes. He looks at his watch. He knows he can't have slept longer than three or four hours, but he feels rested. As if someone has sucked away all his memories, his anxieties and guilt. As if he has been resting for ever. As if the night has lasted an eternity. So much has happened, so many lives lost on the way. Enemies and friends. But he is still here.

He rolls over to sit up on the king-size bed. His artificial leg stands by the night-table in its shoe. It looks lost there, all by itself. The sun streams in through the half-open plantation shutters. In spite of the loneliness and last night's shooting, he feels happy. As if he has been on a long journey away from himself. A spectator's self-search, a cleansing trip into his own past.

He will stick to the past for a little longer, before getting up to go to the flea market. He saw a pretty Japanese vase there a week ago. At the time he was told it was an original Imari design. With luck it will still be there.

He will stick to the past. Not all of it good. Not all of it innocent. But now he is home and it's so good to be home. There is nothing to do. The servants won't be back before Monday. Only the Haitian gardener is out there somewhere. The man has an uncanny way of knowing when to be seen, when to make himself scarce. His mere existence wipes out the loneliness inside the house. Sometimes he leaves a flower or a feather or some liquid brew for him to find. Sometimes a string of dried apples he has learned to make and leave about just when Cunningham feels peckish. As if he can read his mind. He is thirsty now. He can get himself a coffee in the village.

It's good and comfortable to be rich. He does not need to feel guilty about it. El Gordo did not, nor did the Miner, or the Chief of Police. Back where his past lived, people were not ashamed of their wealth. Enjoy, boychick. That was what the colonel had told him when the last deal was signed. It was not that long ago. Eighteen years? Enjoy.

It was at Miami airport. They were standing outside waiting for the colonel's habitual chauffeur-driven limousine. They had just landed from Managua and were about to go to Palm Beach for a few days. The colonel kept an apartment there, overlooking the sea. Outside, orderly traffic of clean, new cars and groomed roadside lawns and manicured palms. In dead contrast to the topsy-turvy, dusty and disorganized lands of Central America. The car arrived, the liveried chauffeur opened the door, they climbed inside.

The colonel took two glasses out of the bar, filled them up and said, 'This is it, boychick.'

'Your health,' Cunningham said. 'How do you mean, this is it?'

'This is the end of the road for you, boychick. You've done it all. And more.'

'I must be going senile. I don't understand.'

'We have been at it for almost two years, remember?'

'I know. I know. We've sold them enough hardware to kill every red Tom, Dick and Harry south of Key West. Somosa loves us. They all love us. We're heroes. What more do you want?'

'You're beginning to talk like a Jew, boychick.' The colonel fell silent and looked outside. They were turning off the expressway and onto Interstate 195 going north.

'I'm not surprised. There are a lot of Jews here.'

'Yes. And a lot of Cubans. Hard-working guys. Coming up in the world. I'm thinking of employing a fellow I know when you leave. He's ambitious and hungry and politically quite safe.'

'Leave? Who is leaving?'

'You are, Cunningham. We'll be parting company after this little holiday. When we first talked about the job two years ago, we agreed.'

'Is it really two years?'

'Almost to the day, boychick, but don't interrupt. You said you needed a rest then, remember. Because you were confused or something. Because you'd finally killed a man.'

'Balthasar.'

'Yes. Balthasar. The guy you buried somewhere and no one knew. Please let me finish. You said you needed a rest. Well, friend, you're getting one. After this weekend, you can go back to England.'

'England? You're mad. Anyway, I like this job. I wouldn't know what to do with myself without it.'

'Sorry, boychick. An agreement is an agreement. You will go to England and you will visit the Provost Marshal in his office. You will be taken ...'

'Arrested?'

'Dammit, Cunningham, will you please listen. You will be taken into custody and stand trial. It will all be very quiet. The press will know nothing of it. You might get a ten-day suspended sentence or perhaps you will sit for a week. Something of that sort. After that, boychick, you will be free. With your money, you won't even stop to piss on me in the street.'

'How did you ...?'

'Exchange deal, I think they call it. We had some information your people needed. We both have terrorists to deal with, you know.'

He listened and he knew it was the end of an association. Give and take and all that.

'Don't pull such a face, Cunningham. Where's your sense

of humour?'

'Lost it, I think. I don't know what to say.'

'Then don't say anything. You're a fabulously rich man now, Cunningham. You can do what you like. Live where you like, screw who you like. But as a favour to me, and above all to yourself, go back home. The English can return from a lifetime in exotica only with money. Life in the cold is bearable then. Get yourself a place in the country. Enjoy life. For a few years your income will continue to roll in. Look, you've done your bit, we've done ours. Time's up.'

They passed Fort Lauderdale and Boca Raton. They drove along the coast and watched the wild surf devour the sand. They were both silent until they got to the apartment.

'We are changing our headquarters, boychick. I don't need this place any more. I think you should take the lease over. You can afford it. You can buy it if you want.'

'Where are you moving to?'

'What you don't know won't hurt you. Forget all about it.'

'You're pushing me aside like some discarded whore.'

'Don't be a shmuck, Cunningham. I love you, you know that. But we must stick to the arrangement. I really sometimes wonder what sort of an officer you were.'

'It was all too short and a long time ago. If I hadn't lost my foot, I would have found out.'

'We would never have met.'

'I suppose you're right.'

'Come on, Cunningham. Don't look so miserable. We Jews say that things can always get worse. You are not even fifty. You are handsome. On top of that you're going home and you're filthy rich. Enjoy.'

It's nearly nine o'clock. He'd better get dressed and go out now. He'll sort it all out later. Must get to the flea market before eleven. Most of the good stuff is snapped up before then. He goes into the shower. He does not feel happy unless he has one at least twice a day. A habit he acquired in the tropics. Oh well, he does have a couple of hours. It takes only a few minutes to get to the high street.

But the man in the window comes back into his mind. He checked the spot during the night. There was nobody there. Whoever hired the bastard must have taken him away. They might be back. Tonight maybe. Who knows.

Outside, the sun floats lazily over the endless greenery of his garden. Too peaceful and beautiful to worry about bodies. He's had enough excitement for one man's lifetime. A hundred men's. And yet there was a time when he craved action. Impossible. No, true. There was a time when he tried to settle down and be a nine-to-five business executive. Buying and selling shares. Meetings with the bank. It was a slow death in a three-piece suit.

He did try. For at least two years. A long time at his stage of life. Right after the desertion business had been cleared. The Israelis had done it again. He never found out what exactly it was they sold to the powers-that-be. It must have been something important for the military to have let him off the hook. Two weeks in jail. He only served one week behind bars, but the experience depressed him. He had never been deprived of his liberty before. Not since the hotel in Port-au-Prince, but that was different.

When he was released, he felt humiliated and alone. He thought of moving to Spain. Somewhere warm and Latin and European. It was the colonel who had talked him out of that one. He was waiting for him outside the jail. Right after the sound of the heavy doors clanging behind him. As always, in a hired spacious car.

'You are suffering from a bad case of self-pity, boychick. Just imagine. It could have been five years or twenty years. You must stop running now.'

'What are you doing in England? Aren't we finished, you and I?' The colonel's face was downcast. 'Smile, Colonel,' Cunningham said as the car started moving. 'This is supposed to be a happy reunion.'

'It is supposed to be and it is.'

'Then why the long face?'

'I have just lost my wife.'

The South African Mama was no more. 'I am a selfish arse-hole,' Cunningham said.

'Maybe you are and maybe you aren't. When a man has a problem he thinks it's the only problem in the world. You can feel for another, but you can never be inside another.'

'But you ... look at you. You came here today.'

'Perhaps I came here because I'm selfish. I'm lonely, boy-chick. There was such a lot I could have told her. Things always remain unsaid. But it's over now. She's better off where she is. And me? Well, a pretty face like yours makes all the difference. You an ex-con. What is the world coming to?'

'I have plans for you,' Cunningham said resolutely. 'We're going to Florida. We'll spend some time in the apartment. I have plans.'

'What plans?'

'First you've got to agree to come with me.'

'This sounds familiar.'

'I'm glad you remember. Are you game?'

'Have I got a choice?'

'That's hitting below the belt.'

'Okay, I'll come.'

'I knew I could count on you.'

After the month he spent with the colonel in Florida, Cunningham returned to England. Marina had told him about Gerald's brother-in-law, the banker. It was a way of keeping in touch with Marina and his love for her and the Dominican Republic and Francisco's memory.

On that first meeting with the banker, Cunningham did not say anything about her. The man was too keen and too clinical and too shy to bring up any sort of family connection with him. He was helpful, though, and Cunningham became quite fond of him. In his simple, square way, Gerald's brother-in-law the banker had tried to help him.

* * *

It's nearly ten o'clock in the morning. Sundays fly. Cunningham is fully dressed and checks himself in the mirror. He is trim still and after the week he has just spent in Marbella he is tanned. He does not look tired and the lines under his eyes do not show. He feels fit. He will walk without his stick today. The grey flannel jacket hugs him like a glove. He has most of his hair still. Not bad for sixty-three. He will buy that Japanese vase. Why not? *Porque sí.* That's why. Because he wants it and likes it and can afford it.

At eleven o'clock on Sunday morning, Cunningham walks down the high street. No cars are allowed around the market and he walks along the pavement enjoying the bustle. Women smile at him and he smiles back.

He has left the car a mile up the road and has walked all the way. He has left his walking stick behind, too, but he feels no pain and he walks without a limp. As he stands by the window, playing with his car keys, he looks at the vase. It's not quite as immaculate as he thought. Imari, all right, not that old. Should he or shouldn't he? Let this one pass, he thinks. Some other time maybe, he says to her, and she waves. What a beautiful day this is.

Cunningham walks to the kerb. He looks left and then right, but there are no cars about and he crosses with a smile of well-being. As he gets to the first stall, he has the feeling that someone is watching him. He looks around. Not a familiar face in sight. He walks into the labyrinth of stalls. The ground beneath his feet feels like a cushion of air. He looks around again. Nothing. *Pues, mañana otro dia.*

It is afternoon by the time Cunningham arrives back at his house. He has a leisurely lunch at the Italian restaurant. The Soave he has with his scampi has a good flowery bouquet and it makes him feel even lighter on his feet. He could go out tonight. See how his luck goes. The Rendezvous Casino by the Hilton Hotel was good to him last week.

The gardener has spread a shovelful of earth on the little step at the entrance. An old brass spoon lies in the centre. He must not touch a thing. He steps over it carefully and lets himself in. He has learned not to interfere with the little chap's eccentricities.

CHAPTER THREE

■

SUNDAY 22 JULY, 1984, 3 P.M.

We are sitting at the table and I have just carved the roast. I am good at that. Over the years I have made an art of carving meat. There is never a mess and the slices are solid and even and just the right thickness. She has often complimented me on it. We eat in silence. I like a bit of a chat over a meal, myself, but she goes all quiet. Perhaps it is a legacy of business lunches, where you're expected to tell jokes and talk and make decisions you'd never make in the office.

Her table manners are impeccable, like Cunningham's. I hear her knife hit the plate as she cuts through the broccoli and I admire the look of complete concentration on her face. There is something different about her. A strain of sorts. As if there is something on her mind. As if she wants to tell me something and cannot find the words.

'Is anything the matter?' I ask. She shakes her head. Her beautiful, full lips open into a smile. God, she is so attractive. I wish I had told her that more often. She is wearing a thin, silky blouse and her wonderful breasts push through the material. They move with her arms. Her skin is soft and pale and my hands itch to touch her. I suppose Cunningham knew how to make her happy that way. With all his exotic experience, he'd know how to please a woman.

How long will I go on thinking of him, now that it is all

316

over? My appetite fades as images devour my mind. I see them together, walking through the black iron door into the Albany. They are in his bedroom and she undresses in broad daylight the way she never did with me and she smiles as he compliments her. They embrace. I can see him slip into her body and hear her groan with the pleasure of it and I want to die. I can see her hips move towards him and somewhere bedsprings creak. I cannot breathe for pain. It surges inside me as I struggle to keep a straight face. Surely something of my emotions must leak out. Why do I think of this after all this time?

They used to meet at his flat a few times a week. I think it lasted three or four years. It all began when she was in London for the sales. Harrods. Oddly, she was in the men's department buying me a pair of pyjamas or a tie. She told me all about it. She said she saw him try on a camel-hair jacket and he came up to her and asked her opinion. Cunningham was quite vain when it came to clothes. And he knew how to make women help him.

Well, he bought her a coffee at the Kenya across the road. He was kind and attentive. She said she detected a shyness and sensitivity in him that she had not noticed before. I can just imagine how the other women looked at her with envy. How proud she must have been. I remember her talking about that day and I remember thanking him for giving her a lift to Victoria Station. What I did not know was that they went to a film matinee a few days later. From then on, neither of them mentioned their meetings any more.

By that time, Cunningham had tired of his furniture business. He used to complain that his manager could do it all, and better. I do not know why he complained. He could have sat back and relaxed as none of us could. Still, I came up with a few propositions, but nothing seemed to tickle his fancy.

And then came the time when he almost disappeared. Oh, he did make telephone calls and bought and sold a few shares, but for some three months he did not come into our office at all. For six weeks of that time we were away. I took a long holiday and we went to America and stayed with the Buckmasters for a good part of the summer. The longest I'd ever been away from the bank. I couldn't wait to get back. She too was happy to get back because she and Marina did not hit it off.

It was around that time that Cunningham got himself into the wine business with a Mr George Markham. They came to see me at the office only once. I remember remarking to her how charged and alert he had seemed. As if he'd found some sort of fulfilment. I couldn't understand what it was. Not then.

He was travelling to and from France a lot. To taste wines, he said. I think he may have met my wife in Paris on occasion. It must have been very new and exciting for her. Booking into a foreign hotel with another man under an assumed name. Perhaps she fulfilled her fantasies. Did things she did not do when we were young because I couldn't afford to. I remember how lively and energetic and happy she was while their affair lasted. She'd come back from shopping excursions to London dressed like a model, clouded in sophisticated fragrances of rare perfumes.

She learned how to lie. She came back one day and told me how she had browsed for hours and hours in a Knightsbridge store and how she had found nothing. Except that store had gone into liquidation and closed weeks before. I knew because the owner was a customer of ours and we were forced to call his loan in. I did not comment, but afterwards, having hired a private detective to follow her, I felt cheap and cheated and a cheat myself. Later I wished I had never found out.

Lunch is over, thank God. I help her clear the dishes, then I turn the television on and she joins me on the settee. We hold hands as they announce the name of the picture, Humphrey Bogart and Lauren Bacall in *Dark Passage*.

'I do love melodrama,' she says, and I nod in agreement. Anticipation reigns as old-fashioned music invades the silence and the film begins. Throughout, she squeezes my hand as if something is exciting her. It cannot be the film. It is hardly one of their best.

There's been no newsflash so far. I suppose they won't find him before Monday. I am tempted to light one of those Dominican cigars Gerald sent me. They visit us from time to time, but whenever they did, Cunningham was out of the country. Over the years, I have grown quite fond of Marina, though my wife has never changed her opinion of her. I like her outspoken, American ways. She makes you feel that she is truly interested in what you have to say. Gerald clearly adores her and still dotes on her after all these years. Marina, too, showers him with noisy affection. With her naïve charm and his almost audible purr, they look like courting students.

I am not one for displaying such feelings openly and neither is my wife, but that was not the case when she was with Cunningham. I know because the private detective made special mention of it. He nearly killed me in the process.

They used to go to the cinema a lot, Leicester Square being only a few minutes from his flat in the Albany. They were seen and heard there and the private detective said there was nothing reserved about her then. She sits here next to me now, her eyes glued to the screen. She squeezes my hand. She did much more than that to him.

Gerald told me that they, too, had their problems when they first went to the island. I find that hard to believe, but then we see them over here so very rarely and people do not argue when they're on holiday. For many years now, they've lived in Lexington with Gerald running the business. They fly about first class and have a pad in Palm Springs. They keep inviting us there.

When Gerald came to London last month, she went to see him by herself. She spent a whole day with him and came back distraught. She didn't explain. I didn't ask. I thought it odd, though, him coming here without Marina, but I said nothing. In view of what had happened, I should have guessed. I should have tried to help him. But I was obsessed. I was too busy planning this thing for Cunningham.

Strange, that. You never know where life is going to take you. Where would your average nine-to-five bank manager look for a hired killer? The one man with such connections was Cunningham's shady one-time partner, George Markham. I suppose I played an exciting Sidney Greenstreet sort of part and I'll probably miss it when it's over. To arrange things by phone with faceless gunmen and drop wads of cash in secret hiding places is some experience. I used to think it only happened in cheap novels.

I have often asked Gerald if he is happy living in the United States, but one only needs to listen to his accent to know the answer. He has been there most of his life and has become a total American. Marina, now she's different. More cosmopolitan. I think she never quite got over the years they spent in the Dominican Republic. She still speaks Spanish perfectly and they have a maid from there to keep her in practice now that the girls have grown up.

She got quite excited when I told her about Cunningham's Haitian gardener. She asked about him and talked about him later as if she knew him intimately. I like the way she gets excited about things. She can speak a bit of French and wants to spend a summer in the south of France to perfect it.

Cunningham, of course, speaks all sorts of languages. But then he was brought up to be a gentleman. Gentleman. In this country, they believe anything you say if your accent is right. A public school accent still commands awesome respect from people. Perhaps because it makes them feel inferior. That gentleman Cunningham spent most of his time in the wine business on the wrong side of the law. He came out of it unscathed. He left others to take the rap, as Humphrey Bogart would say.

CHAPTER FOUR

■

SUNDAY 22 JULY, 1984, 5 P.M.

Cunningham walks into his house and into his study and sits down behind his desk. He tries to remember the night before, but sees nothing except for Francisco Martinez's smiling eyes facing him from the wall. Yes. He had been thinking of Francisco last night, but why? Why, after all these years away from the Malecon and Antonio's Bar? Did Francisco have anything to do with the shooting last night?

Guilt? No. He was not to blame for Francisco's death. He told him, quite distinctly, to be careful when collecting the Camaro. He told him to inform the Chief of Police that he was bringing El Gordo's car in. The rogue did not deserve to die in a hail of bullets like a mad dog.

Maybe the shooting last night reminded him of Francisco. Maybe he would end in the same way. Maybe it was someone who blamed him for Francisco. Impossible. Impossible, because no one knew. No one could possibly link him with that. No one knew that the man who burned inside the Camaro, flooded by lead, was Francisco. Good God, what a way to die.

Or maybe someone did know and they were avenging him. Ridiculous. Not after nearly twenty years. He must have had too much of that wine. He'd make sure Francisco's widow still received her cheques. He had not thought about that lately. Why not? Because he had been bored until last night. Just as bored as he had become when he had tried to be a run-of-the-mill nine-to-five businessman.

He opens his drawer. Bills paid and unpaid. Income tax returns. Bank statements. That's it. Bank statements. Let's see, now, he mumbles, as he leafs through the printed papers. The figures are small. Reluctantly Cunningham puts his reading glasses on. There it is. The bank had been sending the money to Francisco's widow like clockwork. Anonymous. Blood money. The woman would have no idea where and who it was from. Better.

There is a letter from his accountant about his tax position. You should write your expenses off, it says. Run the car and the electricity on the business. What business? He hasn't got a business now. Investments. He could not spend his income even if he tried. Interest rates on the dollar are sky-high. He is too old to start something else. Nonsense. Bored? Thank God, no. Not now. Not after last night. But, boy, was he bored when he sat in his immaculate office in the City trying to think of something to do.

He did try. *Sí, señor*. He had kept most of his money from the clutches of the Inland Revenue. He started off playing the Stock Exchange. It was exciting. Like playing the roulette table, but just like the casinos it wore off when he was winning and this was not Haiti. You couldn't compare the stock-broker's dry voice to the velvet-covered table or the magic of the wheel.

'A man should have an office to go to,' the bank manager had said. 'There are private companies you can buy. Profitable small companies.'

'Who would sell a profitable company?'

'You never know. Family businesses. Brothers falling out. Widows uninterested. Children uninterested. Shall I ask around? We have our contacts, you know.' Spoken like an Israeli. Like a man who must keep busy.

The bank manager's wife did not agree with him on that. Cunningham knew something about her long before they met. She was Gerald Buckmaster's sister. The bank manager often spoke of her. So had Marina. But Cunningham was not ready for her when he finally set eyes on her. She was intelligent and talkative and startlingly beautiful. She was interested in everything and she was funny. She had a pair of long, shapely legs and her lips were a sensuous revelation carved atop an alabaster face. Hair, thick salt-and-pepper hair, fell on

322

the most beautiful shoulders he had seen. And she was lonely and forty and housebound and married to a bore.

At that time, Cunningham was running a small furniture-importing company which had its own trucks. For a while, he enjoyed the daily routine, but once the office manager proved he was able to manage it all by himself, Cunningham found he had nothing to do. There was no excitement in it. No danger. Orders came in and went out and they were paid.

He was deeply in love with the bank manager's wife.

CHAPTER FIVE

■

SUNDAY 22 JULY, 1984, LATE AFTERNOON

In love, yes, in love. A total, selfless, all-consuming love that completely transcended anything else he'd ever known before. It was a gift from heaven that came to him in the afternoon of life. Once started, it did not stop, and it burned in him with all the passion and fervour of youth. It was romantic and intense and promising and painful with jealousy and sweet with contentment. The bank manager's wife embodied all and each and every one of the women he had known; and more, because with her came the understanding of mature friendship which he had never found in any other woman.

She was soft and compassionate and her passive loneliness soared into exhilaration at the sight of him and being with him and it lifted his sagging confidence. The inhibition he had seen in her when they had first met melted in a shameless carnal fire fed by curiosity and lust.

She had become the only woman in the world. Her cool, reserved exterior would explode into shattering sexuality as soon as they were alone and sometimes when they weren't.

She set him alight every time. He knew no tiredness, no boredom when she was there. She refused his presents and only kept his flowers and she wanted him all to herself.

They soon started talking about going away together and staying together as if it were the most natural thing in the world. They had talked about it only last week. All you need do is look at me, she used to say, and I'm gone. Here, touch me and see how much I want you.

He continued to go through the motions of a business relationship with her husband. He entertained them both and hated it when she went home with the other man. For the first time in his life, he felt like a heel for taking another man's wife and he told her and she smiled and said, 'There's hope for you yet.'

In his drawer there is a picture of her, and he takes it out and looks at it and he sighs. That heavenly animal she had discovered inside herself stares at him from beyond her eyes. He remembers the frustration of listening to her husband talk of her with a maddening, smug expression of ownership. He remembers wanting to grab the man by his detachable white collar and scream, 'She's mine, you fool. Mine. Mine.'

Sometimes he felt she was using him because she was bored and that she hated his drug-like dependence on her and longed to break free. At such times he would sink into helpless dark moods that come of suppressed anger. But most of the time she made him the happiest man in the world. They went to film matinées on rainy afternoons and chuckled and cuddled and kissed and held hands.

She had a depth of learning that lost him and taste that haunted him. She introduced him to the world of art and took him to museums and galleries and antique shops. She helped him form the collection that was his pride and joy. He'd acknowledged that by leaving her everything he owned in a will she didn't know existed. Sometimes he took dark, secret pleasure in imagining her face when she found out how rich she was once he was dead and gone. But then he couldn't imagine going anywhere without her, not even there.

At first he was able to shut her matrimonial bed from his mind. Later, he became envious. He envied the order that surrounded her life. Once, he cursed her for having somewhere to go. Somewhere in which he had no part.

He fought the call of the outside world until he met George Markham, a wine shipper in the City who showed him the road to a new life as exciting as the one he had grown apart from since his return to England. It was profitable and dangerous and had brought the adrenalin of adventure back into his blood.

It started when she went with her husband the banker to stay with the Buckmasters in Lexington. It might never have happened otherwise. That was when his affair with Markham's wife had started. He kept it secret from her. He knew she would never understand that his love for her had made it impossible for him ever to be on his own again.

One day she told him she wouldn't be able to see him for a few days. Gerald was coming, she said, alone, to discuss something important with her. She talked about Marina and her dislike for her. She denigrated her and said she was a superficial, spoilt brat. A selfish bitch who had to have things her own way at other people's expense, including her own husband.

'I wouldn't go that far,' Cunningham heard himself say.

'Are you defending her, Cunningham? Did you know her better than you've let on?' He said nothing. 'Did you sleep with her?'

He was too immersed in watching the rage that engulfed her and he had no thought of lying. 'Yes,' he said, 'I did.' He knew he had made a mistake, but he'd said it and it was stupid, but it was too late.

'Did Gerald ever find out?' she asked calmly.

'No. Not as far as I'm aware. No.'

'I hope to God you're right,' she said, and went very quiet. She turned away from him. He thought she was going to get

325

out of bed. Instead, she turned back and all of a sudden she went quite berserk. She ranted and she raved and she threatened and called him a liar and a cheat and a cad and said it was the end.

He tried to put his hands on her shoulders. She pushed him away. She shouted abuse at him. He had been a shit all along. His father must have been the same. No woman could stand that. That's why his mother had left, she screamed, and he slapped her. She stopped mid-sentence and then burst into tears.

'I didn't mean that,' she said. 'I don't know what I'm saying ... I'm jealous ...'

'You can't be jealous of the past, darling. All this happened years ago, before I even knew you existed. It was another time. Another world. I was another man.'

He looked at her as he spoke. The scorn was back on her face.

'You couldn't care less, could you?'

'I have regrets, too. I can't change the past. I wish I could.'

But she did not listen to anything he had to say. She got up and hurried into her clothes. She grabbed her handbag and her coat and was gone. He did not see her again for weeks.

He puts the photograph down. He slips it along the table and it drops back into the drawer. He remembers how she came back, not four weeks ago, on a Friday. She rang his bell and walked inside and sat down and did not talk. There was, he remembers, something frighteningly sinister about her silence. It lasted for ever.

Then he could take it no more. He got up and she got up. They faced each other. For a moment, he thought she was going to strike him. Instead, she threw her arms around him. Her body shuddered. She buried her face in his neck. She led him to the bedroom. Said she could not live without him. Her eruption was incredible. She could not have faked it. He had certainly been right not to mention George Markham's wife.

Then everything resumed as if they had never talked about

Marina. As if they had never separated. Until her strange telephone call last night, when she rang to tell him it was all over. She wasn't coming back, she said. Not ever.

Oh, she'll call again soon and say it was all a big mistake. She'll say she is sorry and must see him and would he please forgive her. She did not mean a word of it. She only told him it was all over because, because, because. She had done it often over the years. Guilt. Pre-menstrual tension. Could have been anything. Could have been his fault. She always came back, seized by uncontrollable remorse.

She'll call. That's why he is still in his study. God, this wreckage is depressing. He'll have to have the place redecorated. Brighter colours next time. She should have called by now. Maybe she can't. She can't because it's Sunday and she's at home with Him. She'll call him here. She knows he can't bear to speak to her from the bedroom. He cannot stand looking at the soft-coloured furnishings and the prints and the sheets and the bedcovers she chose. Not while she is at home with Him.

Without her there is no light and no air. He's going through a bad time, that's all. He's entitled. If she'd known that someone had tried to kill him last night, she'd call right now. His heart palpitates hard. He gets up to pace the room and his chest weighs a ton. It is a long time since he's been in any real danger. The attack last night must be connected to his past.

How far back should he go? Could it have been someone from his days in the banana republics? Some militant leftist group which had been decimated with guns he'd sold to their government? Lots and lots of them have found refuge in England, but why wait so long? Balthasar? No. The man had no one, and no one knows about him anyway. People think it was the police who killed him. Francisco was never identified. Maybe it was someone in the drug trade. Yes, yes, could be. He might have stepped on someone's toes. They almost caught him then. Just as he was getting out of it. Dover. April or May 1970. He remembers.

The customs officer was young. The clean, hairless chin of a once-a-week shaver. He had a pale, embarrassed, schoolboyish face. He had just reached the gate, having rolled off the ferry.

'Step out of the car, please, will you, sir?'

Cunningham opened the door. He smiled at the young man. He pushed his artificial leg out first, then the stick. 'Sorry about this, officer. I can't sprint as well as I used to. The war saw to that.'

The officer blushed. 'Perhaps, perhaps we can do without ...'

'Oh no, officer. The law must be obeyed. That's what my generation went to war for.' He pointed at his leg. 'See what I mean?'

'I'm sorry,' the young man said. 'Have you anything to declare?'

'No, officer. I have not,' Cunningham barked as he crawled out of the car. His voice was angry. His expression hurt and severe. At the back, the supervisor shook his head. 'Would you like me to open the boot?'

The young man looked around for support. He hesitated. Maybe the tip was wrong. And even if it was right, arresting this veteran for a few grams of powder wouldn't save the world. No one would thank him for it anyway. On the contrary. The look on his supervisor's face spelt a possible telling-off. Let the addicts have their money's worth. Wrong tip. He'd had them before.

'It's all right, sir. Nothing further. Thank you.'

'Thank you,' Cunningham said as he got into the car. There was hate in his eyes and the young man looked and he saw.

'Sorry,' he said. He was the enemy, yet on his cap and lapel was the Crown. No one looked in the back or saw the plastic bags under the spare wheel.

The gate was lifted and other cars were allowed through. Cunningham watched them in his rear-view mirror. As he turned towards the Canterbury road, only one car remained behind him. A large black Wolseley which had not been on the boat. There were no signs on the windscreen and when he stopped by the next traffic lights he noticed that the man at the wheel was wearing some sort of dark blue uniform.

A few miles on, he stopped by a large brick-fronted pub. There was a telephone booth outside. As he dialled the number, he saw the Wolseley enter and park discreetly behind a truck by the 'Hot Food' sign.

'This is the last time I bring the stuff in myself,' Cunningham said. 'You'll have to find someone else. They noticed me at Dover, and now there's a police car on my tail. I'll try and lose them.'

'Oh shit. I've promised to deliver this evening.'

'Don't panic. The car will be at Moon's Garage in Soho. Near the Piccadilly Hotel. I'll stay there tonight. I'll leave the keys with the porter. You go up there and collect them. Tell him your name is Smith. Don't make contact with me. I'll call you later.'

'What do we do next?'

'I've just told you. You collect the keys, get the stuff out of the car, deliver, and wait for my instructions. I'll call you around eleven. I'm going to the theatre tonight. One more thing, George.'

'What?'

'Call Katherine at the house. Tell her I'm not coming home and ask her to join me at the hotel. You get rid of the car as soon as possible. Don't screw up, George.'

'I don't much like the tone of your voice. You've got something to lose too.'

'I'm not sure I heard that.'

'Yes you did. Who the hell do you think you are? You call Katherine yourself. We're still married, in case you forgot.'

'Don't start that again.'

'You never consider other people's feelings.'

'I don't pay you to have feelings, George. I'm in a hurry. Call Katherine. Tell her I'll expect her at six. And don't moan.

You don't care a damn for her anyway. Bye bye.'

That had been a narrow escape, Cunningham remembers. Katherine Markham was just a stop-gap. She lived with him at the house for over two months while the bank manager and his wife were on that intolerable trip to America. Markham used to beat her and then apologize and buy her expensive jewellery. He did not understand how those two ever got together. The way she behaved afterwards was a real mystery. He does not feel guilty about all that now. Markham was careless, that's all. Those were dangerous days. But they were exciting. Much more exciting than strolling around Sunday flea markets in search of vases. Yes. He remembers the Piccadilly Hotel. It rained like crazy that afternoon.

The porter rushed forward with his huge umbrella. 'Welcome back, Mr Cunningham. Are you staying long?'

'Get me a taxi,' Cunningham said curtly. 'I can't take the traffic any more.' The other car was still behind, its windscreen wipers swinging violently. The cab came and Cunningham jumped out of the Jaguar and flew into the back seat. He opened the window and handed the porter the keys and a small khaki bag. The porter handed him his stick.

'Park the car at Moon's Garage for me, will you? Keep the keys. A Mr Smith will come and collect them from you later. Here's ten quid.' The porter saluted.

'Victoria Station,' Cunningham said to the driver, and sank back in his seat. Through the sweeping rain behind, the Wolseley followed.

At Victoria Station, he left the cab and walked slowly up to one of the ticket booths. Beyond the rush-hour crowd, the police car crawled to a stop. They seemed to be in no hurry. He bought a ticket to the City and went to a telephone box.

'George?'

'Yes, Cunningham.'

'Are you still there?'

'Who would you be talking to if I weren't?'

'Listen, smartass, go the hotel now. It's quite safe. The

police are with me. Get the keys from the porter and go to Moon's Garage. Collect the stuff and make the delivery. Then get rid of the car, for Christ's sake.'

'What about the porter?'

'I've looked after him. Go now. Get rid of the car.'

'They'll trace it back to the wine company, Cunningham. They can find bits of the stuff in the back if they look hard enough.'

'Blow it up if you like. Go now.' He didn't ask about Markham's wife.

'That's easy. I used to be in demolition during the war.'

'Very funny,' Cunningham said, 'but I'm not in a reminiscing mood at the moment.'

CHAPTER SIX

■

SUNDAY 22 JULY, 1984, LATE AFTERNOON

She's upset about Gerald. There's nothing she'll let me do or say about it. She is in the kitchen now. I can hear the sound of water and the clatter of dishes being lowered into the sink. The film was so-so. The second part of the Sunday afternoon double feature is about to begin. She said she isn't going to watch because she doesn't like Tony Curtis. I sense a sudden restlessness in her. I saw it growing, but said nothing. It is always better to let her work it out for herself.

So far there's been no news about Cunningham. I am getting a little nervous. I try hard to watch the film. A train steams past with a whistle. Burt Lancaster and Tony Curtis are detonating a load of dynamite. Lancaster pushes the handle down while Curtis picks his teeth. Boom. The train is coming off the rails. Dust and flying earth fill the little screen.

Boom. Crack. Boom. Just like the explosion at Moon's Garage.

By that time, Cunningham had become our most important depositor. I had my own branch, a much larger affair, and he kept moving his accounts with me as he had done from the beginning. There was, at first, nothing to connect Cunningham with that spine-chilling outrage.

Three policemen and two attendants were killed at Moon's Garage and at first they thought the IRA had done it. Then they thought it was a gangland murder, but that was ruled out. They found out that the bomb had gone off as soon as the victims tried to open the boot. Scotland Yard said it was most unusual for the underworld and too professional for the IRA. The Jaguar was blown to pieces along with five other cars. Mercifully, there were no other people about.

It was a repair job done to the chassis that finally identified the owners. A wine-shipping firm owned by George Markham. They were in French table wines and mainly supplied the catering trade. Then it came out that Cunningham had driven the car back from the Continent the same day. He had used it coming back from Paris. The customs official at Dover confirmed his story. He said Cunningham was stopped and searched, but not apprehended. He gave no reason.

I don't quite remember what Cunningham's explanation was, but the police accepted his story. Something about a favour he was doing for George Markham. We at the bank were surprised, to say the least. Cunningham's dealings with us were without blemish. The references we normally give are strictly limited to the customer's business activities and credit. Cunningham did not embarrass us by asking for any. I did offer though. Oh, yes. Cunningham said he was bringing the car back from Paris where it had been stuck for lack of spare parts.

For a while, it looked as if someone had tried to kill Cunningham. He said he did not know anyone who would want to do that. 'But then, who knows?' he was quoted as adding.

He admitted financing George Markham's wine business. Then Markham's involvement in drugs reached the press.

In the end, they threw Markham into jail. He had a record under a different name and got thirty or forty years. I don't remember. The most amazing thing about the trial was how his wife stood by him. She was in court every day and later she moved into a flat close to where he was jailed. She sold the story to the newspapers. Love is strange. I suppose she needed the money, and with that kind of loyalty I, for one, do not blame her. I went to see Markham recently. I joined a prisoners' visiting society when I retired. You meet the most amazing people.

They've just shot Tony Curtis. Burt Lancaster is holding the bad guys back. My wife comes in from the kitchen. Her eyes are red. I feel useless. I get up.

'Where are you going?' she asks softly.

'Oh, just for a digestive walk in the garden.'

I'll do something when it's over. I'll assert myself. Help her. Cunningham is back in my mind. I must get out of the house. I hate him today. If there were a power cut or a thunderstorm, I would blame him for it.

And then my wife says, 'It's weeks since we've heard from Cunningham.' Just like that. Out of the blue. 'Don't they do any business with him at the bank now?'

How sensitive women can be to their own problems. How blind to those of others. I am being a pig. I know she is hurting, but I am too involved with myself right now. I can't do a thing for her.

I make no comment. I'm on my way out through the french windows. She'll assume I didn't hear.

CHAPTER SEVEN

■

SUNDAY 22 JULY, 1984, 8 P.M.

The front doorbell rings and it shakes him. Who the hell could that be at this time? The valet won't be back before Tuesday and the housekeeper took the weekend off. They both have keys. The ring is persistent. He gets up. He is about to lower himself into the wheelchair, but he isn't tired. He might as well walk.

'I'm coming,' he shouts. The bell keeps ringing. Strange. He did not hear a car coming up the drive. He must have dozed off. Funny things happen when you're getting old on your own. No one called to say they were coming. Could be anyone. He opens the front door. The man is young. He has never seen him before. He wears black leather trousers and a motorcycle jacket. Goggles and a helmet in his hand. Boots.

'I have a package for Mr Cunningham,' the young man says.

'Yes, that's me.'

'There you are, then, sir.'

He is handed a white envelope. He can see his name scribbled across it. He searches his pocket for a coin.

'Thank you,' the young man says. 'No tip is necessary. The party will be waiting for your reply.'

'Does that mean you'll be back?'

'Yes, sir. In an hour or so. They will call you on the phone first.'

'Thank you.'

He knows whose writing it is. His curiosity has evaporated. Must be another of her dramas. She is going to tell him all is forgiven. He limps back to his desk. On the way he tears the envelope open. She has typed this one. Large foolscap paper.

He hears the motorcycle coughing into life outside the front door. It roars away into the night. The room is hot.

Cunningham opens the big window behind him. The moon is out and shining. Could almost be a Caribbean night. The lawn stretches outside. It reaches the tall, old trees. The sycamores do not move. There is no sound. He flops into his chair. He reads.

Dear Cunningham. No date. No place. No address. No nothing. Line after line of closely typed words. *Dear Cunningham.* Not darling, not my love. What is she writing for? Why not just call or come in person? She knows he could never turn her away, no matter what.

Dear Cunningham. If only she would stop her nonsense and come and live with him the way they had planned. Maybe he should talk to her husband. Be open. Tell all. There would be a kind of justice in that. Someone had taken his father's woman from him.

Dear Cunningham
I feel lost. I am very up and down. My moods change from hour to hour. Unlike yours. You always knew what you wanted. You have been a butterfly, fluttering from place to place, from man to man, from one woman to another. You have devoured them all. You have used and manipulated and you have taken. You gave nothing. You did not need to, because no one made you. You have been offered unconditional love and devotion and loyalty and friendship free gratis and for nothing. You have been the worst kind of thief, Cunningham. You've stolen trust and love and passion and pity. You did not think about any of the women who cheated on their husbands to be with you, or of the consequences of it to their lives. To their husbands' lives. That never touched you, Cunningham. Dear cultured, lonely, self-centred Cunningham. You were born that way. You were born with the right looks and enough charm to last twenty others a lifetime. Your smile, that superb blend of

helplessness and sexuality and fake compassion, it never ran out for you. You knew it was there and you have always used it. But bills must be paid, Cunningham. Paid when presented. And this is yours. Your time has run out. You have damaged too many people and I cannot stand by and see you hurting still more. I have known and loved two of those people. I want you to go away from here and never come back. And I want you to understand why you must go and why you must keep going. It seems all those I love must go. You have destroyed Gerald, my only brother. I have asked you whether he knew about your affair with Marina and you said he did not. Well, Marina has told him all about it. Of course, it died for you years ago, but it did not die for her. She told him she had always loved you. She said she was coming to this country to see you. She wanted him out of the house and out of her life. Told him he was nothing without her. Gerald was a very proud man, Cunningham. And it has destroyed him. I heard last night that Gerald took his own life. Not worth it, I hear you say, not for a woman's love. But some men care. My husband cares. Yes, my husband. Your dull, trusting banker has in his quiet way shown more grit than a battalion of machos. He does not know about us. I will make sure he never does. He loves me in a way you could never understand, and I will make it up to him. I love him, and I will never leave him for you. Never. I loved you, Cunningham. It sounds so cheap when I write it down, but I have loved you, more than anything. You were the universe for me. I could have forgiven you everything, even giving arms to the people who killed my older brother in Palestine. I would have made excuses for you. But now you have destroyed Gerald and he was all I had left. You have spent your life running, Cunningham, running from yourself. Maybe you really hate yourself. I can't blame you for that, but I can blame you for what you've done along the way. When I spoke to you last night you did not believe it was the end because I did not believe it myself.

*How could I? I have love in me, Cunningham, so much
love it hurts. But I see darkness everywhere. All I am capable of dispensing is rejection. To be a woman again, find
peace, I know I must let you go. Make you go. I was so sure
of that last night, and yet as soon as I finished telling you it
was over my world collapsed. I wanted to come to you and
hold you and tell you to forget what I said. Even now, as I
sit and write all this down, I have this desire to speak to you
one more time. God alone knows what that will do to my
resolve. Still, I will speak to you. Wait for my call, Cunningham. Sometime after nine o'clock tonight ... wait.*

There is more, but he puts it down unread. The woman has
finally gone mad. Only last week in this room they had made
plans and she was loving and passionate and she nearly stayed
for ever. She will call, and he will talk to her and it will be all
right, somehow.

How could she say all those terrible things? None of it is
true. None of it is really happening. It's just a bad dream.
When he wakes, he will tell her how wrong she's been. He'll
tell her there's something wrong with her. People don't behave that way. She can get help. He shouldn't really say anything. He's having a nightmare. He'll wake and wait for her
call and see. Play along with her whims. Wake and wait for her
and hold her in his arms. He won't read any more of that
nonsense.

Ti Allain hears the man on the fast motorcycle go away. He
tries to chase him down the drive, but his legs do not listen to
him the way they used to when he was young. On his way
back to his shed, he passes the front of the house and looks at
the step by the entrance. It is well lit and the spoon is right
where it had been before. There are footsteps on Haiti's earth,
but they do not belong to his one-footed master. He knows
his print better than any other. They belong to the man who

has just left on his machine.

This, he knows, is a calamity. He must get his master to come out of the house again or something terrible will happen. He struggles to concentrate. To search deep in his mind for what he must do. Praying is not enough now. He strains his memory to find how to protect his master, but nothing comes. He must run back to his shed. That is where he'll find the answer.

Ti Allain runs with all the speed his strength can muster. He runs past the large window at the back of the house. He sees his master holding a piece of paper in his hands. He does not stop. As he runs, he concentrates on telling his mirror image of the danger he is in. Soon he reaches his shed.

The moon is in the sky, and at the same time another image of it greets him from the steel face of his shovel. The image of the moon on his shovel is the answer. It tells him what he must do. He must dig the half-faced man out of the ground and watch him and dance over his body and tie him more securely. Make sure neither he nor the spirits who have sent him can destroy his master.

He lifts the shovel and slowly he walks to the flowerbed. He must be careful not to let the moon's image escape the steel face until he reaches the spot. The earth is still soft under the burnt leaves. He digs and he sweats and he digs and calls for the spirits. The face of the moon is back in the sky and smiles. He digs and he hears his grandmother's voice telling him to hurry.

The half-faced man is soon uncovered. There is not a cloud in the sky and Ti Allain is hot. He must not allow any of his sweat to drop on the half-faced man. His sweat is part of him and so, too, part of his mirror image. Just one drop of it would tell the half-faced man where his master is.

Ti Allain stands upon the half-faced man's chest. It is hard to dance and hold back all his sweat. He looks down at the cruel young face and hopes that he is holding it all back. He should run back to the shed and fetch the dead mouse he has there, place it on the half-faced man's remaining eye. But he dare not move. Not one drop of his sweat must fall on the half-faced man. It would transfer some of his own powers to him and help him to come out of his grave and kill his one-footed master. The one-footed man did not touch the earth of Haiti and he is more vulnerable than ever.

'Watch him and be ready, Ti Allain,' he hears his grandmother say.

And then he remembers her last words to him before her body died. How the next time he heard her voice would be the time that he, too, would die. He had cried when she had told him, but she had said there was no reason to cry. For where the spirits were there was no hunger and no suffering and they would be together for many, many days and months and years and for ever. Until all the spirits became people again and went back to the tall black mountains of Africa, where all Haitians came from.

CHAPTER EIGHT

◼

SUNDAY 22 JULY, 1984, 10 P.M.

He takes his glasses off and leans back as the cool breeze caresses his ears. In the silence, he can hear the little gardener digging. How strange. He must still be dreaming. And then the phone rings. He picks it up. He knows it will be her voice.

'Cunningham?' she asks.

'Hello,' he says. His voice is loud. He is almost shouting.

'Are you angry?'

'Of course I'm angry. Why? What are you playing at?'

'Gerald ...'

'Please!'

'I'm so confused.'

'Of course you are.'

'I want you.'

'I love you.'

'This is a nightmare.'

'Don't ever leave me.'

'Burn the stupid letter, Cunningham. I did not know what I was doing.'

'Of course I will.'

'Do it now. Burn it now, and let me hear you do it. I don't want you to see it or remember it was ever there. Burn it now. Take the big lighter by the phone. Let me hear it.'

'All right, darling,' he says, and he holds the pages up over the large glass ashtray. He gives her a blow-by-blow account of how he takes the lighter and how the flame, encouraged by the breeze from the window, consumes the paper in no time. He puts the lighter down, juggling the last burning page, talking to her still.

'Going, going, gone,' he says, bursting with relief.

'All of it?'

'Yes, my love, my only love.'

He is the happiest he's ever been. The wind outside has risen and it howls and the sycamores sway gracefully. She will never leave him. The thump of joy is deafening. He does not hear the sound of footsteps behind him, does not turn to see the young man at the window, half hidden behind the black double barrel of a shotgun. She is speaking now. Cunningham wants to talk. To cry. But she does not give him a chance. She makes little sense. Her voice rattles on. She talks of love. She is his for ever. Silent tears roll down his face. And then, just for a split second, he hears the shot and feels the pain and slumps on the desk. The phone, still clasped in his hand, says, 'Goodbye, Cunningham.'

The motorcyclist mounts the window sill. Inside, he gently pulls the phone away. 'Hello,' he whispers.

'Is it done?'

'Yes.'

'Goodbye,' she says. The dialling tone purrs in his ear. He places the phone back in Cunningham's hand and wraps the dead fingers around it. He helps himself to a cigar and lights it with the table lighter. Outside, the wind has died and the night is still. He reloads his gun, taking his time. He looks at the room once more and turns to leave. As he climbs out of the window into the garden, he sees the strange, macabre little figure standing there, watching him.

Ti Allain mumbles something. He turns around. His arms swing out. He dances. The young man lifts his gun and aims and pulls the trigger. The blast knocks the little man forward and down. Ti Allain is in pain, but he rises and he runs. He runs like the wind that has just died down, because he must get into the grave he has unearthed. He runs as if his shoulder is still where it was. He runs as fast as he did as a child in the village. The man gives chase, but Ti Allain runs faster.

'Run, Ti Allain.' He hears his grandmother's voice and her image comes to him from long ago and he races. He runs as though the top left half of his back had not been shattered at all and he reaches the grave and falls in and with his hand he covers the half-faced man's eye. Another shot shudders through his body, but his hand stays where it was.

'Good,' his grandmother's voice says, and so does another. Could be her friend Monique the black witch, but Ti Allain lies flat on top of the half-faced man, and as the young man stands above the grave looking down he does not see him or hear him or the spirits. His hand holds on to the half-faced man's remaining eye as if it were a claw, trying to dig it out.

The young man shrugs his shoulders. There is a shovel by the side of the great big hole and he pushes the earth down on the two bodies until the ground is flat. He kicks a few leaves over the earth and turns to go. As he starts his motorcycle he looks back at the house. The wind picks up again and it howls and shrieks as if it were winter. As if the sky were angry.

CHAPTER NINE

TUESDAY 24 JULY, 1984, 5 P.M.

The weekend has come and gone and so has Monday. We are going out to dinner tonight. My wife is upstairs dressing. She will take her time. She likes to look her best when we go somewhere special. I've booked a table at the Connaught, near Berkeley Square. Best rib of beef in the world, Cunningham used to say.

I heard this morning. Someone from the bank phoned to tell me. A short piece in the newspaper. I didn't mention it to her. She always reads the papers before I do. She must have missed it. She'd certainly have been upset. I won't mention it for now.

I suppose I am a criminal. I have paid a man to murder Cunningham. I am a killer. But I do not feel like a killer. I am elated. I can walk tall again and breathe the clean country air. I shall order lobster salad first, and a bottle of vintage champagne. Same brand as Cunningham used to drink. It will be expensive, but no matter. I have always been careful with my money. The crowning glory of those underpaid years with the bank is the security of a pension at the end of it. We never talk about money. She gets a fixed allowance and it is generous.

She has been through a lot of anguish these past few days. I am going to take her on a long holiday somewhere. Thailand, perhaps. Or India. Or Egypt. Maybe Switzerland. She doesn't care for the heat. I am pleased she's taking her time up there. I need to be on my own. To digest things.

She acted very out of character on Sunday night. Nothing prepared me for that. She tiptoed upstairs while I was watching something on the box. I heard the phone click and I knew she'd been talking to someone. How long and to whom I didn't know. Then she came down. She wore a pink nightdress and over that a black kimono. She looked ravishing. There was a strange, almost savage look in her eyes. She poured herself a stiff whisky. She drank it down in one quick swig. I'd never seen her do that before. I watched and waited in silent apprehension. She poured herself another and gulped it down. She did not watch the screen. She sat down close to me and held my hand. Then she started to rub the back of my neck. She hadn't done that in years.

Her head dropped on my shoulder and her fingers scraped my thigh. Suddenly she turned her head and kissed me. There was a deep, wild passion.

'Make love to me,' she said. Her voice was hoarse and urgent. Her face seemed moonstruck and her hands were everywhere. I leaned backward and then she came down on me and unzipped my fly and probed.

'I'll get you going,' she said with a lecherous smile. I was in a daze. She began to undress me on the settee and finished on the carpet. Her lips brushed me everywhere. I felt her skin close to mine and my excitement grew until it hurt. 'I must have you now,' she said, her eyes glaring at me. She eased my hand onto her moist nakedness and climbed on top of me. The lights were on and the windows were open, but she did not seem to care. She guided me there with her hand and her body shook as it closed on my throbbing. She moved like a machine and she was screaming shameless words I had not heard her utter before. She bit my cheeks and I watched her face and my body was taken over by powers I did not remember were there.

She wriggled and heaved and her sweat poured down on me. Her nails dug into my shoulder and drew blood. Vulgar obscenities pierced my ear. They sounded like the sweetest music. The bitter perfume of her body came to me and then she shuddered and collapsed on my chest, crying uncontrollably. I lay there, her weight pinning me down, her breathlessness whispering down my cheek. I was still inside her, numb with the power she had unleashed. I could no longer feel much, but I was firm and unfulfilled and kept on moving.

'Come,' she said tenderly. 'Come now.'

Magic. Where have we been all these years?

Now it's Tuesday and she is upstairs getting dressed. I am trying to work out what has happened. I pray it will happen again. Tonight I feel released and relaxed and free and strong. Cunningham is no more. I wonder who will get all that money? No one knows better than I how much there is.

She comes down and she looks like a queen. Her face is fresh and her beauty lights up the room. I have donned a dark suit and a red polka-dot bow-tie. A bow-tie always makes me feel festive. She pours a drink for herself. I decline. I shall be driving tonight and they have become pretty vigilant at testing our breath by the roadside. They have special equipment for it. Science has no limits, it seems.

I feel rich. I am Peter Pan. I could take off and fly, but I must control myself. Perhaps she knows but does not say. Or perhaps she is waiting for me to tell her. Not a chance.

Perhaps we should stay the night in some posh hotel. Splash out a bit. Ask her to pack a few things and a toothbrush. Better not. If I suggest that she will know something is different. God, something is. I feel young and impatient and raring to go like a bull. I could start all over again. Yes, even at the till or sorting out paying-in slips at the bank. Anything. Must find something to do with all that time.

I shall never see him again or think about him again or be jealous of his culture and his class and his life and his prowess again. He is the past. He is yesterday. This will be the evening of a lifetime. When London beckons, you can keep all those faraway places Cunningham always talked about. There are places to eat and drink and there are theatres and shops and a man need never look elsewhere. The best Italian, French and Japanese restaurants are right there. I wonder if anyone will miss him.

Lobster salad, I tell myself as I start the car. I am famished. Lobster it's going to be. Then a steak. I am an early caveman.

I am strong. I feel my muscles tingle. Perhaps I should have been a hunter.

'How about smoked salmon to start?' she asks.

'My sentiments exactly,' I answer.

We approach the main street and I learn how easy it is to lie. I stop the car at the junction and turn to her. 'I must kiss you,' I say, and she leans over. Her beautiful face shines in the moonlight.

I shall be her lover now.